Allie's Angel

Sommy L. Ham

WESTBOW
PRESS

A DIVISION OF THOMAS NELSON

WestBow Press books may be ordered through booksellers or by contacting:

WestBow Press
A Division of Thomas Nelson
1663 Liberty Drive
Bloomington, IN 47403
www.westbowpress.com
1-(866) 928-1240

Because of the dynamic nature of the Internet, any web addresses or links contained in this book may have changed since publication and may no longer be valid. The views expressed in this work are solely those of the author and do not necessarily reflect the views of the publisher, and the publisher hereby disclaims any responsibility for them.

Allie's Angel is a work of fiction. Names, characters, places, and incidents either are the product of the author's imagination or are used fictitiously. Any resemblance to actual persons, living or dead, businesses, companies, events, or locales is entirely coincidental.

Certain stock imagery © Thinkstock.

ISBN: 978-1-4497-1400-0 (sc)
ISBN: 978-1-4497-1399-7 (dj)
ISBN: 978-1-4497-1401-7 (e)

Library of Congress Control Number: 2011923703

Cover image © Natalie Diehl

Printed in the United States of America

WestBow Press rev. date:4/21/2011

For Mom and Dad
with love and gratitude

Much love to my husband, Tommy, and children, Laura Ann, Mark, Katherine and Jeff. I could never have finished this book without your encouragement. A huge thank you to my editor, Rosanne, for her *brilliant* support and tireless enthusiasm. Thank you to Francyne—a writing friend for many years and always a source of inspiration. A special thanks to Roxy Halekakis, a former coach and now a counselor at Magnolia High School, who kindly brought me up-to-date on girls' basketball. And to Natalie Diehl, a fabulous photographer who didn't mind snapping pictures in 99 degree Texas heat! Each of you has inspired me to finish the sequel!

Chapter 1

❦

Allie McCall sat on the porcelain throne, staring at the black marker graffiti on the bathroom door.

"Constance loves Josh."

"Constance loves Buzz."

"Constance loves Paul."

Xs and Os followed each scrawl.

Hmm, Constance sure gets around.

From somewhere near the sink a voice called. "Okay, give it up. Who's the newest name on *that* stall door?"

"Josh." Allie replied, as she untied her shoes. "And all this time I thought she liked Buzz Madison."

"Naw, that was last week. Hurry it up, Allie. Do what you have to do and let's get to class."

"Okay, okay. I am. I am." She pulled off her knee socks, tossing them over the bathroom door.

"Not the knee sock thing again!" shouted Wikki. "If you're just going to throw them away, *I'll* take them."

"Aw, jeez," Allie grunted, opening the stall door before bending over to tie her shoes. "They're socks, for heaven's sake. They creep me out. Mama is so weird. We had another knock-down, drag-out this morning. She said I have to wear them because my skirt's too short." Allie tugged at her hem. "What am I supposed to do? *All* my skirts come to, like, mid-thigh. I can't help it. It's not my fault skirts come in sizes, not lengths."

1

Allie glanced down. "Do you think it's too short?"

Wikki shrugged. "Would it matter if I did? You're like, nearly six feet tall."

Allie rolled her eyes at the reminder. As if any fifteen-year-old girl would want to look like the Jolly Green Giant. In the mirror, she studied her classmate and best friend, Monica Wilkerson. Allie didn't have too many friends here at Friendly High School; Wikki didn't, either. Ironic, huh? Friendly was anything but that. Allie had lived here for five years and gone to the junior high, but most kids still wouldn't talk to her. They all seemed stuck-up. They lived in a town about as big as a frog's fingernail, so what did they have to be snooty about, anyway? Allie couldn't wait to get away.

She glared down at her worn plaid skirt and faded green sweater. Part of the problem was that she hadn't owned anything new in years. Mama said she grew too fast, but Allie knew differently. They barely had enough money to buy food and gas. Everything else came from what Allie called the "Salvage Yard," a secondhand store in town. She hated wearing used clothes, but she knew that, if it weren't for the Salvage Yard, she and Mama and Ben would be sitting, eating and sleeping on a bare floor. She tossed the unwanted knee socks in Wikki's direction.

"Every time we go to the Salvage Yard, Mama buys me knee socks. It makes me crazy." Allie pulled a small, tattered purse out of her backpack and dragged out her eyeliner. "She probably makes me wear them just to make me mad. She has to know I pull them off the minute I get to school." Wikki was giving her *the* look again. Allie grimaced. "What *are* you staring at?"

"You. There you go again. You do it every single day right before Mrs. Timmons's class. Thick eyeliner and blue eye shadow clear up to your eyebrows. It looks terrible and you know it. What is it, your own personal protest again English class?"

"Don't be silly. I *love* English." Allie raked one heavy line over her right eye and moved to the left eye. *There. Just about finished.* "It's Mrs. Timmons I can't stand." She fluttered her eyelashes and inspected the blue smudges of shadow. "I'm sure the feeling is mutual."

"I think she's actually jealous of your mother being the newspaper editor," Wikki commented. "That's why she picks on you in class."

Allie shrugged. Wikki was probably right. Mrs. Timmons gave Allie a much harder time than any other student. She groaned and pointed to the mirror. "Look what that awful woman has done to me! I'm coming apart at the seams. I'm about to *explode*. I've complained about her. I've told people about how mean she is. But nobody listens. Rudy Mae Timmons walks on water."

Wikki ignored the outburst. "I think that shade clashes with your eyes. Do you know how lucky you are to have green eyes? So much better than my please-ignore-me brown ones."

Allie grabbed a brush from her purse, thought better of it and pulled the elastic tighter on her long ponytail. She didn't have time to fix her hair today. Besides, what difference would it make?

"You have beautiful eyes, Wikki. Besides, what are you complaining about? You have long, blonde hair. I've always wanted blonde hair. *And* all the guys talk to you; they think you're cool."

Allie sighed. She felt sick at her stomach—for real. Most days she hated this school. Most days she hated her own life. Except for Wikki, she had no friends, no social life, no money—and she was running out of eyeliner. Could things get worse? *Yes. English class and Rudy Mae Timmons.* At least Mrs. Timmons wouldn't talk so much today. They had a major exam. *Hey, if anybody is listening, please beam me up. A galaxy far, far away is okay. I can handle it.*

Wikki was getting impatient. "Come on, Allie. Stop looking at yourself in the mirror and let's get going."

Allie stared back at her reflection. Skin too pale, long brown hair too straight, some freckles, stubby fingernails. And she was way too tall. She zipped her purse closed and grabbed her backpack. "Okay, I'm as ready as I'll ever be." Allie glanced at Wikki. "Why are *you* in such a hurry? Your father's the president of the school board. You never get in trouble; you won't get a tardy."

Wikki snorted. "Obviously, you don't live in my house."

"Oh, come on. Your parents are way cool. And you don't get in trouble at school, so why the frown? Nervous about the test?"

"Duh, Allie, I've nervous because we're *late* for class. I'm worried about *you*, not the test. The test is going to be one of Timmons' lame essay things where you write everything you know and then write some more. I *hate* that stuff."

Allie groaned. "Exactly."

Wikki held up Allie's discarded socks. "I love your socks, though," she said with a big grin, holding up each forest green cable knit before rubbing one against her cheek. "They're so soft. They'll be a perfect fit—whenever I can wear them."

Allie bent over her friend's wheelchair. "What do you mean, *when* you can wear them? You can wear them now. Want me to help put them on?"

Wikki looked down at her shoes. "No. Besides, I'd feel stupid wearing knee socks under my jeans." She stuffed the socks inside the backpack she kept on her lap and then glanced up with a smile. "I'll add them to my growing collection."

Allie's heart twisted. Her friend had spent the past twelve years of her life in a wheelchair. Allie washed and dried her hands, thinking she loved Wikki like the sister she never had. They both loved reading books and doing nerdy stuff like listening to music, drawing, talking on the phone. Neither one was the least bit athletic.

She put her hands on Wikki's shoulders and gave her a squeeze before opening the bathroom door. "You keep me sane. Never forget that. You're the only one who keeps me from doing really stupid stuff. When you walk again, I'll buy you ten dozen pairs of knee socks."

"Good. I'll need them to go with my plaid skirts. We'll be twins."

Allie didn't have the faintest idea how she could help Wikki walk again, but she planned to do it. Why did bad things have to happen to good people anyway? Wikki didn't have any say-so the day her mother headed to the grocery store without buckling her into her car seat. Wikki couldn't stop the eighteen-wheeler that rammed into the side of their car, nearly killing her mother and putting her in a wheelchair with nerve damage and a crippling spinal infection. Life wasn't fair!

Allie blinked away those thoughts. "You absolutely, positively yes, Wikki, you will walk again and do all kinds of stuff. I believe in you. I pray a lot. Good things will happen."

Allie took a deep breath before pushing Wikki out into the hallway. "I'm going to make sure that you walk again."

Wikki glanced up, smiling. "How?"

"I don't know, yet. I just don't know. But I'm making a plan," Allie said as she picked up speed to get them to class.

"I can't wait to hear about my learning-how-to-walk plan. *Omigosh*, we're sooo late for class. I think we're in big trouble."

Allie groaned. *Ugh.* It was Wednesday and Allie didn't know if she could stand three more days of listening to her teacher's sarcastic remarks. Just yesterday, Mrs. Timmons threw out another nasty comment about Mama being the newspaper editor. "Allie, you of all people should know that this is *not* a sentence. It's a fragment," she had said.

Luckily, Mrs. Timmons didn't know Allie's mom had also been an attorney when they lived in Pennsylvania. That info would blow off everybody's knee socks. The only attorney in this tiny Texas town was the well-despised Jack Morgan, who was as crooked as a barrel of snakes. Everybody just called him Black Jack for short, like he was some kind of pirate—of course, the fact that he wore an eye patch might have something to do with that. Rolling her eyes, Allie mumbled a prayer for courage and another one for strength. *Jeezalu.* It wasn't even 9:30 in the morning and she was bummed out already.

Chapter 2

SURE ENOUGH, HURRICANE Timmons awaited them as they rounded the corner.

Veins bulged in her neck. Fat fingers quivered as she twisted the wobbly classroom door knob. "Girls, I mean it this time. You have absolutely fried my patience. I'm not going to put up with this behavior one more minute." Mrs. Timmons's second and third chins wiggled as she delivered her final remark. "I'm writing you both up for this inexcusable, tardy behavior."

Allie scooted past her with Wikki safe in her wheelchair. *Jeez.* One glance at the wall clock told the story—five minutes past the tardy bell. Allie's eyes circled the room, seeing eighteen pairs of eyes trained in their direction.

Even Buzz Madison, the handsomest boy in the whole school—definitely not in her geeky group of friends—looked at her perplexed. Allie pushed Wikki to her desk then squeezed herself into a midget-sized desk nearby. Just as soon as she did, Alfred P. Twister slid his desk closer. *Oh, stay away, Alfred P.!*

The tick-tock of the clock sounded loud. Not a chair squeaked; not a body breathed. Mrs. Timmons paced up and down in front of the desks. Allie kept her head down. There were ten tiny desks on one side of the small room and ten tiny desks on the other side, forcing the students to face each other. Mrs. Timmons moved the desks around every few weeks, because she said this class was a rowdy bunch of kids. *Rowdy?* The most noise anybody made was an occasional sneeze.

Allie kept her eyes lowered as Mrs. Timmons returned to her teacher's desk.

"Now that everyone is here, we can prepare for our test. Unfortunately, a couple of your classmates have wasted your time by not coming to class promptly, so you will have less time in which to finish this first major exam."

Allie looked up to see Mrs. Timmons' eyes trained on her.

"So, class, if you do not finish your exam today, you can let Alexandra McCall and Monica Wilkerson know about your frustration."

Not wanting to look at Wikki, Allie lowered her lids and took out her pen. Just as soon as Mrs. Timmons began passing out the tests, Alfred P. inched his desk even closer.

"Get away from me," Allie whispered—mouthed actually—afraid she would be heard. "Move away, A.P. You're going to get me in more trouble."

Alfred P. Twister gave her a big, toothy grin, showing off his shiny braces. *He was such a pest. Whispering to her during class. Passing her notes.* Because they had assigned seats, Allie couldn't move anywhere else in the room. There was no way she could say anything to Mrs. Timmons about A.P. today. *Why is he smiling? Eew, he creeps me out.*

Mrs. Timmons handed Allie the last exam. "Good luck, students." She walked back to her desk.

Allie focused on the exam, noticing it was mostly multiple choice. *Mmm, this is cool. Only one essay question on the different parts of speech. I'll do that one first.* Allie absorbed herself in the test, thinking of her sample sentences and word usages. All of a sudden Mrs. Timmons stood before her and grabbed her test paper.

"That will be enough of that, Alexandra McCall. How dare you cheat in my class?"

"Wha-a-t?" Allie gasped. "Mrs. Timmons—"

Glaring, Mrs. Timmons bent her ample body over Allie's desk, shaking the test paper. "You were cheating off of Alfred's paper. I *saw* you!" Mrs. Timmons righted herself, her nostrils flaring. "This is absolutely, positively disgraceful!"

Mrs. Timmons rushed for the classroom door; Allie looked at Alfred P. "I didn't cheat off your paper," Allie hissed. "What is she talking about?"

A.P. grinned widely. "I dunno."

Eew. He was cheating! I knew Alfred P. hated English, but cheating?

Wikki leaned way over. "I saw him, Allie. He kept reading your answers. He liked yours better than his."

Lord-a-mercy. Allie tried to see who Mrs. Timmons was talking to outside. Several other students in class started whispering.

Oh, dirty linoleum floor, please open up and swallow me whole. Get me outta here right now. She shut her eyes, but a man's voice interrupted her thoughts.

"Alexandra, please come with me."

A stern-voiced Mr. Danner, the principal at Friendly High, waited for Allie. A telltale flush crept up over her collar as she detached herself from the midget desk and slung her backpack over one shoulder.

"Wait! I'm coming, too." With a handkerchief dangling in one hand, Mrs. Timmons pushed her way past Mr. Danner, rushing through the doorway. They took a shortcut and quickly ended up in Mr. Danner's office with Mrs. Timmons gasping for air.

"Call her mother right now, Jeffrey Danner. I know that Laura McCall will never believe this atrocity. This is simply outrageous."

"But, Mrs. Timmons, I—"

"Just a moment, young lady!"

Allie slumped helplessly into a rickety chair while Mr. Danner sat behind his ancient metal desk.

Mrs. Timmons paced the floor. "You know I've been teaching for over forty years, Jeffrey, and I can count on one hand the number of students who have cheated in my class!"

Jeez, if Mrs. Timmons has been teaching for over forty years, she was probably the principal's teacher. That's totally creepy, if not illegal.

Mr. Danner rifled through a computer printout and fumbled to dial a number, probably her mother's.

Poor Mr. Danner. I don't blame him for being scared. Mrs. Timmons scared him as much as everybody else in the school–maybe in the whole world. Mr. Danner swallowed hard and tried to hit the correct numbers on the telephone, so he wouldn't be next on Hurricane Timmons's hit list.

Truthfully, Allie liked Mr. Danner. Everybody did. He was, well, *perfect.* And who doesn't admire perfection? Perfectly dressed in his dark suits and white starched shirt, he wore red, white and blue ties every day. Every dark hair stayed in place all day, even on rainy days. His half glasses stayed perched in the exact same position on his nose; his big smile greeted students each day. Everyone said Mr. Danner probably didn't even own a pair of shorts or sneakers or T-shirts. No, Mr. Danner had been born in a dark suit and shiny black shoes with never a mark on them, no mud or dirt. *How did he keep them so clean? Maybe he wiped them off at lunch.*

How could we all not like him just for that? Nobody ever heard Mr. Danner cough, blow his nose, or laugh, actually. *That would not be perfect.*

Allie's gaze shifted back to her totally not-perfect teacher.

"I did not cheat, Mrs. Timmons. Alfred P. must have been reading my answers. I didn't know it. Honest. Our desks are so close together. Every class period he scoots his desk closer to mine—"

Allie stopped when Mrs. Timmons held up her hand. Mr. Danner mumbled something into the phone.

"Now call the sheriff." Mrs. Timmons ordered.

Jeezalu. Wrap me up and throw me away. The sheriff?

"Rudy Mae, we both know that cheating on a test is not illegal." Mr. Danner cleared his throat. "I left a message on Mrs. McCall's cell. I'm sure she'll call me right back. There is no reason to call the sheriff."

"The sheriff will know where Mrs. McCall is. And if she can't answer her phone, the sheriff can get a message to her. Not only did Allie cheat on her test, but she has been misbehaving in class. They both need to be told about this. I won't stand for it anymore."

With a loud sniff, Mrs. Timmons marched from one side of Mr. Danner's office to the other, pivoted and then marched in the other direction.

Misbehaving in class? Part of Allie stared at Mrs. Timmons in horror. The other part wanted to give her a whistle and some combat boots so she could really shout some orders. She looked to be a volcano on the brink of eruption. Her iridescent silvery blue hair stuck up everywhere. Most of Mrs. Timmons's students wondered how she got it that color, but figured it must be some kind of famous old-lady hair color. It went with the huge glasses that covered her eyebrows and most of her cheeks. Unlike the glasses, her flowery dress looked too small. Not one of her students' favorites, it boasted bulging buttons that never closed and huge belt loops that hung empty. The elastic belt had gone missing the first week of class—it flew off her waist during a lecture.

Now, Mrs. Timmons's renewed intensity made Allie sit up straight. *She's going to ruin my reputation and straight-A report card. Well, nearly straight A's. Ugh, math. If we could do away with math, the world would be a better place.*

"Jeffrey, did you make that call?" Mrs. Timmons bellowed, her face redder.

"Yes, Rudy Mae. Against my better judgment, I called Sheriff Logan Anderson. He's on his way."

Mr. Danner made a weak attempt at shuffling papers around on his desk, but Allie could see he was a doomed man, tortured and scared by Rudy Mae Timmons.

Jeezalu, everybody's gone crazy. Even Sheriff Anderson has been called.

Allie had grown accustomed to the idea that the sheriff liked mama. The two of them looked at each other when they thought the other wasn't looking. And then the sheriff's dark brown eyes would get all soft. Wikki thought it was romantic that they'd drink iced tea on Allie's tiny front porch.

A towering male figure in a starched uniform shirt filled the doorway—a strong, athletic man out of breath.

"I got here as soon as I could," Sheriff Anderson said, his voice a deep baritone. "I also left a message on Laura McCall's cell."

Allie wanted to crawl beneath the old spindly chair. Mama rushed in right behind him, her eyes wild with fright and her bright auburn hair tumbling from its tidy bun. Mama looked like she had been in a windstorm. She would faint if she knew how disheveled she looked, but Allie wasn't about to tell her.

The next instant Mama loomed over Allie. In that low, wicked voice that parents use to peel back a piece of skin rather than to ask a question, she whispered, "Young lady, what have you done?"

Nothing would get Allie to raise her head and look into Mama's eyes. Mama's temper could turn away a stampeding herd of wild animals. If they had a television show called "Lions Gone Crazy," then Mama would be the lead lion.

Allie raised her head ever so slowly, scared to speak. "I told them, Mama. I explained I didn't cheat. Alfred P. must have been cheating off my test."

Allie's voice was so soft that she barely heard herself. She awaited the onslaught. Mama opened and closed her mouth several times before she finally placed a hand on Allie's shoulder.

"Well, Mr. Danner," Mama said, glancing over at him, "as the principal of this high school, what do you propose we do? Alexandra is a bright student, she makes exceptional grades and, quite frankly, we've never had this kind of episode before."

Catching her reflection in the glass door, Mama hastily refastened her hair. Allie wanted to hug her mother. She came to the rescue so quickly.

Mrs. Timmons's lips turned up in a kind of snarl. "Episode, Mrs. McCall? Did you say 'this kind of episode'? I would call this outright cheating. As the newspaper editor, you might want to print a full story about this in next week's edition." Mrs. Timmons' eyes narrowed. "Tell everyone about how your daughter was found guilty of cheating on an English exam."

Uh-oh. Not good. Mama's normally bright hazel eyes turned dark and muddy. Allie could see the telltale white line around her lips. *Oh, Lordy, her nostrils flared.* Allie squeezed her eyes shut, almost feeling sorry for Mrs. Timmons. She had never tangled with Mama before and she didn't know what she was up against. Sure, Mrs. Timmons outweighed Mama three to one, but even Sheriff Anderson said Mama could cut a man off at the knees with words alone.

Allie knew she should settle back and enjoy the fight—because, well, she and Mama hardly ever agreed lately. Truth was, most days Mama was so strict that Allie couldn't stand being around her. *Better Mrs. Timmons than me in that fighting ring.*

Mama assumed her lawyer's pose, clasping both hands in front of her. "So, tell me—have you disciplined Alfred P. yet?" she asked sweetly.

"No," Mrs. Timmons replied, glancing at Mr. Danner. "I believe Mr. Danner will speak to him shortly."

"I see." Mama moved toward the window and opened the curtain with her finger for a better view of the ground below. Allie watched the cords in her neck tighten, as her cheeks flushed. *Holy moly.* Mama was so tense and angry. Allie knew she could've ripped out the window, sill and all. Too angry to look at Mrs. Timmons, Mama fixed her gaze on Mr. Danner.

"So—I'm to understand that you, Mrs. Timmons, and you, Mr. Danner, escorted my daughter, Alexandra, from her classroom. You disrupted the whole class—in fact, compromising the exam—to bring her to your office, Mr. Danner. You accused her of cheating in front of her classmates, Mrs. Timmons. And you, Mr. Danner, called the sheriff's office to report this alleged cheating, even though we all know that cheating on a test is certainly not illegal."

Now Mama leveled her furious gaze at Mrs. Timmons, her icy voice barely above a whisper. "I ask you again—is that the way it happened?"

Cool. She's closing in for the kill. Mrs. Timmons nodded quickly and Mr. Danner did the same.

"Excellent," Mama whispered. "Is there someone in your class right now, Mrs. Timmons? Or have you left your class unattended while the other students try to finish this exam…."

Mama's voice trailed off as Mrs. Timmons gasped, one beefy hand fluttering with her handkerchief. She rushed from the room, a nervous Mr. Danner in tow.

Sheriff Anderson walked over to Allie and gave her a big smile. *With his twinkly brown eyes and dark hair, he sure is handsome for an old man. Okay, so maybe he isn't all that old, but real close to Mama's age.*

He gave an easy tug on Allie's ponytail. "I should have known you couldn't stay out of trouble."

"I tried to tell her that I didn't cheat," Allie explained, "but she wouldn't listen."

Sheriff Anderson glanced at Mama, who was staring out of the window. "What do you think, Laura? Should I call out my deputy and lock her up?"

Allie's eyes grew twice their size until she heard Sheriff Anderson's throaty laugh. But Mama was far from mollified.

"I'm furious about this, Logan. How dare Mrs. Timmons do this, embarrass Allie and make such a huge stink in front of Allie's class and with the principal? And then calling you! It's just not fair. Allie would not, ever, cheat on a test."

"It's alright, Laura. I needed a break from my paperwork," remarked the sheriff. "Calling me went over the top, I agree. I'll talk to Mr. Danner later. But I know Mrs. Timmons. She's old. She's fractious. She's got a big temper. She intimidates everybody she meets. And she snapped this morning."

"Ya' think?" Mama snorted, pacing the floor as though trying to reason with the wooden planks.

"I don't think Mrs. Timmons likes you, Mama," Allie spoke up. "She's always making fun of the newspaper in class and trying to find places where you've made grammatical mistakes."

"What?" That stopped Mama cold. Her voice dropped. "What do you mean? She said I've made grammatical errors?" Kneeling next to Allie's chair, Mama whispered, "What errors? What has she found?"

"It was stupid. Really, it was. Don't worry about it. She was telling the class that you were wrong to leave out a comma in a sentence. That's all."

Mama gulped. "What did the other students in the class say? Did they agree?"

"You can't be serious. Nobody in my class cares about commas. They don't care about spelling, or writing, or words, or anything else that has anything at all to do with English. They hate English like I hate math."

Sheriff Anderson took Mama's arm. "Laura, let's decide what to do here. Allie is likely to receive an F on her exam."

"Mrs. Timmons should let her retake the exam right along with all the other students in the class that she left unattended."

"If there's anything I can do—"

"Thank you, Logan, but I can't think of a thing." Mama interrupted, glancing about. "Right now, all I have are questions. What can we do to remedy this situation? What's the next step—and—where in the world is Mr. Danner?"

Chapter 3

❧

ALLIE LOVED LISTENING to the rain. The drip-drip-dripping sounds of the water hitting the leaves beneath her bedroom window lulled her into a quiet meditation. Because of the expense, Mama rarely rarely turned on the heater. It was no big deal, Allie just slept with an extra layer of socks and pajamas.

Tonight's cooler-than-usual September breeze smelled fresh, but it searched out secret passageways around her windows. As the quiet chill seeped inside, she pulled the blankets up around her chin. It was a sad night. After today's horrible ordeal, nothing mattered. Not ready for sleep yet, Allie pulled out an old spiral notebook and pencil from under her mattress and began to write:

Dear Dad:

It's been a while, but I've just got to tell somebody. One awful thing after another keeps happening to me. Nobody listens. It's like my life is coming to an end.

It's eight o'clock, but feels like midnight. I finished my homework and the house is quiet. I've had a horrible day. I was humiliated in every class and laughed at by every kid. How am I gonna face them tomorrow? There's Thursday and Friday to get through and I know I can't, I won't go back into Mrs. Timmons' classroom.

Everybody kept whispering behind my back. They said cheating on the test was Alexandra's "Big Mistake." And then kids started calling it Alexandra's "B.M." Mr. Danner made an announcement over the loudspeaker for everybody to stop—that anyone calling the incident a "B.M." would be written up. All one hundred and five freshman kids laughed out loud. Way too humiliating.

Mama told me tonight about her conversation with Mr. Danner. He agreed with Mrs. Timmons's decision to give me an F on my English exam. Mama protested, but I told her to let it go. I'll take the F and just put the whole thing behind me.

And then there was tonight's dinner. Okay, so I can't cook. That may be part of the reason dinner was awful. I really try. But I can't learn from Mama because she doesn't cook anymore, and we don't have much food in the house. When we do sit down at the table, nobody says a word. Maybe that's a good thing. I read somewhere that families are supposed to talk. I guess we don't have much in common. Ben turned ten years old last weekend, but we didn't have a party or even a cake.

I remember my nine-year-old birthday party was the best ever. Remember it, Dad? Loads of balloons and cupcakes that Mama had baked. I loved our house in Pennsylvania. We played outside and had home-cooked dinners at night, lots of good weekend breakfasts with pancakes and waffles. Mama was happy. You were happy.

Then you got so sick. I heard Mama talking to her friends about your medication and chemotherapy treatments. She said we couldn't pay the bills and there was this house in Texas that had belonged to your family. Then, when you died, part of me died, too.

This house and the ten acres are all we had left. I wonder what life would have been like if you had lived. We'd still be living in Pennsylvania. I would have never seen Friendly, Texas. I would never have taken English from Mrs. Timmons. I would never have been accused of cheating on a test. I would never have worn nasty blue eye shadow and black eyeliner to her class. I would never have slept on this lumpy old bed.

Some days I want to go to sleep and never wake up. There's nothing for me here except another day of humiliation and more awful school. Thank goodness for Wikki. Why is she crippled? Why is life so confusing? Sometimes I want to close my eyes and sleep forever....

ONE LONE TEAR slipped down her cheek, then another. Allie thrust her pencil and paper beneath her pillow. Crying never accomplished anything. *Please, God, please let me be happy.*

Allie never saw the hazy silhouette in her room that night. She never knew that an angel watched over her. In fact, she'd be surprised to know exactly how many nights this tall stranger with silvery hair and blue eyes had kept her company.

Daniel stared down at the sleeping girl, thinking again how much he'd grown to love her. He'd watched her grow from a sweet, loving, shy child into a struggling, disgruntled teenager. Not so sweet now, perhaps, but certainly spirited and courageous. And he would need all of Allie McCall's spirit and courage soon.

"So, tell me, Daniel. How is your assignment progressing?" A second angel materialized.

"Ah, Michael, 'tis you. Everything's going well. Quite well, indeed. I'll meet her tomorrow and lay out the plans."

"She *is* young. Are you sure she will be up to all this? She is a child after all, and you're asking her to take on assignments that would challenge an adult."

Daniel nodded. "Yes, she's young. And you're right. I will challenge her in ways she's never known before."

"True. Very true. I'm worried that she can take the pressure. Her life will change radically, you know that. You've tried this project before and you remember the terrible consequences—"

"I know. I know," Daniel interrupted, "you never quite let me forget it."

Michael chuckled. "You amaze me. You're forever the optimist. You believe so strongly in the very people who may wind up disappointing you in the end."

Daniel smiled. "Remaining optimistic is more important than knowing disappointment. But, in Allie's case, I hope I'm not being too optimistic. I have a strong feeling this young lady will be different from all the rest."

"Ah, well, perhaps you're right," Michael replied. "You know that this could be your last Earthly assignment. Those other attempts at rebuilding local churches took years and still weren't successful. You may simply have chosen the wrong people to help in your quest. So this time Daniel, try harder. *Succeed.* We're counting on you."

Daniel nodded, then sighed. "In spite of my optimism, I don't do well with Earthly subjects. And this is a young lady. You're right about that. Still, she's an excellent candidate. Maybe the best one I've found. But I may have a hard time explaining just how important our project is. You know how clumsy I can be. I scare people. You've seen how it goes."

"Never forget that you're one of the good guys. And this is splendid training for you. Interacting with an Earthly human is never easy for any of us, Daniel. But I do agree that Alexandra McCall is a good choice. Just go easy. You saw what she wrote just now. She's disillusioned and disheartened. It sounds like she needs renewed self-confidence. Put on your handsome face and be your charming self. So, what's your deadline?"

"The end of November."

"Excellent. I think you can do it."

Deadlines. Always deadlines. If anyone could save this dying town and its church, it was Allie McCall. Daniel knew it. He'd bet his celestial ring on it. And, thousands of years old, the ring was his most valuable possession.

Who was he kidding? As an angel, it was his only possession.

Chapter 4

✿

THURSDAY, SEPTEMBER 16

THURSDAY DAWNED COOL and crisp, sunshine reigned everywhere except in Allie's heart. She stared down at the wooden steps of the rotting church, wondering why she was here and not at school. Well, it had been her choice.

Skipping school. A first. Maybe my worst decision. EVER!

She glanced down at her watch. *9:15. Too late now.* Mrs. Timmons would be calling roll and asking anyone if they'd seen her. Allie knew the routine. No one would answer because, truthfully, nobody knew she was at the corner of Main and Pine sitting outside of the old community church—the only church in downtown Friendly. And to think she had walked two miles to get here.

She glanced the hundred or so yards to the empty street. Nope, not much traffic at this hour of the morning. Her gaze traveled left to the backyard areas of the few shops quietly waiting for customers. At the pharmacy, where Nate Sims had filled a cold medicine prescription for her about a month ago, the back door stood slightly ajar. Mr. Nate had already been out once this morning to empty the garbage. He had the prettiest white fence lining the back of his store. Allie found herself counting the sixty-eight perfectly placed picket boards that marched over to Mr. Nate's small café next door. People said Nate Sims made the best homemade croissants anywhere on the planet. His pizzas were yummy, too—all cheesy with lots of toppings and a handmade crust. Just thinking about it made her stomach growl. She had only eaten there only once, but couldn't wait to go back.

She scooted down one more porch step, glancing up at the large cross that had stood in front of the well-worn building for a hundred years. The cross looked stark and lonely, its paint worn away by falling rain and perching birds.

Only a few hundred yards off of Main Street, the church sat on a small knoll, as if to oversee and protect everything below. *A nice location, really.* Allie half-turned, really looking at the church for the first time.

She'd never come this close before; she had only glanced at it from the street. She'd never noticed the ironbound front doors. *Jeez.* They had to be about twelve feet tall, certainly taller than she was. Now gray with age, they looked original. *Old, just like everything else in this town.*

Each side of the building had four windows, the walls dulled by time and weather. *Nothing that couldn't be fixed*, she thought. What songs and services had those windows heard? They'd seen babies baptized, heard choirs sing, watched couples get married, watched others laid to rest. How many years had the church been empty? Allie didn't know.

Most folks in town now attended churches along the new highway. A Methodist church had been built about ten years ago—and more churches were breaking ground.

Allie glanced at the church's front entryway. Out of curiosity, she'd tried to open the heavy front doors moments ago, but they'd been locked.

The phrase "quiet as a tomb" came to her mind, yet she felt completely at home. Her mind settled down from her horrible Wednesday and came to grips with what was going to be a terrible Thursday.

Stay here? Run away?

She leaned over to retie a shoelace and a line of ants caught her eye. Inch by inch, they trekked along the splintered wooden step carrying tidbits of food. *Working all day. No fun. No play. That was an ant's life.* One tear, then another slipped from her cheek to fall near the ants' path. How could her life have gone so wrong?

If only her father were here. She could talk to him, confide in him. Allie's heart twisted as she raised her tear-stained face to the battered cross.

"Daddy, why did you have to die?"

The cross didn't answer. A gentle breeze ruffled her hair. The wind played with a dry leaf that had fluttered from a nearby tree, eventually dropping it on the wooden step where she sat.

Absorbed in her thoughts, she didn't hear the rustling of a broom behind her.

"'Morning," came a friendly voice.

"Uh, hi." Allie turned quickly, wiping her cheeks.

A tall man busily swept off the small porch. When he glanced up, Allie met the clearest, bluest, most gorgeous eyes she'd ever seen.

"I-I-didn't see you," she stumbled.

Allie knew every single person in town, except the new Franklin family twins who were born only a couple of weeks ago. She didn't know *him*.

With a big grin, he hoisted the broom in the air, jumped two steps and plopped down beside her. His ball cap flew off and a lock of silver hair fell over his forehead. Allie felt her mouth drop open, but no words came out.

Blue eyes and silver hair. *Silver?* It wasn't white, exactly. It was shiny, shimmery silver in the bright sun. He didn't look old. She went to school with kids and this was no kid. In Friendly there were kids, then parents and grandparents. But this guy... this guy had high cheekbones, boyish dimples, chiseled features—and those magical blue eyes that looked full of mischief. His inviting grin showed an expanse of even white teeth. He was tall and lean with not one ounce of fat on his athletic frame. His muscular arms filled his old blue T-shirt.

"Who *are* you?" she asked.

He extended his right hand. "My name's Daniel. What's yours?"

Of course his voice would be deep, mystical and beautiful. *Pure excitement. Unbridled energy.* Allie returned his smile. She'd never seen anyone like him before. How old was he? Nineteen? Twenty-five?

Suddenly she felt happy, like a puppy with a new playmate. She shook his outstretched hand with newfound confidence. "I'm Allie. And, er, I'm a student at the high school. I'm, uh, in ninth grade." She her cheeks were hot; she felt foolish and clumsy and totally stupid.

He tossed his head back and laughed before fixing a perceptive gaze on her. "Unless you're on a field trip of one, I don't think you're in high school today. I think you've skipped school."

She wanted to disappear, but the wooden church steps wouldn't open up and swallow her any more than the linoleum floor did yesterday.

"You're a lovely young lady skipping school on a picture-perfect day. Why on earth would you come to this dilapidated church?"

Such a simple question, yet she had no answer. She met his gaze again. *Me? Lovely?* He was a little nosy, but he had nice manners, almost perfect manners. *So polite. Even the way he runs his hand through his silver hair seems perfect. Everything about him is oddly beautiful…so precise. His smile, his teeth, his beautiful face, his politeness—all too perfect to be in this tiny town. He just didn't fit.*

"I…it's complicated. I don't even know you. You're asking all these questions—" She rose abruptly. Suddenly she didn't want this guy around. *He could see too much. He's too perfect. Asks too many questions. Calling me lovely—I'm not lovely.*

She stood over him as he sat on the step. "This church is *not* dilapidated," she blurted out. "It's old and it's beautiful. It's over one hundred years old. I'm sure there were people who loved this church. And, today, well it helped me think. I don't care if nobody goes to church here anymore. You'd think somebody could take care of it, though."

Why am I babbling? Allie met his quizzical stare, but said nothing. She didn't owe him any explanation. *I mean, who is he, anyway?*

"Fair enough," he said. "I'm glad you told me how you feel. As it happens, it is my job to care for the church. Actually, it's my job to care for a lot of things. But after listening to you, I don't think I've done a very good job. I don't think people are happy with this church. You're not happy with this church; you just told me so."

"Just look at it!" she gestured. "Anybody can see it's not being taken care of." She softened, adding, "I didn't mean any disrespect. I'm s-sorry."

His eyes warmed as a smile played on his lips. "Let's make a deal, then."

"A deal?"

"You're suspicious. I understand. You have every right to be. Here I am, this guy, a stranger who's talking to you—a very, lovely young lady…" His smile faded as Allie instinctively took a step away.

He reached to stop her. "Don't be afraid. I mean you no harm. No harm whatsoever. But I may need your help. No, I definitely need your help."

Allie stared hard into those velvety eyes. "My help?"

"My assigned task is clear. I must renovate the church."

She blinked twice. "Renovate the church! Omigosh! How cool! That's wonderful!"

A sudden excitement bubbled up inside her. *Wow. He sounds like he really wants to do something real.*

His smile returned. "So I have an ally? Can I count on you for help?"

"Me? Help you? I don't know anything about building anything. I have no idea how to help you."

"You can be a big help. No doubt, I'm going to need a lot of that. I'll need supplies. Could you direct me to people who could help me?"

"Oh, sure, absolutely. Now that I can do," Allie smiled with assurance. "I know just about everybody in this whole town and where they all live. I just don't know anything about this church—or anything about any churches, really."

Daniel grinned. "Churches are something I know a lot about. In fact, sit down—take a load off your feet, lovely Allie McCall, I'll tell you…"

"What a minute…how'd you know my last name?"

He waved her away. "I know a lot of people."

"Oh, yeah? Well, I bet you don't know my best friend, Monica," Allie said.

"Indeed I do. I knew Wikki before she needed a wheelchair."

Allie gasped. Few people knew Wikki. "You did? You knew her back then? Wow, the accident happened twelve years ago. You are old!"

Daniel laughed. "I am, indeed. Some people call me ancient. Now, test me again."

"Okay…do you know my name, my real name?" she asked.

"I know you as Allie. But your Christian name is Alexandra Antoinette McCall."

"Whoa, Daniel, you're creeping me out. How did you know my whole name?" Allie jumped up and backed away from the steps, dragging her backpack. "Stay away from me, Daniel whatever-your-last-name-is—"

He called out, "Hey, wait, Allie. Don't be afraid. I've handled this badly. I didn't mean to scare you. I'm just, well, not used to talking to people. I say the wrong thing."

I hear that, Allie thought, sympathizing despite herself. *I'm always saying the wrong thing.*

He reached out to her. "I'd tell you my full name, but you couldn't pronounce it."

Still on the broken walkway, Allie faced him again. "You're scaring me, Daniel."

"I'm not going to hurt you. Fear not, Allie. I've worked at many, many churches, remember? I'm supposed to know people's names and faces. It's, well, my job to know about… you."

Allie watched Daniel approach, realizing he was taller than she was. She didn't look him square in the eyes or see over the top of his head. She actually had to look up. *How often does that happen?* He took a few more steps toward her, his gait relaxed, his head held high. Okay, maybe he was right. It wouldn't be a stretch for him to know who she was. Her family had visited the new church; their names would be recorded in the registry. He might know her from that.

"Have you really worked in churches a long time?"

He grinned again. He sure was pretty to look at—though way too old for her. Even Wikki would agree.

"I've been working in churches forever," he said, softly.

"Are you telling me the truth?"

His smile faded and his face grew serious. "I always tell the truth. If you'd like, I could tell you about this church, what work needs to be done and how you're going to help."

"Okay—"

An angry honk interrupted them. Allie whirled around to see the black and white police car idling on Main Street.

Sheriff Anderson leaned out the window and yelled up the grassy hillside. "Come on, young lady. You and I need to talk."

His voice didn't sound a bit friendly. *Uh-oh.* Allie felt faint. Her knees wobbled as her earlier bravado took a hike.

Daniel loomed over her as she turned back around. *Jeez. He's way over six feet tall!.*

"It'll be okay," he whispered.

"Promise?" She grabbed up her backpack to run toward the street. On impulse, she turned back around and yelled, "Bye, Daniel!"

He stood on the walkway with his broom by his side, his other arm waving, blue eyes inquisitive, wearing that enigmatic smile. "Bye!" he called out, "and next time, visit *after* school, okay?"

Next time? She'd probably never leave the house again now. *I am such an idiot! Why did I have to skip school right before I met Daniel?*

Allie braced herself for the interrogation waiting in the police car. Head down, she opened the back door and got in. Sheriff Anderson turned to look at her.

"It's nearly eleven o'clock, young lady. Your mama is worried sick about where you are and why you're not at school. You were wrongly accused of cheating yesterday and I spoke to Mr. Danner about his misguided actions and about Mrs. Timmons's impulsive behavior. But this—this is completely different. This *is* against the law. It's called truancy and you are guilty of it today. So you're going to visit my jail."

Sheriff Anderson put the car in drive and focused on the road.

Allie's mind raced at warp speed. "Me? Jail? For real?"

"Uh-huh. I can't trust you to go back to school today—and stay there. Your mother is away at a business meeting. And I've got to finish some paperwork and escort a prisoner to the Tyler courthouse." He gave Allie a stern look in his rearview mirror. "I have no time to babysit a truant juvenile."

Things had gone from bad to worse. The "cheating" scandal had now progressed to jail time. At least she met Daniel this morning—the day wasn't a total loss.

"Sheriff Anderson, do you know the guy I was talking to at the church?"

The sheriff made his last turn around the square, pulling up in front of the small police station. He sighed and half-turned around. "What guy? There hasn't been anybody at that church in the seven years I've lived in Smith County. Folks say it's been empty for over fifty years. It's not good for much but a historical site, and even then it would have to be rebuilt." He shuffled some papers on the front seat. "The land might be useful—I know the church grounds were once a community garden. Neighbors worked together to grow vegetables."

"But who is Daniel? Who was the guy sweeping the porch? Is he some kind of caretaker? He had a broom—"

Sheriff Anderson got out of the car and made his way around to open her door. "Allie, I don't know of any guy named Daniel anywhere around here."

"Wait." Allie laid her hand on his arm. "You must know him."

Sheriff Anderson grabbed her backpack. "Young lady, I don't know what you're getting at. There was nobody with you at the church. And you need to be careful about that. Don't look so surprised. It looked to me like you'd been up those steps—they're dangerous. In that condition, the old church is not the safest place to be. There's no caretaker, certainly not one named Daniel." The sheriff hoisted the backpack over his shoulder before taking Allie's elbow. "In fact, I don't even know anybody named Daniel," he said, guiding her toward her jail home for the day.

No Daniel? How could that be? Allie entered the sheriff's office, her mind whirring from his explanation. Nobody could miss all six feet-whatever of gorgeous Daniel. Those blue eyes! Silver hair! Every female on earth would remember Daniel.

No Daniel? No broom? Something was terribly wrong.

Chapter 5

"**GOOD MORNING, YOUNG** lady." A cheerful voice greeted her from behind the reception desk.

"G'morning, Miss Matthews," Allie replied, feeling foolish. Miss Matthews knew everybody's business. Word would now spread like wildfire, if the receptionist hadn't been on the phone already. She probably had the whole town on speed dial and would only have to press one button to start the gossip about Allie skipping school.

"Why don't you call me Maggie? Being around your Mama these past few years and talking about you and your brother all the time, I feel like you're one of the family. Would you like a glass of water?"

Maggie moved from her desk to the counter, motioning for Allie to step closer.

Just then, Sheriff Anderson's voice boomed off the walls. "Maggie, put her in the holding area. I thought this file was complete, but I still need to make two more phone calls before I leave."

The ringing telephone interrupted them and bubbly Miss Maggie answered. In her short multi-colored skirt and tight orange sweater, Miss Maggie made a bright contrast to the musty, gray metal desks lining the reception area. The plain beige paint on the walls didn't do much to hide the nicks and scratches from years of furniture moving. Sadly, Miss Maggie's only connection to the outside world came through a skinny dirty window inches away from the ceiling. *Yuk.*

But Maggie's good humor didn't seem to suffer. Rouge crinkled when she laughed, accentuating the creases in her aqua eye shadow. Her orange lipstick matched her sweater, but her hair did not seem to match anything.

Such a strange burgundy color. She wore light blue eyeglasses with crystals buried in the turned-up corners of the frames. *Bright and cheerful.*

Miss Maggie hung up the phone and stepped from behind her desk. "Allie, come with me. I need you to sit in this chair nearest the doorway." She picked up a set of keys. "The prisoner will be leaving us in a short bit."

"Thank you, ma'am."

Miss Maggie glanced at her watch. "Well, I'll be. Nearly lunchtime. Tell you what. I'll bring you back a sandwich when I go out in a minute. Would you like a big iced tea, too?"

Wow. "Yes, ma'am! That sounds great."

Allie stumbled against the chair as Miss Maggie turned to leave, quietly closing the door behind her. *So this must be the holding area.* The grey room was dimly lit and smelled musty. Several of the overhead fluorescents had burned out. *Maybe that's a blessing. Eew.*

"Hey! What's your name?" came a raspy voice from the far end of the room.

This must be the prisoner.

The gruff voice sounded again. "Hey! Answer me." He laughed coarsely. "I can't hurt you. I'm locked up. Hey, girl, can't you see me? I'm in the back of this dungeon. I asked you a question. What's your name?"

Allie peered into the four-foot-square cell, looking through heavy bars that could have come from the Spanish Inquisition. A dark-skinned man stood there, long dark hair falling to his shoulders and one lock stretched across his face. Everything about this guy was dark, except for a flash of white that showed when he laughed. Even his T-shirt was black, except for a small red skull imprinted on the chest. He wore tight blue jeans and, with legs spread akimbo, he looked like a tiger ready to spring. Neither had been washed in weeks.

The cell bars will protect me. Allie edged closer, curious. *Is that a scar on his cheek?* It rippled from the right side of his mouth to his cheekbone. *A pirate*, she thought. *With a scarf tied around his head, he'd be a pirate.*

Okay, I've seen enough. But her feet wouldn't stop. She felt herself moving toward him, as if she had no will of her own—nothing to say about it. Her feet took one heavy step, then another. She grasped her thighs to stop herself, but she couldn't control her legs. Only inches from the bars, she stopped abruptly.

Allie gazed into his eyes—fathomless pits they were—the blackest, most sinister eyes she'd ever seen. Where most people have pupils, he had none. For some reason, *she* now felt like the prisoner.

"I want to know your name," he whispered, white teeth flashing in a mock smile.

He was not nearly as old as he looked from a distance; the gnarled scar looked deeper, uglier. From a lost battle, perhaps. *Why am I thinking of battles?*

She swallowed hard. "Allie," she whispered.

Again, his cocky smile. "Short for Alexandra, I presume. What a lovely young lady you are, Alexandra. Although you do have a smudge of mascara under your left eye. May I remove it for you?" He didn't wait for an answer, but snaked his arm through the cell bars to reach up and trace his thumb across her left cheek. "There. All better."

His brief touch electrified her.

"Alexandra," he cooed, before tossing back his head and giving a hearty laugh. "Don't be afraid of me. Whatever you do, don't stare at me like an innocent child." His lips curled wickedly. "Because you're not innocent, now, are you, Alexandra? You're in jail. With me." His chuckle left Allie feeling covered in slime. "You chose to be here."

Allie gasped. "I do NOT wish to be here. I was b-b-rought here by Sheriff Anderson. I want to be in school."

Her heart raced lickety-split.

He peered through the bars. "You keep thinking those naughty thoughts, Alexandra, because you and I are going to meet again one day."

"N-no way. You're in jail …."

"I'm being moved today."

"I know. I'm glad. I'm glad you're being moved."

"You're not glad. You like me. Admit it."

Allie straightened herself. "No! I do not like you. I--" Her voice broke off. Her mouth opened and closed. *I have no idea what to say…when has that ever happened?*

He turned slightly and relaxed against the cell bars. He feigned a look at his fingernails. *Immaculately groomed. Incredible.*

"You want to know where I got this scar on my face," he whispered.

She could barely pull her gaze from it. *I wonder how the other guy looks.* "Sorry, but I don't have time for stories today."

"Another day, then," he said, cocking his head, fixing his gaze on her. "You have a strong will, Alexandra, a very strong will. Women with such a strong will always pose certain challenges to me." His sardonic smile widened. "They are my favorites."

"Allie McCall!" barked Sheriff Anderson. "Step away from that cell right now."

Sheriff Anderson came up from behind her, carrying her backpack. Leaning close to her ear, he whispered, "You were supposed to wait for me in the chair over by the door."

"Well, I--"

The sheriff took her elbow, guiding her out the door and into his office. "Have a seat please," he said, laying his keys on top of a big file folder. "I didn't want you to talk to the guy. I only wanted you to spend five minutes seeing what criminals look at for years."

"Five minutes?" *Jeez. It seemed like an hour.* She had never met a man who was so disturbing in every way.

"I checked my watch. Five minutes, exactly." Sheriff Anderson moved from behind his desk to tower over her as she sat in a wooden chair. "What did he say?"

Allie had never seen such a dark look on the sheriff's face. *Worry? Concern—fear, maybe?* "Nothing much. He asked me what my name was. He said we would meet again. But how could I meet him again?"

"You won't. There's nothing for you to worry about there. He's going with me in a few minutes."

"What did he do?"

"Ethan Benedict? He's building quite a criminal record for himself. The man is only twenty-five years old and we believe he's wanted for assault and battery in multiple counties. In our county, he terrorized a family because he wanted to run off with their daughter. Ethan and the daughter were making a run for it when the girl's mother and father caught up with them. The father stood up to Ethan. Told him 'no,' that he couldn't marry his daughter. Then and there, Ethan allegedly beat the mother, father and the young girl within an inch of their lives. They all had to be hospitalized. Ethan doesn't know we have a neighbor who will testify that he witnessed the whole event." Sheriff Anderson shook his head. "He's one mean critter. I dread driving an hour to Tyler with him. I've tried to reach Deputy Darrell, but he won't be able to ride with me. Darrell is still in the hospital in Wallisville with his wife. Deidre had surgery a few days ago."

"I had heard about that—"

"Well, Deidre will be okay. But I gave Darrell the rest of the week off to take care of her."

Allie was glad about that. She liked Deputy Darrell Larson and his wife. They were a young couple who had moved to Friendly a year ago. Deputy Darrell visited the high school regularly and knew most everybody by their first names. He worked part-time for the sheriff and was also in charge of the Friendly Fire Department.

Sheriff Anderson bent over her chair. "Listen to me, Allie. I've called your mother with the news that you skipped school today. I've also called the school and talked to Mr. Danner. I explained that I had found you in town and that you'll be disciplined here," he said, standing up. "Don't look so shocked."

Called my mother? Called Mr. Danner? Jeez. Allie thought now on top of the cheating incident, there would be the school-skipping gossip.

Sheriff Anderson opened one of his desk drawers and pulled out a small paper bag. "You knew something would happen when you skipped school today. You knew there would be consequences for your actions. In other words, Allie, you have to take responsibility for what you've done."

Allie closed her eyes. *He sounds just like Mama.*

"Instead of giving you in-school suspension, I've asked Mr. Danner to loan you to me every afternoon. I need your help with a community service project I'm thinking about. The good news is that you'll be helping your community. The bad news is that your punishment will use up your free time in the afternoon."

"You're assigning me something else to do?"

As if watching Ben after school isn't enough? Oh, and doing all of the chores and cooking?

She sighed. "When do I start this project?"

"Next week," he said, handing her the paper bag. "I'll tell you more about it tomorrow. Now, take this cell phone. It's for you."

"But—"

"I know you don't have a cell phone. Your mom mentioned that she wanted you to have one, but I know that your family can't afford to buy one right now. So take this. I'm loaning it to you. I have about sixty minutes left, so don't chat with your friends."

A cell phone? My own cell phone? "But—"

"To have in case of an emergency." He opened the phone for her. "My personal cell is '1' on the speed dial; your mother is '2'. I'm sure you know how to dial '911' in an emergency if you can't reach either of us."

Sommy L. Ham

"But—"
"But nothing. Now, what do you say?"

Chapter 6

ꙮ

ALLIE STARED AT Sheriff Anderson, then at the shiny black cell phone in her hand. For two years she had wanted a phone. She'd even prayed for a phone. Every other kid in her school had a cell phone. Now she had one thanks to the unlikeliest person on earth. She jumped up and threw both arms around the sheriff's rock-solid chest.

"Thank you so much," she whispered into his shirt pocket. "It's the best gift—ever."

Logan chuckled and tugged on her ponytail. "Just be careful. No more cutting school. No failing grades. Behave yourself, Allie. You're in high school. Your mother has raised you to know better, and I expect you to act like it. And, if you make Bs or better on your report card, I'll refill your minutes and you can keep the phone. I'll even add texting privileges."

Woo-hoo! "No way! Are you kidding? You'll buy the minutes and the texting? You've got yourself a deal." Trembling all over, she extended her hand. "Let's shake on it."

He smiled and his big hand gripped her smaller one. They shook, then he picked up his keys and folder.

"I've gotta roll. You sit right here," he said, pointing, "Right here by the door. Maggie!"

"Yes, sheriff?"

"Allie is going to stay here in my doorway where you can see her. I want to give you some privacy while I'm gone." He turned to Allie. "Do you have some homework? Like homework you can do in order to make a B or better in all of your classes?"

"Absolutely. Two long chapters to read in history."

She took her seat while Sheriff Anderson went through the door to get his prisoner. Allie tucked her new cell phone in her jeans pocket. It was so slender she barely felt it at all. *A new phone. I can't believe it.* Allie got out her books, not realizing that Sheriff Anderson would have to lead Ethan right past her in leg irons and handcuffs.

Ethan swiveled his head and stared hard at her before offering a disarming smile.

"C'mon, Ethan. There's nothing to look at," growled Sheriff Anderson. "You've got a hot date with the Smith County judge this afternoon."

Ethan's smile withered. Maggie opened the door as the two men walked into the bright sunlight, making a beeline for the police car.

Allie rushed to the too-high front window and stood on her tiptoes, trying to see through the dingy glass. She watched the sheriff secure Ethan inside the car in the back right-hand seat. *Exactly where I sat earlier this morning!*

Miss Maggie reappeared, closing the door behind her.

"Well, now…while you were in the sheriff's office, I went down to the bakery and bought us a couple of sandwiches. I knew you'd be hungry." Miss Maggie set out two drinks and took out two hot croissants from the sack.

Whoa. Smelling the freshly baked treats, Allie bolted for the wooden chair Miss Maggie indicated. She laid a napkin in her lap before diving into the food.

Miss Maggie chuckled. "Well, I guessed right. You are hungry."

Mmm. Hot ham and cheese. Fabulous. Allie chewed and closed her eyes. *And chips, too. Yummy. And iced tea. This is way better than the awful food at school. Having lunch out and getting a cell phone—today isn't so bad after all.*

"Sheriff Anderson didn't want you talking to the prisoner, Allie. He was real upset about that," Maggie said before biting into a chip.

Allie nodded and chewed. *Ethan.* He was charming, yet disgusting. A real creep. Thank goodness she could forget about him; she would rather think about Daniel. He'd made her laugh.

"Miss Maggie, can you answer a question?" Allie put down her sandwich and wiped her mouth with the napkin. "Do they have a caretaker working at the old community church at Main and Pine? A guy named Daniel? Sheriff Anderson said there hasn't been anybody there in years. But this morning I talked to a guy named Daniel who had a broom and was sweeping the porch."

Miss Maggie finished chewing and gave Allie a quizzical look. "A caretaker? No, the sheriff's right. Ain't nobody goes there nowadays. Floor's rotten on the inside. You need to be careful about the steps, too, Allie. They're half gone. But that old cross is still standing, that it is. That old cross—I declare, that building may fall down in a heap of splinters, but that cross out front will still be standing."

"Why?" Allie took a chip and munched patiently. A juicy story was about to unfold. People in Friendly, Texas loved storytelling, almost as much as everybody loved cell phones. She felt the tiny bulge in her pocket. "Why will the cross be standing?" Allie asked again.

Maggie shrugged and chewed thoughtfully. "Maybe the stories our grandparents told us are true. If you've seen the cross, then you can imagine how big those beams must have been, even though they've been worn away over the years. Folks say those beams came from cypress trees thousands of years old. The story goes that the early settlers to this area found the cross already erected—right on that very spot. Nobody really knows why the cross was put there or who put it there. It's just always been there. That's why folks built the church on that hill. I think that now everybody's afraid to take it down—or take down the church. Maybe it is just a bunch of superstitious gobbledygook."

Maggie took a sip of tea. "You should ask your mother. She knows everything there is to know about this area. I bet you know that your father grew up here and your mother grew up about twenty miles away." Her face suddenly lit up. "In fact, your father was baptized in that old church. My sister Frances—do you know her, Fanny Parker? Well, she and I were just young'uns, but I remember your daddy, Jerry McCall, being baptized there."

"My father?"

"Sure. We all knew Jerry. Your mama called him Gerald, but, around here, we call folks by their nicknames. My sister's name is Frances, but folks call her Fanny. My name's Margaret, but friends call me Maggie. Like you, Allie. People around here shortened your name from Alexandra to Allie. We're all friends." She leaned over and gently squeezed Allie's arm.

Maggie's kindness warmed Allie, like having a picnic in the office did. Nice and quiet, with plain conversation. Allie didn't have to pretend she was cool or smart—or anything. This was different from school. *I'm beginning to like the sheriff's office.*

Between bites, she said, "I didn't know you had a sister. I haven't heard of anyone named Fanny."

Maggie put down her tea. "Shoot, we haven't talked in twenty-five years. We got crossways way back when. My sister knows why. She went off her rocker when her husband died. Lord, but Cecil was a good man, a young man when he died and Fanny—well, Fanny just dove head first into her plants, her roots and—"

"She lives in—plants?"

"No, silly. She has a big greenhouse on her property. Fanny pretty much buried herself in her plants and those herbs she grows. Of course she has her dog, her horse, a few cats and some chickens. Like I said, we haven't spoken in nearly twenty-five years."

Surprised, Allie ventured, "You mean that you haven't said 'hello' to your sister in almost twenty-five years? How is that possible? This town is so small."

Maggie shrugged. "It's easy. I work; she doesn't. Though some say she makes money at farmers' markets during the year, selling her plants and herbal recipes. We know a lot of the same people, but she lives a couple of miles outside of town and I live closer in."

Maggie took a chip from the bag. "In fact, she doesn't live far from you. Y'all live on the old Pierson farm and Fanny lives just across the road at Cragg's Cutoff."

"That's your sister living at Cragg's Cutoff?" Allie asked, not believing it.

For the five years they'd lived there, they'd heard of the crazy plant lady who lived about a half-mile away. A hermit, most people called her. She didn't have electricity, running water, a car, or any other modern conveniences. Most people were scared to get near her place because they thought she was raving mad, a real country pumpkin lunatic. Allie didn't want to think about her right now.

"You said my dad's family came from here?"

"He was born here. In fact, your grandpa lived on that property where y'all live right now. He was a good man—a fighter pilot in WWII. Even got a medal for bravery, as best I can remember. Anyway, your grandpa bought the best ten farming acres from old man Pierson, who was mean-spirited anyway—filthy rich and didn't deserve anything better than he got—which was bursitis in both knees and cattle that constantly ran through fences. Served him right."

Maggie had a faraway look in her eyes. "Old man Pierson died when I was a kid. I remember my papa saying that he was so mean; nobody knew if he had any relatives to claim his money and land. His wife, bless her soul, gladly gave up the ghost long before he did, so he went to his grave alone and despised."

"Jeez," Allie whispered. "There's nothing but a broken down fence by the road and lots of empty land next door. What's going to happen to that old farm?"

"Those three hundred acres? Nothing's far as I know," Maggie answered, chewing on a mouthful of ice. "Place has gone to rack and ruin. There've been one or two investor people who've come through town and asked about it, but this ain't exactly New York City. Nobody's gonna want to come and build a hundred houses in Friendly. And, because it ain't near the main highway, it won't be commercial…. I don't know what could happen to that old property. You know, Tyler's the biggest small town around here and, Lordy, it's not even big. Friendly, Texas is barely a dark spot on the map." Maggie laughed. "Sometimes I think this town is dying."

"Really?" Allie asked.

Maggie took another swallow of her tea. "Uh-huh. Can you imagine nervous Nate Sims trying to serve more than four people in his bakery? That'd be like staring down the barrel of a real dilemma for that crafty old toad who overcharges for his fabulous food. Lordy, he'd be calling Marybelle Hightower at the beauty shop to rush over and help him. 'Sides, Nate's always liked Marybelle, but don't ever say I said that. And Marybelle, well, she's as good as gold, but she'd be hollering orders at her daughter, Bessie, to make sure she worked the barber shop side as well as the beauty shop side of their shop. That a-way Marybelle could grab her cane and hobble down the boardwalk to help out Nate in the bakery. And there'd be Bessie washing some lady's white hair, while trying to buzz cut a man's few strands near his bald spot. We just ain't got enough young people in this dying, old town. What a mess…."

"Maggie, you're funny," Allie said, smiling. "I'd like to see Ms. Marybelle and Mr. Nate together behind the counter. If I know Marybelle, she'd—"

"Be a-fussing, that she would. Marybelle fusses if she don't get her way, and Nate would be telling her how long to cook the bread and Marybelle would be fussing right back, saying that her mother taught her how to cook blah, blah…." Maggie's voice trailed off as she hiccupped from laughing, her aqua eye shadow crinkling. "Golly, but that would be a fun sight to behold. Old Nate," she said, "he's a good man."

Just then, Allie wondered if Maggie might like Nate Sims more than she let on. She finished the last of her sandwich as Maggie finished hers.

The room was quiet again, except for the second hand ticking on the old black and white wall clock.

"Do you have any children?" Allie asked.

Maggie shook her head and focused on the empty waxed paper where the sandwich had once been. "No, not a one. Ain't never been married neither." She glanced up. "What about you? Have you ever been married?"

"Oh, my gosh, Miss Maggie! I'm fifteen years old!" Allie knew the woman was teasing. "I plan on waiting a long, long time before I get married."

"Well, just don't wait over fifty years! That's all I've got to say." Maggie leaned across the desk and smiled. "I'll be sixty-five years old soon. I think I've waited too long. What do you think?"

"Miss Maggie, you're still young. There'll be a man walk right through that door any day; I have a feeling. He'll sweep you off your feet and you'll both run away and get married." Allie started rummaging through her purse. "I've got some money in here somewhere. I just know it. Here it is," she said, pulling out two quarters. "I'll bet you this fifty cents that you'll be married by this time next year. And when I win, we'll both have another sandwich. You on?"

Maggie beamed. "You've got yourself a bet. I've got fifty cents in my desk drawer, but I hope I don't have to use it, 'cause I'd much rather you win this bet. And, from what I hear, you're in a betting mood today. I heard the sheriff talking to you about the cell phone."

Feeling like a conspirator, Allie pulled it out of her pocket.

"Here it is," she whispered, sliding the phone across the desk. "Isn't it beautiful?"

Maggie opened the phone and started punching in numbers. "I'm putting in my phone number as number three on your emergency speed dial. That way you can reach me if you ever need help." She looked up with a smile. "I could also tell you where the sheriff is if he don't answer *his* phone."

Chapter 7

❧❧❧

ALLIE FELT HAPPY for the first time in days. "Will you show me how to program in numbers? I want to get my best friend's number in here."

Miss Maggie nodded. They programmed the phone, then listened to different ring tones. It was nearly 1:30 p.m. when the office phone rang. "Yes, ma'am, she's right here," Miss Maggie said. "We just had a sandwich....Yes, ma'am. I'll be sure and tell her. Bye-bye."

"My mama?" Allie asked.

"Uh-huh. She's picking you up in a minute. Her meeting ended early and she's on her way back to town."

Allie sighed. "Was she mad? I mean, did she sound mad?"

"I just imagine she did," Maggie answered, throwing away the lunch trash and moving the mouse on her computer. "You might want to think about what you're going to tell her."

Allie slumped down in the wooden chair and drew her knees up to her chest. *This floor won't open up and suck me in, either. She will never understand. Her life is so easy. Everybody loves Mama. Everywhere she goes, people like and respect her. If I go any place, I get in trouble instantly.* Allie buried hid face, but still felt Maggie's eyes on her. "What am I going to say?" she whispered.

"You're going to tell her the truth. You and your mother are going to sit down and talk about this."

"She doesn't have time for that!" Allie raised her head. "She's too busy working, writing, typing, calling—anything but making time for me. She won't understand. She never understands. She says to be strong and that

37

everything will be okay. And nothing is ever okay." Allie settled deeper into the chair. "Is anything ever okay?"

"Listen to me, child. If you're asking if bad stuff happens to good people, then, yes, it does. If you're asking if things will always turn out right, then I have to answer, no, they won't. It seems to me that you made a mistake today. You skipped school. You know you shouldn't have done it. Your mama knows it. I know it…. Everybody knows it. But you did it. You knew you would get in trouble and you did. The only thing I know to do now is to take your punishment. Be accountable for your actions. It's what people need to do, no matter how old they are. You're lucky, though. What you did doesn't require jail time. Think of people who do the terrible things that send them to prison. Learn from your mistakes and from theirs. Straighten up now, while you're young, and your life will be so much simpler."

Maggie sighed and rubbed her forehead. "Take it from me. I see bad stuff happening every day. Oh, sure, not bad like what happens in the big cities, but it's still bad. It's terrible what people do to people. But then, I guess if people were always kind and nice to other people, well, me and Sheriff Anderson and Deputy Darrell would none of us have jobs, would we?"

Allie sat for a long moment. "I think you would have a job, Miss Maggie. You'd be behind the counter with Nate, kneading his bread dough."

"Arrgh! Not in a million years would I work with Nate Sims," she barked in protest. "He sat behind me in literature class and pulled my pigtails 'til I wanted to slap him silly. 'Course, back then, he had the prettiest head of hair I've ever seen on a man… thick, black, swept to one side. Lord help us all, if Nate wasn't the handsomest senior in our graduating class of twenty-five students."

Dark hair. Thick. Swept to one side. Ethan Benedict. Would he be handsome with his hair cut? Allie shook away the image.

"Are you kidding? You went to school with Nate Sims? And he's never been married, either?"

"Gracious, no. Nate's an old fuss bucket. He's—"

Maggie was interrupted by the squeak of the office door.

Mama! Allie wasn't prepared. Mama didn't look disheveled today, but businesslike and professional. Her bun was tidy and her clothes were neat, even though Allie knew she'd been behind the wheel for most of the day.

"Hi," Allie said weakly, as Laura McCall advanced.

"Get your things," she growled. Then she smiled at Maggie. "I want to thank the sheriff for his phone call. I apologize for my daughter's behavior and appreciate you babysitting this afternoon." She looked at Allie, emphasizing each word. "We'll make sure this never happens again."

"Oh, Laura, it was nothing," Maggie said easily. "We've had lunch and I've enjoyed myself. I didn't think Allie wanted to open up her school books, so I was gonna get out my deck of cards. I don't have many people stop in and it's nice to have the company."

Allie had picked up her backpack and opened the door for her mother. "Thank you, Miss Maggie," she said before stepping outside. Allie took a few steps towards her mother's SUV and then scanned the sidewalk, curious. She wasn't used to being here during the school week. To the left she saw two people leaving the City National Bank. She looked to the right where someone swept the steps of the Friendly Feed and Seed. He had a familiar smiling face smile.

"Daniel?" she whispered.

He waved and flashed his movie star grin. *Omigosh, he is gorgeous. Who is he?* She took one step in his direction, but mama snarled, "Get in the car, Allie. You and I need to talk."

"Yes, ma'am." Allie opened the passenger door, looking up the street again. Daniel was now leaning against his broom watching her, still smiling. *Jeez. Why does my face always turn red? How old is he?* "Mama, do you know that boy over by the feed store with the broom in his hand?"

Her mother glanced over before making a U-turn in the street. "I don't see anyone, Allie."

"His name is Daniel, but the sheriff didn't see him and now you don't. I see him. I've talked to him. And he told me he works at the old community church."

Laura pulled over, stopping abruptly by the bakery. "You are talking to me about this old church?" She turned to Allie, pointing up the hill. "Young lady, I am furious with you over what happened today. You skipped school for the first time in your life and you're sitting here telling me about some boy you met today, some boy that nobody can see, instead of explaining to me why you skipped school."

Allie threw her hands in the air and turned away. "Because it's always like this. You're always like this. Yelling. Always fussing at me." Allie lowered her head. "You don't know what it was like at school yesterday after the cheating thing." Her voice dropped to a whisper. "I c-couldn't take it anymore. Not today. I just couldn't."

Allie felt her mother's stare boring a hole into the left side of her face, but right now she just didn't care. She opened the car door and got out to walk toward the church. Today, it seemed to be the one place that made her feel safe. She heard the car engine die. Her mother's door opened and closed. Soon the clickety-click of high heels hit the broken walkway.

"Careful!" Mama shouted from behind her. "Those steps up there are rotten."

Allie stopped just past the big wooden cross and stared at the four steps leading up to the church. *They are totally rotten. The second step is broken. How come I never noticed it this morning?*

She turned to her mother. "This is way weird. I sat on these steps this morning. I don't remember… anything… like this." She turned to stare at them again. "Mama, I'm telling you the truth. This morning… I watched the ants."

"Wait a minute. You're telling me this morning you came here and watched the ants instead of going to school? Do you expect me to believe that?" With one hand on her slender hip, Mama took a deep breath. "We're not leaving here until we get this matter settled—*so start talking!*"

Allie looked at the ground, the steps, the cross, the old porch where Daniel had been sweeping, as though wishing him back to start sweeping again. Even the porch had gaping holes in it, holes that could actually break somebody's leg. *The big iron and wooden front doors aren't even there, just old rotten plywood. There's no way that Daniel could have swept that porch this morning.* Suddenly, Allie felt faint, her energy sucked dry. She dropped down to the one step where the wood was partially solid. *I'm going crazy. The kids at school have made me crazy. My mother is making me crazy. This town is making me crazy.*

"I'm crazy, Mama," she said softly, bowing her head. "I'm crazy and I'm sorry. I didn't mean to skip school today. But I hate Mrs. Timmons. She makes fun of me and she makes fun of you, too."

The tears slipped out easily, one right after another, in a steady trail down her cheeks, just like the ants. One tear dropped on the splintered wood.

"I couldn't take another day of the kids laughing at me. I know I made a mistake. I seem to make mistakes every day." She raised her eyes. "Do you know what it's like to not even want to get out of bed in the morning? To not even want to see anybody? To want to crawl in a corner because you just know you're going to make another mistake?"

Allie felt a rush of new tears on her cheeks as she recognized mama's anger. She wasn't listening. Her face had gone hard, cloudy. There was no sympathy, no softness there. No love. Nothing. *It's like talking to a brick wall. A smart, well-respected, perfectly-dressed, everything-proper brick wall.*

"Okay, so punish me, Mama. I've got it coming. Miss Maggie said I had to be held accountable for what I've done. Whatever. So ground me. No privileges, not that I get any, anyway. You can't take away new clothes because I don't have any. You can make me cook more dinners, do more chores..." Allie stood up, defeated. "I'm sure you know that Sheriff Anderson has some kind of community project planned for me. Work your punishment around that. I don't care. I won't go to Wikki's sleepover. I can miss the back-to-school dance. Big deal. Other than that, what else can you take away from me? There's absolutely nothing in this town for me—"

The next minute, Allie was grabbed up in a huge bear hug. Mama squeezed hard, tucking Allie's head against her own cheek. Allie felt drops of water on her face. *Tears?*

"Mama?" Allie pulled away, surprised to see wetness on her mama's cheeks. "Why are you crying? You never cry. You're supposed to be mad."

Mama laughed and sniffled at the same time. "That's the funny thing about people. We don't always do what we're supposed to." She wiped away the tears and sighed. "Look, I know I was angry. Part of the reason I was so angry was, well—I was scared. I didn't know where you were when the school called me this morning reporting your absence. I always call them on days that you're sick. Well, this morning they called *me.*"

Mama chuckled ruefully. "I was so scared and worried about you that I jumped in the car and raced back here. Next week, I'm going to have to re-interview that new district judge in Tyler. I stumbled through my questions. He probably thought I was an idiot. But I couldn't stop worrying about where you were. Then Sheriff Anderson called and my prayers were answered. He'd found you."

Mama took Allie's hand and rubbed it. "Do you know why grown-ups sometimes get angry with kids? They worry when they don't know where their kids are. That can lead to misplaced anger. Do you see? Your safety is everything to me, Allie."

"So, you're not mad—not really—about today?"

"I don't often ask this, but do me a favor, please, Allie? Give me a hug. Today, I need a hug."

Mama hadn't asked for a hug in years. *Okay, we'll do the hug thing.* It felt a little clumsy at first; Allie hadn't had much practice. She wrapped her arms around her mama's waist; her mama's high heels made her seem taller.

"Yes, I'm still mad," Mama said after a long moment, laying her hands on Allie's shoulders. "And there will be consequences. But today, we're not going to worry about the punishment. I'm only grateful that you're safe, that you were found and that we've had a chance to—"

"Reconnect?" Allie smiled at her.

Mama smiled. "Yes, reconnect. That's a silly word. It makes me feel like an extension cord—reconnect. People don't reconnect. I think people communicate. I enjoy talking to you, Allie. I miss talking to you."

Allie's heart lifted. "I like talking to you, too."

"Well, then, I think we should talk more. I would like that."

"Uh—okay."

"What I'm trying to say is that I'm going to try harder to communicate with you, Allie. I have problems doing that. I guess I don't make myself clear, or maybe I don't listen, or—"

"Whatever."

"Yes, or whatever, but I'm ready to learn. I hope you'll just keep talking to me, okay? Just keep talking to me, no matter what. Tell me that you want to talk, and then just start talking. Is it a deal?"

Seeing Mama smile was all Allie needed to know that they were reconnecting—or communicating. *Whatever.* "Do you want me to tell you my feelings, and stuff?"

"Yes, and what's going on in school, too."

"Do you want to know about my friends?"

"Yes, if you want to tell me. I do."

"Wait a minute. You're just wanting to know the bad stuff, right? Like who does what so you can call their parents? I can't do that."

"No, wait! That's not what I mean. I want to know about your life, Allie. I want you to tell me 'stuff' about you."

Allie turned back and looked at the church. "Okay, there is something I want to tell you. I have to tell somebody because otherwise I'll go crazy."

"Shoot." Mama took an at-ease position, which looked a little funny since she was dressed in her plum-colored suit and high heels. "I'm ready. I'm listening."

She is listening. Allie smiled. "This morning, when I skipped school, I came here, to this church. I wanted time to think, Mama, just like I said, to get away from Mrs. Timmons. So I came here."

"Okay. Mrs. Timmons has, er—issues, shall we say. I don't think Mrs. Timmons actually likes too many people, so don't feel too badly."

"Well, I met a really nice guy. He's not like anybody I've ever met before."

"Wait a minute, Alexandra. You met a man—a stranger—this morning at this church?"

"Well, yes, Mama, but wait…. There's more to the story."

"We're in Friendly, Texas. There's always more to the story." Mama sighed. "Go on."

"He was here, with me, on these steps, sitting. We talked. He swept the porch up there—"

Doubt flashed across Mama's face. "He sat on these steps. He swept that porch filled with holes." Mama looked even more skeptical.

"I know it sounds weird. But this morning, there were no holes in the steps or in the porch. The wood looked old, sure, but I walked all around it. Tried the doors to see if they were locked, and they were."

"Wait. You say you tried the doors up there, but they were locked."

"Yes. I wanted to go inside."

Mama looked around, still puzzled. "Sweetie pie, you can see those doors are all boarded up."

Allie really felt light-headed now. "I know I checked the doors. I know I did. I'm feeling really sick, Mama. I think I'm going crazy."

"Wait a minute," she said, putting up her hand. "Just a minute. I know you, Alexandra. You are not crazy. You're one of the sanest people I know. You don't imagine anything and you don't make up stories, either. Sometimes I wish you did—you'd be a good writer. But let's get back to the church."

Mama walked along one side of the church, passing the four windows. "We used to raise these windows during hot weather. Were they open this morning?"

"No. Well…I don't remember. I didn't notice. But I looked inside the church."

Mama seemed agitated. "What did you see?"

Allie thought back to earlier that morning. She had walked up the steps, knocked on the doors and gone to one of the windows. When she peered inside, it had seemed as if she were seeing the church through the viewfinder of a camera.

"There were pews on each side," she began slowly, "Long pews. Dark wood. And a big stained glass window above the pulpit where the preacher would preach. It looked way old. Bright colors of reds, blues and yellows. I wanted to see it up close." Allie turned to see the blood drain from her mother's face.

"Allie, have you ever seen any pictures of this church before? Do you know anything about it?"

Chapter 8

✖

"No, Mama. I'm just telling you what happened this morning. I want you to know in case somebody says I'm crazy or something. I'm not going to tell anybody else about this. Hey!" Allie trotted around to the backside of the church. "Maybe I can see that—"

"Window?" finished her mother. "I've seen old pictures of this church and that window was boarded over fifty-some-odd years ago, before my time. So how could you possibly know there once had been a window there?"

Allie stared at the boards. "How weird. What's going on? No pews? No altar? There's nothing inside?"

Her mother looked around. "Sweetie, there's nothing." She pointed to a lone metal gate attached to nothing and going nowhere but an empty field. "That used to be a garden."

"I know about the garden. Sheriff Anderson told me about it. But it was all so long ago."

A faraway look gathered in Mama's eyes as she squinted against the sun to focus. "Who could forget the garden?" she mused. "It may have been the happiest time this town has seen. Things were simpler back then. I remember coming here as a kid on Farmers' Market days. Back then, Friendly wasn't just the name of this town, it was the way townspeople acted toward one another—friendly and neighborly. There was always enough food to sell, and then enough to share with those who couldn't afford to buy any. The townspeople all chipped in to church food pantries and were as generous as they were kind. They put most of the money they did make back into the kitty—as the grown-ups called it—to buy supplies for the next growing season."

Allie nodded, quietly following her mama's example. She surveyed the church grounds. Daniel would not have been able to sweep the dilapidated porch. The old cross seemed to have aged. She didn't remember it looking so splintery. The ugly graffiti at the bottom was worn and weathered. Did it lean slightly to the left?

"Mama, I can honestly say the church looked a lot different this morning than it looks now. Am I crazy?"

"No. But I do think you've come upon a mystery. You somehow got a glimpse inside the church perhaps the way it looked a century ago. Why? I don't know. Hence—the mystery."

Allie turned. "A scary mystery?"

"I don't know. Tell me about the guy. If the guy is scary, then the mystery may be scary."

"The guy? You mean Daniel? He was the guy I pointed to outside the feed store."

They both walked back to the car as Mama shook her head. "I didn't see a guy outside the feed store."

"Well, Daniel told me he was the caretaker of the church—and I believe him."

Mama stopped and turned. "That is the weirdest thing I've ever heard. You've seen the church up close now. Nobody has taken care of it for decades, so if Daniel is the caretaker, he should be fired. Don't you think? He's doing the worst job in the world."

It WAS EARLY afternoon when Allie and her mother turned onto old Pierce Road. Their house was the first one off the bumpy gravel, about a mile down on the right. They were far, far away from civilization or, at least, from the next farmhouse. No paved roads, no tall buildings, no taxi cabs, no crowded stoplights or people waiting to cross at street corners. *Oh, yeah. This is country, baby.*

As far as the eye could see, dozens of pines and oak trees framed the cloudless sky, outlining acres of farms and grazing pastures. Pierce Road bisected the three hundred dormant acres of empty pasture. Fruit trees, mostly peach, dotted the landscape, struggling to grow as pines sprouted up all around. Folks said there may have been a small orchard here long ago.

Allie knew ranchers rented most of the acreage to graze their cattle and horses. And, like Miss Maggie had said, Mr. Pierce died without any heirs, so the talk was that some rich judge in Tyler owned it now. Yet the man didn't want to live on it and didn't want to keep it up. He just wanted to own it.

"Mama, who owns all this land?" Allie asked as their battered SUV came to a stop in front of their tiny front porch.

Allie didn't really expect an answer; Mama looked preoccupied with her briefcase and papers. With a shrug, Allie grabbed her backpack and trudged half-heartedly inside their white frame cottage.

A modest home, she thought, looking around as if she hadn't eaten breakfast here that morning. Well-worn hardwood floors lay beneath the threadbare braid rugs that attempted to harness the dirt they tracked in. The three-bedroom, two-bath cottage had survived its sixty years fairly well, remaining intact on the dozens of cement blocks that supported it. The yard boasted no flower beds, no ornamental garden design, no fancy gates, nothing special to be proud of, just a sprinkling of grass and pine trees around the gravel drive leading up to the porch. Inside, they had no fancy modern amenities, like a dishwasher or microwave, but they had inherited an old television set with the house when they moved in five years ago.

"Mama?" Allie began, following her mother into her bedroom, which contained the only double bed in the house. "I know we don't have a lot of money... and we don't have anything fancy. But are we poor? Like—beg-for-money poor?"

WITHOUT ANSWERING ALLIE, Laura McCall set her purse down near the bed and said a quiet "hi" to Gerald's picture on the nightstand. Every day since he had died, Laura had said good morning and good night to the only man on this earth she had ever loved. In between she often said "hi." Only Gerald would know that was their secret code for "help me with this problem, please." But he hadn't been around for the five years they had lived here. Laura knew she was procrastinating—she knew she had to level with her only daughter, whom she loved beyond the universe.

Taking a deep breath, she sat down on the edge of her bed, patted the old ivory spread and motioned for her daughter to sit beside her.

"Do you know how beautiful you are? I've told you how pretty you are, but I want to tell you that even with your smudged mascara and streaky eyeliner, you are lovely. Go over there and look in the mirror. Go look at yourself."

Allie got up and went to stand in front of the heirloom dresser. Laura had fond memories of this dresser standing in her grandmother's home. Thankfully, she had held onto it through all their moves.

"Mama, I believe that I'm the only thing in this house that's not ancient," Allie commented, tracing a scratch on the dresser.

Such an honest comment. Laura chuckled.

"You're right, as always. You're too much like me, sometimes. You just blurt out what you think. And you're usually right. You and your brother are the only young things around here. I, like the dresser, bed, dishes, television, rugs and everything else, am truly ancient." Laura stood behind her daughter and they both stared into the mirror.

"I love it when you smile, Mama. You are so pretty."

"Even if I'm ancient?"

"Uh-huh, even if you're ancient. You don't smile much anymore."

"I'll do better, I promise."

"Are you still sad about Daddy?"

"Yes. I'm trying to do better."

"You have a lot of things to work on, Mama."

Another chuckle. "Yes, daughter, I do. I'm so glad you're here to keep me in line."

Mother and daughter looked at each other. Both had tear-stained cheeks. Both had smeared mascara and dripping eyeliner, no lipstick, messy hair and big smiles. Allie noticed that she had her mother's high cheek bones, small nose and perfect teeth. Thank heavens for good teeth. Allie shook her hair loose of its rubber band, getting ready to put it up again.

"I have ugly hair."

Laura fluffed it up around her shoulders. "It's fabulous, thick and a beautiful chestnut brown."

"Like yours?"

"Just about the same color."

"I wished it was silky, like yours. Mine is too thick and coarse."

"Yes, it's thick. And wild, just like your spirit. You have an untamed spirit, Allie. You should wear your hair in all kinds of different styles. Experiment with it. Wear it up with barrettes, bows, scarves, whatever you want. Develop your own style. Be creative." Laura wrapped her arms around her daughter's waist. "Just one more hug and then I'll answer all of your questions."

"All of my questions? What questions?"

"The 'poor' question, for one. The 'property' question for another."

"Really? Can you talk now? Do you have time?"

"No…but I will after dinner." Laura glanced at her watch. "Don't look so sad. It's nearly four o'clock and I've got to run over and pick up Ben. He rode the bus home with Calvin Jr. this afternoon."

Chapter 9

✿

"**You want me** to cook dinner?" Allie asked, following her mother outside. She already knew the answer. Her mother never cooked anymore. They had all grown used to it since Daddy died. Laura McCall could write Pulitzer Prize-caliber stories and articles, but she wouldn't cook anymore—at least, not anything they could eat.

Laura sat behind the wheel, calling back, "Oh, yes, please, that would be great."

Part of the challenge was to find food. Allie tried to think of something different from their usual soup and sandwich menu. She had eaten every sandwich known to man—cheese, tomato, meat loaf, peanut butter, mayonnaise, beans, plain ol' butter, just about anything edible that would fit between two slices of bread. Maybe tonight it could be stew or hash or sausage and eggs or biscuits and beans and fruit. On payday, they might have pork chops or chicken or a casserole with meat. Tonight, though, she knew the fridge was pretty empty and there was not much going on in the pantry, either. Maybe spaghetti….

Allie answered the ringing phone. Wikki was worried. What had happened today? Why hadn't Allie been at school? Was she sick? No. She had skipped school? Allie played one hundred questions with her friend for nearly half an hour before finally deciding that she'd better go find the dog and feed the cat.

Finding Zeus, their mutt dog, and Caesar, their movie star white cat, was always a challenge. Caesar took an hour to amble up the path, as if giving everyone time to admire his beauty.

And Zeus? "Stupid" seemed harsh. Maybe playful, ditsy and energetic were more apt descriptions. When he stood on his hind legs, Zeus could put his front paws on Allie's shoulders. He was choosy about what he barked at; he didn't especially want to waste a lot of energy barking at meaningless stuff like raccoons and squirrels. When Zeus did bark, his big deep voice carried for two miles at least. And every day he had to be caught to be fed. If Zeus didn't eat his food, then the deer or hungry birds would nibble at it, and Allie preferred Zeus get it.

She stepped outside, letting out a big whistle and a bigger yell. "Zeus! C'mere, Zeus!" Their golden retriever mutt had wandered up after a big lightening storm two winters ago. Quite honestly, Zeus, The Particular, had adopted *them*.

She rattled the old metal triangle on the small porch, letting him know it was time to eat. *No answer.* In the quiet, Allie strained to hear an answering bark or the swish-swish of the prairie grass as Zeus galloped home. *Nothing.*

Grabbing her sweater, Allie set off on the old rusty bike they had found underneath the house when they moved in. Like everything else around here, it was old. It also had a too-big chain that rattled.

She made it to the gravel road and stared around. No traffic. No dog. Well, what did she expect? There was Cragg's Cutoff up ahead, which led to plant-lady Fanny Parker's house—the neighbor she'd heard about only today. And she was Miss Maggie's sister? Allie couldn't believe it.

Beyond that, one other family lived on the other side of the Pierce property, but that was four or five miles away. So, yeah, their neighborhood was small.

Sudden raucous barking sent geese flapping. *Zeus!* Allie pedaled faster, straining to see any sign of the dog across a pasture.

A woman's scream. No mistaking that. Allie's feet pedaled faster, the cool north breeze whipped her face. Fanny Parker? Could it be? There was nobody else around here who would scream. Zeus's constant barking spurred Allie's pedaling to top speed.

She veered left onto Cragg's Cutoff as another scream rent the air. Allie hoped the old bicycle tires would hold up on the rocky gravel. She also hoped she could find the old lady's house; nobody she knew had ever seen it. She'd heard folks say that Ms. Fanny hadn't had a visitor in years. She'd supposedly gotten senile. She talked to imaginary friends and grew most of her own food. She even sewed most of her own clothes from curtains and wore the same thing every day. In fact, people said that Ms. Fanny didn't even own a car.

"Fanny Parker? Ms. Parker!" Allie called out as she neared what looked like a driveway.

It wasn't exactly a driveway, just the end of the road. Cragg's Cutoff ended at Ms. Fanny's clothesline.

"Ms. Fanny? Are you okay?"

The bike hit the dirt as Allie plowed through towels drying on the line.

"Ms. Fanny? Where are you?" A frantic Zeus, tongue hanging out and barking wildly, nearly knocked Allie over. "Where is she?" Allie hollered. "Show me."

Another bark. Zeus took off toward an old greenhouse a dozen yards away. Allie ran after him before sliding open a rickety door that must have been off its hinges for years.

"Ms. Fanny? Are you in here?"

Row after row of plants grew in meticulous order on old slatted boards held up by sawhorses. From tiny plants to large potted ones, they filled the place with the smell of flowers, dill, thyme and dozens of other spices.

A whimper came from a back corner. Allie rushed toward the crumpled woman, seeing one heavily booted foot twisted in an odd direction and Fanny's old cotton dress rumpled, the hem torn. The older woman clutched her faded pink apron to her cheeks with one hand and wiped away tears with a gardening glove she held in the other.

"He was horrible! Horrible!" Fanny said, choking on each word.

Deep lines etched the woman's cheeks, and Allie could not help comparing Ms. Fanny to her sister. Miss Maggie seemed young and lively, and Ms. Fanny seemed—well—so old. Her gray hair had been drawn into a tight bun on the top of her head, but straggly curls now strayed from the bun to fall around her shoulders. Dull, green eyes blinked back tears. She looked up imploringly.

"What happened?" Allie squatted down, instinctively taking the woman's hand. "Are you hurt?"

Fanny shook her head, her green eyes guarded. "You're the girl from down the road," she said with a loud sniffle. "You're the McCall girl." It was more of a statement than a question.

"Yes, I'm Allie. Can you stand up?"

Allie took Fanny's elbow, as the other woman struggled to grab one of the poles supporting the greenhouse. She took a deep breath as the color returned to her cheeks.

Allie wanted to reassure her. "I'd gone searching for my dog and I heard you scream."

Fanny shook her head, looking dazed. In the back of the greenhouse, Allie noticed more than a dozen plants had been knocked over. Roots and dirt were strewn everywhere.

"Oh, Ms. Fanny—all your hard work. This is terrible. Who did this to you?"

"If I didn't feel him slap me, young lady, I would'a swore it were the Devil himself. He was that mean. Vicious. Horrible," Fanny said with a shiver.

"He slapped you?" Now Allie could see the mark, angry and red, growing on the left side of her face.

"Darn right he slapped me! He came onto my property, demanding to know where the old cemetery was. He said it was supposed to be on the Pierce place, but he couldn't find it. So he came here. He said I knew where it was."

She shook her head, looking down at her laced boots. "I know where it is all right. I just didn't feel like telling him. That's when he slapped me." Her head shot up and her eyes narrowed. "I'd like to catch that fella one more time for what he did. It's disrespectful to hit a woman. I'm gonna be the one to tell him." She balled up her gloved hand and put her fist in the air. "I promise he won't never slap Fanny Parker twice!"

Ms. Fanny might be slim and fragile-looking, but there had to be an underlying strength of character. *Had she really lived here alone for all those years after her husband died?* Allie had seen the sorrel mare tethered outside the greenhouses, Ms. Fanny's only mode of transportation grazing steadily on acres of wild hay. Ms. Fanny sewed her clothes and grew her own vegetables. *Jeez.* Allie glanced around, thinking she'd stepped back to Colonial times. A few hens and a rooster scratched in an open pen near the greenhouse; a couple of barn cats scooted across the yard, playing tag. Allie had already blasted through the laundry drying on the line, now she spotted an old washtub draining on the back porch.

"I know what you're thinking, girl. Everybody in town says I'm crazy. That's why I don't go to town no more. I don't wanna answer their stupid questions. People are so nosy. I just wanna live in private, right here with nobody bothering me." Fanny turned her piercing green gaze on Allie, a slow smile forming. "But you, young 'un, I think you're different. You're the one who's taken care of my dog all these years."

"Wh-a-t? Zeus is your dog?"

Ms. Fanny threw back her head now and belted out a hearty laugh. "Is that what you call him? Zeus?" She shook her head. "Well, he is a mighty fine dog. I never called him much in particular—mainly 'dog.' I'm glad he's got a name he can be proud of."

Allie couldn't believe her ears. *Jeezalu! Zeus had never been lost. He just lived a mile down the road. I've been so stupid. Zeus never belonged to us.*

"I'm so sorry, Ms. Fanny. I never knew. Omigosh, Zeus wandered up when we had that big lightening storm a couple of years ago. I thought he was a stray."

"Young'un, don't give it another thought." Fanny patted Allie's arm with her gardening glove. "You ain't done nuthin' wrong. Zeus here has had two homes these past couple of years. He's been living here with me and then across the street with you. That dog is one independent mutt, I give him that. He must love you to death, else he wouldn't bother sleeping at your place. Probably likes the change, I expect. He comes to see me for breakfast, and goes back to your house for dinner. I've known men who've done that. Live at two houses at the same time, likin' one just as much as the other." A dark look clouded Fanny's face.

Allie ignored that cryptic comment. *Zeus is always gone early in the morning. He must over here with Ms. Fanny! And at night?* Allie had to always call him home. "So, every day, he came here for breakfast—"

"And slept nights at your house," finished Fanny. "You see, I never let him in the house, and I don't let him in my greenhouse, neither. But he can't stand storms. You must have some place for him to get in out of the weather."

"We do," Allie said, more to herself, than Ms. Fanny. "Our house is built on cement blocks and Zeus sleeps underneath."

Ms. Fanny slapped a gloved hand on her apron. "There you have it! One dog sharing two houses. That's why he sleeps at your house. He's got himself a built-in dog house, safe and sound. Don't give it another thought. If Zeus is happy with this arrangement, so am I. How 'bout you, young'un? Are you happy with your dog eatin' breakfast with crazy Fanny Parker?"

Allie smiled in answer to the mischievous twinkle in Ms. Fanny's green eyes, as she turned to stumble through the greenhouse door. "C'mon, let's get some sunlight and fresh air. I'm wonderin' if I'm gonna tell the law what happened."

"I'll call Sheriff Anderson." Allie steadied Ms. Fanny before petting a tail-wagging Zeus. "I've got his cell number handy."

"Shoot, young'un. I got no phone." Ms. Fanny stared at the acres and acres of dormant field behind her tiny cottage. As far as the eye could see, wild grasses grew in place of crops. Spindly pine trees huddled together every hundred yards or so as a reminder that this had all been farm land years before. "B'sides, wouldn't do no good to complain. Don't know that awful man's name— nor where he come from. Weird one, he was. Dark, long hair on his shoulders. Mean, angry-looking black eyes." She shivered and glanced around at Allie. "And that red skull on his black T-shirt? It gave me the chills."

Red skull on a black T-shirt? Black eyes? Long, dark hair? Allie gasped. *Ethan? But Sheriff Anderson drove off with him earlier. How could Ethan be out here?*

"What else can you tell me about him?" Allie instinctively touched Fanny's shoulder. "What did his voice sound like?"

"It was deep, real pretty-soundin'. When he came in the greenhouse, I just thought he was lost. I didn't hear any car, but then, I don't hear so good nowadays. I thought he just needed directions."

Allie nodded. "He had a nice smile?"

"Oh, he surely did. I thought with all that hair cut off, he might be right handsome. I was transplanting some flowers and stopped to talk to him. He asked me over and over about the cemetery. I kept telling him that I didn't know it where it was. That's when he got mad. I watched him change from a handsome young man into, well—like I said before, if I didn't know any better, I would'a sworn I was staring into the face of the Devil." Fanny turned pale and grabbed Allie's arm for support. "Young lady, if you hadn't come along, I don't know what I would've done, I was that scared. Thank you so much."

Poor Ms. Fanny. Nobody loved her, except for a part-time dog, a bunch of chickens, a horse, a few cats and some vegetables. *I never even knew she lived here.*

Allie took her cell phone out of her pocket and opened it up. *If I ever needed to talk to the sheriff, it would be now.* She pushed '1' and nothing happened. Allie shook her head. "No service," she whispered. *Well, we are out in the middle of nowhere. Of course, there's no signal.* Allie tucked away her phone. "Why was he looking for the old Pierce cemetery? I didn't even know there was a cemetery."

"Well, there is. And it's tiny. But he seemed to know about it. Imagine that. After fifty some-odd years, somebody is trying to find where that old cur was buried. As if anybody cared."

"Where is the old cemetery?"

Fanny shot Allie a stern look. "Lordy, girl, you're not thinking about going down there—not this late in the day."

Maybe. There was something going on here and Allie was determined to find out what it was. Was this the same man she had met in the jail earlier today? It didn't seem possible. She had seen Sheriff Anderson drive him away in handcuffs. The man who had assaulted Fanny was so determined to find the cemetery. What if he had found it? She could see if it was Ethan. But it was a crazy idea to go looking for it, maybe even dangerous. Her gut feeling told her to stay away and her common sense agreed. She should ride home as fast as she could.

Fanny went on, "I don't know what business he has at the cemetery. All who's buried there is mean ol' man Pierce and his wife, Abigail. B'sides, you don't need to go traipsing off through the backwoods—"

"Where is it?" Allie implored. *Okay, so if I don't go today, I'll go another day. I want to find out what was going on. I'll take Zeus for protection.* Allie glanced down at the dog sitting at her side. She reached down to scratch his head.

"Girl, where's your mama? She's gonna be worried about you! Don't be so wrapped up with what you think you gotta do. Going to that cemetery just don't make no sense a'tall."

Ms. Fanny hobbled over to the small front porch to get her cane. Allie blinked at the old house. Was it leaning slightly to the left?

Fanny grabbed the cane and waved it in the air. "Alright, young'un. You keep starin' at me, waitin' for me to tell ya'. And I will one day. But right now I'm gonna follow you down to the main road yonder to keep a'watch out. I don't want you traipsin' off somewhere to investigate. Do you promise me you'll go straight home?"

Fanny ambled out toward Cragg's Cutoff and Allie trotted up behind her. She whistled for Zeus and walked her bike as they made their way along the gravel drive.

"I promise. I'll go straight home," Allie replied. "So the cemetery is on the opposite side of the road?"

"Oh, for heaven's sake! Yes, child. You take this drive down to the Pierce Road. Go straight through the pasture and keep to your left. Go until you see a grove of twin trees. There's at least of dozen of 'em. Big, tall pines. You can't miss 'em. You won't be able to ride your bike through the underbrush, so you'll have to hike it on foot."

Ms. Fanny reached into her pocket. "Here, take this whistle, girl, and keep it. You can't get cell phone service out here but you can blow hard on that whistle. You sound that whistle anytime and I'll be sure to hear it. Don't forget that sounds carry out here. Tuck it in your pocket and keep it handy, just in case. Sound the alarm if you're in trouble. We still don't know where that horrible man has run off to."

The older woman patted Allie's hand. Allie couldn't stop herself from leaning over the handle bars of her bike and giving Ms. Fanny a quick kiss on her cheek.

"Thank you so much. I'll tell Mama what happened to you, Ms. Fanny. She'll call the sheriff. He'll want to talk to you."

Fanny waved away the comment. "What happened makes me madder'n than anything else. If I was ten years younger, I would'a slugged that creature."

I bet you would have, too. "I've gotta go to school tomorrow. Can I come by after?"

"A'course you can. Stop in anytime."

Allie took off, gravel spewing behind her.

Fanny reached up and felt the warm spot where the young lady had just kissed her. It had to be close to twenty-five years since she'd received a kiss from anybody. She kinda liked it.

Fanny Parker began her return trek along the uneven gravel road, not leaning on her cane as much as usual. Her thick boots didn't seem to twist so much on the rough gravel rock that had lain on this road for years. Could the extra kick in her step and her growing smile be due to the sweet young teenager who had just saved her life and touched her heart?

Chapter 10

❀

SETTING HER SIGHTS on home, Allie wasted no time getting to Pierce Road. Her mind raced faster than her pedaling feet as she thought about leaving Ms. Fanny alone. It didn't seem right, not after the older woman's attack.

Suddenly, a sharp scream interrupted the crickets' song.

"Help! Help me!"

Allie slowed her bike. The female cry came from the Pierce property. *It couldn't be Ms. Fanny. Who was it?*

Dropping her bike in the ditch, she ducked under the barbed wire fence.

"Help me!" came the woman's cry.

At a dead run, Allie headed toward the open pasture. Another shriek and she veered left. She had just skirted a heavily forested area when a deep, smooth voice sounded behind her.

"Going somewhere, Alexandra?"

Allie halted in mid-stride. She whirled on one foot. "Ethan," she breathed aloud, backing up and looking around. There was no one else. "I thought somebody was in trouble. That was your voice? You? You sounded like a girl!"

His insidious smile pricked the hairs on the back of her neck. *Creepy.*

"It was me," he chuckled. "I knew you would come. Do you want to know something else, Alexandra? You are quite lovely when you're mad."

Unblinking, Allie stared as he walked—almost glided—toward her. "It's just you and me, Alexandra. Didn't I say we'd meet again?"

Allie tried to lift one foot to run. He was giving her plenty of time to scoot, but, like in the jail earlier, her legs felt rubbery. Her feet seemed glued to the ground.

"Going somewhere?" He stopped only inches away. "You're ready to run again. Always running away...but I can't let you do that. I've been looking forward to seeing you. It's a good time for a visit, don't you think? Nobody around. We're here, all alone..." Ethan's voice trailed off, as his mouth crooked in a sly smile.

Allie could see he had shaved off his stubble. His hair was now short and spiked, but his black eyes still seemed to pierce her mind. Instead of the wrinkled clothes he'd worn in jail, he now wore a clean brown shirt and blue jeans with tennis shoes. Someone who didn't know him would think he was a college kid. *Jeez.*

"Go ahead, Alexandra, blow! Blow on that whistle in your pocket. It won't make any noise." Ethan's laugh reverberated off the grove of tall pines.

Allie jerked out the whistle and blew with every last ounce of air. *Nothing.* Her fingers trembled as the whistle fell to the ground. Her breath caught in her throat. *Think, Allie, think!*

"What are you doing here?" she managed. "The sheriff... the sheriff put you in his car this afternoon."

Ethan spread his feet and crossed his arms. "Yeah, he put me in the back seat. Strapped me in. Buckled me up. Tied me tight. Shackled me to the seat. And do you know what?" He flung his arms wide. "Here I am. Can you believe it?" His thunderous voice shook the pines until needles dropped.

"Wh-where's Sheriff Anderson? Did you hurt him?"

"Oh, he's not hurt. He's a big guy. He's just taking a nap somewhere."

Allie swallowed hard. "I don't believe you. Did you hurt him?"

"Are you prepared to save him? Like you did that old hag down the road?" Ethan sneered. "She's useless."

Allie mustered up some courage. "Don't you make fun of Ms. Fanny! She's my friend. She told me all about you."

"She did?" A sinister gleam lit up his black eyes.

Allie's heart raced. *This guy's wicked. And a liar. He hurt the sheriff, and he slapped Ms. Fanny.* Allie's heart skipped a beat. *What will he do to me?* She twisted her feet every which way and flung her arms wildly, but still couldn't budge. Her feet stayed stuck to the ground. Without thinking, she bellowed out, "Help me! Help me!" Her sounds floated through the breeze like a birdsong.

Ethan let out another raucous laugh. "There's nobody around to hear you, Alexandra. Nobody to save you. Come, take my arm. Walk with me."

"Don't touch me. Don't come any closer. You're a b-bully, that's what you are."

She blinked as his dark good looks turned thunderous. He reached for her elbow, but she kept talking.

"Get mad. I don't care. You've done something to where I can't move my feet. I can't run; but I can talk. I'll talk for hours about school, about m-my Irish ancestors—"

"Are you punishing me? All because I won't let you run away? No, my dear Alexandra, you can't leave me. I haven't had so much fun since the time—"

"Yes, by all means, tell us about the last time you had fun," came a soft voice.

Allie's feet suddenly broke free. She whirled and bolted, running straight into Daniel's chest, choking back a sob as she clutched his T-shirt. He cupped her head to his shoulder with one hand. In the other hand, he clutched the broom.

"Shh, Allie. You're okay." He looked at Ethan. "And you. I thought we were rid of you. Yet here you are. How delightful."

Allie wiggled free of Daniel's grasp, staring up at him.

Daniel and Ethan knew each other? She looked from one to the other. *Completely different in appearance, yet possibly the same age.* Now that she carefully studied them, both were much older than they appeared earlier. These two men looked fully grown, not kids, not teenagers, but grown men who, by the mounting anger on both of their faces, had spent time together. *There was history here, for sure.*

Ethan's cocky smile disappeared. "Indeed, brother, we do meet again."

"You are not my brother," came Daniel's swift reply. "You are Ethan... the putrid."

Ethan's menacing glance never faltered. "Indeed, so you and I are left to settle this... score, once and for all."

"I can think of nothing that would please me more." Daniel gave a rueful chuckle. *Not a happy sound. Half-angry, half-disgusted.* "But this is not the day. Now is not the time. Let's agree to meet another day. To discuss, once again…our differences. You should be the first to leave. I'll remain with the young lady."

"She's mine," Ethan whispered in a guttural voice that didn't sound quite human. His lips tightened, his jaw clenched. "Do you hear me? She's mine."

Allie curled closer to Daniel. "She is not yours," he stated flatly. "She *never* will be yours."

Allie stared at the two men, transfixed by the weird exchange. They had known each other for a long time, she could see that. Daniel's eyes had clouded over to a dark sapphire, his face rigid, his body taut.

With a thunderous look, Ethan swiveled and, in a blur, disappeared into the thick stand of pines.

Allie gaped at Daniel, not sure about what she'd just seen. "Did Ethan just disappear? Or is he just a super fast runner?"

"The good news is that he's gone." Daniel's eyes returned to their normal, paler blue and a smile touched his lips. "I remember asking you to be careful."

"But, Daniel, you weren't here!" She dropped her hands from his shirt and backed away. "I heard a girl's voice call out for help, so I jumped off my bike. I swear!"

Daniel shook his head. "Don't swear, Allie. Never swear before me again. And, yes, I believe you. You heard a voice. But it wasn't a girl's voice. It was Ethan. Don't be fooled by him. Never forget that. He tricked you once."

He'll trick me again. "What if I meet him again, Daniel? What do I do?" *Will he hurt me, too?*

"If you ever meet Ethan again, which I highly doubt, do exactly what you did today. Tell him that you're not going with him. Hold him off, fight him, tell him to leave you alone. You'll be okay."

"You're kidding, right? That guy nearly *kills* people! How can I protect myself?"

"Ah, I see what you mean. Well, here's the difference. The people whom Ethan attacked had once upon a time befriended him. They'd asked him to come into their homes, they'd shared meals together, shared conversation, shared their lives with him. Ethan thought they were his friends."

"That's weird. Ethan thinks it's okay to beat up his friends?"

"He does."

"Well, Ms. Fanny may be right. He sounds like the Devil to me."

Daniel's face clouded over. "Or one of the Devil's disciples. Listen closely: you must never agree to go with him. *Ever.* He wants you, make no mistake. But you can fight him. Do you understand?"

Allie nodded, understanding, but not understanding. She scuffed the dirt with her tennis shoe. *Fallen straight into Ethan's trap.* Yep, she was an idiot—a real klutz. *Lapped up the 'help me' thing like it was pure gospel. Jeez.*

She glanced up to find Daniel smiling at her, his eyes twinkling. What was he thinking? Nuh-uh, she wasn't going to ask. She'd seen an older side of Daniel today, a much more serious side than when they'd first met. *How old was he? Not nineteen.*

"Okay, so Ethan is a creep," she said. "What about Sheriff Anderson? Is he hurt?"

Daniel put one hand on the rubber band of her ponytail and it slid right off.

"Yes, he's fine," he answered, distractedly, as he watched her dark hair fall and billow around her shoulders. "Allie, you need to wear your hair down like this."

"But, Daniel, how did Ethan escape if he was tied up—handcuffed and buckled up inside the sheriff's police car?"

"Why don't you ask the sheriff yourself? I think you'll be seeing him tonight."

"I will? How do you know?"

"Ah, sweet Allie," Daniel said with a sigh, pulling her close and cupping her head beneath his chin. "There is so much I know that it would exhaust most people."

She heard the steady rhythm of his heartbeat. At this point, she didn't want to move or speak. But she still had questions. She whispered into his T-shirt. "Daniel, how did you know where to find me?"

He sighed. "I knew Ethan had escaped. I knew he had roughed up the sheriff—"

"Roughed up?" Allie back away. "You said Sheriff Anderson wasn't hurt."

"Well, no, he wasn't. He was surprised by the whole thing and has a big bump and good-sized bruise on his head. But he's fine. In fact, he's at your home right now. To make a long story short, I don't know what you did to Fanny Parker, but she got her walking cane out again and she's fussing to herself right now. Do you know she walked all the way from her house down Pierce Road? I imagine she's nearly to your driveway by now. She's keeping an eye out for you, Allie. You've got yourself a new best friend."

Allie thought Daniel was even more beautiful in the late afternoon light than in the misty morning sun. *Holy moly. He is pretty, no matter what time of day.* Through the soft and dappled light of the pines his light hair looked even more silvery.

"You'd better get home, young lady."

Allie laughed at the broom in his hand. "Will you drive me on your broom?"

He chuckled. "Nope. Sorry. This broom doesn't fly." He cheerfully twirled the broom like a baton, threw it high into the air and caught it before it touched the ground.

Allie noticed the ring on his third finger, right hand. It was a chunky green square stone in a silver setting.

"How beautiful," she said, holding out her hand, hoping for a better look.

He eased the ring from his finger and placed it in the palm of her hand. *Heavy.* Solid, hammered silver and old, really old. It had an inscription written in a foreign language inside the band.

"What kind of ring is this?"

"It's a type of…uh, ceremonial ring. The stone is an unpolished emerald."

Allie turned the ring over in her hand. *A super antique.* She handed it back to him. "I've never seen anything like it before."

"It's not really mine. It's just on loan," he said, returning it to his finger. He placed one hand on the small of her back and whispered, "Now, it's time for you to get along home."

"But I want to talk to you some more. I want to know your last name. And I want to know how old you really are, because I think you're older than nineteen.

"Whoa, did I say I was nineteen?" He flashed a big smile. "You're the one who said I was nineteen."

"I wanna know why Mama couldn't see you standing outside of the feed store today."

"That's a fair question. The last one I'll answer. Did you see me standing there?"

"Well, yes, but—"

"That's all that matters. Now, I mean it, Allie. You need to get home. Your family is waiting." He turned to walk into a nearby grove of tall pines.

She cupped her hand over her mouth and yelled, "How do you know all these things?"

His answer came in a whisper that seemed to surround her. "It's my job to know many things. Stay safe, Allie. Soon, I will need your help."

Daniel will need my help? Cool. Just the thought put an extra-fast spring in her step as she took off at a dead run toward her bike. Moments later, she spied a slender figure in a faded pink dress on the road ahead of her.

"Ms. Fanny!" Allie called out, slowing her speed.

Fanny stopped, whirled and planted her cane on the gravel road like a sword she was about to wield. "Landsakes, young'un, I was scared to death. Now that I know you're okay, I'm mad enough to spit nails. What in tarnation happened? You didn't go straight home like you promised."

"Oh, please don't be mad. Didn't you hear that awful scream? It came from Pierce's pasture and it sounded like a young girl." Allie paused to catch her breath. "But it wasn't a girl, Ms. Fanny. It was *him.*"

"Not that awful man!"

Allie nodded and reached over to pat Fanny's hand.

"It was him. His name is Ethan. He escaped this afternoon while the Sheriff was escorting him to Tyler. But Daniel came and saved me. It's way too long a story to tell right now. I'll tell you everything tomorrow."

With her cane in the air, Fanny called out behind a pedaling Allie. "And this time, no more stops!"

Allie waved a quick good-bye.

Fanny turned away and walked slowly back toward home. *Daniel? Ethan? Who were these people?* The young girl who brought life and excitement had disappeared for the day. Her bad leg began to hurt until Fanny growled at it, "Just quit yor achin' old leg. We've got lemon bars to make. And a pitcher of sweet tea, too. I've got a guest calling tomorrow and I've got to tidy up the place."

ALLIE REACHED HER driveway, her mind still racing at full speed.

How cool is Ms. Fanny? And thank heaven for Daniel! Who knows what Ethan would have done... omigosh, that creep is still on the loose! What if he goes after Ms. Fanny again?

Allie gasped. *Ms. Fanny may be in danger. Daniel ran Ethan off and tonight he's mad. Would he hold Ms. Fanny hostage?* Allie nearly rode her bike up the front steps when she saw Sheriff Anderson's Jeep parked outside. *Would he help her? Was he really OK?*

"Momma! Sheriff Anderson! Ben!" she called out, slamming the front door behind her.

All three people jumped up from the kitchen table, mouths open. Sure enough, Sheriff Anderson had a big white bandage covering part of his forehead. She rushed to his side and grabbed his arm. "Sheriff Anderson, I'm so sorry. Tell me what happened. What did Ethan do? How did he escape? Omigosh, you *are* hurt. How terrible!"

The sheriff took both of her hands and pulled her down into the chair next to his. "Catch your breath, Allie. We're just glad you're here."

"Oh, Allie." Mama rushed to her side. "I've been so worried."

Allie glanced at her brother, who also looked worried. That surprised her. Ben never looked anything but bored, no matter what the crisis.

"Ethan's dangerous, Allie, and he's still on the loose," Sheriff Anderson said.

"I know."

His face turned as white as his bandage. "What did you say?"

Allie's voice dropped to a whisper. "I-I met him in the Pierce pasture. I'm okay, but I'm worried about Ms. Fanny."

The sheriff and her mother exchanged glances.

"You'd better start from the beginning," he said. "I want to know everything from the time your mother left you this afternoon."

Allie related everything, including hearing Ms. Fanny scream, hearing the cry for help in the pasture, and meeting Ethan and Daniel.

Sheriff Anderson listened to every word. "Where did Ethan go after he left you?"

"He seemed to disappear in the trees. He didn't really *go* anywhere."

"Tell me more about this guy, Daniel. Who is he?"

"I met him this morning at the old church. You know, sheriff—right before you picked me up. You said you didn't see him. Mama didn't see him in front of the feed store, either. But, sure enough, Daniel has to be real because he saved me from that creepy Ethan." Feeling proud of her story, Allie crossed her arms over her chest and sat back in her chair. "What do y'all think now?"

Sheriff Anderson shook his head as he rose from the table. "I think I'd like to thank Daniel, but first I need to find Ethan."

"What about Ms. Fanny?" Allie followed him as he neared the front door. "Do you think she should have somebody stay with her? Would Ethan go back—"

The sheriff turned and cupped his hand under Allie's chin. "You're reading my mind. But I can't stay with her." He glanced back to the table. "Laura?"

Mama quickly nodded. "Of course, Logan. She can stay here. We've got the pull-out."

"Mama, she can sleep in my bed and I'll take the pull-out."

"That's very sweet, Allie. I'm sure Fanny would like that."

"Wait!" Allie inserted herself between the sheriff and the doorway. "Please tell me how Ethan escaped. You had him shackled in the car."

The sheriff sighed, looking tired. "My car got hit by a dump truck at the four-way stop at Menger Crossing. The truck ignored the intersection and rammed into the driver's side of my car. I guess I was unconscious a few minutes. That's when Ethan escaped, clean and simple. If I didn't know better, I would swear he had it planned. I don't know how he got unshackled. No keys were missing; his shackle key was still inside my boot."

The sheriff shook his head. "Ethan's another Houdini, I guess. My police car is totaled, that's for sure. The truck driver got clean away. Ethan got clean away. We've issued an APB on both of them, so law enforcement in every nook and cranny in Texas will be on the lookout. I notified the FBI about Ethan, along with state police in Louisiana, Arkansas, Oklahoma and New Mexico. Maggie is finishing up the paperwork now." He glanced again at Mama. "Lock the door, Laura. I'll be back in a few minutes with Fanny."

Allie watched as Sheriff Anderson got into his Jeep and drove away. It was dusk now. Surprisingly, Zeus and Caesar had made it home all by themselves. She dished up their food, gave them big hugs and hurried back inside.

So Ethan had escaped, clean as a whistle. Sheriff Anderson had that right. Ethan didn't have one scar or scrape or bloody cut on him. Ruthless, dangerous, scary—that is Ethan. And he may still be in the area.

Allie came back through the front door, and found Mama sitting at the table, staring down at her hands.

"What's the matter?" Allie asked, walking to the near-empty pantry to get the spaghetti noodles.

"I was so worried about you. You weren't here when Ben and I came home. I got a phone call from Logan this afternoon telling me about his prisoner escaping. You left no note…. I didn't know what to think."

"I tried to use my cell phone but there was no service."

Mama's voice dropped. "I was scared I would lose you, too."

Allie turned; Mama had tears on her cheeks. *Mama's thinking about Dad.* Allie turned back to get the spaghetti sauce down from the shelf.

"I think about Dad a lot, too. I miss him."

Turning on the stove, Allie suspected that her mama had wanted to have one of those talks where she was supposed to reveal all—say what was on her mind so Mama could tell her why she was all wrong about everything. They'd had those talks in the past, and everybody ended up mad when it was all over. Thank heavens, tonight wasn't one of those nights. Quite frankly, Allie felt exhausted. Glad, in fact, that she was going back to school tomorrow where she could get some rest.

Think about Daniel. Tell Wikki everything. Get away from the house. The only good thing about skipping school was meeting Daniel. Would she see him again tomorrow? She sure hoped so. While Mama talked, Allie focused on blue eyes, silver hair and the steady heartbeat of one fascinating man.

A honking horn startled them both. Mama answered the front door, welcoming Sheriff Anderson and Fanny Parker. She had a sack in one hand and her trusty cane in another.

"Why, my goodness, if we don't meet again." Fanny greeted Allie with a handshake.

"Hi, Ms. Fanny. Are you hungry? Would you like some spaghetti?"

Fanny grinned and nodded. "That sounds right fine to me. Got enough food for the sheriff?" She looked up at Logan. "He come down to rescue me. Says that nasty ol' convict might come back 'n git me." She elbowed the sheriff and chortled, "as if there'd be anything he could steal from my little hole-in-the-wall."

Mama stepped up. "We're glad you're here, Fanny. I'm Laura McCall," Mama said, extending her hand. "Allie will show you the way to her room. I'll get the food on the table."

ALLIE HUSTLED FANNY back to her bedroom. "I hope my bed is okay. I think it's kind of lumpy."

"Ooh, it's a big bed," Fanny said, running her hand along the worn twin spread. "How pretty it is. I bet you've got indoor plumbing, too."

Allie blinked at the comment. She'd never heard the expression "indoor plumbing" before, but she could figure out what it meant. "Well, yes, we do. It's down the hall. Ben and I share a bathroom, but you're welcome to use it… the toilet, the shower, whatever you like."

Allie remembered that Fanny didn't have any modern conveniences, but she just had to ask. "You don't have water?"

"Oh, sure, I do, girl. Got a bucket and well in the ground that serves me just fine. I pay no bills. Got firewood for my little stove. Tell you what. I can make the best kettle cornbread you ever tasted and the best pot of pinto beans."

She grows so much of her food. That must be it. "What about meat? Do you eat much meat?"

"Well, you saw those chickens," Fanny said with a sly smile. "Let's just say that some of 'em live longer 'n others." She giggled. "But let's not worry about all that now. It's getting late and you probably have homework. Let's have some supper. I bet you can cook, Allie. Why don't you tell me all about the kinds of foods you like to fix."

SHERIFF ANDERSON STOOD in the doorway, surveying the kitchen bustle at the McCall home. Allie towered over Fanny as they talked nonstop about squash and carrots, all the while spooning out food to serving dishes, Ben sat curled up on the sofa, absorbed in a book. Laura was setting the table; he felt grateful that she laid out an extra plate for him. Good Lord, how could he walk away and leave three defenseless women and a young boy with a madman on the loose? Truth was, Logan Anderson knew he couldn't.

"Ladies? This all looks delicious."

Miraculously there appeared some buttered toast, sliced apples and banana pudding that may have been last night's dessert. Logan didn't care. He was so hungry he could eat a horse. He surveyed the table as he waited impatiently behind his chair.

"Laura, Fanny and Allie, would you please get Ben so we can eat. I don't mean to complain, but I'm about to die from hunger right here on the spot."

The three women jumped and stared at Sheriff Anderson like they had forgotten he was there. *Well, they probably had.* But at six feet. five inches, he knew he wasn't invisible.

"I've never fainted before, but there's always a first time."

"Logan, I'm so sorry. Please sit down," Laura said. "C'mon girls. C'mon, Ben. Let's say the blessing. I think we all have a lot to be thankful for after this horrible day that miraculously brought us all together."

For the first time in months, maybe years, Allie agreed with her mama on something. The fact they were all together tonight was miraculous. Today had begun badly—first her decision to skip school, then going to jail, then meeting Ethan. In between, she'd met her two newest friends— Ms. Fanny and Daniel. But she'd also encountered her worst nightmare— Ethan. Allie watched as her Mama moved from the kitchen to the table with speed, her movements sure and fluid. Clearly, she'd done this type of thing before. *Before Daddy died.* Allie let it go. When it was her turn, she took a heaping portion of noodles for herself. It had been years since she had seen five people eating at their table. She kinda liked it.

Chapter 11

❧

ALLIE WOKE UP, feeling like she hadn't slept at all.

Well, she *had* slept—at least until the wee hours. First, there was the awful dream where Ethan slipped through an open window in their house. He cooed in her ear, promising her trips to beautiful lands, a new wardrobe, new friends, the escape from Friendly she'd always wanted. But Allie had pushed away the menacing evil and screamed, *"Get away from me!"* His face came within inches of hers, his rancid breath spilling onto her cheek. When she pushed him away, fighting against his tightening hold, he abruptly released her and left. Breathing hard, Allie opened her eyes and struggled to sit. She exhaled hard before blinking at the strewn blankets, sheets and pillows. *Had it only been a dream? It seemed so real! He seemed so real.* After a long while, she dozed off again until Ms. Fanny did her best tiptoe routine at four-thirty, when she snuck into the living room.

What had Ms. Fanny wanted? To ask permission to use some of the "sweet smelling" bath salt crystals. Allie smiled when she remembered the excited look on Ms. Fanny's face when she was told to use all she wanted. And the rose milk soap, too? *Absolutely. Help yourself. Use it all.*

Well, things sure smelled a lot sweeter at breakfast the next morning. There had been a distinct aroma about Ms. Fanny the day before. Maybe Ms. Fanny didn't use any soap at home. *I'll give her the extra soap I hide in my closet.* Allie stirred, catching a whiff of the great homemade smells coming out of the kitchen—biscuits, gravy, grits and scrambled eggs.

"What's wrong, young lady? Can't eat anymore?"

70

Ms. Fanny had wrapped an old towel around her thin waist as an apron over her faded pink dress from the day before. Both were dotted with flour and sugar. Did Allie smell a fresh homemade pie in the oven?

"I watched you eat that big plate of food, Allie, and I'm just teasin' you about wantin' more." Fanny beamed as she busied herself washing dishes. "I guess I have to admit that I love cooking for people. Even though it was just me and Cecil for many years and I never had any young'uns, I always made extra for folks who'd stop in."

She turned to Allie and put down her dish rag. "Thank you, child, for letting me stay here last night, givin' up your bed and takin' your bath salts, 'n all."

Allie's shocked expression gave away her thoughts. "Ms. Fanny, thank you! I'm so full, I could pop. I never get a homemade breakfast like this."

Fanny reared back her head and laughed. "I'd say that was the truth. Your brother done eat two big platefuls and took off lickety-split toward the bus stop. He gave me a big ol' hug, he did. Cute young'un, that one. And the sheriff done eat and is doing some paperwork out in his car. Bless his heart, you know he couldn't have been comfortable sleeping behind his steering wheel all night. And your mama done eat and said this was her deadline day. She gave me a hug, too, and then took off. She was the one who let you sleep in a little this morning."

Fanny wiped her hands on her towel apron, got her coffee cup and sat down at the table across from Allie.

"I can bring over some vegetables and that'll save you folks some money. 'Sides, I want to repay you for your kindness to me. And some eggs, too. My chicks have been layin' good these past couple of weeks. I can't eat all them eggs I got."

Allie couldn't believe her ears. *New food! No one's ever done that before.* Ms. Fanny's face was all rosy as she beamed from ear to ear, her long silver hair today barely staying in the bun held by old hair pins.

"I'm baking one of my special apple pies. Later on, if y'all like, I'll make my blue ribbon skillet cornbread—"

"Ms. Fanny, that sounds fantastic. But you don't have time for us." Allie hid her crossed fingers. "Do you?"

"I surely do! Nothing better than cooking for people who'll eat. I love this just as much as I love tending to my herbs and plants."

Sheriff Anderson came through the front door, ducking his head. "Good. Allie, I see you've finished eating. When you're ready, I'll drive you to school this morning. We've got things to discuss."

Uh-oh. Her punishment. This was Friday and the sheriff had promised she would know what kind of probation she would get for skipping school. Allie nodded, excused herself from the table and ran to brush her teeth. The food in her stomach started to churn just thinking about all the possibilities of the sheriff's community service project. Would she have to clean the jail? Pick up trash by the side of the road somewhere with dozens of other convicts wearing ugly orange suits? Would her mother really have to write an article about her in the newspaper? All of it made her sick.

"Ready?" the sheriff called from the kitchen.

Allie didn't answer, but hurried to get her backpack. She moaned, remembering that she had been too tired to do any homework last night. *Would that mean she'd get Fs in the other classes she'd had homework in? Ugh. Something else bad. Yesterday had been insane. Nobody would believe her if she told them what had happened.*

Fannie waited by the front door. "I'm gonna get the pie out of the oven in a bit and finish doing the rest of the dishes. I'll lock the door when it's time for me to leave—"

"Hold on, Fanny Parker, we've already been over this." Sheriff Anderson leveled a stern gaze. "I mean it when I say you're not to go back to your house until I give the okay. I'm running Allie up to the school and I'll be right back. I'll be no more than ten minutes, max. Don't you go anywhere, is that clear?"

Fanny wiped her hands on her towel apron. "Lord'a mercy. All this fuss about me. Y'all don't need to concern yourself with me."

Allie spoke first. "Please, Ms. Fanny, would you cook dinner for us tonight?"

She twinkled up like a Christmas tree. "Oh, you know I will! Oh, my goodness, but I've got to get busy. Now, y'all run along. Fanny's got things to do here. Sheriff, you take your time. I'll be inventorying these cupboards to see what I need to bring over for later. Now, y'all get going," she said, waving them away and turning back to the kitchen. "I'm just too busy to visit."

Allie thought she heard Fanny humming a tune as they closed and locked the front door.

Not long after they'd gotten in the Jeep, Sheriff Anderson scooted a newspaper clipping toward Allie.

"I'm having this golf cart delivered to your house today," he said. "It's for Fanny. Even though we don't have any golf courses nearby, I know the man who sells them. It's a motorized cart she can use to get around. The white top will keep the sun off her face. She can drive it to and from her mailbox. Plus she can get back and forth to your house without having to walk with her cane. The roads out here are too rocky for her to walk, anyway. I got a phone call early this morning that Ethan was sighted near the Oklahoma border. It looks as though he's left the area. I'll be calling the authorities today to follow up." The sheriff stopped at a stop sign and looked at Allie. "Until then, I have to keep Fanny safe. I'd like for you to help me."

"Me? Wh—"

"Hold on, let me finish. I want you to take this," he said, handing her a booklet, "read all about the operation of this golf cart. You have to plug it in at night. I'm working with Otis Spinkle to run an electrical pole out to her house. She needs electricity. We're in the twenty-first century and she's still using candles. I didn't even know that until I picked her up last night. Otis will get with the light company and get the pole run, probably today. But somebody has to show Fanny how to operate the cart. And… that person is you." He nailed her with one of his *disobey-me-if-you-dare* looks.

They had pulled up to the school parking lot. Allie had kept quiet, but she still didn't know what she was supposed to do, or even how she could keep Ms. Fanny safe.

"Is this my punishment? For skipping school?"

"No." The sheriff pulled his Jeep to a stop outside the school cafeteria then turned to look at her squarely.

"YOUR PUNISHMENT IS more of a job, Allie. You won't get paid, but you will be busy. If you've got enough free time to skip school, then you've got enough time to help me with the garden. Don't give me a shocked look, young lady. That whole area does look dilapidated. So let's revitalize the old garden in the back of the old church. I'd heard it once was one of the finest in these parts of East Texas. Too many residents around here need food and…if they don't have the money to buy it, then they need help growing it. I've already talked to Fanny. She's agreed to oversee the project, but I want you to get some volunteers at school to help her. You can help her, too. There's enough work to go around. She making plans to grow vegetables, herbs, whatever she decides, but I've made it clear that I want something done with that land. Mayor Hinkley agrees with me. He unofficially asked me to take charge of the project. But I'm delegating that privilege to Fanny. You coordinate everything with her. Is that clear?"

"Y-yessir."

"Do you have any questions?"

"Yes."

"Good. Make a list of them and we'll all get together this weekend and go over everything. I've already briefed your mom and she's for the project one hundred percent. Do I have your complete cooperation?"

"Well, sure, but I don't know if I—"

The sheriff sighed, interrupting her. "Don't give me all the 'don't knows' and excuses. I want a positive answer, Allie. Can you help Fanny with this job?"

Allie swallowed hard and nodded.

"Good. I've been in touch with Mr. Danner. He's given his approval for you to post signs around the campus—whatever you need to do to get Fanny some help. I need you actively involved in this community effort. I will *not* expect another phone call from the school today. I expect you to stay in class all day. I expect you behave yourself. Is that clear? Nod your head if you agree. Good. I'll see you later, Allie."

Feeling totally sick at her stomach, Allie grabbed her backpack and fled the car. Well, what did she expect? She knew there was going to be a punishment. Hot tears stung the back of her eyes.

Help Fanny with a garden? *A garden?* What did she know about a garden? She didn't like plants, knew nothing about vegetables. Herbs? They were dried things that came in a jar. This was stupid. *Stupid. Idiotic. Dumb.* She was supposed to become a farmer?

Wikki nearly rolled her wheelchair over Allie's shoes. "Hey, yoo-hoo, it's me! What are you doing standing there, looking really weird? Are you okay?"

"Uh, yeah—no, not really. Hi, I didn't see you." Allie's jumbled thoughts came to order as she looked down at her friend.

"You what? You didn't *see* me?" Wikki whispered, conspiratorially. "I'm the one in the wheelchair! Something's happened. I just know it. What's going on? You didn't call me back last night. Why weren't you at school?"

"Shh," Allie whispered, wheeling her friend to a quiet corner of the cafeteria. "Not so loud. I couldn't call you back last night. We had a houseful of people spending the night. It was like a giant sleepover. Even now I can't believe all the stuff.… Sheriff Anderson slept outside in his Jeep."

"What!" Wikki shouted, before dropping her voice to a whisper. "Everybody's saying that you skipped school and went to jail. Is that true?"

Allie nearly tripped over one corner of a lunch table, then slumped down next to Wikki. "Yeah… kinda."

"Wait a minute." Wikki surveyed the big room like a secret agent on a mission. "You're saying you went to jail and that's just part of it. Holy cow! If I went to jail, that would be the end of it, the end of everything as I know it, finito, the end-o—"

"Shh. There's so much. You don't know about Daniel—"

"You go to jail and there's a guy?"

"And Ethan."

"And another guy? This doesn't sound like you. Two guys? Somebody's in Allie's body, but it's not my friend Allie. Holy smokes! You went to jail with two guys? I bet they're older. I heard your mom was so mad when she came up here yesterday. Holy cow, I can't believe this. And the sheriff had to sleep over—"

"No, wait. That's not how it was. Listen, Wikki. I'll explain."

So Allie did explain, in short, fast sentences, with one eye on Wikki and the other on the wall clock. She only had a few precious minutes to get out her story before the first period bell. She told her about Ms. Fanny and left nothing out about Daniel or his blue eyes.

"You are, like, grounded forever, for rest of your life. I know the deal. Is your mom still furious?" Wikki's eyes brimmed with energy.

"Jeez! Are you wanting me to be in super-big trouble? Well, I am in trouble with the sheriff. I'm getting punished for skipping school. I thought I'd be put in jail or something, but he's making me find kids to volunteer to help grow this garden in the back of the old church. You know, the old falling-down one that's on the square? This is so lame, Wikki. I don't know anything about gardens. It's stupid."

"A garden, like to grow lettuce, radishes, carrots and stuff?"

"Well, duh, what other—"

"That's great! Gardens are so cool. My mom and I have a garden on one side of the house. It's small, but we always get tons of red potatoes. We sell the ones we can't use."

"Wh-a-at? You never told me that. In all the time I've known you, you never mentioned having a garden."

"Well, it's not like I'm out there doing the hoeing. Mom takes care of most of it. And, well, you don't really know my older sister, Jeannette. She's grown and all, but when she comes to visit, she helps mom out."

Allie shook her head. "So you know how to grow plants? Do you know what I need to do?"

"Heck, yeah. I'll tell mom. You'll have tons of help."

Allie nodded slowly. *Hey, maybe Mr. Danner would let the kids who volunteer get community service hours for their work? That would be cool. A win-win situation for everybody.*

THE FRIDAY SCHOOL day flew by and, before long, the 3:20 dismissal bell rang.

Allie had suffered through Mrs. Timmons' class, ignoring the teacher's squinty-eyed glances at her. She'd gotten a zero on the big exam that she was supposed to have cheated on two days earlier. No amount of extra work was going to undo that grade. She was likely to have a C on her midterm report card. But even that didn't matter right now.

Allie was focused entirely on this garden thing. She couldn't get it out of her mind, even though Fanny would plan it. *How does anybody make a garden?* After lunch, she wanted to go to the library and look online, but never made it there because the lunch line was too long; she couldn't stay after school because today she had to ride the bus home. She had about a dozen kids come up to her after lunch to ask about the garden. They all seemed ready to help.

Even class clown Marvin "Messa" Kess was interested. Of course, he wasn't talking to her. He was way too cool for that. He stood to one side looking disinterested as he designated Tooley Branson to do the talking.

Still, Allie was excited about the prospect. She knew Messa lived on a two hundred acre farm, so he must know a lot about gardening. And while Tooley was puny and skinny, Messa was muscular and bulky.

But who cared? Tooley could use a hoe and dig a trench, or whatever gardeners called the gully where they planted their seeds. *Ugh.* She had her homework cut out for her. Thank goodness Ms. Fanny was cooking supper. Whatever was on her plate tonight, as long as it didn't move by itself, she vowed to eat it.

Chapter 12

༺∞༻

ALLIE HOPPED OFF the bus and braced herself for the half mile walk to her house. She spotted a tall figure in the trees.

Daniel.

His smile widened as he gave her a wink. "How was school? I assume you went today."

"I certainly did go to school. And guess what? I stayed the whole day." *And* you *wandered in and out of my mind all day.* Now he leaned up against a pine tree, arms crossed wearing his trademark blue T-shirt and jeans. She walked toward him through the underbrush, not caring if she got poison ivy all over her body. "Where's your broom?"

"Well, it just so happens," he said, turning to reach behind the tree, "I have my broom right here." He held it up for her to see. "Why do you ask?"

"Because every time I see you, you have your broom." Allie knew she was gazing up at him in what must look like total adoration. "What did you do all day?"

Daniel looked around, pushing away from the tree. He stepped toward her until she felt the warmth of his breath.

"Let's be serious for a minute. We laugh together and I wouldn't want to change that—"

"Okay."

"Shh. Listen." Daniel placed two fingers over her lips and leaned close to her ear. "Ethan has left town. He's traveling north. He's crossed into Wyoming. He's far, far away. Isn't that good news?"

Allie nodded and mumbled behind his fingers. "Does the sheriff know?"

"No. Why don't you tell him? He'll breathe easier; Fanny will breathe easier. Tell her that Ethan won't be coming to look for her ever again." Daniel had pulled his fingers away from her lips. "And Allie—?"

He paused as she drank in his good looks. *Could he? Would he kiss—?*

"I'm not who you think I am."

Her knees buckled as his warm gaze met hers. "You're not?" *You're not the most handsome guy ever?* "You're not Daniel?"

"Yes, well, I am called Daniel. But...that's not my real name."

"It's not?" She nearly choked on the words. *I don't care if your name is Bill or Tom or Ebenezer. You're inches away from me.*

Daniel wrinkled his nose. "You wouldn't be able to pronounce it. What I'm trying to tell you is... I'm not just a regular guy."

"Oh, for sure!"

"C'mon, don't laugh. Allie, I'm an angel."

"Oh, yeah? An angel?"

"I'm serious."

"I believe you," she said, returning his big smile. *You can be whoever you want to be. Just kiss me. Right here. Right now. Your lips. My lips. It's so easy.*

"Why do you think nobody else has been able to see me?"

She shrugged. "Because you're –"

"Not here. To other people, I don't exist. Only you can see me."

Daniel touched her cheek and moved a stray lock of hair away from her face. "Did you feel that?"

She thought she'd died and gone to heaven. *If all the angels are like you, Daniel, I can't wait to get to heaven.*

"Oh, Allie. You've got a long life ahead of you. Don't be thinking about heaven right now."

She took a step back, startled. "No way! You can read my mind? That's not fair!"

He chuckled, as he reached out to touch her hair again. "That's why I can't kiss you."

"Daniel," she gasped, "you really can read my mind. Omigosh...this is so creepy. Stop it. Stop it right now." *Unbelievable.* "So...so it's true?"

He nodded, whispering, "this may be the last time you'll see me for a while. It takes so much energy to support this form."

"This… is not what you look like?"

"You like my blue eyes. Yeah, I know. You like my silver hair, too." He rubbed his chin. "I thought you might."

"Daniel! Please!" Color flooded her cheeks.

"Shh," he said, pulling her close. "Nobody ever thought I was handsome in that way. Too bad I don't get a material form to live in. I might like it. Just so that you know, this is my first one—my first man body—uh, human form."

"Really?"

He set her away from him. "Really. I'm invisible to those on Earth. As an angel, I'm really just a spiritual being."

"A see-through angel? A spiritual being."

"I know it's confusing and I'm explaining it badly. I exist in another plane, another dimension. You would never know I was there."

Allie shook her head. *Life was getting difficult.*

He leaned closer. "Listen, my energy is nearly gone now. Just know that you can always talk to me, even though there will be times you won't be able to see me."

"W-hat?"

"I'll be here, but I won't be here. Do you understand?"

"Uh, no, not really. If you're not here, how can I talk to you?"

He smiled. "Just open your mouth and talk. Or talk through your thoughts. Talk to me as much as you want. I'll hear you and you'll hear my voice," he touched her forehead, "in your mind."

Allie put her hand on his shirt and pushed. While he looked real enough now, she felt his chest give way, not feeling as solid as it did before. Soon, she would grab on to nothing but air.

"Daniel," she pulled away her hand. "I'm so sorry." She looked up to see that his reassuring smile, like his whole face, seemed to be fading.

"Like I said, I don't have much energy left, but what I had, I wanted to share with you."

"You're a ghost. I can't believe it."

"I'm an angel, not a ghost."

"Ghost. Angel. What's the difference?"

Daniel closed his eyes and pretended to pull a dagger from his heart. "You wound me, madam. Do you not know that an angel lives only by the goodness and grace of God?"

"Oh, Daniel. I didn't mean to say that…didn't mean to get it wrong. Please don't go…." She reached out to him as he faded, lighter and paler, much like the afternoon sun.

"Just remember. You're in charge of rebuilding the church. I am personally assigned to this task and will need your help. Get volunteers and donation money. I've left the architectural plans under your front porch. On Monday, in English class, tell Buzz Madison that he must be the contractor—"

"Daniel, wait! I can't. I don't know anything about building anything. I'm supposed to help Fanny get volunteers to make a new garden in the back of the church and I can't even do that."

He had all but disappeared.

"Out of everyone on this Earth I could have chosen, Alexandra Antoinette McCall, I chose you. Don't disappoint me now. Have faith, Allie, faith that you can do this. Have you not prayed for courage in the past? Did you think no one listened? Now I ask for your help. It is vital that this be done. In return, I will guide your hand in righting an old wrong done to your family. One involving your father…"

My father…. Allie's mind whirled. "S-sure. Yeah. Okay, I'll try."

Allie groped the air where Daniel once stood. *Nothing. No one.* Allie missed the man who had just vanished.

Daniel. She spoke his name in her mind, still feeling his presence.

"I'm here."

"You'll help me?" She gulped.

"I will."

A honking horn sent Allie a foot into the air. She whirled to see her mother rolling down the car window.

"Honey, are you okay? You're staring into space."

She probably did look goofy, now that she thought about it. Allie opened the car door and jumped inside. She couldn't say one word to her mama, so they rode up the driveway in silence. What would she say? *Oh, sure, Mama, I was just talking to Daniel, my own personal angel that nobody else can see.* She'd have to have a long talk with Wikki on the phone tonight. No, on second thought, she'd better just wait until she could tell Wikki this story in person. She wouldn't believe it anyway.

"Sheriff Anderson told me about how you're going to help Fanny create a new garden at the community church. What a challenge!" Mama pulled the car to a stop near their small front porch and picked up her briefcase and purse. "Can you get some help from the kids at school? I hope so, Allie. I wish I could—"

Looking for any reason to escape her mother's watchful eye, Allie jumped out of the car. "It's okay. I know you don't have time to mess with it. I didn't expect you to."

Allie bolted through the front door, interrupting Fanny singing in the kitchen. The luscious aromas of fresh baked bread and chicken and dumplings assaulted her senses and reminded her how hungry she was. Pots and pans filled with vegetables crowded the stove; Allie picked up each lid. *Yum.* And the woman behind it all, Fanny Parker, stood there in an old calico dress with a faded apron tied around her slender waist.

"Ms. Fanny," she said, bending over to plant a kiss on her cheek. "This smells fabulous. Thank you so much. I've starving to death. I don't even recognize the pots and pans or even the plates. And I don't even care. They've been sent here from Heaven. Just like you. The food is wonderful. Where did you get it all?"

Fanny put down the wooden spoon and stood with her hands on her hips. "Oh, for goodness sakes—saying such sweet things to me." She blushed, before a sly expression crossed her face. "It's all on account of Otis Spinkle putting in my light pole today. Thanks to Sheriff Anderson, I've got an electrical line run to my house."

"Oh, Fanny! The sheriff told me this morning that he hoped to do it." *But I'd forgotten all about it until now.* "How exciting! You've got electricity."

Allie gave her a big hug and then pulled away, feeling like a giant next to petite Fanny.

"You can get a refrigerator, a washing machine, a dryer, all sorts of stuff."

"What's this I hear? Fanny, this is fantastic news! You have lights now?" Mama had come in and put down her briefcase and purse.

"I'll have lights one day," Fanny said with a smug nod. "I can put away those awful candles...and Otis said he would even pay my light bill." Fanny smiled wistfully. "He only asked me to cook him one meal a week. He's says he misses home-cooked meals since his wife Clarice died. And I do love to cook. So I figured it was a good trade."

Allie glanced at the table. "Is he coming to dinner?"

"He is. He said he wanted chicken and dumplings. Now don't faint on me, young'un. This ain't one of my chicks in this pot. I told Otis that he'd need to bring me a store-bought chicken. It didn't take any time at all for him to show up on the porch with one in his hands. Oh, and Sheriff Anderson is stopping by for dinner, too. Ben wanted to have supper with his friend, Jacob, and I told his momma that you would pick him up tonight about seven. If all that's okay with you, Laura."

Mama gave Fanny a quick hug. "That sounds perfect. Oh, Fanny, you've not been in our home twenty-four hours and we're so organized. You've given us the best meals we've ever had! Thank you so much."

"Mama's right. Can you take care of us every day?" Allie asked excitedly, looking anew at this woman who everybody called a "crazy lady" because she grew plants, herbs and chickens. It would be great to have somebody else who was crazy in their house, besides them.

Fanny smothered a laugh. "Y'all, there is one more surprise I got today from Sheriff Anderson. I parked it on t'other side of the house, out yonder. It's my very own golf cart. The sheriff says I can drive it back and forth between your house and my house. He said I can drive it on the side of the road, where it's grassy."

Omigosh! Allie rushed out the door and around the house, nearly falling over the dog. "Zeus! Are you protecting Ms. Fanny's golf cart?"

Sure enough, the cart was big and green, with a white seat and a sturdy plastic top. Fanny had it plugged into the outside electrical box to charge up the battery.

"How cool is this? Aw, c'mon, Caesar," she said, scooping up the fluffy white cat. "I don't think Ms. Fanny wants you sleeping on her new golf cart. You think everything belongs to you." Allie nestled Caesar in her lap as she took a seat. "This is so way cool. Now Ms. Fanny can bring over more of her pots and pans and do as much cooking as she wants."

"I can indeed, child," Fanny said, as she quietly padded toward Allie. "But I do my best cooking when I have a partner. I do believe it's time to start some canning. Have you ever done any canning? Mmm, I thought not. Well, we've got bread and butter pickles to make and some jellies, nothing too hard. 'Sides, we've got lots to talk about with this here garden project. Won't it be fun? I guess it's been fifty years ago since I was in that church, singing and listening to the preacher."

The church! Allie jumped what seemed a foot in the air and Caesar leapt from her grasp. *Daniel, I'm sorry! I nearly forgot.* She ran to the front of the house, scrambled around the porch and peeked inside the long, narrow space beneath the wooden porch steps, where they kept a spare key. Allie touched several sheets of thin old parchment paper.

"What in heaven's name are you doing underneath those steps?"

How would she explain this? Allie pulled out the papers, and they were indeed fragile. The cursive writing flowed beautifully. She'd seen copies of the United States Constitution and the handwriting looked similar. Her eyes focused on a scale of dimensions, a list of materials and a date—1894.

Chapter 13

❧

"Ms. Fanny, can you read any of this? I don't understand one word," Allie said, handing over the plans. The handwriting was too ornate and, besides, she had no idea what a mortar was.

"Lordy, no! Child, let's go inside. I'm afraid to touch it. There's cooking grease on my hands, and those papers look important. Let's go show your Mama."

They both went inside, washing and drying their hands before unrolling the old parchments on a narrow coffee table.

"Mama!" Allie called out. "You might want to see this."

"She's probably changing out of her work clothes, Allie. Why don't you and I take a quick look?"

Allie smiled as Ms. Fanny's curiosity.

Fanny rummaged through her apron pocket for a pair of eyeglasses. "Oh, Allie, I can't believe what I'm looking at. These must be the original plans for the old church. There's no name at the top, but from this sketch, these here are the original plans…well over one hundred years old."

Fanny smiled and smoothed out the paper, eagerly pointing to the diagram. "Oh, Lordy. I remember the choir singing every Sunday. There'd be maybe twenty people in that choir. In fact, some Sundays there were as many people in the choir as in those ten pews," she said pointing to the upper left area of the building. "A'course the pastor would preach from the front of the church. But this drawing looks to be a window right behind where the Pastor stood to preach. Oh, howdy, sheriff. I didn't hear you come in."

Fanny jumped up from her place on the sofa. "Sit down and take a look at these plans that Allie found 'neath the front porch. Can't say as how she'd know they'd be there. It's a mystery to me. Y'all handle it, while I go finish supper. Otis said he'd be here by five-thirty. But then he also said he'd be early to eat my chicken and dumplings.

Sheriff Anderson smiled hello to Allie and then to Mama, when she walked into the living room.

He took a seat on the sofa next to them. "So, Allie, helping Fanny with a garden isn't enough?"

Allie caught the stern tone in the sheriff's voice. "I know. It's just that—" She jumped up and started to walk away. "I've wanted to tell y'all. So you have to promise not to laugh at me. And not to tell Ben. He'd go and tell everybody at school. Then all the kids would think, like, I'm super crazy." She turned, peering at Sheriff Anderson and mama's puzzled faces.

Fanny came around from the kitchen. "Well, dearie, you've got three people here who care about you. I'm not gonna laugh. Heck, you were the one who knew where these plans were hidden. Ain't that right, Laura?"

"Why, y-yes, Allie. What's going on? Does this have anything to do with what happened yesterday?"

"Oh, Mama, it has everything to do with yesterday. That's when I met Daniel. Remember? He was standing outside the feed store, only you couldn't see him. Well, the reason you couldn't see him is because he's… an angel."

Three puzzled faces stared back at her.

"No kidding?" remarked Fanny, walking all the way into the living room.

"That's what I said." Allie bit hard on her lip. "I didn't want to tell you. It all sounds so dumb. You don't believe me, but it's true. Daniel really is an angel."

"Oh, for heaven's sake! This is silly," scoffed Sheriff Anderson. "I've never heard of angels talking to people. Does he have wings?"

"I just knew it. See? Y'all are already laughing."

"Now, just hold on a minute," Fanny said, stopped her. "Catch your breath. This angel thing is gonna take a minute for us to wrap our brains around."

Allie faced down their disbelief. "Okay, I can prove it. Sheriff, remember when Ethan escaped and you couldn't figure out how? Remember how he didn't get your keys, but he slipped clean out of his handcuffs? I know that

Ethan and Daniel know each other. And from what I've seen, Ethan must be a fallen angel, or maybe one of the Devil's disciples. Anyway, Daniel told me to tell you that Ethan is not a threat to us right now, he's traveling north and is somewhere in Wyoming."

"Daniel said this," the sheriff said solemnly.

"Yes, he told me this afternoon just before he told me about the church construction project," Allie answered.

"Well, ladies, Daniel—whoever he is—does have the correct information. I found out just before I came here that Ethan has been spotted heading north, only now he's made it up to the Canadian border. I hope he's not coming back anytime soon." Sheriff Anderson stood up. "What did your Daniel say about this church project?"

Allie sighed. "He is not 'my Daniel.' He's been assigned the task of rebuilding the church and he needs my help. Oh, and he wants me to talk to Buzz Madison in English class on Monday. Daniel says that Buzz is supposed to handle the construction."

Allie knew her story sounded too bizarre to believe, but she continued, "I don't know why or how Buzz would have anything to do with it. He doesn't even know I exist. He's said 'hi' to me exactly one time this year and that was at the water fountain. And I don't know why he would have anything to do with a construction project. Then again, I don't know anything about building."

"But the Madison family sure does," Sheriff Anderson said, thoughtfully. "You probably don't know this, but Madison Construction is one of the leading commercial builders in East Texas. Besides being Friendly High's up-and-coming Varsity basketball player this year, Buzz also works construction during the summer with his dad. He'd be a good one to have on any project. Did Daniel say why the church needed to be rebuilt?"

Allie shook her head. "I guess because it's old. Daniel said that after I helped him with this, he would help me right an old wrong done to our family." She turned to her mama. "Daniel said that it involved Daddy."

Mama turned pale; no one spoke for a long minute. "Logan, I can't believe this," she whispered from the sofa, holding out her hand to the sheriff. "Could this be… do you think—"

"Don't get your hopes up, Laura. You've been researching documents for months now. Hang on. Be patient. First things first. I don't know how this is all going to shake out, but I think we're going to be busy for the next few weeks. Allie, tell me again what Daniel said about the church."

She sighed. "He said he needed my help in the rebuilding of it. Oh, and I needed to get volunteers and donation money."

"Well, ask him to elaborate. I'm not sure about this angel stuff, but if you are going to take on rebuilding that church, then congratulations to you. I can easily make that your community project instead of helping with the garden."

Whew! At least she was off the hook for something! "I talked to kids at school today about the garden," she interjected. "A bunch of them want to volunteer. Maybe Wikki can help make signs and work with Fanny."

"Maybe she can. For now, I want you to turn your attention to the church project," remarked the sheriff. "I, for one, am not too clear on this man, Daniel. He's certainly a person of interest. I'll check around...yet another mystery."

"A mystery? Can I do something?" Ms. Fanny echoed from the kitchen.

Everybody answered in chorus. "Cook!"

"Well, Fanny Parker can do that! Oh, boy, I hear a knock on the front door and I know who that is," she said, bustling over to turn the doorknob.

"Hold on, Fanny," the sheriff cautioned. "For right now, I think it's a good idea for everybody here to keep quiet about Allie's angel friend. Can we agree on that? From what I understand, she's still having trouble at school with the other kids making fun of her from the cheating incident on Wednesday."

"Gotcha. I've lived alone for over twenty years by telling nobody nothing. Allie's angel is a secret with me."

Fanny feigned a wink and opened the door. "Well, I declare. If it ain't the handsomest line puller in all of Texas. Come on in, Otis, and say 'hi' to everybody. Dinner's ready. Do you need to wash up? No? Well, then, I'm gonna need your help in running some wire to our new garden out back of that old community church. Will you volunteer for that? And our Allie is gonna work on rebuilding that old church. Won't it be fun, Otis? Just like the olden days when I'd sing and you'd shoot spitballs through a straw at me during church service. Everybody here is all down in the doldrums about it; they think it's just a bunch of hard work. But me? Shoot, it's an adventure!"

OTIS SCUFFED HIS feet, pulled off his ball cap and blushed all the way up to the top of his bald head. He was deeply suntanned with lines etched around his twinkly hazel eyes. As Fanny bustled around the kitchen in her old, faded blue dress, Otis admired her every move.

"Thank you for having me to dinner, Mrs. McCall. 'Evening, sheriff," Otis said, shaking hands with Mama and Sheriff Anderson.

"Oh, for heaven's sake, please call me Laura. And this is my daughter, Allie. It's a pleasure to have you. Fanny's been a lifesaver to us. We are so grateful to her, and to you for running that electrical wire today."

"Yes, ma'am. I had no notion that Fanny didn't have electricity. We grew up together, but," star struck, he looked at Fanny, "we hadn't seen each other in years until this morning."

"Funny how that works, ain't it, Otis? Here we live in this small town and don't ever see each other. Kinda sad, really. I guess folks are that way."

"I'd heard that since Cecil died, you'd stayed at home, to yourself. Didn't want to be bothered by anybody," Otis said, taking his seat at the table.

Fanny paused at the kitchen stove. "That's true. I didn't want to be bothered by anybody until yesterday. That horrible man attacked me in my greenhouse. I told you that story, Otis," Fanny said, her eyes filling. "And our Allie rode her bike to my house after hearing my screams. It was a miracle she heard me."

A miracle? Daniel? Hmm, Allie wondered.

"Fanny's told me a lot about you, Allie," Otis spoke up. "But I didn't know you planned to fix up the garden and the church. Fanny, remember how we'd have to help our grandpas work in that garden?"

"Lordy, do I ever!" Fanny laughed.

Otis smiled. "Only I remember diggin' in that garden more'n you. Weren't there about two acres in the first one we made? My grandpa tried to work all that land by himself, but he couldn't till it all. I remember him trying to borrow mean ol' Pierce's mule, but that crazy ol' coot wouldn't let him borrow nothing." Otis' big laugh carried throughout the house. Allie was startled to see him look ten years younger. "But we don't have to worry about one single mule. I've got a tractor powerful enough to till a row clear to Dallas. It can handle a little two or three acre tract—no problem."

"Then it's settled, Otis. You're my number one volunteer on gettin' this garden up and runnin'." Fanny's grin spread around the table. "Allie's got her hands full rebuilding that church."

Otis frowned. "Tell me again--why are you rebuilding that church?"

"Uh…uh," Allie stumbled, not wanting to spill the beans about Daniel.

Sheriff Anderson saved her. "It's like this. Allie's interested in the church because it's old and…well, not being used. We shouldn't have an eyesore like that in our downtown area. Mayor Hinckley has said the same thing, but most folks are too old to tackle the chore of remodeling, since the town doesn't have any extra money. So, yesterday, when Allie skipped school, I decided to give her a community project –"

"Well, mercy me." Otis smiled. "Allie sounds exactly like Fanny. Do you know how many times she and her sister, Margaret, skipped school?"

"You hush up, Otis Spinkle. Don't go spreading rumors. 'Sides, that was years ago. We lived in a different time. We only had about fifty kids, total, in all the grades, remember? Friendly was a teeny town then. Nobody went to college, and most everybody who was old enough to do anything helped their families on the farms."

Otis chuckled. "But you still got in trouble more times than not, Frances Parker."

Standing over his chair, Fanny clutched her wooden spoon. "We're going to change the subject now, Otis, or I won't be serving you any more chicken and dumplings."

Everybody at the table laughed when Otis bowed his head and smiled, "Yes, ma'am. I'll be quiet."

Dinner was delicious. Everybody talked, telling stories about the past. Allie noticed that even Mama seemed younger and happier than she had in months—maybe years?

When Fanny got up to serve the pie, Allie noticed some tired lines around her eyes.

"Here, Ms. Fanny, I'll do that," Allie said, jumping up from the table. She leaned over and whispered, "I'm washing the dishes, too. Thank you so much for such a wonderful meal."

Fanny turned; their faces were just inches apart. "You're a good girl, Allie," she whispered. "You've got a good heart. A free spirit…just don't skip school again. It didn't do me any good and it won't do you no good, neither. You've got the brains to go to college."

Allie smiled at Fanny's little fussing. Well, didn't she deserve it? It was nice to know that somebody cared. She reached over and gave Fanny a quick kiss on her cheek, smiling at the whiff of rose petals. Fanny had definitely been into the bubble bath again.

"Yes, ma'am. I'll behave," she said, before picking up the pie and some clean plates. "Okay, everybody, this is Fanny's world-renowned apple pie."

"Oh, my gosh. You're going to make me blush. I don't make anything that is world-renowned." Fanny laughed.

"Well, then it should be," Allie quipped.

Sheriff Anderson ate his pie the fastest of anybody and used his napkin to wipe the remaining crumbs off his cheek. "Fanny, my compliments to the chef. That dinner was superb!"

Fanny blushed again at the compliment. "Goodness, y'all, I'm turning beet red. It's just a bit of food."

"It's better cooking than I get at the boardinghouse," Sheriff Anderson said, pushing his chair back from the table. "Marybelle does most of the cooking—"

"Omigosh. I didn't know the boardinghouse was still around. Are you talking about Marybelle Hightower?" Fanny asked.

"Yes, ma'am, she's the one running it now, at least for the time I've lived there. And we still refer to it as the boardinghouse. It's sure not some fancy hotel," the sheriff said. "Even our, *ahem*, friend Rudy Mae Timmons has cooked a beef stew on occasion—"

Allie's fork rattled as it fell on her plate. "Not Mrs. Timmons! My horrible English teacher? Mrs. Timmons lives in the boardinghouse?"

Sheriff Anderson smiled. "She does. I thought you knew."

Allie gulped. She didn't want to know anything about Mrs. Timmons, except when she would be leaving town—preferably soon, and for good. "No, I didn't know. H-how can you stand … living there… with her?"

Fanny leaned toward Allie. "Rudy Mae Timmons has always been a little uppity, if you ask me. Nobody but her ever had a good idea when she was around. It's always been her way or the highway."

Sheriff Anderson looked at the clock. "Laura, why don't you and I drive over and pick Ben up at Jacob's house? It's nearly seven o'clock."

Mama quickly rose from the table. "Logan, I completely forgot the time. Thank you for reminding me." She got her purse and turned to Fanny, Otis and Allie. "We'll be back in a minute."

Fanny waved them away. "Y'all take your time. I think the three of us can hold down this fort."

When they left, Allie shooed Fanny and Otis into the small living room. "Why don't y'all go sit in the living room? Ms. Fanny, you've been on your feet all day."

"Thank you, child. I am a bit tired just now." Fanny moved slowly toward the sofa, with Otis in tow. Allie smiled as she washed the dishes, listening to the couple talk and then laugh with their heads bent close together. It was fun to have a lot of people at the dinner table. Maybe the sheriff and Otis would come back for dinner tomorrow night. She'd talk to Fanny about that.

Chapter 14

✧

SATURDAY, SEPTEMBER 18

ALLIE AWOKE TO a bright and sunny Saturday. With a yawn and a stretch, she jumped out of bed. A beautiful day. *A fabulous day. A great day to be alive.*

The sound of sizzling bacon and the fresh aroma of homemade biscuits filled the air. Fanny was in the kitchen again.

"Yesss!" Allie raced the few steps into the kitchen, ready to sample anything within reach.

"Hold on," Fanny said, as a sneaky hand dug into the bacon. "Put your clothes on and help me set the table. I think your Mama and Ben are sleeping late."

Allie grinned and gave Fanny a swift kiss on her cheek. "I love you, Ms. Fanny." She trotted down the tiny hallway. "C'mon, Ben! C'mon, Mama! Fanny's fixing breakfast and I'm setting the table. It's a terrific Saturday morning. Time to get up!"

Ben opened his door an inch. "It's not even six o'clock in the morning. What are you yelling about?"

"I'm telling YOU to get up and come eat some breakfast, Einstein. It's time you joined the family, Benjamin Franklin McCall. Stop moping around, put all your books away and get some clothes on. Don't be so depressing. Be happy. We have Ms. Fanny here with us and she's cooked more food than we've ever seen before. What is so terrible about that?"

Allie passed by her Mama's bedroom, not bothering to knock. Why keep trying?

Instead, she called Sheriff Anderson and left a message, asking him to breakfast. She had a church to renovate. There wasn't a moment to lose.

Moments later, Allie put down her fork. "Mmm, Ms. Fanny, this is the best ham and egg omelet ever," she said, taking another biscuit. "I'm so hungry, I could eat ten breakfasts!"

"I can see that, child. I don't know what's come over you, calling Sheriff Anderson so early this morning."

"And Otis, too, if he wants to come. Will you call him?"

"Oh, my," Ms. Fanny said, patting her apron pocket and pulling out a rumpled piece of paper. "I have his telephone number right here. I s'pose I could call him."

"Please do, Ms. Fanny. Y'all need to start your garden and I need to work on my church project." Allie pondered over another bite of biscuit and jelly. "Fanny, do you know any rich people who would make a donation to help rebuild the church?"

Fanny nodded. "First things first. I'll go call Otis and be right back." It didn't take her long to hang up the phone. "Well, I'll be! Otis said he'd be over in a jiffy. Said he needed to talk to us anyway about where the electrical needs to be run for that garden and if you need some electrical for the church."

Allie sighed. Of course she needed electricity. So many details!

"Now, you asked me about people who'd donate money," Fanny said thoughtfully. "People who have money generally have businesses. There's the bank, the feed store, the newspaper in town. There's that sneaky-looking attorney Jack Morgan, who I wouldn't trust at'all. Then there's Nate Sims and his café and pharmacy, and Marybelle Hightower's boardinghouse. That's about it, Allie. Slim pickin's for sure."

"I'd ask Mama, but she's too busy."

"Don't be too sure about that," Allie heard Mama say as she entered the room. "You know I care about what goes on in your life."

There came a knock on the door, probably the sheriff. She watched her Mama, dressed in a pair of blue jeans and a T-shirt, pad over to open it in her bare feet. *Mama with no shoes on? Holy smoke! This had to be a first.* Even Mama's hair was sticking out in every direction, and she didn't seem to care.

"Hi, Logan," she said, turning back into the room.

Allie couldn't help seeing last night's mascara and eyeliner under her eyes. Mama looked tired and haggard—maybe even old.

"I'll be right back, everybody. I'm going to go wash up."

Sheriff Anderson eased over to the breakfast table, removing his hat. "G'morning, ladies. You're up and at'em pretty early." He smiled down as Fanny poured him a cup of coffee. "The food looks great, Fanny. Thank you."

"I want to get started on the church today," Allie told him. "Can you give me some ideas of how to get people to donate money? Fanny's already run down the short list of businesses in town."

Sheriff Anderson turned his smile from Allie to Fanny. "Do you think she'll stop asking questions long enough to let me eat?"

Fanny sat down and poured herself a cup of coffee. "If I were you, Allie, I'd start with the bank. Sheriff, who's in charge of that bank now?"

Sheriff Anderson finished chewing. "That would be Mangus Sinclair."

"Oh, no! He must be a hundred years old by now."

The sheriff's eyes twinkled as he sipped his coffee. "He may be ninety-nine. Still as ornery as ever. Certainly not a generous man, Allie. Don't get your hopes up."

Allie rolled her eyes. Another huge battle. "Well, if everybody in town is ancient or mean or stingy, how am I supposed to get money to rebuild this church?"

The sheriff looked surprised. "You're asking me? It's your project, not mine. How did Daniel tell you to get the money?"

"He didn't. Exactly. He...er, wasn't clear on that. He just told me to get donations," Allie replied, crestfallen. "Now what am I supposed to do?"

The sheriff laid his napkin on the table. "You could always ask Buzz on Monday. Give yourself a little time. Make a plan. Write down some ideas and questions. Since Buzz knows the construction business, he knows the people who sell the lumber and materials. Maybe they can help you."

"Sounds like a good idea to me," Fanny chimed in. "In the meantime, Sheriff Anderson, I've thought about the garden and think we should grow flowers along with vegetables. We had rose bushes growing up. That's why I love your bubble bath so much, Allie. It reminds me of when I was a young girl. My sister, Margaret, would press the oil from the roses and we'd use that in our bath water."

"You mean, Maggie, Sheriff Anderson's secretary?"

"She's not my secretary. She's the dispatch operator," the sheriff inserted.

Allie was interested in Fanny's answer. "Maggie knows how to grow roses?"

"She does…or she did. I haven't talked to her in—"

"Twenty-five years," Allie interrupted. "Maggie told me the whole story last Thursday when I skipped school. I know about your feud."

"Hrumph," Fanny growled, sipping the coffee. "It's no feud. She was after my Cecil, make no mistake. All prissy she was, wearin' all that makeup and her fancy clothes…. Well, look at me, child, I didn't have a chance. I'm just a year older than Maggie, but she got the looks in the family. And I'll never forget the day I found them together in the hay barn."

Sheriff Anderson stood up, took his plate to the stove, and scrounged around for more eggs. "Fanny, there's no sense in getting yourself all worked up about the past. Allie doesn't need to know all of this—"

"Sheriff, this girl's part of my family. She saved my life. 'Sides, she loves my cooking and eats pert near anythin' put on her plate. Too many young'uns today are so picky, but not my Allie. She's smart and funny and spirited."

He was now eating the eggs straight from the skillet. "Admit it, Fanny. She reminds you of you when you were young."

"That she does," Fanny said, wistfully. "But I never was as pretty as Allie."

"Oh, stop it. I am not pretty. I'm too tall and my hair is too thick. There's nothing pretty about being a giant."

"There is if you need your cupboards cleaned out. And I just happen to need some help with mine, young'un, if you wouldn't mind," Fanny said, grinning.

"Oh, phooey, you know I'll help you. Sit still, Ms. Fanny, I'll do the dishes. You've been cooking for the past twenty-four hours straight. Sheriff Anderson's doing a fine job of cleaning all the plates and the skillets for me, anyway," Allie teased. "Are they not feeding you at the boardinghouse?"

"Not like this," he said, washing his hands. "Fanny, I have an idea. We've got a nice stretch of good weather ahead of us and I think you should get to work on this garden while Allie works on the church. Could you lend a hand and help her get started with some ideas about getting donations?"

"Uh, well, sure, I'll do what I can."

"One more thing. I'd like for you to stop by the office. I know it's Saturday, but Maggie's working until noon—"

"No, sirree, I ain't gonna—"

"Wait just a minute, Fanny. I'm asking you as a personal favor to talk to Maggie. Take Allie with you. Maggie can be a huge help with finding volunteers and suggesting people to help. I honestly think we could furnish food to many of our senior citizens in town who can't afford it right now. Besides, they might want to do a little gardening. I think a flower garden along with the vegetables would be a good idea. The gardeners could sell the flowers and a good bit of the vegetables. We could put in a picnic table nearby. Nate Sims has always wanted a picnic area behind his shop. I know the boardinghouse residents would like to sit on the back porch and talk about the garden." Sheriff Anderson paused to wipe his mouth on a nearby napkin. "Good luck, ladies. Looks like you two will have a busy day. Allie, please let your mama know that I'll call her later." And with that, he left, closing the door behind him.

"How can he just do that?" Allie turned to Fanny. "He issues all these orders and then just walks away."

"He's the sheriff. That what sheriffs do," Fanny remarked.

"Well, it's not fair." Allie banged the dishes in the sink, sending soap suds flying. "It was like a command."

"Has Logan left already?" Mama scurried into the living room with fresh makeup and brushed hair. "Did I miss him?"

"Yes, you did," Fanny replied. "He left a minute ago."

Allie chimed in. "He wanted me to tell you that he'd call you in a while."

Mama focused her attention on sorting through her messy purse, which was nearly the size of her briefcase. She had everything in there but an extra change of clothing.

Allie stepped closer for a peek inside. "What are you looking for? Are you going to work?"

"Allie," she began, distracted by a bundle of papers. "I'm sorry, but I didn't finish an important story yesterday. I met my press deadline, but I'm in the middle of something...er, that needs finishing. I want to help you—"

"I know. It's okay. You're busy. Fanny said she'd help me."

"Great! Oh, thank you, Fanny. I'm taking Ben over to Jacob's house now. I know it's early, but they're going to ride horses all day and he's been asked to spend the night. Ben! Are you ready?"

"Coming!"

Moments later they were both gone.

Allie washed another of what seemed like one million glasses and plates. "Why does she always do that? She disappears whenever I need her help."

Fanny was wiping off the tablecloth. "She's busy. Your mama runs the weekly newspaper. It's a big job."

"But she's never here for Ben and me! She's always gone, busy, can-this-wait-ten-minutes, can-you-wait-till-tomorrow. It's been like this ever since Daddy died. She doesn't want any part of our lives" Allie stretched out the dishtowels to dry. "Sorry for complaining. Thank you for helping me, Ms. Fanny."

"C'mon, child, put a smile on that pretty face. I thought Otis would be here by now for breakfast."

Aw, geez. Allie had completely forgotten about Otis. And she'd washed all the dishes.

As if reading her mind, Fanny waved her away. "I got it handled. I hear his truck on the gravel outside. I'll just pop some eggs in the skillet and bread in the toaster and whip up some hash browns in a jiffy. Otis will love it all."

"If I ever do get any money, the first thing I'm going to buy is a dishwasher," Allie growled as she trudged down the hallway.

Her excitement slipped as she contemplated her day, suddenly feeling sorry for herself. Ben got to ride horses all day. She had to do homework and then work, work and work some more on rebuilding a church. What in the world was fair about that?

ALLIE LIKED THE easy way that Fanny and Otis laughed and talked in the kitchen. They were friends. Good friends. Allie hurried to finish brushing her teeth.

"Did y'all say something about a dance?" she asked, trotting back into the kitchen.

Fanny was holding court at the stove. "Landsakes! Otis asked me to the Smith County Lineman's Benefit Auction and Dance next Saturday. I don't know what in the world he's thinking. I can't go to a dance."

Allie shouted out happily as her earlier self-pity vanished. "Sure you can! It'll be fun. Otis, I think it's a great idea. Ms. Fanny needs some fun and I can't think of anybody she'd rather go with than you."

Otis blushed a beet red from his shaved chin to the top of his bald head.

"I don't even know how to dance," Fanny said, laughing as she beat the scrambled eggs to death in the skillet. "Well, maybe.... Lordy, I ain't been to a social in years and years." She piled enough food on his plate for ten people. "I ain't got nuthin' fancy to wear."

Allie thought fast. That was true. As far as Allie knew she had an old pink dress and an old blue one. "That can't stop you from going, Ms. Fanny. We'll just fix that problem."

"Fix it? Child, you have to know that dresses cost money."

"Now, Fanny, if it's money—"

Fanny silenced him with her spatula. "Listen, here, Otis Spinkle, don't you worry about my dress. I'll take care of getting my own dress."

Allie smiled. It was working. "And I'll help you, Ms. Fanny. We'll work on your dress today."

"What about the church? And the garden?"

"We'll work on the dress, the church and the garden. We'll do it all!"

From her place at the stove, Fanny shot Otis a big grin. "Well, it's settled. We'll go to your soirée, Otis. If Allie says she'll help me, there's no excuse. Can you give us a lift to town later this morning?"

"Sure can," he answered. "But in the meantime, will you let me inside your house to run the electrical wiring?"

"Now that I can surely do." Fanny took off her apron, and moved a few hairpins around to straighten her bun.

Allie leaned over and whispered, "Remember the sheriff's office before noon? I'm going with you to talk to Miss Maggie."

"Don't remind me, child, don't remind me. That—above all else—puts me in a sour mood."

Chapter 15

LATER THAT MORNING, Allie and Fanny strolled into the downtown Friendly police station.

"Hi, Miss Maggie," Allie called, pulling on Fanny's arm to get her inside.

Maggie stood by the file cabinet, looking more like a spring bouquet than a dispatch operator. She wore a white dress covered with yellow and green daisies and accented by a shiny yellow belt. Her wine-colored hair was piled high on her head, her stiletto heels barely kept her standing upright, and her war paint today included false eyelashes that Allie could see from fifteen feet away.

"Well, how-do, Allie, it's good to see you," Maggie said with a smile. The smile dissolved when Fanny poked her head through the doorway.

Allie had never seen anyone turn as white as a ghost—especially somebody wearing all that makeup—but Maggie did. Her eyes flew open and her false eyelashes popped up on end.

"Well, I'll be," she whispered. "If it ain't the spitting' image of my sister, who I thought sure was dead and buried by now."

Fanny's eyes narrowed. "Don't you say that, you red-haired floozy. You know I ain't neither dead nor buried. You ain't been invited to no funeral yet."

"Might as well be dead and buried, the way we ain't talked for twenty-five years. Why you silly old fool! There I've been living in Mom and Dad's house all this time and you ain't stopped by—not one time—to visit."

"You ain't come by my house, neither. Not since Cecil died. I've been living there all by myself, you...you hussy."

"Stop calling me names, Frances Parker, I mean it. I did not, repeat, did NOT do anything with Cecil that day in the hay barn. For heaven's sakes! You'd been married to him for twenty-something' years at the time. Why would I wait so long after you were married to chase him?"

"You still deny it?"

Maggie slapped a file on her desk. "How dare you! Waltzing in here, digging up the past like this...you've got your nerve!"

"I'm here on account of the sheriff asked me to come and bring Allie. So don't get all uppity with me! Just forget it. What's past is past."

Maggie rolled her eyes. "Really, sister? Do you believe that? We haven't seen each other in years—"

"And after today...we'll just forget this ever happened." Fanny took Allie's hand, "C'mon, let's get outta here. I tried. I really did. I'll tell the sheriff, I've done all I can do."

"Wait!" Allie pulled on Fanny's hand. "We can't leave now," she whispered, "you haven't asked her—"

"And I'm not going to," Fanny hissed.

"Ask me what?" Maggie smacked one hand on her hip. "You come here to ask me something? Well, get it out."

"Margaret, we've taken up enough of your time." Fanny's snootiness was unmistakable. "It's time for us to leave."

"Wait! Miss Maggie...Fanny! Stop...please!" Allie glanced from one to the other. "I l-love you both." Allie shocked herself by her own admission. "I don't know either one of you really...but I almost feel like part of your family."

"Oh, Allie, nobody wants you in the middle of this squabble." Maggie plopped down in her desk chair. "Y'all please sit down. I simply can't stand up anymore...my shoes are killing' me." She refastened a hair pin while Fanny and Allie sat.

"Fanny, for Allie's sake, let's stop fussing'—at least for five minutes. The simple fact is that you've listened to too many stories." Maggie sighed. "Okay. I admit it—for years I thought Cecil was the handsomest man I'd ever seen in Smith County. Every girl around these parts was after him when y'all got married. But then years passed and the younger girls were still chasing' him. We were middle-aged when he took me into the hay barn that day to tell me how much he loved you!" Maggie exclaimed.

"Are you listening to me? He told me in the barn how much he still loved you! Sure, me and Cecil were great friends, but he told me you were the only woman he could ever love. He wanted all the girls and their flirtin'

to stop. And he thought I could, somehow, end it all. That next week…
the tractor accident happened.…

"You haven't talked to me since. Now, if I were you I'd be mighty
happy, because nothing ever went on between us. I swear it on a stack of
Bibles."

Allie watched the blood drain from Fanny's face. She looked tired,
older than Maggie. Worn out by too much stress. Arguing for all those
years. And for what? A family feud. Just plain stupid. People say and do
the strangest things.

"Why should I believe you now?"

Maggie glanced away. "Because… I have no reason to lie. I feel like I
lost my dear sister the very day that Cecil was buried."

Fanny caught her breath. "That's cruel. You didn't lose me."

"I feel like I did! We were so close—you remember—like twins."

"Why wouldn't I believe those rumors? You were always so much
prettier than me."

Maggie sighed. "I was never prettier than you. You just never wanted
to pretty yourself up. Never wanted to wear makeup…or style your hair.
But Cecil didn't care. He loved you exactly the way you were."

Fanny pushed away a tear. "I wanna believe you. I do—"

"Then let it go. Forget about the past."

"But now I don't know where to turn. You were always the one who
knew about these things. How do I say this? I'm supposed to go to a dance
next Saturday with Otis."

Maggie began to giggle, her wine-colored topknot shaking. "Well, if
that don't beat all. Otis Spinkle? He must be sweet on you. I suppose he's
getting' lonesome since his wife died."

Allie chimed in. "He ran an electrical wire yesterday for Ms. Fanny. He
said he'd pay her electric bill every month. He came to dinner last night
and breakfast this morning. I think he likes Ms. Fanny's cooking."

"Are you kiddin'? Everybody in Smith County likes Fanny's cooking.
I bet Marybelle at the boardinghouse would like you to cook over there,
but I wouldn't if I were you, Fanny. There's just a bunch of fussbudgets
what live there—except the sheriff, of course. There's no pleasing them,
no way."

But Fanny wasn't listening. "I don't have a dress to wear."

"A dress?" Maggie chimed in.

"To the Smith County Lineman's Benefit Auction and Dance,"
answered Fanny, "with Otis."

"Well, that is one big soiree. But, if a dress is what you're looking for, you've come to the right place."

"To a sheriff's office?" Allie asked.

"No, silly. To me." Maggie stood up and adjusted her belt.

"Can she wear your dresses?" Allie knew the answer was no. Where Maggie was curvy, Fanny was straight up and down skinny.

Maggie was eyeballing her sister now. "I see what you're sayin'. You ain't got no bosom at'all, Frances. We don't wear the same size, but I've got an idea."

"I thought you'd have an idea." Fanny eyed her suspiciously.

"The three of us are gonna visit Marybelle at the boardinghouse."

"Marybelle's got dresses for sale?" Fanny asked.

"No, but she knows people who do. There's no time to waste. I heard that her sister, Lorraine Lamonte, from Tyler is coming to town today."

"Does she have dresses?" Allie asked.

"Lord-a-mercy. Lorraine's got dresses like Bayer's got aspirin. She owns Dress Express up in Tyler—just about fanciest, prettiest dress shop in East Texas. I'd die and go to heaven right now just to own one. The sheriff said this morning that he'd heard Lorraine was coming for lunch today at the boardinghouse. I say we hustle over there right now and get some ideas."

"Wait," Allie interrupted, "what about the office?"

"Don't you worry. I'll just close up early," Maggie replied. "This is serious business. Fanny needs a dress. And I mean it when I say that Sheriff Anderson likes her cooking way too much to have Fanny upset. He does go on about it, too." Maggie glanced at her sister with a lopsided smile. "I've been hearing nothing but praises from that man for the past two days. I'm sick to death of it. Seriously, sister. Men everywhere are falling at your feet. Can't you ever burn your blue ribbon biscuits just once?" Maggie grabbed her purse, turned out the lights and slipped the key into the door to lock up the building.

Allie and Fanny waited for her on the sidewalk.

"I'm gonna trust you this time," Fanny said flatly. "You do know about style. However," she pointed to Maggie's shoes, "I ain't never in all my days seen shoes with heels that high in such an ugly green color before."

"Oh, shush. Y'all wanna walk?" Maggie asked, grinning. "You know I can't go fast in these heels. We'll go slow in front of Nate Sims's café and see what his desserts are today."

Fanny harrumphed. "Flirting as usual."

"Some Saturdays he has homemade chocolate éclairs and they are the best ever. I just can't resist Nate's creamy inside fillings."

"Nate's creamy inside fillings?" Fanny barked out a laugh. "Did you just say that?"

Maggie flipped up her hand and stuck up her nose. "You know exactly what I'm talking about. The whole fabulous thing about the éclair is the creamy inside filling. Y'all know what I mean; it's like a filled donut. They're so yummy."

The three smiling females rounded the corner to see Nate out sweeping the front doorway of his café.

"'Morning, ladies!" he hollered, waving. "How y'all doin' this pretty Saturday?"

Allie lagged behind for a moment, glancing up at the old church. How in the world was she going to rebuild it? *A plan. I need a plan.*

"C'mon, young'un, quit your daydreaming!" Fanny called out.

"What did I miss?" Allie hurried to catch up.

"Nothing. Just watching Maggie make a fool over herself. She's absolutely smitten with Nate Sims. There's no doubt in my mind."

Fanny turned to Maggie. "I can't believe my ears. Asking him to set aside an éclair for you. Even fluttered your eyelashes at him. You do beat all. Positively shameless."

Allie laughed. "And to think that you two haven't talked in years? You're going to be the best friends ever. Just like before."

Maggie smothered a smile with her hand. "It's true, Fanny. We let a man come between us. And a dead one, at that!"

"Maggie, hush this minute. I'm trying to forgive you for betraying me. Which now you say you didn't do at'all? Landsakes, I can't sort it all out in my pea brain. Don't you dare say one bad word about Cecil!"

"I mean that in a kind way, sister. Cecil would want us to be friends. If it wasn't for that farming accident, Cecil would still be alive today. I say it's time we buried the hatchet just like we buried Cecil. And I hope you forgive me for doing something I never did. Let's put the past behind us 'cause neither one of us is getting any younger."

Fanny grimaced. "God knows that's a fact. And here I need your help in starting the old garden up again and this young'un needs help to rebuild the old church."

"What?" Maggie paused on the steps of the boardinghouse, looking from her sister to Allie. "A garden? A church?" The remaining glue on her fake lashes gave way completely. "Oh my gosh, what fun!"

Maggie pulled hard on the iron doorknob before the two older ladies and one half-scared girl stepped inside. Allie had never been inside the boardinghouse. Such an old-timey name for nothing more than a big three story house with ten bedrooms, two bathrooms on each floor, a big kitchen, dining room and a great room they called the "entertainment area" with a television nearly as big as a movie theatre.

Marybelle Hightower, a widow, and her daughter, Bessie, had inherited the big house from Marybelle's daddy, who had been a lawyer in Tyler. Marybelle had transformed one of the downstairs rooms into a beauty and barber shop that Bessie ran.

"'Morning, y'all," Marybelle said as she hustled across the entertainment area. "Well, I declare! Fanny and Maggie? This is a sight for my old tired eyes. I never thought I'd see the day when you two buried the hatchet and made up."

"That's exactly what I told Fanny. My exact words," Maggie said.

"What can I do for you? I don't have long to chit-chat because my sister Lorraine is coming down to visit—"

"She's the reason we're here."

"Lorraine? Really?"

"Oh, hush, sister. I'm embarrassed," Fanny whispered. "This was a bad idea."

Maggie patted Fanny's hand. "Marybelle, we need your help. Fanny, here, has been invited to the Smith County Lineman's Benefit Auction and Dance next Saturday. Otis Spinkle asked her."

Marybelle gasped. "Well, I'll be."

"And she needs a dress."

"I guess she does! That's the most talked about dance every fall."

Marybelle gave Fanny a quick hug, grinning from ear to ear. "Oh, dear, this is happy news. I cannot wait to tell Lorraine. She is marvelous about these things. She always has tons of dresses and ideas, Fanny. You just wait until she hears the about your date. This is so exciting! Y'all come with me. I've got my sister-in-law and niece in the kitchen and we'll visit." Marybelle turned to lead the way.

"Oh, for heaven's sake, I've completely forgotten my manners," said Maggie. "I haven't introduced you to Allie McCall. Marybelle, have you ever met Allie? She's Laura McCall's daughter."

Marybelle blinked and swiveled around. "No dear, I don't believe we've met," she said, extending her hand. "Why, what a lovely and very tall young lady you are. Very pretty, indeed. We're so glad you're here."

Allie smiled her thanks and followed the others. She had heard kids at the school talk about how snooty Marybelle Hightower was, but she seemed really nice. She had short brown hair, rosy cheeks and a round face...well, she was a little round all over, but Allie just thought of that as being pleasantly plump. Ms. Marybelle seemed like a genuinely happy person. Now she pushed open a swinging door to reveal a massive kitchen.

"Everybody... take a look at who's come to call! Can you believe it? And they walked in together. Fanny Parker and Maggie Matthews. Now y'all tell me if you thought this would ever happen." Allie watched in awe as a peal of laughter greeted Marybelle's remarks.

"Holy smoke!" Allie cried, rushing forward to wrap her arms around her best friend. "Wikki, what are you doing here?"

She giggled. "I'm Marybelle's niece, silly. I thought you knew that. Papa is Marybelle's brother."

"Oh, for heaven's sake. No, I didn't know that." Allie grabbed a chair and pulled it over to sit beside her.

"Now, girls, we'll have none of that. It's time that you two pulled your chairs up to the table like the ladies that you are. Don't sit huddled in a corner. That is not seemly for genteel young ladies," Marybelle said.

"Oh, pshaw," said Jessica Wilkinson, Wikki's mama. "These girls may not even know what 'genteel' means." Mrs. Wilkinson gave Allie a big smile. "Hi, Allie, it's good to see you again. You haven't come by much since summer ended and school started. Have you been busy?"

"Yes, ma'am, I have... and, well, Mama is always busy—"

"I know. I know. You can't drive and don't have a way to get over to our house. That's okay. I'm working most afternoons at the feed store, but I'll see what I can do to have you and Wikki see each other more. She just loves it when you come for a visit."

Beaming, both girls pulled their chairs up to the table, now covered with a white lace tablecloth. Fanny and Maggie were deep in conversation at one end of the table. Mrs. Wilkerson helped Marybelle finish putting out the casserole dishes hot from the stove.

"Lorraine just called and she'll be here in a jiffy," said Marybelle.

Moments later, Allie heard the big front door in the main lobby open.

"Yoo-hoo! Anybody home?"

Lorraine Lamonte swooshed into the kitchen, looking as stylish and elegant as the next cover of *Vogue* magazine. Not quite middle-aged, Lorraine Lamonte had virtually no wrinkles and creamy skin. Allie guessed she might be in her thirties. She had on a forest green suit with a slim skirt and fitted jacket. She wore a scarf wrapped around her blonde hair, as if she'd been out driving with the top down. Yes, Lorraine Lamonte looked the type to have a silver Jaguar convertible tucked away somewhere.

"Ladies, it is so fabulous to see everybody again. I just love these get-togethers," Lorraine said as she placed quick kisses on everyone's cheek. "Oh, goodness, are you Maggie Matthews?"

Maggie giggled and grinned. "Lorraine, you look fabulous as always."

"Oh, you are too sweet." Then she smiled at Fanny. "Have we met before?"

"I'm Fanny Parker. I haven't seen you since you were a teenager. You sure are pretty."

"Oh, dear me! You all put me to the blush. Oh, yes, please tell me how much I've changed since I was a teenager. I looked so dreadful in those days! It's a pleasure to see you, Fanny."

Lorraine moved around the table and fastened her eyes on Allie. Her smile faded, and then reappeared.

"Goodness, what a beauty you are. Stand up. Stand up," she commanded.

Allie, feeling a deep blush rise above her faded shirt collar, slowly stood up, towering over everybody in the room.

"Oh, my," Lorraine said softly, placing her hand under Allie's chin and turning her face to the left and then the right. "You are lovely."

"This is Allie McCall," said Wikki from her wheelchair. "She's my best friend at school."

"Hello, my sweet," said Lorraine, bending down to give Wikki a swift kiss and cheek hug. "You're looking wonderful. Rosy cheeks, and your hair looks so soft and shiny." Lorraine turned back to Allie. "Very pleased to meet you, Allie," she said, extending her hand.

"I have a surprise for you. I've been working on this for a long, long time. Just ask Mama," Wikki remarked.

"A surprise? Oh, goodness, but I love surprises. Let me grab an iced tea—oh thank you, Marybelle. I'll sit here by you, Wikki. Please, whenever you're ready. Surprise me all you want."

Lorraine took a seat next to Wikki, looking genuinely interested. *Compared to Lorraine Lamonte we all look out of style.* Yet nobody seemed to care.

Wikki put both of her hands on the arms of her wheelchair. She lifted the flaps where her feet normally rested, putting her feet on the floor. She pushed herself up nearly to a standing position, held it for a few seconds and then dropped back down in the wheelchair.

She smiled at the gasps heard round the table.

"Wikki, this is fantastic!" Lorraine said, clapping her hands together. "This is the best news I've had for months and months!"

Allie sat, dumbfounded. Wikki could nearly stand. *And to think I promised that somehow I could help her walk. I'm such a dummy. Wikki is working on this all by herself.*

"I'm trying to build up my strength. The doctors in Houston say I have a chance to walk with a special operation," Wikki said.

Her mother added, "It's true. We got this fabulous news last week. Several doctors want us to bring Wikki down to Houston for a series of x-rays. They'll determine if they can fuse together certain vertebrae." Jessica Wilkerson glanced at her tea glass. "It would be simply amazing, really. Experimental—and terribly expensive. But, to think, after all these years, what the wonders of science can do nowadays. It's like a true miracle."

Allie laid her hand on Wikki's wheelchair. "This is amazing. I'm so happy," she whispered. "See? You'll wear all those knee socks, after all."

Wikki looked up, her eyes clouded. "Will you help me, Allie? I'm kinda scared about the operation. The doctor says I'll need to make sure my friends help me through it."

"I'll be there, don't you worry."

Chapter 16

❦

MAGGIE CHIRPED UP. "Could I make an announcement? Did y'all know that Otis Spinkle ran an electrical line for Fanny last week? She's finally going to have electricity in her house! And she's officially coming out next Saturday. Otis asked her—"

"Sister, stop!" Fanny gasped.

"No." Maggie gave her elbow a shove. "Otis asked Fanny to the Smith County Lineman's Benefit Auction and Dance."

"What?" gasps echoed all around the kitchen table.

"I know—the Lineman's dance," Maggie said, nodding, "except that Fanny doesn't have one nice dress to wear. We stopped by today to ask Miss Lorraine if we could visit her dress shop in Tyler. I'd like to buy something beautiful for Fanny."

Lorraine sat up. "Oh, this is so exciting! I know the perfect dress for you, Fanny. You're so slender. A size four, perhaps? I have a belted sage green with chiffon sleeves and a fluttery collar that is just waiting for you in my shop. You would look marvelous in it. And, if that's not what you want, I have a new shipment coming in Monday morning. Just pick out your favorite and it can be my present to you."

"A present? To me?" The color drained from Fanny's face. Her hand fluttered to the top button of her worn out pink dress. "But why?"

Lorraine swirled the tea around in her glass before looking across at Fanny. "Because any woman who can go for years and years without electricity deserves to have a new dress, new shoes *and* a new purse. You've earned it, Fanny Parker. You've earned the opportunity to have a good time. And I just happen to know Otis. He's a kind man."

"He likes Ms. Fanny," Allie said, conspiratorially. "You should see the way he looks at her. When he knows she's cooking, he comes right over."

Fanny brushed aside her comment. "Oh, Allie, you're just saying that. I've been staying with them for the past couple of days and—"

"Doing all of our cooking," Allie interrupted. "She's so fabulous. I don't know what we'd do without Ms. Fanny."

Marybelle began putting the casseroles on the table. "Fanny.... are you really a good cook? Because if you are, I could sure use some help with lunches most days. I can get the breakfast going and make dinner, but my feet have been giving me trouble and I really need to rest some during the afternoon. I guess what I'm saying is that if you'd like a part-time job, I'd sure like to have you help me."

Maggie gave Fanny an elbow jab in the side again. "Sister! What luck. Can you do it?"

"Marybelle, I'd love to help you, but I don't have a way to get into town. I think it's too far even for my golf cart to drive on one charge of electricity, and all."

"Golf cart?" someone asked.

"It's a long story," Allie answered. "The sheriff got it for her safety."

"I'll come and pick you up at 11:00 every day," said Maggie. "I'll take an early lunch. Shoot, you're only five miles away. It's no problem. Or Otis will drive you. From what Allie says, he'd be crazy excited to pick you up and bring you to town."

Fanny hesitated for a second. "Fine, I'll do it, Marybelle. I can start whenever you say. Would Monday be too soon?"

Marybelle had finished putting the fifth and final casserole out beside the big fruit salad and freshly baked bread.

Mmm, it smells fantastic. Allie watched Lorraine from the corner of her eye, placing her napkin in her lap when Lorraine did. *I never thought all this would happen. How fun!* Lunch with the ladies was just as special as she had imagined. Allie never got to meet many of her Mama's friends; she never got around grown-ups very much at all. Now she felt like part of some new extended family. She was a stranger to all these women, yet they included her in everything.

Allie studied how easily the women talked to one another, laughing, sharing jokes, serving food. Lorraine kept adding more to Wikki's plate, but Wikki pushed it away.

"No, Lorraine, no more, please!" Wikki said, laughing. "I'll get too roly-poly to ever walk."

"You're so thin that I think you're gonna dry up and blow away."

Allie smiled at that; Wikki was forever talking about how fat she was. She looked over to see Fanny and Maggie laughing and talking about something—maybe nothing—but she hadn't seen either woman look so happy.

Maggie spoke up. "Fanny also has some news about rebuilding the old church and garden."

"Did I hear somebody say 'garden'?" Marybelle asked.

"Oh, dear, that's right," Fanny interjected. "Allie's assignment is to rebuild the old church and I've promised to make a new community garden. Won't it be fun?"

"Well, for heaven's sake, I'll help with the garden. I don't know anything about church construction, but I sure can grow things," said Marybelle. "Besides, it's just a hundred yards beyond my back porch."

That was certainly true. Because the church and the grounds sat off Main Street, all the shops backed up to the nearly three acres of land that would encompass the new community garden.

"I'm gonna help," Maggie chirped.

"Count me in," said Jessica.

"I'll shop there," said Lorraine. "I'd love some fresh herbs and green beans. Would y'all grow those for me if I pay for the seeds or plants, or whatever it is you need to grow it with?"

"Sounds like you'll need to make some decisions about how all this will work, ladies," Lorraine said, eyeing the gooey, delicious-looking chocolate cake that Marybelle had just set on the table. Six heads nodded, as they took turns slicing the cake.

"We all think so much better when we eat. It must help our brains," Marybelle said, the last to pick up her fork.

"Oh, you're silly. Admit it, Marybelle, you just love to eat," chuckled Lorraine.

"Okay, I admit it. You can see by looking at me that I don't miss too many meals. Now everybody pass these plates around and y'all sample this new recipe."

The rooster clock on the kitchen wall showed an hour had passed when the conversation finally slowed. Allie turned to Wikki, speaking quietly. "All this stuff with the church rebuilding just happened yesterday. I haven't had a chance to tell you about it."

"Yeah," Wikki looked askance at her. "What's going on? Your punishment for skipping school?"

"Yes. No…I don't know. Jeez, Wikki, it's a long story. I'll tell you later. I don't know what I'm supposed to do at that church."

"Another fine mess." Wikki ducked her head and smiled. "Count me in."

"Thanks, I will." Allie slowly rose from her chair. "I'd like to walk over to the old church… if y'all don't mind. To look at what's there."

"I can't believe you're gonna take on that job, Allie. Do you know how much work that'll be?" Maggie asked.

"No…yes…" Allie sighed. "I guess I'll find out."

"You run along, young'un," Fanny remarked. "We're gonna sit here a while longer."

Wikki was finishing her cake. "I wanna come, Allie. But lemme visit with Lorraine first."

"Sure, take your time."

Allie left as she had come, through the big double front doors. *Golly, this house is big.* Three stories tall, it was the largest house within thirty miles, and Allie knew it didn't take care of itself. That's why Marybelle loved having Sheriff Anderson as a boarder. *I bet he does repairs, paints and also protects the place. He probably gets his room free for all the work he's done for Marybelle.* He said he spends so much time at the sheriff's office there wasn't a need to buy property. Besides, he'd been divorced for years and his only son lived in Connecticut.

Allie glanced up at the enormous, white pillars that lined the stately front porch. Several empty rocking chairs waited for a tired passerby and potted geraniums welcomed guests who climbed the porch steps. *Gone With the Wind*, Allie thought. *Tall and stately.*

She walked along the sidewalk, finding an opening between two shops where she could climb the small knoll leading up to the church. She stopped about a hundred yards away, looking at the church that even Daniel had called old and dilapidated.

"How do I rebuild a church?" she asked herself.

"It's not going to be easy. You'll have to find volunteers and get the materials."

"Daniel," she sighed.

"Hi, Allie."

There was no Daniel in person today, only the pleasing tone of his voice in her mind. She paused to listen, thinking she could hear him better if she stood still.

"I don't know what to do."

"You have the plans. That's step number one. Next you need to talk to Buzz on Monday. Tell him you need his help. He's going to be the contractor. Tell him you need his friends to help."

She mumbled out loud. "Oh, sure. Like they'll all rush to help me when I snap my fingers. C'mon, not Buzz Madison. He's one of the most popular guys in school. The girls fall all over him. He'll laugh at me. He's said 'hi' to me exactly one time this year. He barely knows who I am."

"He knows you. He's in your English class. He'll help you. Have you forgotten who I am?"

She smiled. "Well, yeah, kinda." She giggled. "You're an angel. Somehow you know he's going to say 'yes.'"

"He'll say 'yes'. Now here's the plan. I'll provide some basic building materials. Tell Buzz there will be a lumber delivery at the church."

"You're going to deliver lumber?"

"Some of it. Not all of it, of course."

"So…what exactly do I do if Buzz is doing all the construction work?"

"You've got a big job. You make sure Buzz comes to work and that he brings his friends. You've got to get more people to volunteer. You have to encourage people to donate money so you can buy supplies and more materials."

"I don't know anything about—getting donations. That's hard."

"It may be hard and, yes, it's a lot of work. So… are you ready to quit?"

Yes, Allie thought. "No," she replied. Then, exasperated, "I don't know. What I mean is… I don't know how to get people to donate money. I don't know any rich people, Daniel."

"I'll explain it this way—you'll need volunteers to work on the church. But it's your responsibility to get the building materials and supplies. Buzz can help you determine what you need. Your mother can guide you to those who can donate the money. Fanny is working on the garden, but you know she'll help any way she can. You can do this, Allie, I know you can."

Allie shook her head with the enormity of it all.

"And one more thing…"

"Only one more thing?"

"Don't get mad. Am I not the handsome guy with beautiful blue eyes anymore?"

"Oh, stop it!" She grinned. "You're giving me all this really hard work to do. It's like I don't have any control over my life. Between you and the sheriff—"

"What are you saying? You have complete control over your life. You have control over how this project works, who's involved—"

"But you're telling me to do all this stuff and I don't know how to do any of it."

"It's called delegation. You're going to be the master of it when you're finished. And you may not know what to do right now, but you'll learn. We all have to learn and you're a fast learner. That's just one of the many reasons I chose you."

Allie rolled her eyes.

"And another thing..."

"Hurry up. My brain is about to explode."

"Visit Fanny's house and go inside."

"And do what, exactly? Clean it?"

"That would be nice."

"Is that all?" Allie was almost afraid of his answer.

"No. Look around. Take a long look around her house. Then make your own decisions."

"Daniel. Tell me now. What's wrong with her house? Are there rats or big bugs? Will I be creeped out?"

"No, no, nothing like that. Just take a look around. She needs some help."

Allie was getting more and more used to helping people. "What am I supposed to do? Can you give me a hint?"

"Not this time. Trust your good judgment. I'll leave it entirely up to you."

Allie shook her head. *Jeez, another decision.*

"Hold on. There is one decision you won't have to make, dear Allie."

She smiled at the old softness in his voice. "Really?"

"Ah, we're friends again. Excellent. You will not have to decide about installing a window in the back of the church."

"Window?"

"Yes. The building plans call for a window to be installed on the back wall of the church. Am I going too fast for you?"

"Er, yes, Daniel. So, we're back on the church. I have to know about windows?"

"Yes, haven't you read the plans?"

"NO! I don't know how to read plans!"

"*Alright, take it easy. Ask Buzz to show you where the windows go. Believe me, he will be delighted to explain everything to you. In fact, I know for certain that he can't wait to explain everything to you.*"

Allie heard the chuckle in his voice. "It's easy for you to make fun of me, Daniel, but it's not helping me understand anything. You might know how all this will turn out, but I sure don't."

"*No, you wouldn't. And I'm not making fun of you. You're doing splendidly! I have complete faith in you to handle all the details. Just tell Buzz that the big window in the back of the church is on its way. Tell him it's on its way from the factory.*"

Daniel let out a hearty laugh that Allie had never heard before. "*The factory. That's a good one. Yes, tell him it's coming from the factory.*"

"Okay, Daniel. I'll tell him it's coming from the factory. When will it be delivered?"

"*In a couple of weeks. I don't know if I can get it ready before then.*"

"Hang on. Are you making this window? Do angels make windows?"

"*Shh, Allie. It's fantastic. It's my special contribution to the church. Just wait. It'll be our secret. You'll love it, I promise.*"

Allie sensed his excitement. Her angel was having the time of his life.

"*But remember—and this is important—make sure that Buzz cuts the window opening to the exact dimensions on the building plans. It must be exact, or this window won't fit.*"

"Gottcha. Measure for the window. Exact measurement. No mistakes."

"*You got it.*"

Allie grew quiet. "Daniel?"

"*Yes?*"

"There's something I've wanted to ask you about last Wednesday, when we met. How come I was able to see inside the church that morning? To see the beautiful pews and the stained glass window. A few hours later when mama and I stopped by, the windows were busted out, the porch was rotten—"

"*I wanted to you to see how beautiful it once had been. I gave you a special peek inside the original church—call it a window into the past.*"

Allie smiled. "The pews were dark wood with fancy carvings. They would be so expensive now."

Allie's Angel

"Mmm, good point. Those pews were carved by hand. A big task for sure. Only…don't think about them right now. Just focus on building the church and… don't give up. I'm supporting you on this project, Allie."

"Can I really do it?"

"Of course you can! Why do you keep questioning me?"

"Because…you just suddenly appear in my life one day and everything changes. Why choose me?"

"Allie, it was because of your belief in the goodness of your fellow man and your total faith and trust in the Lord."

"Really? You know this?"

"Of course I do. I've watched over you since your birth. I've seen your energy when you work. I know your fears and your strengths. I've heard your whispered prayers at night and throughout the day. And even though your family hasn't always attended church services regularly since your dad died, you haven't been any less faithful, or prayerful, in your daily life. Your disgruntlement only shows your frustration and your rebelliousness. That doesn't hide the perpetual happiness you keep locked inside your heart. And when you get tossed a curveball, you struggle and fight for answers. Can't you see? You have so many of the fine qualities I need to make these important projects happen."

Allie blinked. *Wow.* "But I can't make anything happen. I can't drive. I'm only fifteen years old—"

"Oh, so you can't make things happen now? You just need a little confidence. Look at all the changes in your life in just the past three days. It all started when you supposedly cheated on your English exam and then you met me, then met horrible Ethan, and then met your new best friend, Fanny."

"Horrible Ethan. I'd forgotten about him."

"Well, I haven't. I'm keeping up with Horrible Ethan. He's one worry you don't need right now."

"And Fanny. She's so cool."

"Isn't she? She's been lonesome for years. Yet you ran to her aid when she called."

"I've thought about that and something's bothered me. How do you think I heard her yelling all the way from her house? It has to be a mile."

"Sound travels. You know that."

Allie smiled. "Does sound travel as fast as an angel flies?"

"Uh-oh. I'm not going to admit to anything. You heard her scream fair and square. I had nothing to do with that. You ran to help her and the rest is history. You two have become so close. She loves you like the daughter she never had. Look at how much fun she's having. She's working on reuniting with her sister, she's getting a new dress for the social, and she's the only one within miles who drives a golf cart. It's fantastic! Funny how that worked out. But, if you love her, then check out her house."

"Okay, I'll check out her house."

"*There you go, pardner. Ha! Like my new Texas accent? I dig the lingo here.*"

"Daniel, like, 'dig' went out ages ago."

"*Oops, then teach me new 'stuff.' Until then, little missy, stay steady in the saddle. See ya' and stay busy.*"

And Daniel was gone.

"Hey, Allie!" Wikki tried to roll her chair up the grassy hill. "Are you okay? You look like a statue staring at the ground. Why are you smiling?"

Allie didn't dare say that it was because she'd been called 'little missy' by her angel.

Chapter 17

❧

"It's so bumpy," Allie said, helping Wikki maneuver her wheelchair the rest of the way up the hill. "How did you even make it up this far?"

"I wanted to come with you, remember? But I also wanted to visit with Lorraine. She's so cool for a grownup."

Allie nodded. She didn't have much family anymore. She never really knew her grandparents and, with her father dead, she only had Mama and Ben. She looked down at Wikki. Should she tell her now about Daniel being an angel? Maybe not today.

Allie dropped down to the grass, facing her friend. "I didn't know you'd been trying to walk. It's so cool! You nearly stood by yourself at the table. I feel so like a dork, saying I would help you walk. I'm *so* stupid."

Wikki grabbed Allie's hand. "You are *not* stupid," she smiled, "you're my best friend in the whole world."

"Are you really getting better?"

Wikki shrugged and laced her fingers together. "Yes. No. I don't know." She shifted her gaze to the grassy field. "Mother's talked to a doctor in Houston who specializes in paralysis cases. There are some new techniques now. Allie, are you sure you're interested in all this—"

"I am. I promise. Tell me."

"They say now that I have partial paralysis. For as long as I can remember, I've been in a wheelchair. It hasn't been a lot of fun for me to grow up like this."

Allie covered her friend's hand with hers. "I can't imagine it, Wikki."

"I was so little when the accident happened, and doctors didn't know much about spinal cord injuries. There was no stem cell research, no nerve connection research. You can see Mother still drags her right foot. She can't walk much some days and her right hip hurts a lot. I know she can't stand in one place for very long."

Allie blinked at the clear honesty in Wikki's dark eyes. "I think you're amazing," she said, "and if I can do anything to help you, just tell me."

"You can find me a miracle," Wikki said, laughing, "that's what Mother says we need right now."

"Okay, one miracle coming up!"

"No, really, I'm not kidding." Wikki's shoulders drooped. "I know I was talking big and brave in front of everybody in the kitchen, but mom and dad say they're scared for me. They say it would take a miracle to get the kind of operation I need. They don't think I should have any operation right now. The doctors in Tyler say it's too experimental, but the specialists in Houston say I'm ready. I say, let's do it. Sure, I'm scared. But I'd risk anything to be able to walk. If there's any chance—"

Allie whispered, "Wikki."

"I mean it. But the cost...it's so expensive. You wouldn't believe the money. We don't have it. Nobody has it." Then came her unexpected smile. "That's why I need a miracle. See?"

"Yeah, I see."

"I keep hoping. It's all I have right now. Mother called the Houston surgeon, but he hasn't called her back. She was going to ask him more about the cost. We have a pretty good idea...but, even with a loan, we can't make a down payment." Wikki looked away. "So it doesn't matter if he calls or not. It won't happen. I won't walk and that's that."

Allie put her hands on the grass and stood with one fluid motion. "Don't be so sure. You've asked me to find you a miracle and that's exactly what I'm going to do."

"Really?" Wikki asked, glancing up at her.

"Really. I'm kinda into needing some miracles myself."

Allie's brain worked to process all this new information about Wikki's paralysis. Her best friend had never confided this much in her before. Allie moved the wheelchair forward, looking at Wikki's shiny blonde hair. *If anybody deserves a chance to walk, she does. She is so kind, so nice to everybody. I said I would find a way and I'm going to. I don't know how, but I've got to find a way.*

"C'mon, let's see if we can get back down this hill." Allie pushed Wikki to a rickety old iron gate that stood alone, without a fence. *This must have been the entrance to the garden years ago.*

Allie's eyes scanned the plot. "Jeez. It's a lot of land. Fanny's got her work cut out for her." *Just like me,* Allie mused. She could still make out faint glimpses of rows that would have been carefully maintained once upon a time.

Wikki half turned in her chair. "I wanna help with the garden and rebuilding the church. Can we start on Monday? Should we tell our teachers what we're doing? If these are community projects, then kids should be involved, right? Maybe they won't give us so much homework."

"I'll do anything to stop homework." *I'll be so busy with the church that I won't be able to help Fanny with her garden. Shoot! I love working with Fanny.* "Otis will *have* to help plow up this land," she whispered.

"That he will, young 'un." Fanny and Maggie, whose stiletto heels were sinking into the soil, trudged to the top of the hill.

"In fact, I just talked to Otis," Fanny went on. "Can you believe he tracked me down at Marybelle's place? Called me on her telephone, he did." Fanny shook her head. "That man. He surely is insistent. Says he'll be plowing this land for me on Monday morning, if not sooner."

"Then what?"

Fanny and Maggie exchanged glances. "Then we plant some vegetables," answered Fanny.

"Come to think of it, sister, we need to talk to Marybelle about that," Maggie said. "Let's go back and see if she's still got that pen and paper. We've got to make sure we get the right crops for the fall season. We won't get any really hard freezes for another few months. We should be able to get something growing before then."

"Please talk to my mother," said Wikki. "She's been gardening since before I was born."

"Good idea," Fanny said. "Girls, we're going back down the hill to Marybelle's and talk plants...and money!"

"Plants and money," Allie whispered. "Two things I know very little about."

"Omigosh, look who's coming up the hill! If it isn't Nate Sims," cried Maggie. "What's that he's carrying?"

"Probably your desserts," whispered Fanny. "He knows how much you love them. I wouldn't be surprised if you loved Nate Sims more'n you love his homemade desserts."

"Shhh, sister, keep your voice down. He'll hear you. I do not love Nate Sims. Besides, he likes Marybelle. Everybody knows that."

"Ha, you're not looking in the mirror when you say his name. You should see the high color in your cheeks. I know that ain't *all* rouge." Fanny turned back to Allie and Wikki. "Are y'all listening to this? My sister has head-over-heels gone crazy for the town baker and pharmacist. Who'da thought it?"

"Howdy, ladies!" Nate called out. "I brought each of you a little something to take home. I heard y'all are bringing back our community garden. I sure am glad to hear the news. You know I'd love to get the freshest vegetables for my sandwiches. I'll add them to my lasagna and pasta sauces, too. How do I join?"

"It's easy, Nate." Fanny spoke up. "Just provide a service or lend a hand. I think that's right. Would you like to help?"

"Sure would. Don't know if I've got the time, but I tell you what. I'll make free sandwiches for all the helpers. How does that sound?"

Maggie jumped on that. "Oh my gosh, Nate! Those delicious sandwiches of yours? With iced tea? Your tea is marvelous."

Nate smiled. "Just for you, Maggie. Oh, alright, and I'll throw in some chips. How does that sound? Now who do I give my vegetable order to?"

"To me," Maggie said, passing around the sweet treats that Nate had brought. They smelled wonderful. "Y'all, let's walk down the hill. C'mon, Fanny. We'll talk as we walk. Let's go and tell everybody the good news. Nate Sims wants to be a part of our community garden!"

Nate and Maggie turned to walk toward his bakery, but Fanny stayed behind.

With a wicked grin, she leaned over to Allie and whispered, "Don't tell me he likes Marybelle Hightower. Look at him smiling at Maggie. He's like some lovesick hound dog. And she's just as bad. Those two are crazy about each other. Think we should tell 'em we know?"

Wikki giggled. Allie did, too. "No!" she mouthed. "C'mon."

ALLIE AWOKE ON a bright, sunny Sunday to the aroma of bacon and eggs frying. *This fold-out sofa sure is hard and lumpy.* She had given up her bed to Fanny what seemed like years ago and now had to rub her back for the umpteenth time.

"Mmm, something smells great," she called out.

Even though Allie couldn't exactly see the stove, she knew Fanny was there. Nobody else would be cooking at this early hour—or cooking at all, for that matter.

"We must've gotten a cold front last night. I'm freezing." Allie wrapped herself up in the old comforter and staggered into the kitchen.

Fanny had her wooden spoon out and stirring something yummy. Allie moved closer to see. "Did you sleep good?" she asked. "I was out like a light. But I sure had fun at Marybelle's."

Fanny stopped stirring and put one hand on her small waist. "I agree. I ain't had so much fun since Maggie and me were young 'uns like you, and used to swim in the rice pond down Cragg's Cutoff."

She opened the oven. "I hope you don't mind cherry pie. Maggie and me went by my house yesterday afternoon before she dropped me off here. I grabbed these cherries, 'cuz they don't stay fresh forever."

Allie drank in the delicious aroma of all the food and especially the perfectly browned crust on the freshly made pie. Fanny had to nudge her to one side so she could get to the sink.

"Come to think of it, you and I need to be cooking together in this kitchen. You're certainly old enough. Maybe we can cook up some food today that'll last you all week." Fanny pulled the oven mitt off her hand. "I'll be needing to go on back to my own house this afternoon."

"But—"

"I've had the absolute best time ever staying with you and your mama—and Ben, when I get to see him. But I've outstayed my welcome. I'll be just fine with my golf cart and all. You remember I have a horse? Well, old Miss Lizzie misses me. I checked on her yesterday and her water tub was nearly empty. I refilled it and filled her feed trough and gave her some hay. I hugged her neck while I was there. It felt so good to see her."

"But Fanny—"

"No 'buts' about it, young 'un. If you'd like to ride back with me on my golf cart, though, I'd appreciate the company. I've been keeping the battery charged. Otis even installed an electrical outlet on the outside of my house, just so's I can keep it charged there, too."

This news nearly broke Allie's heart. "You'll come and visit, won't you?"

"Wild horses couldn't keep me away. Are you kidding? I love y'all. It's like my second home here. And the sheriff, too. He's just like a son I never had, giving me the golf cart. He's a sweet one, he is. Your mama needs to hang on to him." Fanny ladled some grits onto a plate. "Don't go all quiet on me, Allie. You know they like each other. But for some reason, your mama's holding back. I think the sheriff would like to court her right and proper, but she's—"

"Good morning, everybody." Laura McCall entered the kitchen, stretching her arms and yawning at the same time. "Ooh, I'm so sorry about that. But I slept so good last night. Allie, are you cold?"

"Aren't you? Burr, I'm freezing."

Mama laughed and pulled up her long-sleeved shirt to reveal another one. "And there's one on under that one, too. I have on three shirts and two pairs of pants, so I'm just toasty warm. This smells fabulous, Fanny."

"Fanny says she's going home today."

"Oh, no! Fanny, say it's not true. Besides, it's not time. Sheriff Anderson said he'd let us know when it was safe."

Fanny spooned out scrambled eggs onto three plates. "I don't have time to wait around any longer, Laura. It's time for me to move back home. Is Ben here? I can get out a plate for him, but I didn't see him last night."

"No, he stayed another night with Jacob. He's over there so much I might have to pay them rent. He loves their horses and says he wants to be a veterinarian when he grows up. I think he and Jacob sleep in their horse barn."

Allie grew quiet as the two women talked about breakfast in general and the new garden in particular. She knew she had to get over to Fanny's house and take a look inside. She would have a chance today—Daniel had been right. It was yet another Sunday when they wouldn't be going to church. They hadn't been to many services these past five years. After Dad died, Mama was so sad all the time that she'd cry during the service. Allie and Ben were too embarrassed to go to church alone, so nobody went. *How sad*, Allie thought. And yet she had been given the project of rebuilding an old church. *How odd.*

"Fanny, would you ever let Ben ride Miss Lizzie?" Allie asked. "He loves horses so much. I know he'd like to ride and feed your mare."

Fanny slapped down the wooden spoon. "Why, young 'un, that's a fantastic idea! Why didn't I think of that? I would love it if Ben would feed the chickens and Miss Lizzie. She's old now, and still so gentle... he'd fit my small saddle with no problem. She'd sure love to get her fur rubbed with a currycomb now and again... what do you say, Laura?"

Mama flashed her a genuine smile, one Allie hadn't seen in years. "I think it's a great idea, if Fanny likes it."

"I do and it's done. Y'all can talk to Ben whenever he gets home today. See what he says."

"Oh, and Mama," Allie interrupted, "I need to ask a favor."

Mama sat at the breakfast table, took a sip of coffee and put down her cup. "Go ahead. Ask away."

"Would you please call Mr. Danner at the high school and ask him to give everybody working on the garden community service hours? Could he also give hours to kids working on the church, too?"

Trying to focus without her contacts, Laura McCall looked up at her daughter standing next to the stove. Allie seemed to have matured since the cheating debacle. Her long brown hair fell in softer waves around her shoulders. Her smooth, porcelain skin highlighted bright, eager green eyes—questioning eyes, judgmental eyes. Oh, yes, Allie was a teenager and had definitely grown up from the little girl who'd curl up on her lap for a bedtime story. Laura knew she hadn't been the most understanding mom in the world. She knew she'd disappointed Allie by not giving her new clothes to wear, or the latest shoes, or even enough food to eat.

But now was not the time to think about what she'd done wrong. Allie had just asked her for a favor. She had chance to do redeem herself, to do something right—to work on rebuilding their relationship.

"Community service hours? I can do that, Allie," she said, taking another sip of coffee. "What are your plans for rebuilding the church? What's happening with that project?"

"Nothing... at least not yet. Now, don't laugh when I tell you this, but Daniel talked to me yesterday at the church right before Fanny and Maggie came up the hill. He said some materials for the job would be delivered. He told me to talk to Buzz on Monday about being in charge of the construction."

"So, you're telling us that your angel is going to deliver some building materials to the church."

"Laugh at me, if you want, Mama. I don't care. I'm only telling you what he said. I believe in Daniel. I have to do what he says."

Fanny passed around the breakfast plates. "What about you, Laura? Do you believe in angels? I sure do. There's no way I could have lived alone for as long as I've lived on my itty-bitty place, if I didn't have some guidance from the Almighty. There are angels on this earth just as sure as I have about twelve chickens, a couple of barn cats, a horse named Miss Lizzie and a part-time dog named Zeus."

"Well, Mama?" Allie whispered, "Do you believe in angels?"

Mama laid her fork down and stared at the scrambled eggs. "I suppose. It's a little hard for me to admit. I guess I'm not comfortable confessing that I do believe in angels." Mama glanced from Fanny to Allie. "Since your father died, it's been so hard for me to juggle… everything. I don't know if Gerald is an angel, but I know he's helped us over the years. He's been there for us. I know he's helped me… helped us. But I don't see angels like you do, Allie. No angel has ever asked me to do anything."

"Daniel said I was chosen. He said he chose me."

Mama smiled then and gently squeezed her hand. "I think Daniel chose well."

"He said I have courage."

"You do. Don't you think so, Fanny?" Mama asked. "I think you have a lot of courage. In fact, I think you have more courage than I do."

All those years, Allie thought, *for all those years I thought that mama never cared about me.* Now Allie could see the love in her mama's eyes.

Fanny passed a napkin to Mama before dabbing at her own eyes.

"Lordy, there sure is a lot of smoke in the kitchen this morning. Why else would everybody's eyes keep waterin' like this?"

"Aw, Ms. Fanny, are you crying?"

"For heaven's sake, this is so silly. But I guess it's because I see two people sittin' here talking about how much they care about each other. You and your mama love each other, but sometimes life gets in the way of that love. It's hard to always know what to do, how to say the right things. Sometimes crying is just a good way of cleansing the soul. It makes us feel better. I love you two like you were my own family and now I'm happy that we're sharin' all this—"

"All this?" Allie wondered.

"This family stuff," Fanny finished, then laughed.

Allie and Mama joined in. The tears were gone and the eggs were cold, but there was no warmer home to be found in Friendly that bright Sunday morning. Three women from three generations, reached out and held hands as they bowed their heads in prayer at the breakfast table. Nobody cared if the tablecloth had tattered edges, or if the plates were mismatched, or if the stove had a broken burner. This was family. And on this Sunday morning, family was all-important.

Chapter 18

❀

SUNDAY, SEPTEMBER 19

WHEN THE BREAKFAST dishes were done, Fanny took off her apron and announced, "I'm ready for the trip back home. Anybody wanna come?" She smiled at Allie. "I sure could use some help cleaning out my tippy-top cupboards."

"Sounds good to me." Allie smiled, and then said to Mama, "Who were you talking to on the phone just now?"

"Sheriff Anderson," she said, tidying up the sofa where Allie had slept the night before. "He...he asked me to go on a picnic today." Allie thought Mama paid too much attention to folding the sheets. "He said he'll make all the food."

Fanny and Allie exchanged glances before rushing into the living room.

"Did you say 'yes'?" Allie ventured.

"I said yes."

"What was that?" Fanny asked, in a teasing voice. "I didn't quite hear that—did you, Allie?"

"No, ma'am. Didn't hear Mama's answer at all."

"Okay!" Mama dropped the folded sheet with a giggle. "I told him I would go. I can't be sure, but I think he dropped the phone."

"I knew it. I just knew it," Fanny said, snapping her fingers and twirling around. "Sheriff Anderson's come a'courtin'. *Woo-hoo!* This is the best news yet this morning—besides our talk about angels. Don't you

125

worry about trailin' off after me to my house. You and the sheriff have a wonderful day. Right, Allie?"

"Absolutely!" Without thinking, Allie rushed over to give her mama a kiss on her cheek. "Have a great time."

Mama whirled around and grabbed Allie up in a bear hug like she hadn't felt in years.

"I will. And you two have a beautiful day." Mama quickly hugged Fanny and gave her a kiss on the cheek. "Thank you *so* much. You've given our family so much happiness. I don't know how to ever repay you."

Fanny, who was never at a loss for words, blushed and looked away, "Oh, my goodness. Y'all are gonna make me cry again. I ain't done this much cryin' since my Cecil died." She stomped her foot. "Y'all quit this right now."

"Okay, okay," Allie said, rushing over to gently squeeze her arm. "We just love you, that's all."

"Well, let's finish our chores and get goin'. We need to spread some of this love to my chickens and Miss Lizzie. And, come to think of it, where is that lazy dog, Zeus? He ain't barked one time this morning."

FANNY AND ALLIE arrived at the house at Cragg's Cutoff shortly before noon. Fanny had packed up her old dresses and aprons in her sack, along with her toiletry items and bedroom slippers. Allie was amazed that Ms. Fanny could fit so many of her favorite things into such a small bag. Zeus barked cheerfully, running alongside the golf cart as they rolled along the grassy edge of the gravel road.

"It seems like we've known each other for years," Allie thought aloud, stopping at Fanny's mailbox. "But we met only four days ago." Allie shielded her eyes from the bright sun as she climbed back behind the steering wheel.

"It's sure been fun, dear." Fanny glanced through the mail as they turned left and lurched along the Cutoff Road. "I've enjoyed every minute of it—meeting you, and your mama and the sheriff, seeing my sister who I missed so much. And, of course, seeing Otis again after all these years. Allie, sweetie, please don't make the same mistakes I did and let time eat away at your happiness."

Allie watched as Fanny grew quiet. Zeus was happy enough, the birds were singing, the sun shining. Allie wanted to erase Fanny's melancholy.

"But you've been happy this week, haven't you? Things are better?"

"Oh, sure—they are. But look how much time I wasted being mad at this stupid thing or that stupid thing—at my only sister, for heaven's sake. I've got to get over my anger at Maggie. Old wounds cause harmful anger. And wasted years. When you stop and think about it, really think about what happiness is, it's being surrounded by family and friends who love you. It's helping them any way you can. Do you know what I am sayin'?"

Allie pulled the cart to a stop in Fanny's yard. "You're saying that true happiness comes from helping other people. That's the secret? Kids at school say that happiness is getting a car, or buying the right clothes or going out with the coolest guys."

"But it's not. Think about it, child. Think about your life before all this happened with me and your exam. Were you happy?"

Allie shook her head. "Not really. Mama never talked to me. She never had time for me. I was lonesome. I was really lonesome. I talked to Wikki on the phone, but I didn't have friends, there was nowhere for me to go… I must've been angry most of the time."

Fanny slid her arm around Allie's shoulder and pulled her close. "You're a beautiful young lady with a boatload of spirit. You remind me of myself, but I weren't near as pretty nor as smart as you are. About the only thing I was talented at was coming up with dinner most days. I could pick off a rabbit a hundred yards away with one shot. My mama taught us girls how to cook, but Maggie liked foolin' with flowers 'n' roses more'n food, so I was always the one stuck in the kitchen. I remember we each owned one pair of shoes that we wore to church every Sunday. Most kids even went barefoot to school. And you know what? I was always happy, Allie, even though we were dirt poor. I never knew what I didn't have."

Allie thought about the truly happy time she'd had the day before, having lunch with Marybelle and the other ladies. Maybe she had changed a little over the past few days. She'd been happier being around Fanny, for sure. Fanny was like a sister she'd never had, yet before, she had judged Fanny to be that "crazy plant lady who lived down the road" just because she'd been different. Fanny had wanted to be left alone. That was her only crime. Allie knew she and all the other townspeople had judged her too harshly. Shame on her. Shame on them. Allie wrapped her arms around Fanny's neck.

"I love you, Fanny Parker," she whispered. "You're the best friend, ever."

Allie pulled away to see the tears sparkle in Fanny's eyes.

"That'll be enough of that, young 'un. You ain't gonna get my faucet turned on again today. I hear a couple of dirty ol' cupboards calling me from inside that house. Let's go tackle some chores. How 'bout it?"

"Sounds fine to me." Allie jumped from the golf cart, hugged Zeus and took off for the back door. "Do you want me to feed Miss Lizzie?"

"Not just yet. I'll check on her once I get you started on the kitchen. I need to gather up the eggs, too," she said, unlocking the door.

Happily, Allie bounced inside the old kitchen. The white paint was chipped here and there and the linoleum on the floor was old, but there was no mistaking Fanny's touch. Pink sprigged curtains covered the window. *Wasn't that the same material as her pink dress?*

Three cabinets hung on either side of the window, and canning jars were set out on the white tile countertops. A big wooden work table stood at the ready in the center of the room, probably doubling as a dining table. Allie could imagine Fanny eating her scrambled eggs here, or rolling out her bread dough, or even carving a roasted turkey for Thanksgiving dinner.

Fanny had pulled a wooden step stool from around a corner and set it up near the kitchen cabinets. "If you would, dear, please pull down the rest of my canning supplies. There is a cook pot, and lots more jars up there I'll need. I'll go check on the animals."

Allie climbed up one step and easily reached the top shelf of the cabinet. Fanny hustled out the back door. Moments later Allie finished her task, stepped down and decided to look around.

She peeked into Fanny's bedroom. *What?* Allie did a double take. Fanny slept on a hay bale, with only a sheet to cover the hay. Her makeshift pillow consisted of hay stuffed into a feed sack and covered with a scrap of faded white material. The tiny corner closet held a brown dress and an equally faded grey dress with an extra pair of shoes beneath them. A scarred nightstand with a floral washbasin told the story of Fanny's indoor plumbing.

The floor plan was simple. The front door opened to a living room, a small hallway led to a total of two tiny bedrooms, then ended in the kitchen, clearly the largest room in the house. As she came back into the kitchen, Allie looked around more carefully, noticing that the large white sink had no faucet.

The door burst open and a rosy-cheeked Fanny rushed inside. "Got my jars down yet?"

"Here they are—all twenty of them. Fanny, where is your water faucet?"

"Aw, shoot, I've got a well out back. It's as good as any faucet inside."

"And your bathtub and toilet? Where are they?"

"Well, my bathtub is right outside on the back porch and my toilet... well, the outhouse is on the far side of the house; you can't really see it from here. It's hidden in that grove of trees yonder," she said.

"An outhouse? You can't be serious."

"I am serious," she said, grinning. "Now you know why I loved your bathtub so much, Allie. The water came from inside the wall and straight into the tub, already hot. I didn't even have to boil it."

Suddenly Allie wasn't happy. Her friend's house might as well be an 1800s log cabin.

"Where are your lights? Your light switches? I thought Otis ran electricity to your house."

"Well, he did. He put in a receptacle outside so I can plug in the golf cart."

"You need some light switches, light fixtures and some running water, Ms. Fanny. This is crazy!"

"Crazy? Don't I have anything to say about it?"

Oops. "I'm sorry, but...but I'm upset. Don't you want electricity and water in your house?"

Fanny looked around and shrugged. "I suppose I do."

"Good. Then let's get that done. If I can rebuild a church when I know nothing about construction, then I certainly can install light switches and running water when I know nothing about electricity and plumbing." *Daniel!*

Fanny nodded. "That sounds about right. When are we gonna do all this?"

Allie's prayer was answered when a familiar white truck came bouncing up the road and into the yard.

"I say we get started right now," Allie said, thanking Daniel just in case he had anything to do with this stroke of luck.

Fanny raced outside with Allie trailing behind her. "Otis! It's Sunday. What in the world—?"

"Hey, Fanny! You weren't at the McCall house, so I came looking to see if you were here. 'Afternoon, Allie," Otis said, tipping his ball cap. "I've been thinking that today would be a good time for me to plow some of that garden. I got a last minute call to do a job on Monday. So I figured

I'd better do this plowin' before something else pops up. Right now, I'm good to go and my tractor's ready, but I need some help from somebody on where y'all need me to plow."

"I'd like to come, Otis," Allie said. "Coming, Fanny?"

"Sure. Give me a minute and I'll get my bonnet."

Allie watched as Fanny went back inside the house before turning to Otis. "I know you ran the wire, but there are no lights installed in her house. Did you know she also doesn't have running water or a toilet or bathtub? Is there anything you can do?"

Otis rubbed his chin. "I know. I haven't gotten the light fixtures yet. Got all the wires run…Lemme see what fixtures I can pick up. I'll make a phone call and get somebody out here to put 'em up maybe tomorrow afternoon. Do you think Fanny will be home? He'll need to get inside."

"I can come over after school. I'll make sure she's here."

"The guy I'm gonna call is a smart kid… my apprentice. Taught him everything he knows. He'll do a good job."

Allie impulsively hugged his arm. "Thank you, Otis. I don't know what we'd do without you."

The screen door banged shut as Fanny hurried outside, waving a brightly colored red and yellow bonnet. "Sorry it took me so long!"

"Now all you need is a Conestoga wagon," Allie said, smiling.

"A what?"

"You know. A covered wagon…like the pioneers in the old days."

"Oh, pshaw," Fanny said, fastening the strings under her chin. "It'll keep the sun from burning half my face."

Otis smiled wistfully at her as he took her hand and led her down the porch steps.

"Why thank you, Otis. How kind."

"My pleasure. You sure do look pretty in your bonnet. I like it."

Allie felt her mouth drop open. Fanny looked like an elderly prairie woman in that bonnet. But Otis—so doggone smitten—just grinned.

WHEN THEY REACHED the church and community garden, Allie jumped out of the backseat of the pickup. She spotted a red tractor in the distance. *It's really gonna happen. Fanny's garden and my church.* Pure adrenalin sent her charging toward the tractor and then scrambling up onto the seat. She'd never mowed anything in her whole life, never been on a tractor, never driven a car, never even ridden a horse—not in all the years she'd lived here.

"You wanna drive?" Otis asked, as he pushed back his ball cap and looked up at her.

"No way! Yes. No. I don't know. I've never driven anything in my life. I'm too scared."

"Sure, she wants to drive it, Otis. Look at her face," Fanny said, standing next to him. "She's scared and excited all at the same time. Allie, you stand behind Otis and watch what he does. He'll show you how to work it, so pay attention. It's loud, so get ready. Then you can drive it and Otis'll stand behind you."

Allie nodded, way too excited to speak. She easily slipped around the seat as he climbed up into it. She obediently stood on the platform behind him as he put the key into the ignition.

"What do you think, Fanny? Make it about an acre for right now? Should I keep the same pattern that we had in the old days?" he asked.

Fanny strained her neck to look up at him, shouting over the engine noise. "That sounds good. I don't wanna think about it too much. It brings tears to my eyes just thinking about all the old folks who used to work this garden. Wouldn't they love to see us now?"

"That they would," he said, putting the tractor into gear. The smoke stack puffed and off they went.

"Stay close, Allie," he said. "Hold onto my shoulders and stand still with your feet on the three-point hook up back there. Got it?"

She nodded. Fanny wasn't kidding. The engine noise was deafening. She could hardly hear Otis when he was yelling instructions at her. There were gears and a clutch and she would have to press on the clutch to shift gears. This would take some doing, but she was determined to handle it. They made one complete circle—well, not a circle, but more like an oval. Then he rolled up next to Fanny and killed the engine.

"Ready?" Otis asked, settling Allie securely in the driver's seat. "You remember what I said about pressing the clutch before shifting gears? It's gotta be one fluid motion or the tractor will buck and die."

"Got it," Allie answered with confidence. *Now or never.*

Otis took his place behind her as she turned the key. Off they went, lurching forward as she plowed nearly the same route as Otis had done the first time. Getting the rhythm of the clutch and shifting took some getting used to. She heard Otis chuckle, between hollering for her to speed up or slow down as she made each turn.

Allie pulled the tractor even with Fanny, only to see Buzz Madison standing there.

Omigosh! I don't have on any makeup. My hair's falling out of its ponytail. I've got on the oldest of my old clothes. We were supposed to talk tomorrow. I wasn't supposed to meet him today! This can't be happening...I look terrible. Buzz Madison can't see me like this! She wanted to dig a hole in the tractor seat and disappear. Buzz stood there, waiting, legs akimbo and arms crossed, grinning from ear to ear just like he'd heard a juicy joke.

"Hey, Otis! I saw your truck parked along the street," Buzz hollered before Otis killed the engine.

He turned to Allie. "I didn't know you drove tractors."

"I-I don't," Allie said, ducking her head and slipping down from the driver's seat.

"Yes, you do," Fanny interrupted. "I just seen you do it. Heckfire, young 'un, we all seen you do it. You're a regular pro at this now. You know Buzz Madison? He just introduced himself to me, Allie. He says he goes to school with you."

Still smiling, Buzz muttered near Allie's ear. "I do know who you are. I'm in your English class."

"Uh, yeah," she replied her head down. "He's in my English class. He's gonna be on the Varsity basketball team."

"Well, I expect so. Look how tall he is. How tall are you, son?"

"Six-three."

"Well, I'll be. Otis, did you hear that? This young'un's six-three. That is tall, ain't it? How tall are you, Allie?"

Eight feet. Allie raised her chin. "Five feet, eleven inches."

Fanny laughed and slapped her thigh. "Well, Buzz Madison, it looks like you've got yourself a dancing partner. All the boys in Friendly are too short for Allie and all the girls are too short for you. You'd break your back trying to dance with some of those little short things in your class, I'd expect."

Allie and Buzz exchanged glances; she tried not to let her mouth drop open. *He's even better-looking up close!* Without his silver-rimmed glasses, his blue eyes blinked at Allie from under long lashes, highlighted by a stray lock of black hair falling across his forehead.

He hadn't stopped smiling since he'd seen her. *Why?*

"Are you laughing at me?"

He kept his grin. "No."

She leaned closer. "Fanny's going to make a new community garden."

"Oh, yeah?" Buzz straightened and his smile faded. "Does she need some help?"

"From you?"

"Maybe. We all heard about the community garden project on Friday. Mr. Danner came into the locker room and talked all about it."

"Wait… you're telling me that Mr. Danner told you—told all the jocks—about the garden? Why would he do that?"

"You know how it is. Everybody knows everybody else's business almost before they do. Mr. Danner said his grandparents tilled this garden years ago. He thought it was a good idea to bring it back."

Allie thought for a minute, nearly biting a hole through her bottom lip as she wondered if now might be the right time to ask him. They were alone, except for Fannie and Otis—no other kids to overhear and laugh. Buzz was definitely out of her league. She wasn't part of the jock groupies that hung around him every day. She knew she looked as ugly as a mud fence, but she couldn't worry about that now. She had to get the church built—and that meant she needed somebody to hammer the nails.

Impulsively, she laid a hand on his arm. "Buzz, I've got a bigger favor to ask."

Allie glanced around and saw Otis and Fanny had climbed up on the tractor. It looked as though Fanny was driving it this time, with Otis behind her. Allie smiled. "That woman is amazing. She's not going to be left out of anything. I already know what's going to happen. She's going to till the rest of this garden with Otis standing behind her. She is so cool. I just love her to death."

She glanced up again at Buzz who was grinning his toothpaste commercial grin again. Then she glanced down at her blue jeans with holes in the knees. She laughed nervously. *I look so awful.*

"Would you stop grinning? I know you're laughing at me."

"I'm just waiting to hear what the favor is. Remember? The favor you wanted to ask me?"

"Oh. Oh! The favor. Uh, Buzz, would you …would you walk with me up to the church?" She pulled slightly on his arm. "The one…the one up there?"

He chuckled. "I know the one. What's at the church?"

"That's where I need your help."

"My help? At the church?"

"Well… I'm, uh, supposed to rebuild the church."

Buzz's eyes grew to the size of silver dollars. "Are you kidding? You've got to rebuild the church?" He started to chuckle.

"Yeah. I bet Mr. Danner didn't know that."

Buzz shook his head. "No, he didn't."

Shielding his blue eyes from the afternoon sun, he stared at the church again. "There haven't been church services there since before my dad was born. Nobody's stepped foot in there in years." His voice dropped. "Why do you have to rebuild it?"

She sighed. "It's what I have to do. It's...my assignment. I don't know what it's called, Buzz. I'm just supposed to rebuild the church. Will you help me?"

Buzz Madison stared at the girl who wore too much makeup at school. He kind of liked having her in his English class; she was smart and funny. He knew Mrs. Timmons couldn't stand her, didn't like her at all. He also knew the cheating thing was Alfred P.'s fault. Buzz felt badly when he found out she had to do community service for it.

But rebuilding the church? Well, that just wasn't fair. She shouldn't have to rebuild a church just because Mrs. Timmons accused her of cheating. That punishment was way out of line, but Allie looked like she could handle it.

Buzz studied her up and down, deciding she had spirit, for sure. No fingernail polish for Allie McCall, and today she didn't have on any makeup. Her hair blew all around her face. It was shimmery reddish-brown in the sunlight. Buzz liked it. He kinda liked her. Unlike Constance, she was real. Constance was even mean to her own friends. Oh, yeah, he was ready for a change.

"Okay. Tell me what you want me to do," he said.

Chapter 19

❦

Allie gulped in a mouthful of air. "Really? You'll help me with the church?"

Buzz smiled. "Yeah, only do me one favor—don't wear any more of that black stuff on your eyes. They're pretty. They, like, match your shirt. I like them plain, like now."

Allie screwed up her face at the request. *Buzz likes my eyes plain?* "No eye makeup? That's it?"

"Yeah, pretty much. Depending on what you need done, I'm going to have to tell my parents about it. When I'm not practicing basketball, I help my dad with extra work in the afternoons. If I'm not there, he's going to want to know why."

Allie grinned, feeling butterflies. "Good. Great! Absolutely!"

She grabbed his arm and linked hers through his. "C'mon. Walk up there with me and I'll tell you all about it."

They walked the hundred or so yards to the church grounds. She told him about having the plans and how they looked to be the original ones. Buzz then asked her about the building materials.

"Some stuff will be delivered—"

"Hang on. Are you paying for this?"

"No! No, it's nothing like that. The materials...I'm not paying for the...they're going to be...donated. All the materials will be donated. I'm going to find people who will donate money to help—"

"Oh, no, no, no, Allie. You're kidding, right? Do you really think that people 'round here are going to fork over enough money to rebuild this church? Do you know how many thousands of dollars it's gonna take?"

She gulped and shook her head. "No, not really," she said in a small voice.

He seemed preoccupied with looking beneath the cinder blocks of the church, running his hands along the wooden planks. Allie had never noticed before how big his hands were. Rough, too. Hands that were used for construction and playing basketball. Allie wondered what it would be like to hold his hand in hers, or slow dance with Buzz, his arm wrapped around her waist. She blinked. *What was she doing?*

Nervously, she shook away the idea, while Buzz, who had crawled partway underneath the church, reemerged. He jumped up, sneezing.

"Cobwebs," he said with another sneeze.

Allie reached up to brush dirt from his shirt as he slapped it off his ball cap and shook the dust from his hair.

"I wanted to see under the floor. To see how much of the wood was rotten."

"Is there a lot?" she ventured to ask.

"Oh, yeah, Allie—all of it. To do this right, we've got to rebuild the floor in addition to everything else."

Her spirits sagged. *More work.* The more she tried to do, the more new work was left to do.

"Hey," Buzz said, patting her shoulder. "Don't look like that. It's easier to rebuild the floor than to build around something old like this. We've got to add plumbing anyway."

Allie's head shot up. "Plumbing?"

He barked out a laugh. "Sure, what's an extra couple grand, right? Back in the old days they had outhouses, but now, it's kinda nice to have an inside toilet if you need to go during church."

She laughed with him. "I didn't think about a bathroom."

"We'll take a look at the plans and figure someplace for a bathroom—"

"Wait… are you showing the plans to somebody else?"

"Sure. When my dad hears you're rebuilding the church, he's gonna want to see the plans. He liked the garden idea. He's gonna go for the church idea, too. If we get more people to help, it'll go faster. He might donate his crew for a couple of days if he's between jobs. I can ask. You know we're not gonna have these sunny afternoons for long. It's September already. When it starts raining, it usually lasts for days. In the construction business, that sets everything back weeks—maybe months. We'll have to work fast to close in the church in. That means completing the roof and the exterior. Otherwise, we'll have to give up any hope of finishing in time for winter."

Allie took in this news. Buzz was right. Winters in East Texas were notoriously rainy and cold. The fact that it was still in the seventies and sunny right now was rare indeed. They'd have a little more than sixty days to get all this work done before the weather turned completely.

"When can you start?"

"Tomorrow's Monday. How about after school? You bring the plans and I'll see if Dad can meet us here."

Allie grinned, her fingers crossed that she'd find a ride to town. "Sounds great! Tomorrow, then."

He glanced at the church again. "The problem is the price tag. It's gonna be hard to find the money to pay for it all. But, who knows? Miracles happen every day, right? I already know one person you can talk to."

"Oh, yeah?" Allie's ears perked up.

"Curly Lively. He's got his own lumberyard outside town. Dad's done business with him for years. He's honest."

Allie smiled her thanks and they both turned to walk up the hillside to where Fanny and Otis were still plowing. *Tomorrow afternoon,* she thought. *I'll see him again tomorrow. Here, at the church, and away from other school kids, I can talk to him.*

"Allie!" shouted Buzz, grabbing her hand as she stumbled and nearly fell. "You okay?"

He pulled her up even with him and they walked hand-in-hand for a moment longer than they needed to. Allie didn't mind. *Why, oh why do these things happen to me?* Not only did she have more work than she could possibly finish, but she was falling for a guy who would never ask her to a dance or walk her to class.

MONDAY MORNING DAWNED bright and beautiful. Not a cloud in the sky. Allie jumped out of bed, grabbed a bowl of cereal and was hunting for her coat when the telephone rang.

"Hello?"

"Is this Allie?"

"Yes."

"This is… Buzz. Remember me?"

She smiled. *Duh. The answer would be yes.* "How are you?"

"Well, I can't make it to the church until about five-thirty today. Okay?"

At least he didn't cancel. "Sure."

"Okay. Bye." And he hung up. *Did he hang up fast? Maybe. Shoot, he hung up too fast.*

Mama brushed by her in the hallway. "Sorry, sweetie, I'm late. Do you remember what we talked about? That you're going to be at Fanny's this afternoon? Marybelle's driving Fanny to Tyler to get her party dress. Remember? Otis is sending somebody over to install her light fixtures. You're going to open the door?"

Allie realized her mind must have gone blank yesterday when she agreed to meet Buzz after school. Thank heavens he changed it. "Uh, yeah, I'm supposed to be at Fanny's this afternoon. Sure. Right after school."

Three-thirty. Two hours before I need to meet Buzz at the church. "Mama, I need to be at the church at five-thirty today. Can you take me?" she asked.

Laura McCall gathered up her purse and briefcase. "I think so. It's Monday and I don't have anything special going on." She brushed a kiss across Allie's cheek. "You sure look pretty today. Your cheeks are rosy. And your hair looks—well, have you done something different with your hair?"

Today, Allie wore a headband, the same one she had on when she saw Buzz yesterday. Her hair looked a little wild and unruly, but he'd seemed okay with it.

"It's a new style. I know it's ugly."

Her mother laughed. "It's not ugly. You're lucky to have naturally wavy hair. It's beautiful. I've always told you that—you just never believed me. Bye, dear." Mama was gone.

Remembering Buzz's phone call, Allie grabbed her purse and backpack, locked the door and almost skipped to the bus stop. She would have plenty of time to take care of Fanny's electrician before going to see Buzz.

For the first time in three months, Allie was not even close to being late to Mrs. Timmons's class. In fact, she and Wikki were the first ones in the classroom. Thankfully, Mrs. Timmons was nowhere to be seen.

"Okay, I'll ask you again," Wikki whispered across the two rows of desks, "why are we in here so early? Omigosh, we've got four whole minutes until the bell rings."

Allie swiveled around in her chair. "I don't want to get in trouble again. I know you don't get in trouble—but I get in trouble so fast in this class.

Besides, if I get another community service project assigned to me, I'm gonna lose my mind! No kidding!"

Allie carefully avoided thinking of other reasons to be in English early—like not missing one second of Buzz Madison. She'd barely slept a wink. She smoothed down an annoying lock of hair. She had on no eye makeup, like he'd said, and nearly no powder on her cheeks. Just a hint of pink lip gloss.

The tardy bell jerked her back to second period. Alfred P. deliberately bumped into her desk. "Hey, Allie. Cool hair. Didn't know it was that long."

Allie wanted to slap him. "Thanks," was all she offered.

A tall boy in a tan jacket and blue jeans filled the door. His black and silver glasses safely guarded the most beautiful pair of blue eyes she'd ever seen. *Well, except for Daniel.*

Allie averted her gaze, trying not to follow him as he crossed the room to his desk and laughed at something Creepy Constance said to him. Everybody knew that Buzz and Constance had been going out until Buzz suddenly dropped her a week ago. Nobody knew why. Constance acted like she cried one day in the bathroom, but Allie knew she was just putting on a show for her friends. The only person Constance liked was Constance.

Mrs. Timmons charged into the room, barking orders to open their English books, and start copying down what was written on the board. Allie complied, but when she looked up again, she caught Buzz's glance. One corner of his mouth turned up in a half-smile and he winked. Allie coughed a couple of times to hide her nervous laugh. *That wink was better than anything he could have said.*

Her spirits soared throughout the whole class. Mrs. Timmons answered in her usual rude way when Allie asked two questions. Today she just didn't care. Today she would get to talk to Buzz later on at the church. Today she was floating on top of the world.

Allie wanted to run all the way to Fanny's house after school, she had so much pent-up energy. Instead, she pedaled her bike so fast her tires barely touched the road. She pulled the key out of Fanny's special hiding spot and unlocked the door. Feeling the need to do something to take her mind off Buzz, she started cleaning the countertops, work table and cupboards. During this whirlwind of activity, she heard a loud knock on the back door.

"Anybody home?"

Allie nearly fell off the short ladder she was standing on. "Hang on. Just a minute," she cried, rushing to open the screen. A crimson blush flooded her face. "Buzz? It's you?"

He grinned back. "You again?"

"Buzz, no way! You're the electrician?"

"Yes, ma'am, part-time," he said, playfully.

"I was supposed to open the door—"

"So you're the cleaning lady?"

Allie realized she had one rag slung over her shoulder and another in her hand. "Part-time cleaning lady."

He set his toolbox on the kitchen floor and raised his own taller ladder. "I'm supposed to install the fixtures that Otis bought this morning." He removed the overhead light from its carton and glanced at her with a grin. "I can't talk long. I've got a date at the church."

His smile was infectious. "Oh, yeah? A date? With a….a girl?"

"Yep," she heard Buzz say from the ladder's top step. "A real pretty girl. I'm gonna help her rebuild a church."

Yes!

Chapter 20

❦

Buzz worked in quiet, moving from the kitchen to the tiny living room and then to Fanny's bedroom, installing overhead light fixtures. He finished off the job by making sure she also had a few wall sockets before closing up his toolbox.

"Just about finished," he said, passing through the screen door to the porch. "I can drive you down to the church. Might as well—long as you're here." Another disarming white smile. *How am I supposed to fight that smile?*

The sound of tires on the gravel interrupted her thoughts.

"Yoo-hoo!" called out Fanny's happy voice. "Lordy, mercy! Wait 'til you see the beautiful dress Lorraine picked out for me."

Buzz backed out of the way as Allie hurried past him into the yard. "Fanny! Ms. Marybelle!"

Marybelle Hightower turned her cheery red pickup around in the drive, waved and said howdy before she took off down the gravel road.

Allie grabbed the packages from Fanny. "You got your dress?"

Buzz looked amused, but puzzled, so she filled him in. "It's been the talk of the family. Fanny's going with Otis to the Smith County Lineman's Benefit Auction and Dance next Saturday, and she's been so worried about not having a pretty dress to wear. Ms. Marybelle's sister, Lorraine, owns a ladies dress shop in Tyler and that's where Fanny went today." She turned to Fanny. "Was it fun? Did y'all eat lunch out? Tell me *everything*."

Buzz sighed. "I can tell y'all have a lot to discuss, but, Allie, we don't have time for *everything*. We're supposed to go to the church, remember?"

141

Allie jerked the rags off of her shoulder. "Oh, shoot, I know it. I'm ready. Can we stop by my house so I can pick up the plans? I'll need to tell Mama. She was going to take me today."

"Oh, goodness, young'uns, I'm keeping you from your business. Y'all run along."

Allie took one look at Fanny's drooping smile. "You want to come. I know that sad, pitiful look."

Fanny clapped her hands and grinned. "I would love to come! Thanks so much for asking me!"

And with that, she climbed into the back seat of Buzz's green truck while Allie tossed the cleaning rags on top of the wash tub outside and locked the back door. They were winding their way along the gravel road in no time.

Allie bounded inside her house to see mama working at the kitchen table.

"I've come to get the plans for the church. Buzz is driving me. He's outside in the truck with Fanny."

She hurriedly gathered up the big rolled parchment sheets, carefully cradling them in her arms.

"Allie, who is Buzz? Does he have his license? I've never met him before. How do I know he's a safe driver?"

Four hundred questions. Allie rolled her eyes. "Mama, he's in a 1950-something, beat-up green pickup that probably can't hit forty on a good day—after an oil change. Fanny's in the backseat talking faster than the truck can travel. There's no way Buzz can take advantage of me on the two-mile trip to the church. He's in my English class. He's going to help rebuild the church. That's why I'm in a hurry. We're meeting his father in a few minutes."

"Oh. Oh! Yes, run along. I'll be down there in a few. Just one more phone call to make."

Allie pivoted at the door. "Why are you coming?"

"Why, to meet Buzz. I like to meet all your friends."

Allie left her mother musing over a stack of papers. She jogged to the truck and climbed in. "I got the plans, Buzz, but get prepared. Mama said she's coming down to the church, too. She says she wants to meet you."

"Oh, yeah?" Buzz smiled as he turned the key in the old contraption, making it buck and sputter.

"She wants to protect her only daughter," he said, glancing at Allie. "She must've heard all those bad things about me. They're all true, you know. I take advantage of every damsel I meet, or at least try to."

Allie chuckled. "Right. Somehow I don't think I'm one of those. Every time we've met—like, outside school—I've been learning to plow or cleaning a house. Damsels wear fancy dresses. You don't even *want* to see my closet. I don't own one fancy dress."

He shot her a perceptive look. "You won't need one for a while with the work you've got to do."

Allie knew what he meant. She'd be way too busy finding donation money for the church project.

When they reached the church, Buzz's truck rattled to a slow stop all by itself. Every eye on the grassy hillside looked their way. Allie thought Buzz muttered something under his breath. He shook his head, looking down at the steering wheel.

"Allie, just so you know, I had nothing to do with this. My mother is here…. I asked her not to come—I just can't believe she's going through with it." He looked away. "Please say you understand it wasn't my idea."

Allie glanced from the crowd of people back to Buzz. "Oka-ay—you didn't have anything to do with what?"

"C'mon, let's get this over with," Buzz said in disgust. "Just don't be mad, Allie. Make your own decision. I'm okay with whatever you want to do."

Allie tried to match Buzz's long strides as he walked purposefully up the broken sidewalk toward the church. She turned back to check on Fanny, who waved her on.

"Y'all go ahead. It'll take me a minute to catch my breath."

Allie trotted up to see small stacks of lumber and a few supply sacks littering the ground. *Daniel! You've been here! And so soon!*

"Hi, Allie!"

Oh, Daniel, you didn't forget! Supplies. Lumber. Thank you so much!

"Thank YOU. You're doing quite well. You've got lots of help. These people support what you're doing. Take charge of the meeting."

Me?

"Well, certainly not me. It's up to you. Make it happen, Allie. This is your project. Just remember the most important thing. Make sure that the carpenters leave an opening for my special window in the back wall using the exact dimensions on the plans."

An opening for your special window.

"*That's right. It will be beautiful. You'll love it. Trust me.*"

She smiled. *Of course I trust you. You are such an angel. Wish me luck!*

Allie squeezed through the crowd, spotting Buzz talking quietly to his father. Without thinking twice, Allie summoned up her courage, stuck out her hand and found herself staring up into an older pair of blue eyes rimmed in black lashes.

"Hi, Mr. Madison. I'm Allie McCall. Thank you for coming today."

Todd Madison had his son's crooked half-smile. He shook her hand. "Young lady, do you know what you're getting yourself in for with all this?"

Allie's confidence wavered. The crowd quieted and she glanced around, seeing their puzzled faces. Everybody probably thought she was crazy. *Well, wasn't she?* She didn't have a clue what she was doing, but she couldn't lose her courage now.

"No, sir, I don't. But I'm hoping you and Buzz will help me to…uh, understand it."

He rocked back on his heels and laughed. "I expect we will. What I mean is, this isn't nearly enough lumber and materials."

"How much more do you need?"

"Give me those plans and we'll take a look." Then he looked around at the crowd. "Y'all give us some room over here. I expect every one of you knows how to use a hammer. Just write your name and phone number down on the tablet my wife is holding. Everybody who's able to, please meet back here tomorrow morning at six-thirty sharp. We've got some tearing out to do."

He turned to Allie. "I don't know why you've decided to do all this, but I've got to tell you, I'm happy to help. It's time we set things right and gave a little something back to our community. I remember my daddy talking about the old days of the potluck dinners and gardening with his parents." Mr. Madison unrolled the plans a bit and whistled. "By the looks of these plans, this is the original church. Well, I'll be. I never would have thought these plans would be preserved in such good condition. Amazing."

Mr. Madison spread the parchment out on a folding table that he'd brought. "Look here, Allie. These plans called for square nails. Buzz, c'mere. We've got to put a bathroom off of one of these corners."

"Wait, Mr. Madison," Allie interrupted. "There's one important thing." She pointed to what she guessed was the back wall on the plans. "Please make sure you leave an opening on the back wall for a special window.

It's so important—I can't begin to tell you—that it be the size specified on the plan."

Mr. Madison nodded. "Sure, no problem. One opening for a special window coming right up."

When someone called her name, Allie left them leaning over the plans.

"Excuse me, Allie, I don't believe we've met before. I'm Buzz's mom," said the tall, attractive PE coach at her school.

Allie smiled. "Yes, ma'am, I know who you are."

"Well, I know you've asked Buzz to help with building this church. That's fine. He'll help you. In fact, my husband wants to donate his time, too. You see, we all talked about it last night. But, there's one…condition. In order to have my support—and for me to agree to have both my son and my husband involved in this—I'm asking for your help."

"You want my help?" Allie's ears perked up.

"I'd like for you to play on the girl's varsity basketball team this year."

Allie laughed. "Me? Play basketball?" *Should I tell her I'm so clumsy I can't walk in a straight line?* "Coach Madison, I would be a terrible player." Allie struggled to control her laughter. "You don't want me on your team. You'd lose every game."

"Nonsense. I'd have you work out. Train. Learn the skills. Honestly, Allie, what I need from you most of all is your spirit. Look at what you've done right here. You're rebuilding this church and dozens of people will be turning out to help you. They know they're not going to be paid, but it doesn't matter to them. You've inspired a kind of team spirit in our town. Nobody's been able to do that for years. And in our high school, well, you know we have the worst—well, I shouldn't say that, but we don't have a strong girls' team right now. I'm asking you to give them team spirit. They need someone to look up to. A team member to give them confidence. Will you do it?"

So this was it, this was what Buzz meant in the car. Allie surveyed the scene until she found him, standing shoulder to shoulder with his father studying the plans. What would he want her to do?

"Umm, okay," Allie said, almost without thinking. "I'll do it. I'll play. I'll just be so terrible, Coach Madison. You need to know that. But I do need Buzz's help with this project. So for that reason, I'll do what you ask. You have no idea, though. I've never played basketball. Really. I've never played. Never even picked up a ball. I don't even know the rules."

"Oh, dear." Allie watched as Coach Madison bit hard on her bottom lip. "I didn't—"

"Allie! What wonderful news!" bubbled Fanny as she gave her a sideways hug. "The girls' basketball team. She'll do fabulous, won't she, Coach Madison?" Fanny turned to the brunette coach. "Your husband can put in a little basketball court right next to this church and Allie can practice while Buzz works. He can coach her every afternoon, ain't that right, Allie? Heck, Buzz can be your trainer. You'd get a jump on the basketball season. I can't wait. As soon as everybody here learns about this, there won't be an empty seat in our little Friendly High School gym. I could ask Nate Sims if he'd pay for the electricity if Otis ran a high-powered light out here so's you could practice at night. I think it's a heck of a good deal, don't you, Coach?"

"Y-yes, why yes, it's a great idea!" Coach Madison's look of confusion turned to determination. She called her husband over. "There's one more thing, dear, to add to this church project."

Todd Madison looked questioningly at his wife. "And that is?"

"A basketball court. Buzz can teach Allie to play while he works. Todd, don't you see how perfect this would be? Allie can get a head start on the season. She can practice here and not feel like she's being watched—not like practicing in the gym after school. I think it's the perfect place for her to gain confidence. Buzz would be a great trainer. What do you think?"

Mr. Madison looked across at Allie. "Have you agreed to this? Seriously? You've agreed to play on the team?"

Allie nodded, red-faced and embarrassed. "But I told Coach Madison that I don't know anything at all about basketball. I don't...well, go to any games."

He chuckled. "Then I guess you do need your own private court to get started." He took a few steps back, kicking and eyeing the ground. "Yeah, I think we can do it. We can get a pump truck up here with no problem for the concrete. Lemme work on it."

Just as quickly, he turned to leave.

Allie didn't think she could handle any more, but she had to smile when her Mama rushed up. "Hi, I'm Laura McCall," she said to Coach Madison, then turned to her daughter. "Did I hear correctly? Fanny just told me that you're going to play basketball this year. Allie, I can't believe this! It's fantastic!"

"Aw, jeez, Mom, don't get so excited. I think I'll be terrible, but Coach Madison must have enough faith in me to think I can learn to play."

"This is great news," Laura said, looking at the volunteers still milling around. "Not only that, but I just found out there's going to be a workday here tomorrow—and Nate Sims said he'd make free sandwich plates for everybody helping. I know it's a school day and you can't make it, Coach, but I sure plan to."

Keeping her smile, Mama turned back to Allie. "Even Sheriff Anderson said he'd be here. Lots of people are just waiting to help you, honey. You should be so proud." She gave Allie a quick hug. "I know I am."

Allie beamed. "Mr. Madison said he would build a practice court up here, Mama. Maybe I can learn how to play if Buzz helps."

"Omigosh! Buzz Madison!" She turned to the coach. "How silly of me. Of course, Buzz is your son. Obviously, a fantastic player in middle school...there will be colleges waiting to draft him!"

"There are," Coach Madison said with a laugh. "Right now, Buzz only cares about playing high school ball and passing his classes." She smiled at Allie. "But, if you're serious about playing, then I have Buzz's word on it that he's serious about teaching you." She glanced over to where Buzz was buckling on his tool belt. "Only, don't think that it's going to be easy, Allie. He'll be tougher on you than I would be. He trains hard and he works hard. You've got to show him that you really want to learn." She turned back to Allie. "Can you do that?"

Allie stared at Coach Madison, suddenly feeling the impact of the woman's words. Did she want to learn basketball enough to put on a show and convince Buzz that she was interested? She had to get this church built and he was one of the main builders. *Aw, jeez. Basketball...why me? I don't even like basketball.*

*"Allie, you **do** like basketball."*

Daniel?

"Of course, it's me. Now, quickly, agree with Coach Madison. You'll learn how to play."

I can't act like I like something. I hate basketball. I hate sports.

"No, actually, you don't hate sports."

Oh, really? Are you sure?

"I can't believe you asked me that! Seriously?"

Allie grinned at the coach. "I'll do it. I'll work hard, I promise. I only hope that Buzz has a lot of patience. I hope he doesn't have to yell too much." *That was stupid.*

"Don't worry. Buzz still plays a lot with younger kids on Friday afternoons. He's used to working with beginners."

Moments later, as Allie mingled with the dispersing volunteers, Buzz came up behind her.

"What did you say? I didn't hear you yellin', so I guess you're not mad."

She turned to watch him tip back the brim of his red ball cap, mesmerized by his eyes and smile.

"I am… No, I'm not, er…. What I mean is that, yes, I'm going to play. And you'll teach me…" Her voice trailed off.

His grin widened and a dimple flashed. "Oh, yeah? Did she tell you how mean I am to beginners? Did she say how hard I train? Do you think you're ready for that?"

Allie fidgeted, uncomfortable. "Don't make fun…of me," she whispered, glancing first at her tennis shoes and then back up at him. "I can do this, Buzz. Well, at least I think I can. Don't think I'm going to quit. I'm not. If I say I'm going to do something, I'm going to do it."

He teased her. "So—bring it on?"

Resolutely, she fired back. "Bring it on."

Chapter 21

❧

"Good!" he said, straightening. "Dad says he'll have the basketball court poured by tomorrow afternoon. It needs to cure for a couple of days, then I'll stripe it and we'll be ready for play. In the meantime, we'll meet out here tomorrow morning at six o'clock. You'll get to train for nearly two hours before school starts."

Allie took a step back. "Two hours? Are you crazy? School starts at eight-fifteen. I'll be dripping wet, and maybe dead—I've never exercised for two hours in my life!"

"Whoa! Okay, so you wanna train like a girl? Fifteen sit-ups and twenty push-ups, then head for the showers? No way. If you train with me, you'll be the best girl player that Friendly High ever had. You'll even be able to make it to district track if you want to."

"Track? Good grief, Buzz."

"You sound just like Fanny."

"No, what I sound like is stupid," she shot back. "Plain ol' stupid. I'm trying to learn basketball and you're talking about track." She held up her hand. "Whoa. One sport at a time."

"Okay. Okay. Have it your way. The first practice will last an hour. We'll see how you do. No fancy clothes. No jeans. Wear some athletic pants."

"I don't have any."

"I do. We're about the same length in the legs. Mine might be too long, but…we'll figure something out. Just make sure that you eat something light in the morning. You'll be hungry after the workout. You can eat something then, too."

He readjusted the hammer in his tool belt. "I'm going back to work. No need to waste any more daylight. Remember…six o'clock, sharp!"

He disappeared into the crowd of people pretending not to listen to their conversation.

Todd Madison approached her. "Allie, I've made out a preliminary list of supplies and materials we'll need to get this building started. I've probably got enough electrical wiring in my own inventory to donate, plus I have enough roofing materials to finish the project." He folded the list away in his pocket. "I'll ask Buzz if he can think of anything else. You might want to visit Lively Lumber and talk to the owner after school. See if Curly wants to donate any money or supplies to your project. You've got the hardest job of all in getting donations. This'll take a lot more money than you could raise with any spaghetti or pancake supper." He tipped his cap and walked away.

Allie wanted to crumple over somewhere and cry. She spotted an overturned log and slumped down on the dry bark. Why did she agree to all this? It was crazy thinking she could learn how to play basketball and help the girls on the team. She hated sports!

This is just great. Build a church and find the money to pay for it all. Plus, how in the world can I become Coach Madison's newest, greatest player? Ugh. She buried her face in her hands just thinking about it. *Talk about ugly.* She'd look terrible after training for an hour in the mornings. *Sweaty, hair sticking up everywhere, no makeup, tired. No chance now of Buzz ever looking twice at her. No, not Buzz. He was way too popular.* Allie sighed.

Boys. All they care about is sports, sports and more sports. Basketball and track. She'd bet all his conversations with guys were about basketball and track—but mostly basketball. He probably slept with his basketball. Ate breakfast with it. Carried it around the house. Carried it everywhere he went. He probably loved to train and workout and, well, sweat. Allie stopped for minute. If he could work that hard, it seemed strange that Buzz struggled in Mrs. Timmons's class. English was probably his hardest subject.

It was no use. Her thoughts zoomed back to how she'd fall flat on her face trying to learn to play basketball. She should just give up. Even if she could learn, would she become "one of the boys?" Would Buzz ever look at her like a girl? *Arrgh, I don't know if I can stand it. He's so determined to succeed, to win. I don't have that determination.*

"I know what you're thinkin'." Fanny said, sitting down next to her on the log. "You're already doubtin' whether or not you can do all this."

Allie blinked away unwelcome tears. "Oh, Fanny. I can't do it all. Buzz wants to train me so hard. He'll be watching me. Judging me."

Fanny leaned closer. "Honey, there's only one person who can judge you and that's the good Lord who's sittin' right up there above us all. Nobody else on this Earth matters. Never forget that. Just do your best. That's all anybody asks. Just do your best."

Allie felt a gentle breeze caress her cheek. Instinctively, she reached up.

Daniel?

"Listen to Fanny. Wise words from a wise woman."

Her courage bolstered. "How do you know all this stuff? I don't always like listening to grown-ups, but what you say makes sense. How'd you get so smart?"

Fanny chuckled. "Just because I don't talk as refined as most folks don't mean that I'm stupid. Oh, no, it surely don't. I learned most of what I know just by livin' every day. A lot of my life I lived alone and…I thought a bunch. I figure that thinkin' sometimes gets me in more trouble than just doin'. But you, Allie, why, you've got your whole life ahead of you. You've got such a grand start. Looky here, all these people wanna help you build this church, and help me plant this garden. All you gotta do is thank them. You're helping them learn how to be helpful to others. That's a gift."

"But, Fanny, you're making me sound like such a good person. I'm not good. It wasn't my idea to do this stuff. It was Daniel who told me to build the church. I'm not doing all this because I want to!"

"Hold on. I don't know anything about your angel, Allie, but lemme ask you a question." She leveled a serious look. "What would happen if all of a sudden Daniel disappeared right now…today. Would you stop everything you've started? Would you call it quits? Tell everybody to just go home?"

Allie glanced across the field at the church. One man was measuring, another man laughed as he pulled off rotted boards, and a couple of volunteers studied the plans. She honestly couldn't answer.

"These people are rebuilding this church for themselves, make no mistake about that," Fanny said. "There's a little selfishness in all of us, never forget it. Most people don't do anything without first thinking about how it's going to help them. I honestly think these people would continue to rebuild this church even if you told them you weren't going to head up the project. I've been watchin' their faces. Happy folks and happy faces, the likes of which I haven't seen in years."

Allie wanted to believe her. "Do you think so, Fanny?" she whispered. "Do you honestly think this makes them happy?"

"Ah, child, I do," she said, before patting Allie's knee. "You're just the breath of fresh air that Friendly needed most, the only one with the courage to just keep going and not stop."

"Daniel said I had courage."

"Well, then listen to Daniel. Angel or not. He's one smart cookie."

Allie chuckled. "That's exactly what he said about you."

Fanny was smiling as she struggled to stand. "Ah, my legs are tired today. I need to rest awhile. But I like your Daniel. I like your angel. Maybe one day I'll get to meet him," she said turning to leave.

"Not too soon, Ms. Fanny. Please not too soon."

ALLIE HAD FINISHED giving Coach Madison her phone number when she spotted Nate Sims throwing out another bag of garbage. She quickly trotted down the grassy hillside.

"Mr. Nate, thank you so much for making sandwiches for the workers this week!"

He opened the back door and ushered Allie inside his shop.

"Don't mind doing it at all, young lady. It's the least I can do. That old building has been an eyesore for years. It's good to get it replaced."

Allie turned to him, suddenly interested. "Do you remember the old church?"

"Lord, yes, in all its splendor. That was a happy time in this town. The church potlucks on Sundays started the week for our families. All of us kids would spend hours playing games outside. Grown-ups brought blankets and played dominoes or cards. Families would make a day of it."

Allie smiled, turning when the bell on the door tinkled. She saw a face she'd only seen on television; Myron "Stingy" Jenkins, Friendly's one and only furniture shop owner, had just walked in. Folks said if "Stingy" loved anything more than furniture, it was money. Allie had seen his commercials when he'd crash through a big paper dollar bill, shouting, "You can trust me. I'll be stingy with your money!"

But what nobody could forget was that he had moved his store out of town. He had built a bigger, more expensive store on the interstate to attract more business. Evidently his plan had worked because, from all the talk, he was more successful than ever—and maybe more stingy. Allie had never met him in person before, probably because they never bought anything new.

"Stingy" Jenkins's trademark black silk bow tie and white starched shirt, made Allie think he was another perfectionist, like her principal. She did like his red, white and blue suspenders. They coordinated with his navy blue suit pants. He had a shock of white hair and round eyeglasses, rosy cheeks and a ready smile. Allie liked the way he looked like Santa Claus without the beard—more friendly than stingy. He stuck out his hand in welcome.

"You must be that young lady who's in charge of all this building around here. I don't know, Nate, but I think I might've moved out of town too soon. It gives me a good feeling to know that the church is going to be put back to rights... and after all these years. You must be Allie McCall." He eagerly pumped her arm.

"And to think we owe all of this to a young lady. You're the only one who could get the old folks energized about something again. Folks around town call me Stingy Jenkins, and it's a pleasure to meet you."

Allie felt her arm go limp after such a handshake workout. "It's a pleasure," she smiled back. "I've heard all about the pretty furniture in your store, Mr. Jenkins."

Nate Sims was busy bundling up what looked like several sandwiches and stuffing them in a too-small bag when Stingy replied, "You're welcome to stop by anytime. Pick out something you like. No charge."

Allie's jaw dropped as Stingy Jenkins accepted the large dill pickle that Nate offered him and took a huge bite.

After a minute of chewing, he said, "There's nothing you need in a big furniture store? A pretty dresser? Nightstand? Stand-up mirror?"

Allie gulped, thinking of the first thing that popped into her head. "Mr. Jenkins, I would like a new bed," she whispered in awe. "A big bed. A double bed. Could I have that, please?"

"For you? Yes, ma'am, anything. One double bed coming right up," he said, beaming from ear to ear. "Would you like this bed delivered, too? Free of charge, naturally."

"Oh, it's not for me. Not really," she quickly added, "It's for Fanny. You know Fanny Parker? She lives on Cragg's Cutoff, just outside of town."

Stingy glanced up at Nate. "Would that be little Frances Parker that went to school with us way back when? Lord, I haven't seen her in over forty years, Nate. I heard she got married, but then her husband died. Does she still live on that gravel road to nowhere?"

Nate Sims nodded. "She's stayed on that land ever since. Allie and her family live in the old hunting cabin just t'other side of the old Pierce property. They've been living there over five years now."

Stingy nodded, turning back to Allie. "So you want to give this bed to Fanny Parker? Mmm, I don't know about that."

Allie beseeched him. "Mr. Jenkins, please. It's just like me asking for the bed for myself. Fanny...Fanny sleeps on a hay bale with nothing but a thin cloth. It's not fair. You don't know what she's done for my mom, my brother and me. She's cooked for us and helped us...you just can't imagine how important she is to me. I think she's my best friend, next to Wikki. Please, Mr. Jenkins, please let her have this bed. It'll be such a big surprise. I can't wait to see her face. Please..."

Stingy Jenkins straightened his suspenders. "Well...I've never—"

Allie pleaded. "Otis Spinkle ran electricity to her house today. She'd been using candles all these years. Fanny's going to have electric lights and now she can sleep in her very own beautiful bed. Can you throw in some new sheets? Maybe a couple of pillows? Please Mr. Stingy, er, Mr. Jenkins?"

"Little lady, it is you who I wanted to give the present to. Now you're asking me to give a new bed to Fanny Parker. I've never heard of anything like this. Don't you need a bed? You're so tall, I bet you need a longer bed. And I heard you're going to be playing basketball. Heaven knows, you'll be tired from that. I don't know about a bed for Fanny —"

"Oh, please, Mr. Jenkins, I'm begging you." By this time Allie had gripped his arms, imploringly. "Please let Fanny have my new bed. I'll even make you a promise. I'll work so hard at learning basketball and becoming the best player ever that maybe the girls will win more games. How's that?"

Stingy Jenkins looked up over the tops of his glasses. "Maybe go all the way to District?"

Allie gulped. "Yes. Okay. Maybe go to District. Now, will you please—"

"Okay, okay," Stingy said, picking up his sack of sandwiches. "As you wish. I'll give Fanny your new bed. But...don't think I'm happy about it. I was trying to give you something new as a special thank-you for all your hard work. But, no, if you want to give away your present, then go right ahead. Just remember, I tried to give you something."

"Oh! Mr. Jenkins!" Allie threw her arms around his wide shoulders. She'd buried her face into his shirt before she realized what she'd done.

"Jeez, I'm so sorry," she said, brushing away any dirt she'd left behind.

"No bother, young lady. If it makes you that happy to give a bed to Fanny Parker, then who am I to take away your happiness? You're a fine friend, Allie McCall."

"So are you," Allie replied, her smile hiding the wetness she felt behind her eyes. "Thank you so much. You're not stingy at all. You're a wonderful man."

Nate Sims burst out laughing. "Did you hear that, Myron? This young lady called you 'wonderful.' Can you believe that? Better go tell your wife. It'll be a surprise to her!"

Stingy Jenkins chortled at his friend's remark. "I'll have Fanny's bed delivered tomorrow. Will somebody be there to let us inside?"

"Yessir, I will. For sure. If you can make your delivery after school."

"We can do that. We'll plan for it."

Allie grabbed his hand in hers. "I can't thank you enough. I won't forget my promise to you, either, Mr. Jenkins. I'll work so hard at basketball. It's the only way to pay you back."

The next thing she knew Stingy Jenkins had placed a sack in her arms. "Allie, why don't you take these sandwiches home to your family tonight? It's getting late and your mom will be too tired to cook. I think there's enough food in here to help with your dinner. Nate won't mind making me a couple more to go. Now, you run along, do your homework and get a good night's sleep."

Shocked again, Allie could only mumble more thanks as she stumbled out the door and up the grassy hillside to where her mother and Fanny were deep in conversation.

Back inside the sandwich shop, Nate looked across the counter at his longtime friend. "Well, what are you going to do?"

"What do you think? I'm going to ask you to make me two more sandwiches."

Nate rolled his eyes. "That's not what I'm talking about and you know it."

"Oh, *that*. Well, I'm going to get a new double bed and some new pillows and sheets over to Fanny Parker's house tomorrow."

Stingy took a package of potato chips from the rack, opened it up and pinned his gaze on the perfect chip inside. "And then, I'm going to deliver a new double bed to that wonderful girl who just left here with my dinner tonight. She's going to also get new pillows, sheets and comforter—the works—delivered to that broken down old cabin where they live."

Nate blinked, seeing the sadness in his friend's eyes. "Myron, why are you doing all this?"

"Because…because it's just fine with me to be generous with people who are so generous with others. Okay, Nate, so maybe I can be stingy, but there are times when I try to remember the Golden Rule. And this is one of those times. That young girl wanted me to give her new bed to somebody else. How unselfish! A remarkable girl, she is. She gave me a big hug for it, too. Lord, I haven't had a hug like that since our Tina was in high school. Now my Tina's all grown up with a husband and family. I hated it when they moved up North. I sure do miss her and the grandkids."

For a long minute, Nate Sims studied his old friend. "Well, that'll mean giving away two new beds."

"I know that," Stingy replied, biting into another chip. "I think it's money well spent…er, maybe not money spent, but it's the right thing to do. I know you're closing up, Nate, but, no kidding, do you think you could make two more of your famous chicken salad sandwiches? I'd better not go home to Gladys empty-handed. She'll scorch me for sure."

Nate Sims smiled his answer as he got to work behind the counter. "I guess you know that I'm feeding the workers every day. I'm glad to do it."

Stingy nodded. "I heard that. I also want you to feed Allie in the morning after practice. I heard about those early morning practices with the Madison boy. Feed her whatever she wants. Oh, what the heck…feed him, too. I'll pay for it…just don't tell them. And give me the bill. If she's going to take the team all the way to District, then I have to be a part of that. It'll be fun. Gladys will be delighted."

Nate put down his knife. "Well, I'll be. You're thinking of Tina again, aren't you?"

"I am. And basketball was Tina's love all her years in high school. The year Tina graduated was the last year that any of the Friendly girls' teams went to District. That was over ten years ago. It's time we changed that statistic, don't you think?"

"Absolutely. Between the two of us, our little Allie will be well fed."

"And she'll get a good night's sleep every night on her new bed!"

Windows were lighting up everywhere in the sleepy little town as shopkeepers closed and locked their doors for the evening. Two older gentlemen strolled along side by side, sharing a joke, a laugh and a special bond about a young lady they both admired.

Allie McCall never knew that she'd been the subject of their conversation that night. Instead, she lay in her too-small bed worrying about how she could exercise without sweating in front of Buzz Madison. Across town, Buzz paced his bedroom floor, wondering how he could shorten the legs on his training pants for Allie. And Daniel? Daniel was wondering just how hard it would be for Allie to find—without heavenly intervention—all the donors and the money to get the rest of the materials delivered, pronto.

Chapter 22

⟨⚬⟩

THE SUMPTUOUS SMELL of frying bacon tickled Allie's nose. Her early morning alarm hadn't even sounded, but she sat upright in bed.

Fanny?

Allie grabbed her bathrobe and padded down the short hall, hearing the soft clatter of plates.

"Fanny, is that you?"

"It sure enough is me," she said, wearing her white apron and pink floral dress. "I thought you might like a little snack before your first workout this morning."

Allie grabbed a piece of bacon. "Mmm, how wonderful! But Buzz said I'm supposed to eat light. Maybe I should just have cereal?"

Fanny got down a bowl and pulled the milk from the fridge. "Here you go, child. I want you to have a great morning."

Sleepily, Allie staggered to the table. "I'm so nervous. I could hardly sleep last night. It was awful, Fanny. I'm so tired." She poured the milk. "Thank you for coming by."

"I expect your Mama will be up to drive you to the church." Fanny coaxed the bacon out of the skillet and laid it on a stack of paper towels. "She might like a little breakfast herself this morning. She's gonna work with the other volunteers."

Lost in thought, Allie stared at the different cereal shapes circling each other in her bowl. *Rebuilding the church.* Could she find enough donors—and money? *And then basketball.* Could she actually learn how to play and be good at it? Would she learn to like it? Would the kids at school laugh at her?

She'd fallen into bed last night and never got a chance to call Wikki. *Okay, so maybe I put it off, kinda on purpose.* Allie knew Wikki would be upset when she found out about the basketball. The two had forged a pact a couple of years ago never to play sports. Naturally, Wikki would have a hard time playing any sport. And Allie had been fine with their pledge to run away from anything in which they had to sweat.

"Are you about ready, honey? It's nearly five-forty-five. Allie? Are you awake? I'm going up to the church to meet with volunteers."

Brought out of her reverie, Allie saw that Mama had pulled her long hair back in a ponytail, her usual up-do gone. This morning, Mama had on blue jeans, an old flannel shirt and jacket, very little makeup and she looked...relaxed.

"Uh, sure, Mama, I'm ready. I-I need to brush my teeth. I'll meet you outside."

Allie jumped up from the table and gave Fanny a quick hug.

Mama pivoted in the kitchen. "Allie, I've been thinking about how you're going to drum up support for this church and get all the money you need to buy building material."

"Mr. Madison said I should talk to the lumber company."

Mama took a piece of bacon. "Uh-huh, but I was also thinking about talking to the banker, Magnus Sinclair. You've seen the bank. It's down the street from the newspaper office. I could take you tomorrow after school... maybe you could get an appointment with him."

"Sure. That sounds good." Allie knew she'd need all the help she could get, her mind bouncing from learning to play basketball to building the church. The memory of seeing Mr. Madison's long list of supplies worried her. "Maybe I won't need an appointment," she mused over her bowl, "maybe he'll have time to see me tomorrow."

"Mmm, maybe," came Mama's reply.

Fifteen minutes later, Allie's stomach churned with anticipation and fear as she walked up the tiny hill toward the church.

This morning Buzz wore a blue ball cap and warm-up suit. He looked tall and serious. Allie trudged over the damp grass, the hem on her blue jeans getting so soggy she prayed the sun would stay hidden behind the clouds. *Ugly.* That's what *she* was. Wearing no makeup at all.

"Hey!" Buzz called out, tossing her a pair of athletic pants. "My mom took up the hem so they'd fit you. She guessed at how tall you were. They may not be perfect."

Allie smiled, trying not to look at him as she caught the pants. She wanted to keep her face hidden as long as she could. "Where do you want me to… change?"

"Uh… could you go back down to your car?"

Allie took this opportunity to pivot and run back down the hill, feeling like she was going to throw up any minute. The pants in her hand seemed to burn a hole through her skin. *What was she doing here? This was ridiculous!*

"**Alexandra, I can't** believe this. Are you sleeping? *Alexandra!*"

Allie's eyes flew open as Mrs. Timmons' angry voice boomed through the classroom. *Sleeping? No way.* She jerked herself upright and cleared her throat. "Yes, ma'am?"

"Alexandra, we are turning in the rough drafts of our research papers. Where is yours?" Mrs. Timmons glared at her, as she clutched what had to be everybody else's papers in the class.

Rough draft? Blood whooshed to her feet. *Oh, no! Today? Tuesday? That's right! A major grade. A huge project. Inexcusable.*

Mrs. Timmons approached her desk. "Alexandra, you have had nearly a week and a half to complete your rough draft. Judging by your surprise—you're as white as a sheet, by the way—you have forgotten your paper. You probably haven't even finished it. Well, young lady, what is your excuse?"

Allie struggled to remember the assignment, but her brain was at a complete stop. She was just exhausted after this morning's workout with Buzz. *Had it only lasted an hour?*

She gaped at Mrs. Timmons, trying to blink away her horror at forgetting to finish her homework. *Embarrassed didn't come close. Humiliated was more like it.* Every pair of eyes trained on her; some people hid their smiles. Unbelievably, Alfred P. was the first to her rescue as he raised his hand.

"She's been really busy, Mrs. Timmons. I bet you've heard Allie's helping to rebuild the church—"

"Oh, yes," Mrs. Timmons interrupted, her cold, steely gaze never leaving Allie's face. "I've heard all about her brave attempts to save that dilapidated structure. What exactly does that have to do with English? Alexandra, I ask you, what does that have—"

"Excuse me, Mrs. Timmons." A virtually unknown voice sounded from the other side of the room.

"Who spoke?" she demanded, whirling around.

Silence. Nobody moved. Allie wished once more for the dingy linoleum floor to open up and suck her in. She took a moment to exhale now that she was free of Mrs. Timmons's angry stare. Swiveling about, her teacher crept ever so slowly toward the other half of the class, staring quizzically.

"I asked you a question! Who interrupted me just now?"

Buzz Madison unfolded his long legs and got up from his desk. "Me. I said that Allie has worked hard on the church project—"

"Buzz, you of all people. You never speak in class. No wonder I didn't recognize your voice. Do you want to fail my class? If you take up for Alexandra, I guarantee you will fail my class. And do you know what that means? No pass, no play. You won't play basketball."

Buzz kept his composure. "Allie will also be part of the girls' basketball team—"

Audible gasps rippled through the class. Some students clapped. A few yo's and yeah's rang out. Mrs. Timmons shushed everyone.

"Perfect! So now *she* will be exempt from turning in her class work?"

"No, ma'am. I just wanted to tell you—"

"Buzz, I don't want to hear what you have to say. I'm going to write you a pass to Mr. Danner's office. I don't want to hear any of your backtalk again this class period. Allie, I'm writing you a pass to the principal's office, as well. There will be no sleeping in my class."

Mrs. Timmons grabbed the white pad on her desk and scribbled each a pass. Buzz and Allie gathered their books and walked to the front of the classroom.

A moment later, Wikki rolled her wheelchair up to Mrs. Timmons's desk. "Please write me a pass. I want to talk to Mr. Danner. I'm helping to coach Allie in basketball. I don't know about anybody else in here, but I'd like to explain to Mr. Danner how much Allie has been helping this town by rebuilding the church and trying to learn how to play basketball all at the same time. I'd like to tell Mr. Danner that Allie is a straight-A student. That she loves English more than anything, and was probably too tired to finish her rough draft."

Allie took a step toward Wikki and whispered, "It's no use. Don't get in trouble because of me. Please."

Alfred P. stood up. "I'd like a pass, too, Mrs. Timmons. I wanna go to the principal's office. Shoot, I ain't been there in two days. I bet Mr. Danner's plum forgot what I look like."

Kids started to chuckle.

Messa Kess stood up. "I'm goin', too. Allie's gonna play ball? Cool. I'm working with Buzz. Rebuilding that church. Yeah. Everybody's gonna be there," he said, high-fiving another basketball buddy, Billy Richardson, who unfolded himself from his desk to stand.

Dismayed, Allie watched her classmates one by one, as they rose from their desks, books in hand, asking for passes to the office.

Mrs. Timmons smacked the pad down on the desk as the bell rang. "I will see all of you in detention if this episode ever repeats itself. Is that clear?"

Allie watched as everybody nodded and then left through the doorway.

"Alexandra?" Mrs. Timmons called out. "I need to speak with you. Yes, stop right there, thank you. Completely against my better judgment, I might add, I will give you a one week extension on your rough draft. Will that be sufficient time?"

Did Mrs. Timmons almost smile? No, of course not.

"Yes, ma'am. I'm sorry… er, thank you. I'll…I'll have it by then."

"Good. See that you do. Now, hurry to class. I'm sure Wikki is waiting for you in the hall."

Allie scooted toward the doorway.

"Alexandra?"

Allie turned slowly. "Yes, ma'am."

"Will you practice basketball every morning before school?"

"Yes, ma'am."

"Then, by all means, get your studies done the night before. Is that clear?"

"Yes, ma'am, Mrs. Timmons." She hustled out the door. Seeing Wikki sitting in her chair and grinning from ear to ear, Allie poked her friend gently in the shoulder. "I could kill you," she whispered. "Don't you ever do that again. Don't you dare get in trouble because of me."

Wikki whirled on her as she was being pushed forward. "Just because I have to practically live in this wheelchair doesn't mean I'm not a strong person, Allie. I couldn't stand anymore of it—the way she beats you up like that with her mean talk. I'm sick of it. And from the looks of everybody else in class, they're sick of it, too." Wikki laughed behind her hand. "And did you hear Buzz? O-mi-gosh! He stood up for you. It was way cool. I've never seen him do that for anybody. Not even Constance."

Allie grinned, her tension gone. "It was way cool. He was being nice."

"No way. I think he likes you."

Allie whispered, "Don't be silly. Hey, are you mad about me playing basketball?"

Wikki waved her away. "Heck no! If you're going to play, I'd like to watch."

"Really? Cool."

Wikki nodded. "And ya'know what? If you had texting on your phone, you could text me all this stuff."

"I know, but I don't get cell service at my house, anyway. Here's Mr. Becker's room. C'mon, we need to get to class!"

"Allie, we've got to talk!"

Allie whispered. "I know. We will—after school. No, wait! I can't. I'm getting a bed delivered. No, not a bed for me. Oh, it's supposed to be a surprise. Don't worry, Wikki, I'll call you tonight on the house phone. Promise!"

Allie scooted Wikki to her assigned desk and then rushed out of the classroom, eager to get to her third period class. Her feet barely touched the ground as she thought about how Buzz had spoken up on her behalf. How cute he looked with his serious face and his silver glasses. *He came to my rescue!*

Allie tried to calm her pounding heart as she half-jogged, still grinning, straight into Mrs. Rice's history class. With her teacher nowhere to be seen, she swooped into her desk and hollered out to her classmates. "Hey, everybody!"

She was instantly seized by a dozen kids.

"Hey, what happened in Mrs. Timmons class?" "Everybody's talking about you being on the basketball team. S'up?" "Is Mrs. Timmons gonna fail Buzz Madison?" "Is Mrs. Timmons gonna fail you?"

Allie's heart soared; she barely heard Mrs. Rice greet the class and take roll moments later.

Still daydreaming, Allie remembered how they had started the workout with fifty sit-ups. Luckily Buzz had brought a tarp with him to lay across the wet ground. She did five sets of fifteen pushups, military style, nearly falling on her face. Back to more sit-ups and jumping rope as fast as she could, then jogging the entire perimeter of the one-acre garden area.

When she finished, Buzz set up orange cones. She raced from one cone to another and then to another. He'd shift the cones, change up the route and she'd do it again. She almost kissed Nate Sims when he brought their hot breakfast croissant sandwiches and large orange juice bottles. That meant the workout was officially over.

On their drive back to school, both of them tired and drained, they ate in silence. Thankfully, Coach Madison let Allie have a private shower in the locker room before any of the first period girls came in. Allie smiled to herself. She certainly needed that shower.

"….clearly the Colonists didn't like the English rule. Allie, can you tell us why?" Mrs. Rice finished her sentence in front of Allie's desk. *"Allie?* Are you with us today?"

"Yes, ma'am. The colonists, uh, the colonists didn't like the British style of taxation without representation."

"That's a main reason. Any other ideas?"

Thankfully, Mrs. Rice called on Rueben Carnes as Allie straightened herself, determined to keep her mind on the class. But it was no use. This day kept getting more and more perfect.

Even waiting for the bus, her mind whirled. She lost herself, thinking about how Buzz had walked Wikki and her to lunch. He had even eaten with them. Messa Kess had come over and flirted a little with Wikki. Talk about blushing—Wikki's cheeks had turned bright pink but she kept on laughing anyway at Messa's super worn-out jokes.

By seventh period, her energy sagged as she reviewed her homework calendar. She'd make sure she finished all of it tonight. She'd also penciled in a phone call to Wikki. They had lots to talk about. Hopping off the bus, she raced to the house, eager to get on her bike and ride to Fanny's. She didn't want Fanny to turn the delivery away, thinking the driver had made a mistake. She dropped her books on the kitchen table, locked the front door again, and pedaled away down the road.

Fanny was clucking and tossing hen scratch to her chickens as Allie approached.

"Hey, Fanny! Got any more chores?" Allie propped her bike up against a wire fence.

"Not right now," she called out. "I could use a little company. I kinda got used to staying with y'all. There's nothing busier than a house filled with kids. Somethin's going on all the time. It's kinda lonesome 'round here."

"Will you plant some of your herbs in the church garden?" Allie asked as she and Fanny walked toward the greenhouse. "It would be so cool if everybody could have fresh herbs."

"I've been thinkin' on it." Fanny slid open the greenhouse door. "Here, sit down on this old stump. I'll lay out my plan." Allie quickly complied.

"While you were at school today, I drove up to the church in my golf cart. Bless its heart, that little battery has been through the mill, it has. Nate let me charge it in his bakery while I was at the church. And then it nearly plum died again just before I got home. I've got it recharging now. Your mama and the sheriff was at the church, and so was Wikki's mama. Well, shoot, what am I saying? There must have been a couple dozen people gathered 'round, including Marybelle and Bessie Hightower from the boardinghouse, Nate Sims…just about every business owner on the town square came up to see about the church building and the garden. Your mama kinda got everything organized and we had a sit-down meeting. Everybody saw how we'd done tilled up the soil, and then we started making a plan about what to plant and when to plant it.

"But the main point is that we took a vote and decided to set it up as a CSA project. That stands for Community Supported Agriculture. All it means is that folks around town, even outside of town if they want to, can become shareholders in our garden. They pay a certain amount of money in advance and then come pick up their produce. The garden will make money—don't know if it'll make a profit and right now, we don't care—so at least we'll be paid back for seed, plants, fencing and whatever else we're needing to buy. They elected your mama as the treasurer."

"Really? Mama?"

"I guess these folks must really trust her."

"Fanny, that's so cool."

"And…well, everybody thought that we should elect a president of the community garden. And so…they chose me."

Chapter 23

✦

"Omigosh!" Allie cried. "I'm so happy!"

Fanny started to laugh. "Now don't get so excited. I was the one who took the project on in the first place. But now I'm feelin' a little old for this responsibility. I asked Wikki's mom to help me out and be co-president. Don't know if I've ever heard of that, but I want her workin' side by side with me. And do you know what? She's got the best ideas for growing radishes and squash… I've never thought of that particular soil mix before. And she's a real rose grower… grows patented roses, grafts them herself. Wouldn't that be something? Jessica said maybe one day she'd start her own flower business. She's amazing. We'll have to build a fence for them roses, too. Maggie will love her ideas." Fanny took a deep breath. "Now that we've got all this garden stuff squared away, I'm ready and willing to help you get this money together for the church."

"Great!" Allie threw her arms around Fanny's shoulders and gave her a kiss on her weathered cheek. "I need all the help I can get. Mama's taking me to meet with the banker tomorrow afternoon."

"Lemme know what he says." Fanny's eyes lit with laughter as she patted Allie's arm. "Oh, this is all such an adventure. Is that somebody out there on my gravel? Do you hear that noise? Sounds like a truck. Shouldn't be nobody here today." Fanny stood up and made for the greenhouse door. "Lord'a mercy. Am I seeing right? What the devil is he doing here? That's ol' Stingy Jenkins's truck. It says it right there on the side of the door. He surely ain't got no business with me."

Allie grinned and rushed to her side. "This is all my doing, Fanny. I hope you're not mad. I got you a bed. Your very own double bed, brand new. With sheets."

"You wha-at? A bed? But why, child?"

"Because I didn't want you sleeping on that nasty old hay bale anymore."

Fanny chuckled. "Listen, that hay bale is getting' smaller every day. Money's been tight and I've been using it to feed Miss Lizzie. My bed don't even hold up my legs anymore. Maybe that's why they're so tired. I just can't believe this. A bed? For me?"

As Fanny chuckled, her eyes brimmed with tears. "There ain't nothing I would like more than to have a honest-to-goodness bed."

Allie grabbed Fanny's hand and pulled her along. "Well, in that case, don't you think we need to accept this delivery?"

"I surely do. Would that nice delivery man carry my hay bale to the feed shed?"

"Let's go ask him."

Minutes later, Fanny's hay bale was moved out of the house and Allie was sweeping hay from the wooden bedroom floor. She opened the window a little more to air out the musty smell, while Stingy Jenkins and his driver carried in the bed frame and then the bed.

"Mr. Jenkins, it's beautiful!" Allie cried, seeing first the box springs and then the mattress.

"It's a blessing, for sure," Fanny whispered, almost in awe. "I can't thank you enough, Myron."

"Oh, Fanny, you've known me umpteen years. You know I ain't been called Myron since grade school," Stingy said, after the bed assembly. "Allie, here are sheets and pillows. I'll let you ladies finish up with this."

He turned to his husky driver. "Billy Ray, I need for you to bring in that recliner, too. There's room for it in the living room."

"Sure, boss. Weren't that delivery going to the Turner house?"

"It was, but I'm making a change. I've got another one at the warehouse for Mrs. Turner."

"Sure, boss." Billy Ray turned to leave.

"Stingy, what are you doing? First, a bed. Now, a chair? I don't need no chair."

Raking one hand through his hair, Stingy sighed, "Fanny, this bed comes to you courtesy of this young lady. I had offered to give her a bed for all of her hard work, but all she wanted was to give the bed to you.

And the chair? Well, the chair is from me. You don't have one comfortable chair in this little cottage of yours. And everybody needs at least one easy chair. There must be nights when your legs hurt. Mine sure do. We're not young anymore, Fanny Parker. Use this recliner and I guarantee your legs will feel better right away."

Allie rushed to throw her arms around his shoulders one more time.

"Thank you so much. Mr. Jenkins! I don't know how I'm ever going to repay you."

He pulled away and pointed his finger. "Yes, you do," he whispered. "It's District for you, young lady. Live it. Think it. Breathe it. Do it, Allie. You know you can."

She grinned and nodded. "I will. Thank you again. The bed is beautiful. Her chair is beautiful, I bet."

And it was. Moments later, Stingy Jenkins and Billy Ray had carried in a velvety, blue-cushioned recliner for Fanny. She sunk deep into it, propped her feet up, closed her eyes and smiled.

"This ain't no ordinary chair. It's a cloud from heaven." Fanny reached up and took Allie's hand. "Thank you, my dear. I don't know when I've had such wonderful presents."

Satisfied that all had gone well, Allie pedaled faster to get home. Tonight, she'd have to make dinner. Okay, so she wasted a little extra time feeding Miss Lizzie and the other animals before she'd left Fanny's house. But once Fanny sat in that chair she wasn't getting up. She just called out instructions as Allie ran in and out of the house, filling up the bucket from the well to water the yard animals. Even though Allie had made up the bed with the new sheets, Fanny said she might sleep in the chair tonight. Allie smiled, happy. A perfect ending to a perfect day.

She pulled up to her house to see her Mama's car and Sheriff Anderson's jeep. He was carrying a bundle of hamburger sacks.

"Hungry?" he called out.

"Starved," she yelled back, storing her bike near the house. She rushed in the front door to find everybody in a huddle.

Ben was pleading. "Why can't I have her old one?"

Everyone turned to stare at Allie.

"Old? Old what?" She looked from her Mama to Ben, then to the sheriff. "What are y'all talking about? Everything I have is old."

"Not anymore," her mama said, a slow smile forming. "You, my dear, are the proud owner of a brand new bed—extra long, too."

Allie's heart stopped. "Whaaa—"

Mama waved her through. "Right this way, please. New bed, sheets, and comforter. Mr. Jenkins said you needed extra pillows, too."

"Me? But…but…but I gave my bed to Fanny," she whispered.

"Tell me your version of this story."

"Well, uh—yesterday, I thanked Nate Sims for making sandwiches for the church work crew. Mr. Jenkins was in the sandwich shop and talked to me about playing basketball. He asked if there was anything I wanted from his….well, store. I told him that I wanted a bed, only for Fanny—"

"No need to replay it again, Allie. That's exactly what Stingy told me. I didn't believe him at first, so I appreciate you confirming it. It's all unbelievable."

Still shaking her head, Mama led everyone down the short hallway. Allie gasped when she saw the gorgeous Queen Anne double bed frame. Hand-rubbed mahogany accented the head and foot railings. The lacey white comforter reminded her of a frothy concoction ripped from the pages of a fairy tale. Never, ever, not even in the movies, had she seen anything more beautiful.

"It's fit for a queen," she whispered, running her hand along the sleek smoothness of the fine wood. "I'm scared to sit on it, Mama. I can't imagine what this bed costs."

But Allie knew. Stingy Jenkins laid the cost out plain and simple. *District.* That was the price of this bed.

"I don't know if I can learn to play and get good enough in time for District," she whispered.

"District? Allie, I think you need to worry about getting your homework done so you can rise and shine for another morning workout. Come wash up. Sheriff Anderson was kind enough to bring us dinner tonight. I've got a ton of work to do. But we had a great workday at the church, didn't we, Logan?"

"We got a lot more finished than I thought we would. The tearing out is just about done," he replied.

"Well, I enjoyed every minute of it. Ben! C'mon, get your hands washed."

"Aw, Mom, pulleze? Can I have Allie's old bed? Just this once?"

Mama ruffled his hair. "I don't see why not."

Ben jumped two feet in the air, pumping his fist. "Alright! Let's eat!"

The four of them had a fun, lighthearted dinner. Mama and Sheriff Anderson tried to explain the progress on rebuilding the church while Ben interrupted them every few seconds with ideas about moving the furniture around in his room.

After dinner, and after Ben was comfortably settled in his "new" bed, Allie wanted to relive her most perfect day ever. But when her head hit the cushiony pillows she hardly had the strength left to say her prayers. Tonight, she had tons to thank Heaven for. So, with her eyes closed, she settled for a running 'thank you-thank you' mantra in her mind.

It was cut short by Daniel. *"The new bed suits you. A queenly bed for a queen."*

Allie mumbled into her pillow. "Daniel. I've missed you. What are you doing?"

"If I told you, you'd never believe me. Bottom line? I've been busy. You've been busy, too. I see their lists. I hear their conversations. You've assembled the busiest bunch of workers I've ever seen. And, believe me, I've seen my share over these thousands of years."

"Thousands of years? Daniel, are you really that old?"

"Give or take."

"You don't look old."

"My heart is young, Allie—and my spirit? Well, a spirit is all I am. I don't have a body, except when I visit you."

"Pretty hair. Pretty eyes. And, you're funny. Thank you for your help. I pray to God every night. During the day, too. But I forget to thank you, my BFF. Maybe more than Wikki, more than Fanny. I wouldn't be doing all this stuff, if you hadn't made me—"

"Oh, no. Not made *you, Allie. I didn't make you do anything. I chose you. There's a big difference."*

"Okay. Okay. But at least you stuck by me. Helped me. Always there. Just one more thing…I'm awfully tired, but I want to know if I finish the church…can I really get people to donate all that money?"

"That depends on you."

"So I can't give up. Gotta keep going. That's it?"

"That's it."

"I won't give up. Won't stop trying. And the basketball thing? Will I learn basketball? Keeping my bed depends on basketball."

"Same rules apply."

"The don't-stop, keep-going thing? Yeah, sure. In that case, I need more strength…need to get through Buzz's workouts. He says they'll get harder. Stay close. Don't leave me. I need you. 'Night, Daniel."

"*Goodnight, dearest Allie. Rest well. And do not doubt yourself so. You already possess ample amounts of everything you need—strength and courage, faith and devotion. These admirable qualities are a part of you. I can only help develop what you already possess. My role is small. Yours, however, takes center stage. You'll have self-doubt. Your courage will waver. Say no to the nay-sayers. Hang on with your strong heart. Above all, do not give up. Repeat after me, 'I will not give up.'*"

Allie mumbled, "I will not give up. I will not give up. I will not give up."

Laura McCall stuck her head in the tiny bedroom next to hers, hearing some mumbled nonsense. She padded softly over to where her daughter lay sound asleep and stroked her silky brown hair.

"Shh, Allie, it's only a dream."

The young teen quieted in seconds and Laura padded back to her bedroom, closed the door and breathed a heavy sigh.

She followed her nightly ritual, making her way into the tiny room she called her "private bath," which consisted of a stained claw-foot tub, a corner sink and a toilet—all of which, to her surprise, still worked most of the time. She glanced at her husband's picture on the towel stand as she slipped out of her tattered robe. Turning on the faucet, she sprinkled a few drops of lavender in the tub of warm water and began her nightly conversation.

"I'm tired tonight, Gerald. Not just tired the way I am when I work behind a desk all day, but physically tired, like I used to be when our kids were little. It's a different tired. A good tired."

Laura slipped into the water, sinking down deep so that it lapped against her shoulders. She closed her eyes and inhaled the floral scent.

"I feel like I'm doing something productive, something with meaning. I really enjoyed my day. I liked it so much that I wanted to tell you I might do it more often. Have fun, that is. Too much work and no play makes Laura a very unhappy mom. And Allie still will not open up and talk to me. I'm trying to repair the bridge between us, but the damage goes back to when you got sick. Ben hides in his room or over at his friend's house most afternoons…I'm at a loss to know what to do. I've talked to your picture for the past five years, but I've never asked for your help. Now I'm asking. Please, if there's any way you can help me reach out to Allie, please send me a sign. Tell me something. Draw me a picture…anything. She's tackling all these projects, bless her heart; she's going to collapse. How can I let her know I'm there to help? I mean, really, Jerry, isn't she a blessing? She's talented, smart and pretty. You've always been as proud as I have of her."

Laura smiled as she washed her face. "And now basketball? God help her learn that one. Remember how our daughter could hardly run down the hall without falling all over her feet? She's going to have to learn coordination—and fast."

Laura stood up and grabbed a nearby towel, dried off and put on her pajamas.

"Jerry, there's one more thing. It's about Sheriff Anderson. This is harder for me to talk about. But since you've been gone, I haven't looked at men, Jerry—I haven't been interested. But Logan is persistent. Sure, we've sat on the porch with our iced tea. We've gone together to city functions. But I found out today that Logan likes me. What I mean is that, well, he wants to date me. Today when we were working on the church with the sun shining and the birds singing— you can understand, everybody was so happy—Logan asked me out on a date. Good grief, I felt like a teenager again." She smiled.

"It was…well, fun. I feel guilty admitting it, but today I laughed and had so much fun working hard and visiting with other people, for the first time in years. I said yes to him, Jerry. I'm forty-two years old, but I still feel young and—he's a good man. He likes me. And, well, I like him. For some reason, I wanted to tell you all this."

She glanced again at the picture of her late husband, the man she had pledged to love forever.

"I don't know why I need your approval, but I guess I do."

Chapter 24

❦

WEDNESDAY, SEPTEMBER 22

BUZZ STARTED ALLIE on dribbling. As uncoordinated as ever, she stumbled over her feet, unable to hold onto the ball. *He makes me so-o-o nervous.*

"Okay, stop right there," he told her. "This isn't going to work. Let's try something else. We've got another month or so before real practice starts and your ball-handling is so not ready."

Allie's shoulders sagged. "I know. I'm awful." Maybe it was the two mile run or the one hundred and fifty sit-ups and one hundred sit-ups. They had started thirty minutes earlier, too. "It's not your fault, Buzz. It's me. I'm terrible."

And her forehead was sweaty and her snarled hair was falling out of its ponytail. What she had thought would be a fairy tale experience was unraveling fast. She was *not* learning how to play. She would *not* become a star. They would *not* go on to District. She would let Buzz and the coach down, not to mention her friends and her teammates. Even Stingy Jenkins would be disappointed. *Jeezalu, I'll have to give the bed back.* Allie plopped down on the church's basketball court. "It's no use."

"What are you doin'? You're not quitting." Buzz held out his hand. "C'mon. Get up. We're gonna change priorities, that's all." He pulled her to her feet. "Don't say you're awful, okay? You're not. You're learning. As my mother says, 'don't confuse the two.' Just work on hitting the basket, making free throws, mid-court shots…under the basket. Work on scoring points. Dribbling can come later."

Embarrassed, Allie stood at the free throw line next to Buzz as he demonstrated. Giving the ball two bounces, Buzz effortlessly made the shot. "See? Work on hitting the basket."

"You make it look so easy, Buzz."

"Hey!" he laughed. "I know it's not easy, okay? It just takes practice. That's why we're here, right? And while you're practicing on this end of the court, I'll practice at the other. Just keep on shooting, shooting and shoot some more. Pick out your favorite positions on the court and shoot. You'll learn where you get your best shots. Me? I'm no good past center court. I'm better inside the free throw line and under the basket."

Allie nodded. For the final thirty minutes she devised her own system while Buzz worked closely on his own game. Allie shot from different vantage points and averaged making one shot out of five—plus she didn't trip over her feet quit as much. Buzz was right. It was slow going but there was no need to give up, at least not yet.

Mama greeted Allie when she got home from school. "I've got to run back to the office to pick up some papers. Do you want to come along and talk to Mr. Sinclair about a building donation?"

The banker. Ugh. She knew she had to go, but she dreaded the thought of doing it and she had shoved it from her mind. *It was now or never.* "Sure… but I don't know what to say or how to say it."

"I know, sweetie. Jump in the car and we'll talk about it on the way."

Fifteen minutes later Allie had introduced herself to Mr. Sinclair's secretary.

"Glad to meet you, hon. M'name's Daisy," the woman said in between gum smacks, "I heard about that church-thang. Y'all really rebuilding it from scratch?"

Allie wondered if the orange streaks in Daisy's brown bouffant came from a beauty shop or a can of special hair paint. "Yes, ma'am, and I'm here to see if Mr. Sinclair would like to contribute to the project—on, er, behalf of the bank."

Daisy rolled her green-shadowed eyes and tossed her orangey bouffant at his closed door. "Him? Seriously?" She leaned over her desk and whispered, "I've never seen Mr. Sinclair give one penny to the hundred scout troops who've traipsed in here wantin' donations. If I were you, I wouldn't waste my time."

Oh, no! Well, hadn't Mama warned her it would be an uphill battle? Could he really be that mean? She needed thousands—tens of thousands— of dollars. How would she get it if the bank president wouldn't help?

"Uh, Miss Daisy, I really need his help. Could I talk to him just for a minute?"

Daisy's lips thinned, her fuchsia lipstick all but gone. "Tell you what. I won't say why you're here. I'll just say you're Laura McCall's daughter and have a question to ask him." She smiled and spread her arms wide. "It's not like I'm lying now, is it?"

Allie returned her smile. "No, ma'am! And thank you!"

The next moment Allie was escorted into Mr. Sinclair's office and seated in a cushiony leather chair. She gazed at the man who had the most money to give to her cause. He hadn't looked up from the papers on his desk, his glasses perched low on his nose, his bald head glistening beneath the fluorescent lights. Mama had said he would be formidable, if not downright nasty.

Allie cleared her throat.

"Well? What is it?" he barked without looking up.

"Mr. Sinclair… I'm Allie McCall." She swallowed hard. "I'm here… I'm here…."

He slammed down his pen on the majestic oak desk and glared. "Yes? Why are you here?"

"To… see if you would…could contribute to the church rebuilding project."

"To what? Are you kidding? Do you really think I'm going to donate money to rebuild that worthless pile of…that rotting bunch of lumber—"

"Mr. Sinclair… please, there are volunteers. People are working right now. I just need money—"

"Of course you need money! Everybody in this dying town needs money! That's the only reason they come to see me. You're not the first one with her hand out, young lady. I can't afford to give to every little cause—"

"Excuse me, sir, but we're not a little cause. This is a big effort. The whole town is turning out for this p-project. Mr. Sims is donating sandwiches. Mr. Madison is handling the reconstruction, even Ms. Marybelle and the sheriff are helping—"

He waved her away. "Spare me the details. It's never going to happen. Just another pipe dream from somebody—maybe you—some idiot fool who thinks that old wood pile can be rebuilt. I don't care if there's a host of angels with sign-up sheets out there. I will not donate one thin dime."

A host of angels? Was he kidding? What nerve! How dare he call me an idiot fool! "Do you know what? Everybody's right about you. I don't blame the scouts for being too scared to ask you for donations. You *are* mean. And a bully!" Allie blinked. Had she just called the banker a bully? "B-but thank you for your time." She turned on one heel, left his office and closed the door behind her.

His secretary glanced up. "Not go well?"

"Oh, Miss Daisy, it was awful. He's so mean, he growls." Allie leaned on a nearby desk for support. "And I interrupted him. I try never to do that."

She shrugged. "Don't take it so hard. He's not much of a people person." Then Daisy gave her a knowing smile. "Sorry, Allie. I wish you luck."

"Do you know anybody else in town I could talk to?"

She shook her head. "Not really. Just the feed store and the attorney. Them's about the only two businesses left, aside from the newspaper."

Allie nodded. Maybe Mama could use her influence with the newspaper owner to get a small donation. Wikki's mom worked at the feed store. Maybe they'd donate a little.

But she needed big bucks....

"Thank you, Miss Daisy," Allie said before leaving the bank. She met her mama on the sidewalk.

"Well, how did it go?"

"Exactly how you thought it would." Allie shook her head. "What am I going to do, Mama?"

"Keep trying. You're going to keep trying."

HER HEAD WASN'T in the practice early Thursday morning. Allie plopped down on the basketball court, hands in her lap. "It's no use, Buzz. I went to see the banker yesterday. He told me—flat out—no. If I can't get money from him, then who?" She retied her ponytail. "Do you have any ideas?"

Towering over her, Buzz tucked the basketball under his arm. "Yeah, one. You can't hit the broad side of a barn this morning and your head's not in the game," he said, glancing at his watch. "It's almost seven and Curly Lively's opening up his lumberyard. Wanna go?"

"Now?"

"Sure. Curly will've had his first cup of coffee in a few. And early's always a good time to do business with Curly." He grinned and held out his hand. "C'mon, Nate Sims's light is on. I bet he can give us something to eat."

Allie jumped up, trotting after Buzz. They were traveling the highway in no time, headed for Lively Lumber, about ten miles away. Allie and Buzz rode in silence as Buzz's green truck spit and sputtered on the asphalt. Allie tried not to think about their sweat pants and t-shirts as they entered the lumberyard office.

"Hey, Buzz!" came a friendly voice.

A squat gnome of a man in denim overalls approached, his hand outstretched. "It's been a month of Sundays since I last seen you. Say, have you gotten taller! How's your daddy?"

Buzz shook Curly's hand. "He's good. Real good."

"You tell him I've got that material he wanted for the Tyler job. I'm ready to deliver anytime." Curly turned to Allie and looked her up and down. "You sure know how to pick 'em, Buzz. Gotta say that for ya'. This one's awful purdy," Curly said with a wink. Allie blushed to her toes and shook his hand.

"I'm Allie McCall." She couldn't help but smile. *What a flirt!* Curly seemed to be in his fifties, and his twinkling brown eyes and bald head barely reached her waist.

"Say...I heared about you. Ain't you the one who's trying to rebuild that church out yonder on the square?"

"Yes, sir," she spoke up, "I need—desperately need—donations—"

"Aw, shoot, girl, why didn't you speak up?" Curly reached for the three-ring binder that stood at the ready on a nearby counter. "Lemme look at my inventory. I'm not much on donatin' money, but lemme see what I've got on hand that you'll need." Curly donned his reading glasses and flipped through the binder.

Buzz raced outside. "Buzz? Buzz?" Curly called after him.

"Yessir. Got it right here. The list...was in the truck." Breathing hard, Buzz handed it to him.

"Okee-dokey, lemme look …." Lost in thought Allie glanced up at Buzz who smiled and winked at her. *Omigosh, what an improvement over yesterday. Buzz may be way handsome, but now I think I'm now falling in love with Curly Lively, the tiny lumberyard guy.*

"Oh, Mr. Curly, whatever you can do to help, I would greatly appreciate it."

Not looking up from Buzz's list, Curly nodded. "No problem, missy. If Todd and Buzz are doing this building, well, I gotta be helping out, too."

Curly slipped off his glasses. "Okay, son, tell you what. You know I can't give you everything on this list, but count on all your framing supplies, roof trusses and any electrical."

"Alright!" Buzz straightened. "Dad's gonna donate insulation, dry wall and what roofing and some electrical materials he's got on hand. It's not a big building, maybe two thousand square foot—"

"Wha-a—" Allie began.

"But you still gonna need siding and plumbing and windows and doors and air conditioning and heating," Curly interrupted. "Now I can order all that—but not for free." He leaned over the counter. "What about you, little lady, can you get some money in here so's I can get these materials ordered?"

Allie looked into his questioning eyes. "Y-yes sir, I-I can."

Curly's big laugh bounced off the metal walls. "You ain't soundin' so sure about that, now, are ya'? Nobody's helpin' you get this money?"

"She's pretty much doing it all by herself," Buzz interjected. "And learning how to play basketball at the same time."

"Oh, yeah?" That piqued Curly's interest. "You gonna be a Lady Lion? You got the height for it. And you got the coach here and his mother on it, too, I bet." Curly nodded assuredly. "Tell you what—and this is my final offer—you get me one or two of them big cloth banners with my business name printed on it, real pretty-like. And you hang them banners up in the high school gym, so's everybody knows I'm a supporter of this town and the Lion team and—I'll donate the tiny dab of plumbing materials you'll need. That's the deal. Take it or leave it."

"We'll take it," cried Allie and Buzz in chorus.

"Good! Lemme copy that list and pull the materials. Buzz, let 'em know they can pick up what I've got on hand after lunch if somebody's makin' a trip up this way."

"Thank you, Curly. I'll let Dad know. He'll be at the job today."

"Good. You'll talk to your mother about them advertising banners, okay?"

"Yessir, I will."

Curly came from around his counter. "And you, little lady who's learning to play basketball—I heard about your bargain with Stingy Jenkins. You're gonna take this team to District, right? Help put us back on the map?"

Allie's mouth dropped as she towered over him. "Y-yes sir, I'll try."

"No, little lady, the correct answer is 'yes, I will.' He grinned at her. "Be positive. Believe in yourself. Heck, I do and I don't even know ya'."

He sounds like Daniel! "Oh, Mr. Curly, thank you!" Impulsively, Allie bent over and gave him a tiny hug. "Thank you for being so nice."

Slapping a nearby cap on his head, Curly hid his blush and smiled. "Just a bit of supplies. Nothin' more." He hobbled over to a copier machine.

Allie grinned up at Buzz who grinned back. "See?" he whispered. "It's all good." Moments later they were winding their way to the high school to make their first period class.

"Buzz, I still can't believe your dad is going to donate all that stuff!"

"He's got odds and ends in our shop from completed jobs. He said he'd donate what he had. And he always has roofing materials on hand." Buzz donned his sunglasses. "And, just to prepare you—we may not have time for a shower today."

"I know." *And I don't care. I'll wear these clothes all day, I'm so happy! Donations, finally!*

School couldn't end soon enough. Allie jumped from the bus and dashed to the house, where she found the sheriff's car and Fanny's golf cart.

"What's going on?" she cried, bursting in the door.

Three surprised faces turned in unison. "That's what we want to know," said Sheriff Anderson. "Todd Madison picked up a boatload of supplies from Curly's lumberyard today. Great job! We heard all about how you and Buzz visited him early this morning."

"Congratulations, Allie!" said her mama, hugging her.

"I knew you could do it," chimed in Fanny.

Grinning, Allie dropped her backpack and took a seat on the sofa. "He was so different from the banker. Mr. Curly is such a great guy!"

The sheriff laughed. "He's had that lumberyard for years—in fact, he inherited it from his father. He's a good man."

"But I still don't have near enough money." Allie turned to mama. "There's siding and windows to buy—"

Mama patted her hand. "I know. You can make an appointment with the newspaper owner, Mr. Donnelly."

"I know, but he can't give me as much money as I need." *Why, oh why does this have to be so hard?* "What am I going to do?"

"Can you go back to that mean ol' banker?" Fanny asked.

"No, I can't." Allie bowed her head. "I was…rude to him. I told him he was mean."

"Oh, Allie, I can't believe that," chided Mama. "You've never talked disrespectful to any adult before. What got into you?"

"Mama, you have no clue! He called me an idiot fool—"

The sheriff laughed, then Fanny began to chuckle. "And you had the nerve to call that nasty ol' coot a meanie? My, oh my, but you've got some of your mama's Irish in you, young'un. Ol' Sinclair is a meanie, he's always been a meanie—and what's worse—he knows it!"

Allie sighed. "It's not funny. I was so embarrassed. I know I shouldn't have called him that—out loud, at least."

"What's done is done. You'll have to ask him a second time," said Mama. "Maybe the second time's the charm."

"No! I can't. I'm embarrassed. He hates me!"

"No." Mama waved away her protest. "He's got thick skin. He probably laughed—later. I don't believe anyone has ever called him mean before." She smiled and said, "You're right, Allie. What you did was disrespectful, but he was also out of line with his rudeness. If I were you, I'd go back down there. Give it one more shot."

"You've got nothing to lose," Sheriff Anderson said.

"That's the right of it, child. You need the big bucks that only Sinclair can donate," said Fanny. "Who knows? Maybe he'll give in."

"Fanny's right. He also may feel guilty about his rude behavior," Mama interjected. "Give it another try, Allie."

"I've gotta think about this. I don't know if I can do it." Allie shook her head and turned away mumbling, "But what other choices do I have?"

"Not many," replied Mama. "Tomorrow's Friday and the bank closes early but Mr. Sinclair is usually there with his BMW parked in the street until about four o'clock. I'll pick you up here after school and hopefully you can catch him before he leaves for the day."

Allie nodded, grabbed her backpack and headed to her bedroom to bury herself in homework. *Enough already! I don't want to do this anymore. I want to go back to the way things were two weeks ago. Eew! I can't stand Mr. Sinclair!*

Chapter 25

⚜

THE SCHOOL DAY DRAGGED. Allie watched the second hand on the clock in each classroom, her nerves nearly to the breaking point... waiting... waiting... for the time she'd have to face the unlikable Mr. Sinclair. As promised, Mama was ready for her when she got home.

"I know you're dreading this, sweetie, but it's one of those must-do things. You must apologize for being rude to Mr. Sinclair and ask again for his help." Mama draped her arm around Allie's shoulders. "I know you'd rather be—"

"Boiled in oil!" she hurled back. "I'd rather walk the plank! Ooh," she shivered, "he's awful... creepy. I nearly failed my math quiz because I couldn't stop thinking about seeing him again."

"Oh, dear, how terrible," Mama sighed, "this is too hard for you. I've been wondering about this project, all this work, this huge responsibility of getting money. Do you want to forget about the whole thing?"

Allie whirled around. "What? Forget about the donations? Forget about the church? Forget about talking to Mr. Sinclair?"

Mama nodded. "I'm worried about you. This is nearly impossible for a grown person to do, much less a teenager. I admire you so much for taking on this job, but if you want to quit—if you decide it's too much to handle—believe me, Allie, I'll understand. How many times have I bitten off more than I can chew?" Mama's voice dropped. "Well, more times than I can count. I know how it feels to be overburdened with too many projects."

Allie looked at her mother. For the first time perhaps, she felt one bit closer to the woman she'd always lived with, but never knew very well. Today another layer of Mama's hard outer shell had fallen away. "You'd let me quit? Really?"

She nodded. "I would. Sure I would. It might be awkward for you at first. But people would understand. Maybe somebody else would pick up the ball and find the donations to finish the church. But, believe me, Allie, nobody would ever say any of this was easy. Nobody. They would never blame you for halting your involvement."

"You mean, they wouldn't blame me for quitting."

"Okay, yes—for quitting. I know people say to never quit anything and ideally they're right. We shouldn't quit. We should all be determined to succeed in everything we try. Sometimes though, the going just gets too rough and we think we'll go crazy unless we quit. When that happens—or if that happens—then quitting whatever you're doing would make sense. Do you understand? Quitting something, in and of itself, is not always such a terrible thing. It's possible to stop, reposition and then move forward in another direction."

Quitting. Allie had never thought about just walking away. She complained to herself and fussed about all the hard work—but to quit? She would save herself agony, frustration and lots of stress. *Then there's Daniel. Quitting would be hard to explain to Daniel.* He believed in her so much. He'd chosen her. How could she tell him? Surely, he of all people—er, angels would understand. He would know what was in her heart. Surely Daniel would forgive her. Mama would forgive her. Fanny and the sheriff loved her, she knew that. They would forgive her. *What about Buzz? Mmm, he'd be tough. I bet he'd hold a grudge. And Wikki? She would understand, but she wouldn't like it if I quit. She thinks I'm strong. Dependable. Well, what's it going to be?* Now was her chance. She dreaded meeting Mr. Sinclair again. This was the perfect opportunity. *Quit and run the other way!*

After a long moment, Allie caved. "I c-can't, Mama," she agonized. "I can't quit. I don't know if I can do this…this thing with Mr. Sinclair today, but I know I have to keep trying…it may sound weird but I just have to…."

Laura McCall pulled her daughter close, willing all of her strength to be shared in that one brief hug. How proud she was! Allie had moped around the house with a long face and been as cross as a bear since the encounter with Sinclair. "Don't be afraid of failure, sweetie. We're human.

Failure is something we're all guilty of. People who never try anything never succeed at anything." She cupped her daughter's cheek. "As Fanny would say, 'life is all about the tryin'.'"

"That sounds just like Fanny." Allie smiled. "Thanks... thanks for understanding."

"Oh, Allie. I do understand." Mama hugged her again, then grabbed the car keys. "We're alike in many ways, you and I. We're both stubborn, independent and have pride in what we do. Sometimes that pride can get in the way of making good decisions. Try not to let that happen, Allie. Above all, don't ever have too much pride. Learn to ask for help." She paused. "Ready?"

Allie took a deep breath and nodded. *Get this over with....* The conversation that had seemed to take hours had actually lasted only minutes. Allie found herself alone in their car parked on the street, gazing at the bank ahead. Mama had gone inside the newspaper office, but Allie wasn't quite ready to face Mr. Sinclair.

What would she say? Would he yell at her again? *Okay, if he does yell, this will be the last time I ever listen to him. It will be over in a minute.* She could handle one more tongue-lashing. *Mama said I'm strong. I can do this.*

Allie got out of the car just as Miss Daisy and Mr. Sinclair appeared on the sidewalk. They walked around from the back of the bank, Miss Daisy furiously scribbling on a tablet while Mr. Sinclair's mouth moved a hundred miles a minute.

"Mr. Sinclair!" cried Allie on impulse. *"Wait! Mr. Sinclair!"*

Sinclair pivoted, then spied her. "Halt, young lady! Stop right there! Don't come any closer."

Embarrassed, Allie looked around. She'd acted too fast. *Should have waited for him to return to his office.* They weren't even close to the bank now...more like front of Black Jack Morgan's office.

"Please! Mr. Sinclair... I've come... I wanted to apologize for the other day—"

"For what?" He had closed the gap between them. "You didn't intend to call me mean *and* a bully? Fine. Now leave me alone; don't ever come back!"

He stormed back to where Miss Daisy was fumbling with her notebook. She glanced up, throwing Allie an understanding look before turning away.

That went well. Allie slumped down onto a nearby bench. *Failed again. Totally. Now what? There will be no money. No church. No supplies ordered from Curly's lumber yard.* She didn't have to quit. Mr. Sinclair had just made that decision for her. She'd failed. *Ugh! Which was worse? Failing? Quitting? Failing. Failing was far worse....*

"Psst, girl, over here!" The voice seemed to come from nowhere.

Allie swiveled on the bench. A stooped man with gray hair appeared in a tiny doorway.

"Come here!" he beckoned, whispering loudly. "You were talking to Magnus Sinclair just now—this town's idiot fool banker."

"That's what he called me two days ago," Allie scowled. "He called me an idiot fool." She got up and moved closer.

"He needs to learn better manners than to call people names. That's never a good idea. But in the spirit of conversation, I'll tell you my name if you'll tell me yours," he said, holding out his hand, his back resting against the door jam. "I'm Jack Morgan."

Whoa! This was Black Jack Morgan? Allie tentatively reached across to shake his hand. "Uh...Allie McCall."

The town attorney had a reputation of being as mean-spirited and stingy as the banker. Even with his black eye patch, he didn't look as fierce as his reputation. In fact, he looked much older with his walking cane and thinning gray hair.

Now, he gestured for her to come inside his office. "Consider me a friend, Allie McCall. I know your mother. Nice woman. One of the smartest women in this tiny town. Good writer, too. I read her stuff all the time. Here, I'll leave my door propped open a bit. Don't be afraid... never hurts to have a little fresh air."

Allie cautiously peeked inside the spacious room. Surprised, she stepped all the way inside. *A tiny museum! In Friendly!* The dark paneled walls boasted hundreds of books—and, where there weren't books, maps of the world, of oceans and of continents lined every inch of every wall extending upwards to the twelve foot ceilings. Everything looked old and slightly dusty, but smelling of lemon oil and fine wood. Creamy lamplight bathed dozens of war pictures in a delicate glow. Model ships, carefully assembled, held places of honor on perfectly matched tables. *There are six, seven—no, eight of them!* Spanning the length of one wall rested the biggest vessel in the whole office. Naval memorabilia—plaques, diplomas and medals—lined the walls of Jack Morgan's office in the same way that American history filled the halls of the Smithsonian.

"Wow," she exhaled.

"Like it?" He grinned.

She nodded. "It's awesome! I've never—" Allie moved from frame to frame, picture to picture, surveying everything before stopping in front of the huge model ship.

"Know anything about warships, Allie?"

She shook her head.

"I thought not." He chuckled. "Allow me to introduce you to the sloop-of-war, USS *Constellation*. First launched on August 26, 1854, this little lady was the last sailing warship built for the United States Navy and the last naval vessel active during the Civil War." He smiled at his prize. "Is she not beautiful?"

"A sailing ship? It is…she is beautiful." Incredulous, Allie glanced at the older man. "Did you—"

"Did I put her together? Indeed, I did. Took me nearly ten years and boatloads of patience. Had the table custom-built for her, too." He gently stroked the dark wood of the ship and fingered one delicate mast and billowing sail. "I do love my *Connie*."

How cool! What a project…talk about patience. Tiny model pieces filled every nook and cranny, guns, people, props, thousands of them, glued, sewn, strategically placed—and all separately painted. *Omigosh!*

"I usually cover her with a special glass top to keep the dust off. I had just removed it when I overheard some of your conversation outside." His eye patch made his smile crooked but pleasant. "I'm glad you got to see her."

"Me, too." Allie glanced again at the old black and white photos showing uniformed men on ships. "So you were in the Navy?"

"I was," he said, resting his cane against his desk and slowly taking a seat. "Sit down, Allie. You're probably wondering why I asked you in here. Typically, I don't invite anyone inside my office. I use the conference room for meetings, and consider this a private place for me to work. But I thought you might enjoy seeing my most prized possessions," he said, his eye glistening, "and this afternoon I felt like a little company. I'm glad you trusted me enough to come inside and look around."

Allie sat on the other side of his desk, noticing a special frame holding a medal on his credenza. The ribbon was navy blue with a white center stripe. "That medal… behind you. It's beautiful. It looks important."

"Oh, it is… but," he sighed and bundled some papers together on his desk, "that happened a lifetime ago. Today is what's important. This very day. Because today you and I have business to discuss, Allie McCall." He refocused his gaze. "Now tell me what was so all-fired important that you risked humiliation by speaking in the middle of the street to that wickedly mean Sinclair!"

Allie caught the twinkle in his one good eye. *Should I tell him? I met him moments ago. Now he's asking to know my personal business, my personal mortification…my personal failure. This man, Mr. Morgan, is steely tough. Oh, yeah, he must be a great lawyer. Ugh…telling him how I messed up is asking too much.*

"C'mon, Allie, don't be embarrassed. We all make mistakes. Heck, I'm nearly ninety years old. Don't you think I've made one or two in my lifetime?" he chortled. "God only knows how many… and He quit counting long ago."

She softened. "It may sound stupid now, but I visited Mr. Sinclair earlier, asking for a donation to help rebuild the old church. He said the project was probably some stupid idiot's idea and pretty much yelled me right out of his office. I, uh…called him a name…I called him mean. I shouldn't have said that. I came back to apologize today…I thought maybe he would have changed his mind about the donation. You, uh…heard the rest."

"He's still as disagreeable as ever?"

Allie shrugged. "I suppose."

Morgan grinned, the black eye patch stretching the right corner of his mouth. "Tell me more about this church project of yours." He fingered a silver pencil on his desk. "Tell me your plans."

Allie quickly outlined Buzz's involvement, his dad's involvement, how volunteers were working at the church every day, Nate Sims was providing sandwiches and everyone seemed eager. She even told how Fanny and Otis were re-creating the church garden. Mr. Morgan let her talk; she found herself completely exhausted—just from explaining it all!

Only when she fell quiet did he glance up. "That's a great story, Allie. I love the characters, the people in it, all their motivations. It's pure. It's simple. It's well told." He paused. "But now, I want you to tell me why you want to fix the church. There is a reason and I want to know what it is."

"Why?" She pulled back. "Well…because…it needs to be rebuilt."

"No, that's not the reason. I want the real reason. What made you decide to rebuild this church? Why are you—a young teenager, I presume—going to all this trouble? What makes you so determined to get it done?"

She gulped and searched about for a quick exit. He could sense her hesitation…could probably smell her fear. She didn't know him. *I can't trust him. He'll laugh. He has an office lined with medals and awards.* He would know if she lied. He'd see right through her. She needed to get out—now. She rose from the chair. "It's not important."

"Sit down and listen," he said, leveling his gaze. "Please. It's important—to me. I brought you into my private world where I keep my most precious possessions. I can count on one hand the number of people who've seen these things. I already believe in you enough to show you this collection. Now, I want you to share something with me—I want to know your real reason for building this church. You see, I might just be that one benefactor you need."

Her mouth dropped. "Really? You would…could help me?"

"I think so. But I want the truth. So don't be afraid. Look around. It's just you and me, Allie. Be honest."

She stared at the wizened face of Jack Morgan. *He's started twirling that pencil in his hand again. Can I tell him? No nonsense. Just the facts. The old church has already been torn down. There isn't enough money to rebuild anything now. What was one more humiliation?* She had nowhere else to turn.

A familiar voice intruded. *"Tell him, Allie. It's okay."*

Daniel?

"In the spirit! Tell him the truth. He'll understand."

She shifted in her chair. "It's because of Daniel. It was Daniel who told…er, asked me to build it."

"Daniel's your friend?"

She nodded, leaning forward. "He's wonderful. He's my friend, he's, well, actually, he's my…my angel." She paused. "Please don't laugh—"

Morgan's pencil hit the desk with a thud. His face froze for a moment. "And you saw him…this Daniel?" Morgan glanced up from beneath one hooded brow. "You actually spoke to him?"

"Yes…several times. He says an Earth form requires so much energy that he can't always, well, materialize. Now when we talk, I hear him through…my mind."

Morgan nodded slowly, digesting this news. "And…you still talk to Daniel? You two communicate?"

Allie smiled. "Yes, but not every day. He says angels are busy, so—yeah, I'm sure he's busy."

Morgan cocked his head. "At least you're honest." He glanced up at the ceiling and rocked back in his chair, lacing his fingers behind his head. "When I heard people talking about how you wanted to rebuild that old church, I wondered why…what your motivation was in tackling such a big job. I enjoy understanding people's motivations." He glanced at her briefly, "but this… this angel story—"

"I knew it! I knew you'd think I was crazy," Allie interrupted, "I shouldn't have told you. I'm sorry, Mr. Morgan. I'll get my backpack. I just thought—"

He moved to stop her. "It does sound… unbelievable."

"I know! That's why I haven't told anybody but my family and closest friends. You… you wanted to know. And, besides, Daniel said I should tell you."

He sighed. "Daniel told you to tell me."

"Well, yes, he did."

Morgan leaned back again in his chair. "Well, if Daniel told you, then maybe I've finally found someone who might understand." He stared up at the ceiling for a long moment, catching and releasing his bottom lip as he pondered. "There's really no use in not telling you. After all, Daniel might expect it…. if, indeed Daniel does exist…." He lowered his gaze at her. "Remember that other lifetime I was telling you about? My story happened in what seemed like a split second…."

He rocked forward and faced her. "Honestly? My story is as unbelievable as yours. Even now, I wonder if it ever happened… it was during the war…I was a cocky twenty-two-year-old with a big attitude. A Navy Lieutenant JG stationed aboard a sub-chaser several hundred miles off the Hawaiian coastline. I had just been installed as the executive officer since our commander lay in sick bay with an intestinal virus. So I wasn't at all ready for the sudden *whoosh* of torpedoes. Men scattered. An enemy midget sub had attacked us out of nowhere. Another explosion and *boom!* A dozen sailors flew up and over the sides of the ship to sink beneath the water. Another hit, only this time more solid and I was airborne, my head and shoulders cracking against the ship's forward gun mount. I hit that icy water and sank fast, conscious enough to know I was facing sure death. I told myself to swim, to use my arms. I was young, healthy, and an excellent swimmer, but my arms and legs were of no use. I dropped below the fish, below the plants and the seaweed, until the water grew murky, muddy, black as pitch. I kept telling myself it was *not* my time to die! I envisioned my future—I had men to save, battles to fight, ships to command, my whole life ahead of me…a million thoughts raced through my head. Then *she* appeared."

Morgan caught his breath and slowly exhaled. "A woman …at those incredible depths… pale and fragile, a cloud of silver hair floating all around her. I stared as she held out her hand, the phrase 'not yet' running through my brain. She nodded as though understanding. 'Help…' I begged, now trying to reach out, desperate to use my limp arms. My whole body—lifeless. My lungs collapsed. My eyes closed. The next moment she had my hand. Her fingers warm and safe. Mine felt cold by comparison. She pulled on my arm. 'Come and live,' she whispered. Those words stirred some energy back into me. In the dark recesses of the ocean I was saved by a miracle. Was she an angel? I thought about it. She had to be. Magnificent. A radiant angel whose face I'll never forget." Morgan blinked.

Allie reached out to him. "Mr. Morgan—"

He waved her away. "I know it sounds crazy." His voice cracked. "Can you… believe me?"

"Of course I can. I do believe you!"

"Good." He heaved a heavy sigh, "because I don't think I've told five people that story besides my wife, God rest her soul, and my grown sons. I knew people would make fun of me. They'd tell me it was my imagination, the shock of hitting my head that made me hallucinate…." He scowled, still reflecting. "But I know what happened. I also know it was scientifically impossible for me to have survived that plunge into the ocean. As somebody who's always believed in science, I know I faced death head-on that day and I should have died. I experienced the suffocation… the moment of my last breath. Yet that woman…whoever she was, that angel perhaps…pulled me up so fast from rock bottom in the blink of an eye, my body popped up sputtering and spewing water amid a dozen of my ship's lifeboats.

"Sure enough, my men had chased off the sub with enough firepower to light up Las Vegas. Every sailor who had gone overboard had somehow made it safely to the surface. We had minimal damage done to our ship, which was also unbelievable. It was as if the whole incident was never supposed to happen." He gripped his forehead. "I couldn't get the story out of my head. I stayed in sick bay until I got stateside and doctors were able to operate on my shoulders and neck….I'm so lucky I was able to walk again. In the beginning, they said I'd be paralyzed. It would have been terrible for me to be confined to a wheelchair all those years. I dreaded thinking about it."

Wikki. Allie's heart softened. "I'm so glad your story had a happy ending," she whispered.

"And yours must, too. Naturally, I ask you to keep my story private as I will yours."

"Yes, sir, I will and thank you."

"And I'm feeling generous today. Not only do I detest Mangus Sinclair for refusing me a loan when I moved here ten years ago, but I'm also happy to report that, if I wanted to, I could buy his bank outright. Nothing gives me more satisfaction." Mr. Morgan sat up straight. "And because Sinclair was so mean to you—yes, you were right, he is mean—I'm going to call up Curly and tell him I will personally pay those invoices for your building supplies."

She gasped. "But, Mr. Morgan! It'll be too much money! We need siding, air conditioning, light fixtures—"

"Very well." He waved her away. "I'll get a list from Curly. I'll let him know I'm donating to this project. The main thing is that I want you to work hard in school, get more donations from that feed store across the street and your mother's newspaper, everybody needs to contribute to this," he chuckled, "and to make it extra hard for them to refuse, tell everybody you meet that you got a hefty donation from Black Jack Morgan. See how much money they'll hand over then!

"Oh, and I'm going to ask a favor, Allie. I want you to... thank Daniel for me," he said, "would you do that? I've been thanking God all these years, but it wouldn't hurt to thank somebody who serves Him on the front line, now would it?"

Allie smiled. For his story, for his generosity, for his gratitude, she wanted to rush over and give Mr. Morgan a giant hug.

"Allie, tell him he's welcome. We've heard his prayers."

Daniel?

"Tell him McGuinty ended up with ten kids. He'll understand."

"Uh, Mr. Morgan? Daniel wanted me to tell you that they've heard your prayers and you're welcome—and that—McGuinty ended up with ten kids—"

Morgan spit and sputtered before belting out a laugh. "McGuinty? Goodness knows, I haven't heard his name in sixty-some-odd years! What a great guy! He was the petty officer onboard that ship. His wife was pregnant when we deployed and the whole crew cheered when we got word she delivered their first baby. Had a real party that day. Our chief cook made a huge cake," a faraway look gathered in his eyes, "best cake ever." His gaze shifted back to Allie. "So… this Daniel. He really does exist."

She nodded.

"Extraordinary…."

"Yoo-hoo! Hel-lo?" came a tiny voice from the entryway. "Allie, are you in here?"

Allie spun around to see Mama walking through the door. "Sweetie, I've looked everywhere for you…the bank, the feed store. I never realized… Mr. Morgan, it's nice to see you. My, what a gorgeous office!" No one was immune to the magic of Mr. Morgan's museum. "Oh, Allie, I know he's been telling you fabulous stories. Mr. Morgan, you were a captain in the Navy?" Mama was speed-reading all his diplomas and plaques. She even picked up the small frame on his credenza and gasped, "You were awarded the Navy Cross?"

He smiled at Allie and winked. "Yes, ma'am. That particular battle happened some years after my near-death experience. I was just telling your daughter about it."

"For heaven's sake, you're quite the celebrity. These ships—"

"They're models, ma'am, and yes, I built them. It's a hobby. Gets me away from these dry, dusty law books."

Allie laughed. For once, Mama seemed flummoxed. Couldn't find a word to say that Mr. Morgan couldn't answer with a better rebuttal.

Mama smiled uneasily. "It's getting late. Come along, dear, we'd better let Mr. Morgan get back to his work. Thank you again—"

"Wait! Mama, listen; Mr. Morgan is going to donate a lot of money to help rebuild the church."

She hesitated. "Really?"

Allie nodded. "He also wants to make sure we spread the word that donations—"

"Are pouring in from everywhere," he interjected. "Can you help do that, Mrs. McCall? I want to make sure that old Sinclair knows that I'm supporting Allie's project. It will eat him alive," he chuckled. "Sinclair thinks I'm the most miserly person on this planet. I can't wait to see what he'll do when he learns the news." He gestured to Allie. "I bet he donates double what I'm donating. We'll wait and see, eh?"

Allie grinned. *Fabulous!*

"Honey, I'm going to grab my purse from the office and meet you at the car." Mama shook hands with Mr. Morgan. "It was good to see you again and thanks for spending time with Allie."

"The pleasure was all mine, Mrs. McCall. She's a remarkable young lady."

Allie beamed under his approving gaze as her mother left.

"She's lucky to have you," he said, fingering the cane next to his desk. "I never had a daughter. I've always missed that. It's just me, this office and my ships for company. My sister doesn't live far from here, but, other than that, my sons and their families are scattered across the country."

Allie, tell him not to worry about being alone. He saved the lives of thirty-five men. Their families thank him every day. Their grandchildren and great-grandchildren thank him, too.

She blinked at the message. "Mr. Morgan? Daniel just told me that you saved the lives of thirty-five men. He wants you to know that they thank you every day. Their grandchildren and great-grandchildren thank you."

His mouth sagged. "He...Daniel said this?"

"And the medal?" she pressed. "Is that why you were awarded Navy Cross?"

He nodded. "Another battle...years later. The Korean War. A rescue at sea. Awful conditions. So many men died. Lost my eye that day. Save a life; lose an eye. At the time, it seemed like an even exchange."

"No, it was a great sacrifice." Allie laid a hand on his arm. "In the end, you saved the lives of thirty-five men. That's why you were saved by the angel. You had to live in order to save. That was the even exchange."

Chapter 26

❦

SATURDAY, SEPTEMBER 25

ALLIE PEEKED AT the illuminated dial. *Eight o'clock?* Too early to get out of bed. Yet the delightful aroma of breakfast tickled her nose. Groggily, she slipped on some socks beneath her pajamas.

"Ms. Fanny?" she called out, knowing that no one else would be cooking.

"Hey, young 'un! I couldn't sleep. I've got so much work to do at the garden today. My mind was full of people to meet and seeds to order...I'm as jumpy as a long-tailed cat 'neath a rockin' chair." She cracked a couple of eggs in the skillet. "You sure are sleepin' late."

Allie smiled as she put bread in the toaster. "Fanny, anytime after four o'clock in the morning is late *to you.*"

"Ha! No sense wastin' time by layin' up in bed all day." She laid two perfectly cooked eggs on a plate for Allie. "What are you up to today?"

"I'm going to ask Mama to take me by Curly's lumberyard. I need to check on some supplies." Allie set silverware on the table. "You'll never guess who's going to donate money—Black Jack Morgan!"

"Oops!" Fanny dropped the serving spoon with a clank on the floor. "No way!" she exclaimed, retrieving it. "That ol' hermit?"

"Allie, are you awake?" Mama came in with rumpled hair and two layers of pajamas. She yawned, then mumbled, "Hi, Fanny. What have I missed?"

"Not much, just your coffee," Fanny said, pushing a cup in her direction. "Allie wants to drive up to Curly's lumber to check on—"

"Supplies. Mr. Morgan's supposed to have faxed Mr. Curly a letter saying that he'll be donating money."

Mama added a spoonful of sugar to her coffee and stirred. "Sure, we can do that. There's a big crew of volunteers working today at the church." She glanced at Fanny. "I understand you've got a meeting about the garden, too.

"That I do. Been up since before the rooster crowed, wringing my hands and pacing the floor."

"What are you nervous about?"

Fanny harrumphed. "I ain't never run nothing in my whole life. Don't know the first thing about—"

"You've run a kitchen!" Allie interjected. "You've run this family... gotten us to school on time and fed every morning and every night for nearly a week."

"You sure have, Fanny, and we love you for it." Laura took another sip of coffee. "I'll be there to help if you need anything."

"Ya' will? Well, in that case, I think I'll cook me another breakfast just to celebrate. I hate to see people eatin' alone, don't y'all?"

Mama and Allie blinked as Fanny cracked three extra eggs into the skillet.

Two HOURS LATER, Curly had Mama, Fanny and Allie barricaded inside his tiny office.

"I just wanted to know if you got the fax from Mr. Morgan," Allie repeated.

"Shh-hh," Curly said, gesturing. "Talk soft. It's Saturday and there's twenty customers out yonder picking up supplies. What we're doin' in here ain't nobody's business."

The three women exchanged puzzled glances.

"Well?" Allie pressed.

"I got it!" He handed the letter to Allie.

She gasped. "Omigosh! It says that Mr. Morgan will donate $20,000 for the building materials!"

"What?" Mama grabbed the letter. "For heaven's sake, she's right. Fanny, take a look."

"Now, y'all wait a minute," Curly said, fighting to get the paper back. "This here is Allie's business with Mr. Morgan."

"I know what it is," Fanny grumbled. "I read it before you grabbed it out of my hand, Curly Lively."

"Why all the secrecy?" Allie asked.

"Because Mr. Morgan's been doing business with me for years."

" Morgan, that ol' miser? He *buys* stuff?" Fanny asked.

"No...he don't buy stuff," Curly retorted, filing the letter. "He *donates.*"

"He donates?" Mama repeated. "How does he do that?"

"The same way everybody does. He gives money to people." Curly rolled his eyes. "Friendly is so full of gossipmongers that people like Mr. Morgan don't want to contribute to anything. The big secret here is that Mr. Morgan is one of the biggest donors within a hundred miles. Do you really think I can afford to sponsor ten Little League teams a year on what I make at this lumberyard? Heck no! It's Mr. Morgan who's sponsoring nine of them teams every year. He hates to say no to kids raisin' money for their projects, so he has me donate to 'em under my name. That'a way people won't be botherin' him all day long." Curly glanced from one female to the next. "Y'all can close your mouths now. I figured that news'd put a wrinkle in your britches." He chortled and turned back to Allie. "What I want now is a list of supplies that Buzz and Todd Madison are gonna need. I wanna place the order first thing Monday morning to keep those volunteers working. Can you get me that list?"

Allie found her voice. "Y-yes, sir."

"Good. Mr. Morgan would appreciate it if y'all wouldn't share any of the information we talked about today. I consider it top secret," Curly said. "He puts a lot of confidence in me to handle his donations. I'd hate to disappoint him."

"Absolutely," Mama replied.

"My lips are sealed," said Fanny.

They all shook hands like they were concluding a business deal before the three ladies climbed into the car.

"My, my, this whole town gets more peculiar everyday." Fanny sighed. "Just when you think you've got this world figured out, something hits you broadside. I could'a sworn Black Jack Morgan was just a slimy old recluse."

Mama turned the key in the ignition. "He fooled me, too. Do you know he was awarded the Navy Cross?"

"Oh, Lordy, so he now goes from good to *gooder*?" Fanny rubbed her forehead. "I feel a migraine coming on. I've misjudged that man somethin' terrible."

ALLIE WATCHED FROM a few yards away, hearing laughter as the volunteer crowd finished their lunch. One by one they picked up boards, hammers and nails and returned to their work. *Making progress,* she thought, noticing how the walls were in place and the outline was taking shape. Mama and Fanny had assembled the garden volunteers for their meeting. She was disappointed not to see Buzz today, but he and Mr. Madison had gone to pick up more supplies for the coming week's work.

"*I want you to meet him, Allie.*"

"Daniel! You scared me!"

"*I usually have that effect on people.*"

"Oh, you know what I mean. It's just that… you pop into my head suddenly. I'm not always ready."

"*Ready now? Good. I want you to meet him—Jonas Smiley. He was the pastor here over sixty years ago.*"

"Sixty years? Jeez, that's forever ago. Is he even alive?"

"*Believe me, sixty years is not forever. And…I would know if he were dead.*"

"Uh, that's true. Do you know where he is?"

"*His nephew is Walter Hagen, the pastor of the United Methodist Church. You and your family have been there several times.*"

"C'mon, Daniel, just tell me where Jonas Smiley is."

"*You find him.*"

"Why?"

"*I want Pastor Jonas to deliver the inaugural sermon. It's important to the reestablishing of the church in the community. He must be here.*"

"Really, but why?"

"*Oh, Allie, don't keep asking questions. You're doing great, by the way. However, I would consider it a personal favor if you were to talk to him.*"

"Oh, all right. There's no use arguing with you."

"*No, there's no use arguing with me. I always win.*"

She had to smile at the chuckle in his voice. *Jeez. Another assignment. Maybe it won't be too hard.*

A sudden flurry of activity behind Nate Sims's café caught her attention.

"Where is she!" bellowed a furious Sinclair, pushing aside young and old, as he stormed through the crowd. "I need to find that McCall girl right now!"

Allie cringed at the sound of his voice, but her mama met him head-on.

"You're looking for my daughter, Mr. Sinclair? Then I suggest you lower your voice. Adopt a more civil tone if you wish to speak to her."

Go, Mama! Allie saw Sinclair glance up toward where she was standing. *I've been found! Oh, whew, mama's following him.*

"Allie…yes, it's good to see you," he said, making his way up the hill.

"What is it you want, Mr. Sinclair?" Mama moved to stand beside Allie. "What could you possibly want with my daughter?"

"Is it true that Black Jack Morgan donated money to this church project?"

Allie glanced at Mama, who nodded, "Go ahead. Tell him."

"Y-yes, sir, he did," Allie stumbled.

Sinclair's eyes narrowed. "How much? How much did that old curmudgeon donate?"

Allie and Mama swapped glances. "We've been asked not to reveal the exact amount," Allie replied.

"Secrets. More of his little secrets." Sinclair clenched his fist. "Curley Lively won't tell me. Now you won't tell me. I bet Morgan's paying for all this—this lumber and materials." Furious and red-faced, Sinclair turned to Allie. "He won't do this to me, won't humiliate me in my town. I'm ready to double what he donated."

"Just like that?" Mama asked coolly. "You're ready to double his donation without knowing the amount?"

Sinclair straightened, his head high. "I just said so, didn't I? You get with Morgan. Have him come to my office Monday morning at ten o'clock sharp. We'll go over the details—and yes, I'm willing to double his donation. In fact, I'll even pledge to pay the monthly bills for the first twenty-four months this church is operational."

Allie gasped. "Thank you, Mr. Sinclair."

He looked down his nose at her. "You're intolerably persistent, young lady." He turned on his heel and left.

"Whoa," Mama breathed. "What a disagreeable man."

"I tried to tell you." Then Allie brightened. "But we got the money, didn't we? Now we can finish the church."

Her mother pondered the question. "Maybe. Perhaps. I hope it will be enough money."

"Should we ask Mr. Curly and Mr. Madison?"

"That's exactly who we'll have to ask."

IN A TRANCE, Allie stared at her dinner plate. Ben had been excused and was reading in his room. Mama was clearing off the table.

"You've chased those peas around your plate for the past fifteen minutes, Allie. What's bothering you? You hardly spoke at dinner." Mama soaped up the dishes, then paused, setting down the dishrag.

"I know it was a big day. Lots of things happened. Fanny's got her garden started and loads of people to help her. She found out today just how many neighbors will need food from our community garden."

"Oh, yeah?" Fanny's name snapped Allie from her reverie. "Is she happy? She was so worried this morning."

Mama wiped down the old countertop. "I think she's really happy. Did she tell you I'm the treasurer?"

"She did!" Allie grinned. "That's great!"

Mama giggled and turned back to wash the dishes. "Believe me, Fanny has an entire board of directors eager to help her. She's so hardworking. Otis was there; he said he was going to plow up another acre just to have enough room to plant all the vegetables they want to grow."

"I'm glad."

"Me, too." Mama dried her hands on a nearby dishtowel and sat down at the table. "What were you thinking about?"

"Lots of things—Mr. Sinclair's donation, Mr. Morgan's donation, if there's enough money. What happens if there's not..."

"I called Mr. Morgan this afternoon as Mr. Sinclair asked. Those two will meet at the bank Monday to discuss their respective donations. I wouldn't even like to be a fly on the wall in Sinclair's office." Mama harrumphed. "Too dangerous with those two titans squaring off."

"Thanks for helping me with that." Allie folded her hands on the table. "Then there's Daniel...today he told me I need to find Pastor Jonas Smiley. He wants Pastor Jonas to deliver the first sermon...." Allie's voice trailed off as she suddenly felt drained. "I feel so tired, Mama. I don't know how to find this man."

She covered Allie's hand. "Now you're talking about something I can help you with. I happen to know that Walter Hagen is Jonas's nephew."

"That's what Daniel said."

Mama smiled. "I also know that Pastor Hagen is delivering the sermon tomorrow at the Methodist church. Do you want to go?"

"Really? You'd do that for me? You'd...go...to church?"

"For you, Allie, I'd do practically anything. I know I haven't been to church in a long time…I've been sad since your daddy died. But sure, we can go. Let's get a good night's sleep and make the early service, okay?"

Chapter 27

❧

AFTER THE SERMON, Allie searched high and low for Pastor Hagen. The departing crowd had dispersed by the time she stumbled into the church office. A lady stood in front of a copy machine with a handful of kids' coloring sheets.

"Can I help you?" she asked, turning to Allie. "There's usually no one in the office during services on Sunday."

"I was looking for Pastor Hagen. I can't find him anywhere. Is he... er, gone?"

"I heard he was called away for a minute. I'm sure he'll be back in time for the next service."

"Oh." Allie felt deflated. "I was—"

"What's your name? I'm Bethany Wilkes. I work in the toddler room."

"I'm Allie McCall."

"It's nice to meet you, Allie. If you'd like to leave him a note there on the desk, I'll make sure he gets it."

Allie stared at the pen and paper. *Should I just write my name and phone number? He wouldn't know me. And it isn't an emergency. But I have to find Pastor Jonas.*

She picked up the pen and took a gamble. In her best cursive, she invited both pastors to attend the potluck supper at the church construction site tomorrow. *There. That should do it. Maybe they'll be interested and come.*

Moments later she met Ben and Mama at the car. "Well, did you talk to Pastor Hagen?" Mama asked.

"No. A lady named Bethany Wilkes said he was called away." Allie stared out of the window as they made their way out of the church parking lot. "The potluck is still on at the church tomorrow, isn't it?"

"Uh-huh. And I'm glad you mentioned that. I've got to put a casserole together tonight."

Allie brightened. "You're going to cook? Really?"

"I am," Mama returned deliberately. "But don't either of you get too excited. It's been years since I've cooked and I bet I won't be any good at it."

ALLIE NEARLY SLAMMED into her mother as she raced through her front door on Monday after school. "You're home early."

Mama grabbed her forehead. "Omigosh, Allie, you have no idea!" She twirled around and plunged both hands into her purse. "I've got so much stuff," she said, rifling through papers, "I-I don't know where to start."

Mama frazzled? This had to be a first. "Here, sit down," Allie said, taking her mother's hand. "You look like you're losing it." She led her to the sofa. "What happened?"

Mama sank into the cushions and raked her fingers through her hair. "You have no idea! I've just come from Sinclair's office—Oh!—and you think you had it bad with that man. I thought I was going to have to sign my life away. Or strangle him, whichever came first." She let out a long sigh. "He is positively the worst, most disagreeable man I have ever met in... my... life!" She rubbed her arms up and down. "I swear, Allie, I can't stop trembling. That man—"

"Mama, how awful." Allie edged closer. "What did he do?"

"You know that he and Morgan met this morning at the bank to discuss their separate donations. Okay, fine, that happened. Then, after lunch, Sinclair called me on the phone. He asked me to stop by because he wanted to give me a letter of credit we—well, you and Mr. Madison—could use for buying supplies. Okay, sure, fine. I met with him...and then he wanted me to agree to be the banker for the church project. He wants a monthly accounting, showing how his donations are being spent, and on and on.

"I explained I wasn't an accountant. I would do the best I could, provide him the information he asked. But no! That wasn't good enough for Mr. Sinclair. We went round and round for a good thirty minutes about how he wanted the information precisely prepared and given to him each month." Mama finally exhaled. "I can feel my blood pressure dropping just now, thank heavens—and our conversation was an hour ago."

She suddenly stood up. "I'm okay, Allie. I can do what he asks. But I'm here to say that I sure wish Friendly had another bank in town because Sinclair needs a little competition so he'll lighten up. Not everyone needs to be clobbered over the head and made to behave! Seriously, if we didn't need this donation money so badly I would have verbally left him standing in the dust today."

She unbuttoned her suit jacket and forced a small smile. "We don't need to leave for another hour. And thank goodness my casserole is made. Right now, I think I hear a hot bath calling my name. It's time to refresh myself after my Sinclair encounter." Mama snatched up her jacket and called out to Allie from the hallway. "Maybe I'll just email him those reports. That way I won't have to cross the street and waste all my *energy!*"

Allie sat alone on the sofa, her shoulders shaking from holding in her laughter. She could just visualize mama butting heads with Mr. Sinclair. Ooh, that thirty-minute brawl must have been a doozie… She could have sold tickets! While probably defenseless against mama's full-blown temper, Sinclair seemed to win the day. Mama must have given in—sacrificing a victory to the more important quest of getting the donation money. *Bravo! Think I'll stay on Mama's team….*

The church parking area was packed with cars at five o'clock that afternoon. *Amazing.* It had only been seven days since the town volunteers had agreed to begin the reconstruction and already so much had been accomplished.

She said hello to Buzz, shook hands again with his parents and gave Fanny a quick hug. Folks busily wandered in and out of the church building, oohing and aahing, laughing and happy. But Allie held back, wanting to step inside alone. Approaching slowly, she saw that the door frame was ready to accommodate a set of double front doors. The flooring was in, and the framing and roofing completed.

Allie stepped over to inspect the four window openings on either side of the small sanctuary, thinking about the cross breeze on Sunday mornings in years past. Thank goodness Mr. Sinclair's donation would help buy all the windows needed for the church.

"Do you like?"

"Daniel?" she whispered, not really surprised by his presence today.

"*In the spirit.*" His twinkly laugh seemed to bounce off the bare wooden floor. "*I like it very much. Thank you, Allie, for your help. What a wonderful tribute. Such a special church to hold a hardworking and dedicated congregation. And, of course, a special window.*"

Ah, the window. Allie looked at the back of the church and the large, refrigerator-sized opening covered with plywood.

Is it the right size?

"*It's perfect.*"

You sound excited. I've never heard you so excited.

"*You have no idea how excited I am. My sole purpose is to complete this project and serve my Lord.*"

Allie turned to see Mr. Madison smiling in the doorway. "D'you like it?" he asked.

"I love it," Allie answered. "It's going to be beautiful. Y'all have done a great job."

She felt Daniel brush against her shoulder.

"*Tell him there will be a church bell. You'll need to order one. Put it on your list.*"

A church bell? "Uh, yes…and, Mr. Madison, there will also be a church bell."

Madison rubbed his chin. "A bell? We didn't allow for a steeple in the plans. I suppose we could always…"

"*Tell him the bell will stand in the front churchyard.*"

"Mr. Madison, the bell will stand in the front yard of the church. It won't, uh, we won't need a steeple…for the bell."

"Well, sure, we can do that. Oh, and, Allie, now that the roof and exterior are completed, we'll get the windows installed and sheet rock up this week. After that we'll stain and varnish the hardwoods and front doors before hanging them."

She smiled her thanks and nodded, not exactly sure what she'd just agreed to. Fanny suddenly called out, "Grab yourself a plate, young 'un. There's lots of great food over here. Your mama's casserole is wonderful. I brought my beef tips and a fair-to-middlin' if-I-say-so-myself apple pie."

Moments later Allie had wolfed down a big piece of that very pie, so delicious that she wanted to lick the juice from her lips, but decided it was better manners to use her napkin. "Fanny, it's wonderful, as usual," she said, feeling full and sleepy. Allie liked praising Fanny's cooking, even though Fanny probably knew she made the best pies in the five counties.

"Thank you, dear. Even I agree—this one is kinda tasty."

"Do you remember Pastor Jonas Smiley?" Allie asked, hoping no one could hear her off-the-wall question. Maybe Fanny could help track him down just in case he didn't show up today.

Fanny swiveled around so fast that she nearly bumped into Allie's pie plate. "Pastor Jonas? Why, Lord a'mercy, a'course I remember Pastor Jonas. He's the one who baptized me an' Maggie." Fanny chuckled until her shoulders shook. "It was just awful. Me an' Maggie were baptized the same day. You should'a seen us. There was Nate Sims in the church with his spit-wad thrower and Maggie an' me couldn't have been more'n six years old, standing tall and skinny as pine trees in Buster Hightower's cattle trough that they'd had to bring inside the church 'cuz it was pouring down buckets outside. We couldn't get baptized outdoors unless every person in the congregation got soaked to the skin. It was way too cold for us all to get soaked to the skin. So, just Maggie 'n me got soaked to the skin.

"Pastor Jonas got the biggest kick out of it when Buster poured two heaping ice cold pails of water over each of us. The wetter we got, he said, the better our chances of gettin' into Heaven. Plus, the icy water would keep the Devil away." Fanny mumbled in a faraway voice. "Hope Buster's cattle didn't miss their waterin' trough too much that day."

Allie smiled. "Do you know where Pastor Jonas is right now?"

Fanny glanced up. "Shoot, child. He's probably dead and buried."

"No, he's not. Daniel wants me to find him."

"Well, I'll be," she whispered. "If Daniel's an angel, why in blue blazes don't he know where the man is? Oh! I really didn't mean to say 'blue blazes'. I hope God and Daniel forgives me on that one."

"Both Daniel and Mama said that Walter Hagen was Pastor Jonas's nephew."

"What? I never knew that. Walter Hagen is the one with the real pretty church up yonder on the Bullard highway."

"I know. We went to services yesterday, but then Pastor Hagen was called away. I never got to talk to him."

"So there ain't no problem with finding young Walter, who I guess ain't so young anymore." Fanny pondered a moment. "Why all the questions, child?"

"I have to find Pastor Jonas. He's supposed to give the inaugural sermon."

"Ah!" Fanny finished the last bite of her pie. "Inaugural sermon. If that don't beat all. Well, it would be easy enough to phone Pastor Hagen, but you might want to ask him in person about his uncle. Let him know why you need to talk to him. And you'd better talk to your mama, too, if you need to go back to that church up yonder. My golf cart won't make it on one battery pack," she said with a wink.

Over at the dessert table, Buzz watched his father take a piece of Fanny's apple pie. After he enjoyed a bite, he looked at his son.

"Allie told me there's a guy named Daniel making the glass for that window opening. Do you know him? I hope he's reliable and gets the size right."

"Daniel?" Buzz narrowed his eyes, curious about this man's relationship to Allie. "No, I don't know him. What's his last name?"

"Dunno. Hard to pronounce, she said. Lots of consonants. Thought you might have heard of him."

No ONE NOTICED the black sedan pull to a stop near the sidewalk. A middle-aged man stepped from behind the wheel. Moments later, he helped an older gentleman exit the car before both made their way carefully up the broken walkway toward the church.

"What do you think of it, Uncle Jonas? I've heard the church is being completely rebuilt."

The older man stopped to straighten his shoulders as he peered for a better look. "Lots of memories here, Walter. I still can't believe all this construction." A gust of wind ruffled Pastor Jonas's thin, white hair as his voice trembled. "It's a miracle, a pure miracle, that's what I think. I can't believe so many townspeople came together to put in the energy, especially after so many years."

Pastor Hagen helped steady his uncle's cane. "Like I mentioned earlier, my congregation told me it was a young girl who started the whole thing... only fifteen years old. She came to the church office yesterday after the early service to talk to me. But that's when you took that fall and the nursing home called. So I missed the opportunity to meet young Allie McCall. But I'm glad she left the invitation to this potluck. She specifically wanted me to bring you."

"Happy that you did, Walter."

"And I'm relieved you're feeling better. Anyway, several of our church members are helping with Allie's church project. She's gotten dozens of volunteers. Seems that people are happy to see the old become new again."

Pastor Jonas kept his eyes on his feet as he carefully placed one foot in front of the other. "Then she's the girl I want to meet. Do you think they'll fix this crummy brick walkway? God knows that would be a blessing. Heckfire, I'll even pay for it. I'm going to fall flat on my face any minute."

Mama first spied the duo and rushed over to greet them. Guiding them to the picnic tables, she cornered Allie first. "It's Pastor Jonas Smiley and his nephew, Pastor Walter Hagen, of the United Methodist Church. Gentlemen, this is my daughter, Allie. Pastor Jonas was once the pastor here. They said you invited them today?" Mama flashed Allie a questioning glance. Allie promptly ignored it.

So this was Pastor Jonas. Alive and in person. Allie smiled and extended her hand.

Pastor Jonas shook it gently. "I'm glad to meet you, Allie. I wanted to meet the person who was in charge of rebuilding my church."

Then it was Pastor Hagen's turn. "It's a pleasure, Allie," he said. "You've done a fantastic job. It looks splendid."

"Pastor Hagen," she remarked softly, "wow, I never thought I'd meet either of you. Thank you so much for coming. Pastor Jonas, I'm so happy you're here."

He chuckled, then wheezed and coughed.

"Well, young lady, I'm here—today at least, but I don't know about tomorrow. At ninety years old, every day counts! My cough isn't any better, so I spend most days cooped up like a caged bird in my nursing home. But here," he said, glancing around with a slight smile, "I feel free and happy. I love that you are bringing the old garden back to life. I can smell the freshly turned soil; you've tilled the rows already. My, my." *Did he tear up at the unexpected gust of wind?* "I have such great memories of this church and garden." His glance slowly traveled back to Allie. He took her hand again and patted it. "Thank you, Allie. Thank you so much."

"It wasn't me, Pastor Jonas. The people here are the workers."

"Ah," his smile widened, "spoken like a true leader."

"Do you want to go inside? It's not completed. You could give me some ideas... ways to improve—"

"Absolutely," he interrupted, burying his cane in the grass while turning to walk. "Walter and I want to see everything."

"We'll have the cross reconstructed," she said.

"Good. Excellent idea. Keep the old one, though. It was the reason those settlers built the church on this very land... they saw that old cross."

Pastor Jonas and Allie slowly walked toward the church as Walter waved for them to go on without him. Clearly, he wanted to shake hands and reunite with old friends.

"We'll have a church bell. Just not in a tower. It'll stand in the front yard of the church."

Moments later Pastor Jonas was standing next to the old cross while trying to visualize the church bell.

"Splendid idea. You can ring the bell on Sundays and other special occasions. You can ring it in case of town emergencies. I'm sure the council could vote on something like that."

"Wow, that sounds great!" Allie glanced around, making sure nobody was within hearing distance. "There's… there's one more thing…it's really important." She bit down on her bottom lip. "Could you preach…er, deliver the sermon?" She took a deep breath and started over. "Pastor Jonas, would you deliver the first sermon? Please?"

Pastor Jonas shook his head. "Allie, you're very kind to offer. But I can hardly stand up straight anymore. I can barely hobble with my cane. My voice cracks and most days I'm hoarse. No, child, you'll need to ask my nephew, Walter. I'm sure he would agree to do it."

Allie's heart raced. "Oh, but Pastor Jonas. It must be you. I'm sure that your nephew gives a fine sermon, but…er, it… it must be you who gives the first one."

Pastor Jonas gave Allie a thoughtful glance. Heavy lines circled his tired eyes and a thin lock of white hair draped across his forehead. He managed a slight smile.

"Tell you what, young lady. Trot over to where my nephew is standing and tell him about this plan of yours. He'd be the one who would have to drive me up here. If he agrees, then I'm all yours. When you come back with his answer, you can finish showing me around. Is it a deal?"

Allie straightened up to her full height. "Yes, sir, it's a deal!"

She swiveled on one foot and began to gallop across the hillside to where Pastor Hagen stood with friends. Pausing to glance behind her, Allie came to a complete stop. *Daniel! What was he doing here? And in person.* Allie couldn't believe her eyes. Pastor Jonas was talking to Daniel. Allie gazed in amazement.

Daniel looked so handsome in his trademark blue T-shirt and blue jeans, his short silver hair sticking up in every direction, just as she remembered. If she moved one inch, would he disappear? Allie decided to watch. She hadn't seen him in so long. And yet, she wanted to argue with him every time they talked. *Stupid. I'm so stupid. How could I ever think of arguing with Daniel?*

At that moment he turned, saw her and winked. *Like Buzz. Daniel winked at her just like Buzz in English class.* Allie couldn't suppress a giggle. *Daniel was too handsome for his own good. Like Buzz. Too handsome for his own good, too.*

Allie watched Daniel turn back to Pastor Jonas. The two men seemed deep in conversation; Daniel did most of the talking while Pastor Jonas nodded now and again. Anybody who saw them might assume Pastor Jonas was merely staring at the church in front of him, when actually he was staring right at Daniel. Moments later, Allie watched Daniel disappear. She couldn't hide her curiosity. She fled back to where Pastor Jonas stood next to the old cross.

"So you met him? You met Daniel?" she asked, breathless. "You met my angel in the blue T-shirt and blue jeans? Omigosh, you're the only other person who's ever seen him! How fantastic!"

"Amazingly, yes, he did say his name was Daniel." Pastor Jonas still had the I-don't-believe-this-just-happened look. "A miracle. But...but there was no blue T-shirt. No, this man had on a white suit, with a white tie. Beautifully attired, really. All of it amazing. He's an angel? Yes, he did say that—"

Allie leaned forward. "What did he say?"

Pastor Jonas blinked. "That... that he wants me to examine the stained glass window he's having delivered for the back of the church. Daniel knew— as an angel, of course, he knew. Gosh, I still can't believe this— that for the past twenty years or more, since leaving the ministry, I'd worked with church curators and historians on dating religious artifacts, stained glass among them. Curious that he would want me to—"

"Don't you see?" Allie gasped. "Daniel wants you to somehow authenticate the stained glass window he's creating. That must be it, Pastor Jonas. Daniel told me it's the perfect window. Now I understand. Daniel wants everybody to know that the window is an inspiration—"

"From God," Pastor Jonas finished in awe. "Indeed, that is what he wants, Allie. He wants congregations everywhere to know that God is ever-present in His house of worship, and we would do well to remember that."

Pastor Jonas took Allie's hands. "Allie, this is a great day for me. The best day in all my life, actually. We have a mission to fulfill and I'm feeling stronger by the minute. Don't you see? Daniel wants us to work together on this project. How could I refuse to authenticate his stained glass window? That being said, how could it not pass all carbon testing with flying colors? After all, with Daniel crafting the glass, how could it not be thousands of years old? I'm not sure I will know how to—"

"Wait. You will perform the tests, won't you?"

He harrumphed. "Of course I'm going to perform the tests. Daniel wouldn't have it any other way. Having only met my first angel moments ago, I certainly don't want to displease him." The older man smiled in satisfaction. "What a day, I've had, Allie McCall. First meeting you and then meeting your angel. Now show me this lovely church. Walk with me and tell me what wonders await me inside."

MOMENTS LATER, PASTOR Hagen had joined Allie and Pastor Jonas inside the framed structure. Using his cane, Pastor Jonas hobbled his way down what would soon become the center aisle.

He turned and faced the sanctuary. "It's much like I remembered. Only now it seems smaller, more like a chapel. To think this church was my very first assignment. Oh, there had been pastors before me, but, back then, I thought the building was huge. And yet it only accommodated about forty people... but never mind that, right? To me, it was the mightiest church on all the Earth." He glanced to his right. "And this is the choir alcove? Very appropriate—small, but powerful."

"Amen to that, Pastor Jonas," boomed Fanny as she strode down the narrow aisle with Maggie in tow.

"It's been a month of Sundays since we last saw you. But you're looking well, ain't that right, Maggie? I know you don't remember us—Fanny and Maggie Matthews?"

Both women warmly greeted and shook hands with Pastor Jonas.

"Do I remember you? I'll say. I never knew two young girls who could get into so much trouble during any twenty minute sermon."

Fanny and Maggie laughed and gave him hugs.

"We hope you'll be back in the pulpit when the construction is finished," replied Maggie. "We loved your sermons on Sundays, no kidding, and we did listen. Honest, cross our hearts."

Pastor Jonas seemed to glow. "You both were too young to know what I was talking about. You rapscallions loved dodging spit balls, playing hide-and-seek and chowing down on dinners after church. Nobody could keep a handle on the two of you."

A smiling Fanny took one of Pastor Jonas's arms and Maggie took the other.

"Well, we've changed a mite since then," said Fanny, "but this whole town is glad that you're here. You are coming back to be our preacher, ain't that right?"

The trio slowly strolled together as Pastor Jonas quizzed them. "You won't mind it if my voice sounds a little raspy?"

"I think that's why somebody invented microphones," Maggie replied, "right, sister?"

Chapter 28

❦

Friday, October 1

Allie squinted at the irritating alarm clock, ready to toss it out the window.

Another frantic basketball practice. A quick shower. First period class. More homework this weekend and, this is Friday—test day.

She rolled over to stare at the ceiling. *I don't wanna get up.* Buzz might be the best looking guy in the whole school—maybe the whole world—but he was an unbelievably tough coach. *I'm getting blisters!* She'd pulled a second pair of socks from her drawer. *Jeez!* She glanced at the papers littering her bedroom floor—another major report due in two weeks in English. *A history paper due next week with tons of research to do, Algebra and biology tests today…* Allie covered her face. *Make it go away!*

A gentle knock sounded. "Wake up!" Mama whispered. "I'm taking you to practice."

Allie sighed, knowing her life had ramped into high gear. Reaching for her tennis shoes, she was out the door in five minutes, sitting in the passenger's seat, half asleep as her mother steered their car through the fog and down the drive. Minutes later she'd jogged up the hill to meet Buzz, who was uncharacteristically seated and already having breakfast on their practice court.

"Hey, 'sup?" he called out, ready for another bite of sandwich. "Sorry to start without you. I was hungry… but got yours right here." He glanced up as he slid a sack toward her. "Yeah… about practice today…it's like, well, it's me this time. I'm pooped. Been a hard week. Hope you don't mind."

She plopped down on the damp concrete. "Are you kidding? I woke up hoping today was over already!" Eager now, she tore into her sack. "Mr. Sims won't mind we're not practicing? Guess not. We're eating… just not practicing."

Buzz smiled. "He doesn't mind. I think he gets up early just to feed us. Do you know his café doesn't open till eight? But he's there at five-thirty every morning."

She finished chewing. "I'm glad. This is great. Really great. Thanks, Buzz. I've got tons of homework, too. *Jeez*. Every night this week. There's the donation work—"

"And basketball," he finished her thought. "Yeah, it's been hard."

"I need to make a list. I can't keep everything straight. I forget what I need to do."

Because he'd started eating first, he finished first. Stuffing his trash into the sack, Buzz pulled out a tiny pad and pencil. Without looking up, he smiled. "Okay, don't look at me like that. I know it's weird, but I carry this stuff around." He finally glanced at her. "I make lists."

Allie giggled. "You… make lists?"

He laughed. "Yeah! If you tell anybody… uh… I'll quit being your coach."

"No!" she laughed. "Don't stop coaching me, *pulleze*. I won't tell. Promise!"

He flipped to a clean sheet. "Okay. Ready."

"Huh? Oh! You're ready for me to—"

"Yeah, tell me what to write, you know, on the list?"

Allie thought a moment. "Well… I know all the church materials haven't been delivered. Oh, no! I was supposed to get Curly a list of materials you need!"

"Don't worry. It's handled. Because Mr. Morgan and Mr. Sinclair donated so much money, Dad ordered the supplies through Curly. You see," he said, a slow grin starting, "I saved you. I was there with *my* list. Everything's due in next week."

"Cool." Allie smiled. "Is there a lot more work to do on the church?"

Buzz chuckled. "Well, what do you think? It's right behind you. Look at it."

She did and glanced away. "Oh, Buzz. I don't know anything about construction. I know what paint looks like and what nails are used for. That's about it."

"Okay." He hid a smile. "We're working on the interior. Will you need furniture?"

"Huh?"

"Pews or chairs?"

"Oh, jeez, I never thought about that." Her gaze wandered. "I'll have to check the money."

"And check with the supplier."

"Wait! I know. I'll ask Pastor Jonas what he thinks."

"Finally. Something to write down on my list."

The next ninety minutes flew by and the good news was neither Buzz nor Allie had to shower when they got to school. Forget that she wore her practice clothes all day. It didn't matter. She happily breezed through her classes, constantly thinking of Buzz. His clear blue eyes seemed to laugh at her, tease her and sympathize with her as they passed each other between classes. He'd even winked at her today in English. With Buzz on her mind all day, it seemed fated that she'd run into Coach Madison after last period class. One more "to-do" list item could be checked off.

"Hi, Coach Madison."

"Allie. It's good to see you."

"I wanted to ask you—when Buzz and I stopped in to see Curly a couple of weeks ago—"

The coach held up her hand. "I know. You wanted to ask me about the advertising banners for Curly." She nodded. "Already taken care of. I called and talked to him personally. Got the lettering down exactly as he wanted. Right now, Curly is one happy man. Everything will be on order soon. Mr. Madison and I will take care of donating those banners. Glad to do it. And I appreciate your follow-up. Good work, Allie!"

Wow! Awesome. "Thank you so much!"

"You're welcome. Just make sure you and Buzz practice hard for me starting Monday morning. And—hear me when I say this!—practice every morning! Focus, focus, focus, young lady."

"Yes, ma'am!" Allie called back, hurrying to snag the bus. Oh, yeah, coach knew they'd skipped practice this morning. *But next week? Blister Town for sure.* Allie would definitely be doubling her socks.

DOODLING WITH HER pencil, Allie glanced up as Mama came through the kitchen to pour a glass of tea.

"Making a list?" she asked.

"Buzz and I started one this morning. I'm adding to it."

"Really?" Mama took a seat at the table. "What's left to do?"

"I'd like your opinion on something. Curly is getting banners hung in the gym for his donation. Do you think we should also do something special for Mr. Morgan and creepy Mr. Sinclair?"

Mama chuckled. "Creepy Mr. Sinclair? Allie, I admit, I was wrong to make those comments about him the other afternoon. I was just so frustrated. But maybe he's just unhappy. And over time he's become—how can I kindly say this?—unsociable. But, yes, I think your idea is a good one. How about a plaque thanking them for their generosity? Both he and Mr. Morgan have given large sums of money to rebuild the church. I'll ask Sheriff Anderson if he wants to share that donation with me. We'll discuss it. And one more thing—" She put down her tea glass. "You've had so much homework this week that I thought I could help out. I talked to the newspaper owner and stopped by the feed store. Both businesses confirmed they will also donate."

"Thanks, Mama!"

"You're welcome. Anything else I can help you with?"

Chapter 29

ख़ॐ

THE UNEXPECTED TELEPHONE ring jarred Allie out of bed.

"Hey, this is Buzz." Then silence. "I know it's not even 5:30. But I want to cancel our practice this morning."

"What?"

"I want you to come to the church anyway."

Allie yawned. "Why?"

"The window's here. The stained glass window, remember? Your guy Daniel must have delivered it last night. I want you to see it."

Again a long silence.

"Buzz, what's wrong? You sound, well, kinda mad."

"Not mad. Confused. Are you coming up here?"

Allie nodded into the receiver. "Sure, I'll get a ride."

She woke mama and grabbed a bowl of cereal. Laura McCall stumbled into the kitchen, yawning while tugging on a sweatshirt over a pair of blue jeans.

"Sorry I overslept, Allie."

"No problem." She put her bowl and spoon in the sink. *I can't imagine what's so important for him to call....*

Mama dropped her off minutes later and Allie carefully stepped up the uneven path to the church. The sun broke through the horizon to cast a luminous glow on the fresh coat of white paint. The building was taking shape. She smelled fall in the air and breathed deeply.

"Over here!" shouted Buzz from behind the building.

Allie found Buzz steadying the heavy stained glass window with both arms.

"This is it, I guess. I don't know who this fella in this picture is supposed to be, but he doesn't look like Jesus and he doesn't look like God."

Bewildered, Allie studied the stained glass that depicted a man on his hands and knees, digging in the soil. The window was huge, so it took both of Buzz's hands to hold it upright.

Clearly frustrated, Buzz added, "This is just a picture of somebody digging in the dirt. Where is God? Where is Jesus? What kind of picture is this, Allie? And who is Daniel? I don't know any glass man around these parts named Daniel. Did somebody sell you some cheap stained glass knock-off?"

Allie gasped. *All these questions. Was he talking about Daniel? Her angel was a cheap glass maker?*

"Buzz, you don't know what you're saying. This…this glass was made by Daniel. He's an angel, Buzz. Everything he does is perfect. Even…even this stained glass."

"Oh, good Lord, Allie. An angel. You're kidding, right?"

Buzz smirked before propping the stained glass window up against the church. The image was a little rudimentary, Allie had to agree. A man digging….

"It's Adam."

Daniel?

"I can't believe I have to explain my window. It's a picture of Adam cultivating the Earth with his hands. He's planting seeds, he's growing food, he's helping to create life, just like this town is trying to do with its garden and the reconstruction of the church. Allie, please explain to Buzz. This window is a metaphor for the continuation of life as humans know it every day."

Allie repeated Daniel's message as Buzz continued to look skeptical.

Yet, there, in the growing light of day, Buzz watched in amazement as the name "Daniel" was slowly inscribed in majestic longhand on the stained glass. "Good Lord, Allie. Are you seeing what I'm seeing?"

She pointed to the name etched across a bottom corner—the stamp confirming Daniel's existence. "Daniel signed his window just to show you—and everybody else who doesn't believe in angels!—that he's real."

Buzz shook his head. "This is weird…this…whatever it is—"

"His name is Daniel. He's the one you want to talk to."

"I…I…." Buzz stumbled. "I still don't believe it."

"You don't believe in angels?"

"Yes. No." Exasperated, Buzz scowled. "I don't know… okay, maybe I believe in angels."

"Good. Because I think you've insulted him."

"I've insulted an angel."

"Say something nice to him."

"Allie, you're serious?" Buzz turned to the glass still resting against the wall in its frame. "You really believe an angel created this window?"

"Oh, for goodness sake. Allie. Tell him that if he would stop playing 'The Sixth Avenger' and 'Titans of War' until two in the morning that he'd make above a seventy-five on his Algebra tests."

Allie giggled. "Okay, Buzz, you're bad. Daniel said if you'd stop playing 'The Sixth Avenger' and 'Titans of War' until two in the morning, you'd make above a seventy-five on your Algebra tests."

Buzz did a double take. "What? How do you know about my Algebra tests?"

"I didn't," she laughed, "until now. Daniel just told me."

"No way! Just like that?"

"He talks to me, Buzz."

"I'm weirded-out. Totally. I don't want to talk about this anymore." He began walking away, then turned. "Why didn't you ever tell me about your angel thing before now? All those early morning workouts? Not one word. *An angel*? Who else knows about Daniel?"

Allie shrugged. "My family. Fanny. Sheriff Anderson. Mr. Morgan. Oh, and Pastor Jonas met him, too."

Buzz took off his ball cap and raked his fingers through his thick hair. "Pastor Jonas met him. You talk to an angel. Well, I never. Ever!" He shook his head. "If that don't beat all."

"Daniel is the first angel I've ever talked to. He's the one who told me he needed help rebuilding this church."

Buzz's eyes got big. "That was *him*?" Buzz grabbed her hand. "C'mon, I'm starving. I've gotta give this some time. Nate's making us breakfast. I forgot to tell him we weren't practicing today. I'd better get a message to Dad. I don't want him to say anything bad about that window. We may not appreciate its beauty— but I bet it'll grow on us. Nobody wants to insult any… angel."

It took only hours for the news to spread. Buzz only told Messa Kess. By lunch, the whole school knew about Daniel, the stained glass window and that they were reconstructing the church as a mission for Allie's angel.

What had started as an innocent project to make something beautiful again had fast turned into a nightmare.

After lunch, Allie escaped to the bathroom with Wikki in tow.

"You can't bolt the door, Allie. Girls need to get in here before class!"

Allie whirled around and barricaded herself against the door frame. "They can go to the one by the cafeteria. I'm sick of everybody laughing at me!" She jerked the rubber band from her ponytail and raked a brush through her hair. "I need to chill. Did you hear Trudy O'Malley ask me to be part of her group? Jeez, Wikki. She asked me if I was a witch! *O-mi-gosh!* Three of her friends came up in the hall and invited me to their next meeting— I heard they're into, like, black magic, or something. She has no idea—" Allie broke off. *She has no idea that I've met Ethan Benedict and I certainly don't want to meet any demon ever again*!

Wikki gasped. "Black magic?"

Allie reknotted her hair. "I told her no! I'm not about to do anything like that. I was nice to her, though… well, Trudy's always been nice to me, but flat out no—" Allie shivered. "The thought gives me the creeps. And then Madeleine from my history class and her friends laughed when I came out of gym. They practically pounced on me… asking me when Daniel and I were going out. Like, duh, Wikki, how lame. Don't they know that angels are spirits?" Allie rolled her eyes. "I'm sick of it. I knew it would be hard once a bunch of people found out."

"But Allie, how could you keep this a secret?"

Allie's face fell. "I guess… I guess… maybe I couldn't. It was just easier before…." Allie dropped down beside Wikki's wheelchair. "I wanted to tell you so many times but I didn't know how. Like, it's not the easiest thing in the world to believe, right?" Allie hesitated. "But you do believe me, Wikki, don't you?"

She smiled. "Of course I do."

"Seriously?"

"Seriously. We're best friends, right?"

"Always." Allie shook off her smile and groaned, "Okay, I'm ready. Let's get to class."

MAMA WAS HOME when Allie got off the bus. "Allie—"

"I know all about it. Totally. I've answered questions all day. Everybody's shocked at first, then they want to talk about it for hours." She plopped down at the kitchen table. "The teachers are looking at me a little weird." She covered her face. "I was so humiliated. Some kids want me to join their group… they think I'm a witch. The other kids think I'm crazy… nobody believes I can talk to an angel."

"It took us a while to get used to the idea."

Allie peeked at her from behind her hands. "I don't have a while! I have to face them every day! Believe me—*I* never mentioned Ethan, who I think is the Devil's disciple. That would have really revved up *some* kids and *terrified* everybody else!"

Mama smiled. "They're trying to understand… nobody else gets to talk to Daniel."

"Pastor Jonas has. Daniel was the one who asked him to authenticate his window!"

"Really? Hmm, that's something for your classmates to think about. You can't be all that crazy if Pastor Jonas has talked to him, too."

"I guess not." Allie sighed. "All I know is that I'm exhausted."

"Well, you may not know everything."

"There's *more*?"

"There is. But relax. It's not bad." Mama poured two glasses of tea. "Pastor Jonas is meeting you at the church this afternoon to look at the window. He called me at the office today. I told him it would be fine. He told me that he had a dream about the window and wants to see it right away."

"A dream?"

"Yes, a dream." Mama held up her hands. "That's all I know."

Allie looked askance. "Okay, you can bet everybody in town already knows about the meeting. Can we get going before the whole town fills up that itty, bitty parking lot?"

Mama and Allie arrived a few minutes later, and their mouths fell when they spied tables piled high with food. People had brought chairs, kids were playing basketball and Allie felt like she was late for her own birthday party.

"Can you believe this?" she whispered.

Mama turned off the ignition and started to chuckle. "I've never seen anything like this before. You remember how dead this town used to be? People never spoke to each other. Nobody came to any town gathering. We almost had to trick people in attending city council meetings. And yet…look at this. There must be forty people out there playing and having a ball."

"All because of a stained glass window?"

Mama shrugged. "I don't know why. C'mon, I'm getting my purse. Let's go find Pastor Jonas. Maybe he can fill in the blanks."

Sure enough, Pastor Jonas waved his cane high in the air when he saw them. "Ladies! Hurry up!"

Mama and Allie danced lightly over the broken bricks to reach the top of the grassy hillside.

"Have you seen the stained glass window?" Allie called out.

"Have I seen it, child? Are you kidding?" He grinned from ear to ear, stumbling in his excitement, almost forgetting to use his cane. "It's absolutely fantastic! Unbelievable. I've sent a message to Bishop Margaret Standley asking her to come as quickly as possible to see this window. Amazing. Absolutely amazing. I cannot wait to authenticate it."

Allie paused as she neared the church. "You like the window, then?"

"Like it?" Pastor Jonas pointed his cane to the sky. "Do you not know? This window was definitely made by an angel of God. By Daniel. It can only be him." Pastor Jonas turned to Allie. "You've probably read about the famous Canterbury Cathedral in England. Well, there is an early series of stained glass panels showing the ancestors of Christ dating from the twelfth century. This window could be another panel from that same collection. It's a splendid piece! Only one other stained glass panel shows Adam delving into the soil, replicating life in the Garden of Eden, and that panel is truly authentic. The remaining panels are reproductions. This could be a missing panel from that collection. Not only that," he jabbed her gently with his elbow, "but, look at the details! I feel sure this one's an absolute original. Marvelous!"

Pastor Jonas coughed and Mama quickly rushed over to the refreshment table to get him a glass of water.

He drank deeply. "I can't handle this much excitement. Excuse me, please, both of you. But I've never, ever in my life seen quite as much beauty as I've seen today."

Mama and Allie exchanged glances as they helped Pastor Jonas walk to the back of the church. People gathered round as the pastor took a seat in a picnic chair facing the window. Pastor Jonas wiped his eyes. "I must confess that Daniel came to me last night," he began, his eyes never wavering from the window that still rested upright against the wall. "He told me that he wanted me to authenticate this window. I agreed, naturally.

"Then Daniel explained that he knew how many umpteen years I had studied the ancient stained art glazing techniques. I became fascinated by glass while traveling throughout the churches of Europe. Glass has been around for centuries, dating back to the time before Christ. While we assume there was more glass produced a thousand years ago than what has survived, we can also assume it must have been broken during the endless tribal warring throughout Europe and Britain. And now—now *this*. This could be one of the missing panes, or simply an original Daniel wanted added to the collection. And, miracle of miracles, such a magnificent window is here."

Allie, Mama and the other townspeople stared in awe at the glass window, noticing the intense colors ranging from royal to navy that dominated the vivid reds and the bright yellows. Pastor Jonas explained how the glass had been cut into shapes and then fitted into an iron framework and then fitted with lead inlays—careful, painstaking work.

He continued, "We should celebrate this window and the fact that God, through Daniel, has blessed our town with His presence. I cannot think of a more joyous occasion." From his chair, he reached up to squeeze Allie's hand. "Can you?"

Buzz interrupted them, stepping forward. "It's beautiful." He turned to Allie. "It's just that… well, this morning I couldn't believe Daniel was really an angel."

Pastor Jonas twisted around in his chair. "Why not, young man? Don't you believe in angels?"

"I—no, yes—"

Pastor Jonas nodded. "I think you do. It's just hard for some to admit. I'm delighted that Allie listened and quickly responded to Daniel's wishes." He smiled at her warmly. "Well done, my dear."

"Thank you," she whispered.

Buzz cleared his throat. "We'd better get it up off the ground now. I'll get my tools. Dad is on his way. Pastor Jonas, do you mind if we get to work?"

"Goodness, no, young man. Let me move this chair."

The crowd dispersed and folks scurried around as conversations began about the window, about Daniel, about how Pastor Jonas had also talked to Daniel, so maybe Allie wasn't all that crazy after all—and, of course, everybody wondered what was for dinner.

Chapter 30

❧

ALLIE GLANCED UP from the dessert table to see Black Jack Morgan using his cane to gingerly make his way up the broken walkway.

"Mr. Morgan!" she shouted, before rescuing him as he stumbled on several broken bricks. "I'm so glad to see you!"

He smiled weakly. "I'm glad to be here. Only… Allie, do you think you could replace this walkway with some of that money I'm donating?"

She chuckled. "Of course! Pastor Jonas also wants to donate money to fix it, too."

"Who is Pastor Jonas?" Mr. Morgan had successfully maneuvered the walkway and now stood on solid ground.

"I am Jonas Smiley!" a bold but crackly voice called out. "I was once pastor of the original masterpiece you see before you— now taking shape again as a lovely church." Pastor Jonas made his way toward Morgan and the two men shook hands. "You must be Jack Morgan, the town attorney. I've heard about you, but we've never met."

Allie whispered, "What you may not have heard is that Mr. Morgan is one of the largest donors to our project."

"Is that a fact? Then we need to circulate the news that you are a great philanthropist!"

Morgan waved him away. "No need. I like the current, antisocial image much better. It's the true me."

Pastor Jonas's eyes danced. "I sense a rare wit, Morgan. I like that."

Allie interjected, "Pastor, do you know that Mr. Morgan predicted that the banker, who didn't want to donate any money at all, would double Mr. Morgan's donation? He did, and we have the letter of credit to prove it!"

Pastor Jonas popped his cane on the ground. "Bravo! Well done! More good news to make my day."

Allie leaned into him. "And I'm glad the two of you are here, because we have an important decision to make."

"Really?" Pastor Jonas winked. "Then I cannot think of three clearer heads or better brains to make it. What is this decision, my dear?"

"Whether to have pews or chairs."

Morgan repeated. "Pews or chairs?"

"In the sanctuary, my good man. The girl's asking whether we want pews or chairs."

"Oh…Oh! Pews. Yes, I think pews," Morgan said, nodding.

"Done!" She brushed her hands together and hugged Pastor Jonas's arm first and then Morgan's. "You both are so wonderful. I don't know what I would do without you." Then to Morgan, "Did you know that Daniel introduced himself to Pastor Jonas? Ask him. He'll tell you all about it. And… you can share your story, Mr. Morgan… that is, if you want to."

She left both men staring after her. When she glanced back, they were deep in conversation. Mr. Morgan tipped his head back and laughed. *Beginnings of a new friendship?* Allie wondered as she spied Buzz taking his second piece of peach pie. She edged in beside him. "Save any for me?"

He cut her a piece and passed her the plate. "It's so good. One piece might not be enough," he said. "We got the window installed. Gotta load up my tools now. Go take a look."

"Sure. Thanks for the pie."

Allie stood on the church steps and took a deep break. The afternoon sun had dipped behind the trees, sending dappled streaks of light cascading through the branches as the yellow glow spilled onto the garden and lawn. She opened the front door and stepped inside, smelling the aroma of freshly sawn wood, of paint and of varnish. Moving slowly along the aisle, she focused on Daniel's window of Adam working the soil. Colored sunlight from the stained glass created a dazzling effect as it danced on the wooden floor.

"Beautiful, Daniel. Just as you said."

"Glad you like it. It's everything I envisioned. Buzz and his dad did a perfect job of building the church and installing the window."

"It is perfect!"

"Allie, I've wanted to tell you for a long time…thank you. Thank you for working so hard. You did a great job. I know it's not completely finished. There's

still furniture to buy, pews, a pulpit... your mother and Pastor Jonas will see that everything gets completed. But I wanted you to know how important you were... uh, you are, and how much I appreciate you tackling this project for me."

"Will I ever see you again... uh, in person?" Allie whispered, crestfallen. "I... miss you."

"I know... it's hard right now. I've been... reassigned."

"Reassigned? To another project? Another... girl?"

"No! No, nothing like that. I can talk to you but not as often."

"Hey!"

Allie jumped as Buzz snuck up behind her. "Do you like it? I do. It kinda grows on you."

He's talking about the window, she thought.

"I like the different colors," he said, glancing around the inside of the church. "Daniel must be one cool dude."

Daniel would love being called a "dude." Allie grinned. "He is, Buzz. Way cool."

"Think I'll ever meet him?"

Allie looked into Buzz's blue eyes. She could have sworn that twinkle was Daniel's. "I hope you do, Buzz. One day, I hope you do."

IT WAS SIX-THIRTY that night when Allie plopped down on her bed. Big day. She was so tired... but thirsty. She trod quietly toward the kitchen. Clad in her jeans and old shirt, her bare feet never made a sound.

She stopped when she heard Mama and Sheriff Anderson having words in the living room.

"Are you sure you've looked everywhere for it, Logan?"

He nodded. "I'm sure."

Mama sighed aloud. "I definitely remember Fanny telling me that the metal box was hidden up in the big oak tree near the old Pierce property cemetery."

Sheriff Anderson nodded. "I know. I remember. I climbed up that tree myself. The box is nowhere to be found. I swear it."

"Omigosh!" Mama dropped down on the sofa. "Logan, what am I going to do? I've got to find that box. If you're right, and the papers are hidden in that box, and the box is missing, those papers could be gone forever."

Allie watched as her Mama's shoulders slumped and her head rolled back. She grabbed her forehead.

"Do you know what those papers would mean to me? To the kids? I've spent months doing that research...my trips to Tyler, even to Dallas. The kids never really knew why I was drove up there so much." Her voice cracked. "And, then, all of your help. Oh, Logan, we've just got to find that old box—"

Allie shifted her weight and a floorboard creaked. Mama jumped up and Sheriff Anderson turned quickly.

"Uh, sorry," Allie said, feeling sheepish. "I...I just wanted to get something to drink, but—" Thinking better of her idea, she fled back around the corner to her bedroom and grabbed her sneakers.

The box. It had to be the one Mama meant. Goodness knows, I must have hidden that metal box over and over again dozens of times. No one else would know where it is now.

Allie fled the house, waving good-bye to the two surprised faces, still standing in the living room. Grabbing the handlebars of her bike, she turned from the driveway onto Pierce Road and pedaled as fast as she could.

How bizarre! Their box was the same box as my secret mailbox to Dad? Years ago she'd found the old metal box when she was poking around what must be the tiny Pierce cemetery—only she never knew it then, because she never saw any grave markers. She'd climbed trees, built forts and thought about how she hated her life. She never once thought the rusty container was important to anybody. *What is so important about that box?*

Allie dumped her bike in the ditch, ducked beneath the barbed wire fence and raced toward the grove of trees a few hundred yards away. Even now, after just a little training with Buzz, she could run so much faster. She wasn't nearly as winded and felt as light as a dove on her feet. Fully energized, she sprinted the final fifty yards to her cemetery hiding place.

Skirting a slender oak, Allie skidded to her knees before the massive oak tree, shoving away the already falling leaves to uncover the hidey-hole she'd found beneath the trunk. Brushing away debris, Allie opened the box. She discarded dozens and dozens of folded letters on the ground—her whole collection of letters to her father. *Pointless, really,* she thought now, as she looked at how many she'd written over the past five years. He can't read them. Why bother?

Nothing else inside. Hmm. Allie tapped on the bottom. Sure enough, it sounded...thick, not hollow. She pushed and pulled. She shook it. Nothing. She pushed on one end, then the other. It gave, slightly, with a squeaky noise. *A hidden bottom?* She pushed harder; it gave a little more.

She gently pushed and then pulled away part of the secret compartment. She managed to see a piece of parchment tucked inside.

"Are you looking for something, lovely Alexandra?"

A cold, watery chill raced down her spine. Allie froze—scared to move, even more scared not to. Recoiling from the sugary-sweet voice, Allie glanced up, trembling.

Ethan Benedict!

"I thought you were in Canada," she whispered.

He stood there, legs akimbo, cocky and confident, his hands on his waist, wearing skin tight jeans and a snug black shirt. Allie couldn't miss his ripped arms or wicked smile.

"I thought you might miss me," he offered seductively, as a lock of black hair fell across his forehead. "I think the scenery down here is much better. Much prettier. Just like your hair, Alexandra. It's a golden copper, long and luxurious. "

Allie gasped, realizing she was alone. Mama and Sheriff Anderson were at the house. No one knew where she'd gone.

He took a step closer. "Looking for something? Maybe I could help."

She clutched the box to her chest. Whatever was inside belonged to her mother and nobody was going to take it away from her.

"You s-stay back." Allie slowly got to her feet. "You stay away from me...."

"Or what, my lovely Alexandra? What on earth can you do? I think it's time that I took you back to Canada with me. I've met new friends there. They'd like you, I'm sure of it. Wouldn't you like to see more of the world than this hick town? Let me show you things you've never imagined."

Again, his maniacal grin seemed enticing, designed to woo her. He advanced two more steps.

Allie tightened her grip on the metal box. It held something mama wanted. She couldn't just hand it over to one of the Devil's disciples. But would he hurt her? He'd had a couple of chances to before and didn't. What had Daniel told her?

"I'm busy!" she yelled with renewed confidence. She pointed to the opposite side of the tree stand. "Go. Now! Leave this place. Get away from me. I don't want to meet any of your friends. Ever! And I'm not going anywhere with you. Not now, not ever!"

He took another step closer, his smile growing.

"I'll protect and take care of you. I'll show you beautiful villages, more beautiful than..."

"Stop right there, Ethan. You know nothing of beauty, of glory, of what is holy, righteous and good. Don't move another muscle toward the girl."

Daniel!

Ethan's grin turned wicked as he swiveled around. Allie glimpsed a light growth of black hair rippling along his neck; his pupils turning a pale yellow. A drippy wetness encircled his mouth.

"Or you'll do what? What can you do, *o brother?*" Ethan's cruel laugh echoed among the trees. "You'll do *nothing*! Nothing as always. I've always known that about you, Daniel. You are such a do-nothing—"

"Hush! Speak not another word." Daniel stepped from behind the huge elm and, in one long stride, stood beside Allie.

She glanced her gratitude at him.

"Are you okay?" he asked.

She nodded, feeling perfect and unafraid. "I've got to get this box back to mama."

Daniel nodded and focused on Ethan again. This time, he radiated a quiet calm she'd never seen before. He locked eyes with his evil adversary.

"How can you say I do nothing when I have been saving soul after soul from you for, lo, these thousands of years? You are the lowest form of life, straight from Hell. Do *not* deny it. You are a liar, a cheat, a thiever of souls. I forbid you to call me brother again. I forbade it once before and yet, you say it again this day. This time is once too many."

Ethan's laugh rang hollow. "What are you going to do about it?"

"What I should have done ages ago."

Daniel threw his broom into the air and balled his right hand into a fist. A thin beam of bright light shot from his ring to the broom and what fell back down was an immense broadsword, larger than Allie had ever imagined. As Daniel grabbed the handle, the whole sword glowed with a crystal-clear light. Emeralds, sapphires and rubies encrusted the hilt as Daniel clutched it with both hands, wielding the golden blade several times as if to get the feel of it once more.

"I vow to protect this town and all who are in it. You are now and forevermore banished, Ethan. This town is off-limits. Its people are off-limits. You are expelled. Is that clear?"

Ethan took a step back.

Daniel took a step forward. "Leave now. Do *not* come here again!"

Ethan suddenly dropped down on all fours. Fangs took the place of his teeth. His hands curved like claws with talons on each finger, and his mouth dripped a reddish ooze.

"Frighten me, Daniel?" came his unnatural growl. "I think not."

Anger settled over Daniel's face as he slashed his sword at Ethan. The next moment an electrical current shot through Allie, tossing her a good two feet away. On her knees, she swiveled, watching Ethan crash into a tree.

Looking more like wolf than man, Ethan pounced at Daniel.

"Try to kill me, brother?"

"Depraved animal!" Daniel's anger shook the treetops. "How dare you tamper with the sight of God! Get to *Hell* where you belong."

In one long stride, Daniel pierced Ethan's shoulder with the golden blade.

The creature howled and covered the deep gash with his paw. He pounced again, rough claws gripping Daniel's throat, paws tearing cavernous slashes down his chest. Daniel's flimsy T-shirt hung in shreds, exposing open wounds on his chest and arms.

With a mighty plunge, Daniel pierced Ethan's jugular as he thrust him high in the air. Daniel twisted the huge broadsword and Ethan roared, flung himself away and ran yelping into the dense grove of trees.

Allie blinked as Daniel swayed. She rushed to his side, trying to somehow cover the claw marks on his neck and chest, wanting to make them disappear, feeling like she had caused their fight—if it hadn't been for her, Daniel would not be here now. There would have been no battle. Daniel would have not been injured.

He leaned against her as she lowered him to the ground. Allie saw there was no blood. Why would there be? Daniel was an angel. It was all true. Yet the claw marks that ripped through his skin and tattered his clothing told the story. Daniel had been right about evil. There *were* permanent scars that Ethan and his followers left on their victims.

"Daniel." She bent over him. "Can you hear me? You're so hurt."

His right hand still gripped the sword that had returned to a broom. Among the leaves, he looked more like a peasant than angel.

"Allie," he whispered, his eyes straining to open.

She put her cheek against his, hoping to feel warmth, but feeling none. She lifted his wrist, but felt no pulse.

"Daniel, what can I do?" She choked back a sob as she laid her hands on his still chest, desperate for any sign of life. She caressed his cheeks—

and still no warmth. "No! she cried, her face turned toward Heaven. "Let him breathe! Please!"

One tear followed another as she buried her face in his chest, clinging to the remnants of his shirt. "No, Daniel, don't go. You can't... go," she whispered.

For the first time in five years, Allie wept. She wrapped her arms around him and squeezed. She kissed his chest, his arms, his cheek and his hands as she cried. She kissed his cuts, his deep wounds.

"Come back. Sweet Daniel."

Yet, despite her pleading, Daniel faded. With his eyes closed and his breathing all but stopped, Daniel slowly disappeared.

Allie rocked back on her heels and covered her face. *He couldn't be gone! Angels don't die. They live forever. Hadn't Daniel been alive for thousands of years?*

"Dear Allie, do not cry so."

She sniffed and wiped her face. A man stood where she had dropped the metal box.

"Daniel? Is that you?" She rose slowly, cautiously. He didn't look like Daniel. This man was middle-aged. He looked familiar, but—

"It's me, Allie. It's Dad."

Her mouth dropped as she took a step forward.

"Wait... stop right there."

She halted and stared.

Relaxing now, the man smiled. "You're so beautiful. So impulsive. So brave. I'm so proud of you."

"Dad, why? After all these years. Why now?"

"Daniel will be fine. He doesn't want you to cry. I was sent to tell you. Plus, I wanted to thank you for all your letters. I read them, each and every one. I've loved watching you grow up."

Still not quite believing, she wiped her eyes and blinked. "Dad, you look... good; you look really good—like you used to."

He laughed. "The pain is gone, Allie. I feel great. Oh, and I have a message for your mother. This may sound strange—"

Strange? Everything about today is strange.

"Allie, she talks to me. You write me letters and your mom talks to me every night. Tell her... tell her it's okay. The sheriff is a good man. Tell her I said it was okay. She'll know what I mean. Would you do that for me, please? Oh, and by the way, I think Buzz is a fine young man, too.

Remember that I love you. I've got to go now," he said, with a small wave. "Bye."

"Dad?" Allie watched as her father slowly traveled backward into the dense grove of trees until he was lost from sight.

Allie rubbed her eyes and looked about. She was alone. Completely alone— no ghosts, no angels, no demons. The forest was quiet, but not frightening like before. One long slender shaft of sunlight shot through the trees to shine on the spot where Daniel had lain. Allie stared at the dry leaves for what seemed like hours before she lowered her head and murmured a prayer of thanks for meeting Daniel, a prayer for his quick recovery and another prayer to thank him for— well— everything.

Chapter 31

✧

ALLIE SHIFTED UNCOMFORTABLY in the tattered living room chair as she faced Mama and Sheriff Anderson. She finished recounting the last hour, dabbing her eyes with a tissue.

"That's quite a story. Honestly, it sounds impossible." Mama glanced from Logan to Allie. "And you say that Daniel is now gone? As in gone *forever?*"

"You know, Allie, I haven't been notified that Ethan Benedict is in our area. I need to contact the Texas Highway Patrol. You're... sure about all this?"

Allie nodded and wiped away a stray tear. "You couldn't have known. He's not even, well, real." She lowered her gaze. "He's not exactly somebody you can chase. He's more like a demon. With fangs and claws." She shivered. "It was awful."

"Whatever he is and whatever he's doing in these parts, it needs to be reported." The sheriff stood up and walked to the door. "I'll be back in a minute. I'll make a few phone calls from my Jeep."

When the door closed, she felt Mama's hand on her shoulder.

"Are you okay, honey? I mean, are you really okay?"

Allie nodded, then shrugged.

"Sad?" Mama asked, as she encircled Allie in her arms. "Come here, sweetie. Give me a hug. I think I need a hug as badly as you do."

Allie felt the old warmth that she had loved so many years ago. She closed her eyes as her tiredness melted away. Mama's arms tightened their hold before releasing her.

"You're so brave," she whispered. "So grown up. So beautiful."

Allie looked down at the tattered sleeve of her shirt. "I'm going to miss him, Mama. I'm going to miss talking to Daniel. I don't want to go back to the way things were. I never thought I'd ever admit that life was so boring." Allie forced a brave smile. "The excitement, the fun—he gave me confidence. I can't imagine life without him!" New tears spilled down her cheeks.

"You've got school and basketball to keep you busy… and, well, things are about to change around here," Mama said, folding her arms. "I'm going to wear my hair down more often and I'm going to, well…start going out with Sheriff Anderson!"

"What?" Allie gasped, "I almost forgot. I s-saw Dad."

Mama crumpled back down onto the sofa. "What on Earth?"

Allie sat down beside her. "It's true. Dad was there after Daniel left. He told me to give you a message. He said something about how it was okay. Something you had asked him. Do you really talk to Dad? He also said you would understand. He said he thinks that Sheriff Anderson is a good man."

Mama blinked a couple of times. "Is that all he said?"

"Well, no." Allie struggled to remember. "He thanked me for writing my letters. He said he'd read them all."

"What letters?"

"That's what I didn't tell you before. I used to write Dad letters and put them inside an old box. I used to, well…I hated it here and so I wrote Dad about it. I know it was stupid. I knew he'd never read them. But today he told me that he'd read every one. He said he liked watching me grow up. He said I was pretty and…and that he liked Buzz."

"Allie, are you serious? He mentioned Buzz?"

"Uh-huh. It kinda surprised me, too." She smiled. "He looked really great, Mama. Like he did before he got so sick. Remember?"

Mama's eyes teared up and she folded her hands in her lap. "I remember. Oh, boy, do I ever remember. And I confess, I have talked to him—his picture, actually. I have missed him so much all these years." She sighed and looked up at the ceiling. "But wishing and hoping won't change anything, Allie. We all have to press on. Life keeps on keeping on, right?"

Sheriff Anderson stepped back through the doorway. "No news on Benedict's whereabouts right now." He looked from mother to daughter. "You're both giving me funny looks. What have I missed?"

"I told Allie that you and I are going to start dating," Mama said, brightly.

"Good!"

"And I was just about to tell Mama that I found the old metal box at the Pierce cemetery," Allie interjected.

"You what?" Sheriff and Mama asked in unison.

"For years I stuffed my letters to Dad in here," she explained, handing over the army-style lock box she'd set next to the kitchen table. "I didn't know this box was important."

"Go ahead, Laura," Logan said, nudging her. "Open it up."

Mama carefully took the box from Allie and returned to the sofa. She stroked it once, as if caressing a prized jewelry box before peeking inside. "Nothing!"

"Check the bottom," Allie said.

Mama tugged and jerked on the bottom latch until parchment papers spilled out over the coffee table. "Wha-a-t? Logan, look! Omigosh! This is the deed to the Pierson land. And look! It's... what is this?" she asked Logan.

He flipped through several pages, reading bits and pieces. "This is Pierce's will. Finally! You found it... wait, did you know that your late husband was Pierce's nephew? Read this, Laura... Pierce specifies that all the land must remain intact, not be divided into parcels. He even names Gerald in his will and specifies all of Gerald's dependents as his heirs... this will was written long before you and Jerry were married." Sheriff Anderson grinned. "Don't you see? Because Pierce's wife is deceased—Jerry was his only heir and relative. Pierce's property should legally belong to you and the kids—all of it! All three hundred acres!"

"What!" Allie jumped in. "Mama, this is our land?"

"Pass me those papers, Logan." Mama quickly scanned them, shaking her head. "I never thought this... all these years. Jerry never said anything about being Pierce's nephew. Unbelievable! I never...wait... Pierce died years ago. Who's been the caretaker? I mean, who's been paying the property taxes?"

Logan turned to pick up his ball cap. "I wasn't going to mention it right now—"

Mama gasped.

"I have," he said, softly.

"What? Were you going to buy—"

"Laura, now listen. A good friend of mine is a retired judge in Dallas. He learned I was moving to Smith County and told me about this parcel of land that went on the auction block many years ago—specifically, the old Pierce place. He bought it for the back taxes, thought it was a good investment, and wanted to retire here. But about six years ago he had a heart attack; now he lives in a nursing home. So I thought, what the heck? The judge said if I kept paying the taxes, at some point I could make an offer, possibly buy the land and transfer the deed. I didn't know too much about the area but I sure liked the land…and all of this happened before I met you—"

"You never told me, Logan! You've been paying taxes on the property right next door to me?"

"Yes, and now that you're a big landowner, you can pay me back." He smiled as he wrapped his arms around her waist. "Or, do you even want the property?"

Laura smiled up from beneath her lashes. "You bet I do! You will never get this land from me, Logan Anderson, so you can just forget that idea." She reached up and kissed him on the cheek. "But—I thank you very much for paying the taxes all these years and, yes, I will pay back every cent I owe you."

"So the land… it's ours to keep?" Allie finally found her voice. "What an awesome day! We're not poor. We just found out we own three hundred acres of land. Did Mr. Pierce have any money?"

Mama and Logan exchanged looks. "Good point. Laura, we'll schedule a trip to Tyler to find out exactly what needs to be done to probate the will and transfer any other Pierce property."

"Good," Allie said, picking up her backpack. "I want y'all to get started as soon as possible. My wish list includes a new house—a bigger house, new dishes and a new dishwasher—all to be built on our new land." Allie glanced behind her. "Any questions?"

Chapter 32

⟢

ALLIE GLANCED AT the gymnasium clock on this crucial, wintry night in late January. Only eight minutes left to play in the District game for the Lady Lions. Would she, could she and her teammates pull it off? Allie's silky new uniform made her feel like a pro, but her tennis shoes were toast. Despite double socks, she could feel the slippery ball court through the holes in the bottom.

They had taken a time-out before starting the fourth quarter. Now she glanced around at her teammates, especially Sarah Johnson, who everybody called Sarah J. for short, and Emma Fox, both seniors, and both serious basketball players. They'd had a hard time accepting her once, and now they were all in District together.

"Like Sarah J. and Emma Fox are just going to let me on the court and play," Allie remembered telling Buzz one morning early in the season. "You're crazy if you think that."

Allie remembered him wiping the sweat from his forehead with an old towel. "You don't get it. They're gonna let you play because they're all so short. Every girl on the team is short, Allie. They're like maybe five feet tall. They need you and they know it. Besides, those girls are seniors and they'd give anything to win District their last year. They're both great ball handlers, I give them credit for that. And Sarah J. will probably get a scholarship just for dribbling. But none of them can hit the side of a barn broadside with the ball. You can." *That had sounded simple enough.* Allie snorted at her memory; nothing was simple.

"And here she is," Sarah J. had called out during one of their first practices, "our new star player." Sarah J. ducked and dribbled circles around Allie. "Not light on our feet?"

Allie remembered shaking her head, feeling humiliated for even wanting to play ball with these girls.

"Everybody says you're our miracle player. You're nothin' but a freshman nerd. Don't look tough to me. And you're supposed to take us all the way to District? Ha!" Sarah J. stopped dribbling and strained her neck to get a good look at Allie. "I say you're a fake, Allie McCall. Besides, I don't believe in miracles. I don't believe in that angel story. He gonna help you out? Hey, I asked you a question, geek." She stopped dribbling and set the ball on her waist.

Allie glanced down at Sarah J., not missing the venom behind her words, knowing the girl would love to claw her eyes out. Allie chose not to be intimidated. "Yeah, I think it's a miracle that I'm on this court. It's a miracle that I've made it this far."

"It's stupid. That's what I think it is." Sarah J. stuck out her jaw, ready for a fight.

Allie didn't take the bait.

Sarah J. shot back. "Look, we know you can't dribble but we're hoping you can at least shoot. Well... can you shoot?"

Stony-faced on the outside, but scared to death on the inside, Allie had held out her hand. "The ball, please?"

Allie remembered that, with her heart pounding, she had somehow made five out of five baskets, two from the free throw line and three from different positions under the basket.

Emma Fox chuckled. "Well, she's looking good to me, Sarah. You might want to believe a little more in miracles."

Allie smiled at the memories of it all. Tonight was the game of games this season. She glanced over as Sarah J. gave her a thumbs-up. Emma Fox did the same.

It had taken some time, but the two girls had become two of Allie's closest friends. In fact, because of their tight teamwork, other schools in the district called them the Lady Lion Steamroller Express. The trio practiced early mornings and late afternoons, thinking up new dribble and pass plays. Coach Madison and Buzz worked tirelessly with them. Then they'd bring in the other two starters and the five would practice pass and shoot plays. Long hours and lots of practice—mo wonder Allie's shoes were worn smooth.

Allie glanced up. Buzz and Mr. Madison sat in the stands near Mama and Sheriff Anderson. *Who'd a-thought it—even Ben is here.* And there was Messa Kess and Wikki—and Mr. Morgan. Allie spotted Fanny and Otis Spinkle, Maggie and Nate Sims, Marybelle Hightower and, gosh, nearly everybody she knew from Friendly, including Pastor Jonas. They all started whooping and waving when they saw Allie looking their way.

She couldn't help grinning. Everybody was here tonight except Daniel. He hadn't talked to her since the night he "died" near the Pierce cemetery. He hadn't been there to help complete the church, which they did just before Christmas. She and the others had taken care of that all by themselves. Allie constantly talked to him, but he never responded.

The buzzer sounded and Allie glanced up again at the clock, just to make sure they had five minutes left. Bullard had beaten them one other time this season, but Allie knew they had fought hard—Bullard had only won by only two points. A real barn-burner.

Tonight was no different. Everybody was on their feet. The stands rocked from the stomping. Voices cracked from the shouting. The cheerleaders fought with each other to be heard above the racket of the crowd. Too tired to be scared, Allie said a quick prayer for courage. She wanted to talk to Daniel, to hear him whisper that everything would be all right, but decided against it. He hadn't responded these past three months. He wouldn't respond now.

She focused on the ball and the game. Sarah J. and Emma Fox dodged the Bullard point guards. Teammates Justyne and Gigi were on their toes to the outside as Allie put the ball into play. Back and forth the ball went. Up and down the court.

Allie felt an adrenaline surge as she slipped into her zone, the zone she'd found in those long ago early morning practices with Buzz. The stop, point and shoot sessions. Bounce, bounce, stop, point and shoot. So routine that now Allie could shoot from anywhere on the court. She'd even made a few half court net-ripping shots. She couldn't dribble worth a flip, but she could shoot nine out of ten baskets, leaving points on the board.

Bullard scored two, then Friendly matched it. Emma Fox got fouled and everybody exchanged glances, knowing Emma would miss those two.

It was Friendly 34 and Bullard 36, but moments later Bullard grabbed it on the rebound and shot off a three-pointer. The crowd roared. Allie turned right around and nabbed a three-pointer as Coach Madison called a time-out. Sweat towels were passed around the huddle and everybody grabbed a water bottle. Three minutes left. *An eternity!*

Allie barely heard Coach's pep talk about who to watch on the Bullard team. She grabbed another sweat towel and looked through the cheering crowd for Buzz. He winked at her, just like she'd hoped. Allie tossed aside the towel. Now, she was ready. She'd played this team before. *They were skilled, tough, and experienced. Everything I'm learning how to be.*

The buzzer sounded. Allie's job was to stay open and be ready. The Steamroller Express was about to explode.

A DRUMMING THUNDER of feet pounded the Lion bleachers when the five girls hit the floor. Sarah J. and Emma Fox went into a figure eight dribbling pattern that Allie knew would mean a three-point shot. She jumped into position, caught the pass and took the shot. *Yess!*

The Bullard starters dragged. The girls were tired; they'd played the same lineup all night with only a couple of rotations. Still, Allie didn't trust them not to score. She gave a nod to Sarah J. *Let's do it again.* Sarah J. grinned, nodded to their teammates and the girls spun into action. On a steal, Sarah J. got the ball, set up another figure eight, only this time the Bullard girls had read the play. Sarah lost the ball, only to have Emma Fox retrieve it again. Yet they couldn't get closer than mid-court.

A hand-off to Allie might open it up for a three-pointer.

Allie shouted, "Now!"

Emma turned, passed the ball hard to Allie. In a flash, Allie twirled, jumped and—*Whoosh!* The ball never touched the rim as the buzzer sounded.

The crowd went wild before flooding the court. The girls clutched Allie, hugging and crying. The final score? Friendly 43, Bullard 39.

Allie found herself grabbed up by Buzz Madison who kissed her cheek right there in the gym. "Yesss!" he whispered in her ear. "Wanna have dinner?" She had no chance to answer as the crowd propelled her toward Mama, Ben and Sheriff Anderson for big hugs, then she turned to see Fanny and Maggie wiping their eyes with hankies.

"Lord a-mercy, child, you did it. You and your team," grinned Fanny. "I ain't seen the likes of this in all my years."

Throngs of well-wishers were pushed aside as Mr. Danner dragged a microphone to the middle of the court. Somebody turned up the volume until it squealed.

"Ladies and gentlemen," Mr. Danner began, "students and faculty members. Thank you for coming tonight. We want to thank our Bullard team members and coaches for tonight's game."

Everybody cheered and clapped.

"But I have to say to our Lady Lions—I sure am glad to have this District trophy back in our trophy case this year!"

The gym erupted with stomping and cheers.

"Wait. Wait. We have a special announcement. Y'all know Stingy Jenkins, a longtime citizen of Friendly and owner of the furniture store out on Loop 95. Well, Mr. Jenkins has something he would like to say. Mr. Jenkins?"

Stingy Jenkins, dressed in his familiar red, white and blue suspenders and starched white shirt took the microphone from Mr. Danner.

"Thank you, Mr. Danner. A big howdy to all you Lady Lion lovers out there." A roar came up from the crowd. "At this time, I would like to make a special presentation. I would like to present a $5,000 college scholarship certificate to the Most Valuable Player of tonight's game."

A hush fell over the happy mob. *Whew,* Allie thought. *$5,000? Nobody has ever done anything like this before.*

"And I would like to present it to our very own Allie McCall."

The crowd went crazy and converged on Allie.

"Now, everybody, just hang on!" Stingy shouted into the microphone. "Y'all need to give the young lady some room. Step over here, Allie."

Allie stumbled forward, Buzz catching her arm, as she walked over to where Mr. Danner and Stingy Jenkins were holding a huge cardboard check.

"You'll only need to write your name in the blank and we'll get you a real check," Mr. Jenkins said. The crowd laughed. "Well, Allie? What do you say?"

She took the microphone and stared at the check. *College money! $5,000. Really?* That was more money than she had ever seen before. *I could have my own bank account.* While her family had inherited Mr. Pierson's land, there was no money attached to his will. They were the same poor family, just living on a lot of land.

A familiar face stood out in the crowd, the face of a friend who had been her support and confidante. She knew what she wanted to do. "Mr. Jenkins and Mr. Danner, I'm so happy to be here tonight, to play with my teammates, my coach and to help win this trophy for our school. And thank you so much for this scholarship and for choosing me as MVP. But, if it's okay with you, Mr. Jenkins, what I would really like to do with this money is to start a new Wikki Walk Foundation so that my best friend, Monica Wilkerson, can have her surgery in Houston." A hush fell over the crowd, but Allie pressed on. "Would that be all right with you?"

"I have the darndest time tryin' to give a gift to this young lady." Stingy Jenkins chuckled and shook his head.

Wikki rolled her wheelchair closer, wearing a look of shock and horror. "Allie, no! Please don't do this!"

Allie rushed over to her and knelt down. "Don't you see? This is the miracle you needed. You asked for a miracle and you got one. This money can be your down payment. We can raise more money, Wikki. Don't you wanna wear all those knee socks? I want you to walk, Wikki. I want that more than anything else in the world."

Stingy Jenkins cleared his throat and took the microphone. "Well, ladies and gentlemen, it seems we have a change of plans. I guess we're starting a Wikki Walk Foundation, and I will be the first contributor in the amount of $5,000. In fact, I will pay for the family's lodgings in Houston during the young lady's surgery."

The roar of applause filled the gym. Somebody shouted from the back, "I'm a bus driver! I volunteer to drive one of the buses to get there. Y'all know one carload ain't gonna be big enough to carry everybody from Friendly!"

The crowd laughed.

"Count me in!"

"I'm coming, too!"

Laughs and cheers went up as Wikki reached up to hug Allie. "I can't believe this. After all this time. Do you think I can really do it? Do you think I'll ever walk?"

Allie studied Wikki long and hard. "Are you kidding me? If I can learn to play basketball, you sure as heck are going to learn to walk. I've got five dollars in my purse that says so."

ALLIE FELL ON the lace and embroidery sheets with a clean body and freshly washed hair. She was tired like never before. *What a night!* They had done it. She couldn't have done it without her teammates, and Allie knew they couldn't have won it without her. *How totally cool!*

Now she could keep her bed. They had won District, even advanced to Regionals. She grinned into her pillows. Buzz had been so proud of her. He kept asking her to go out with him. Even after their dinner tonight, he asked her to have dinner with him on Valentine's Day. He didn't want to stop their early morning practices, either. Allie laughed at the weirdness of it all. They had spent all their waking hours these past three months working out in the gym and playing basketball. There had been *no time* to go on one date!

Yes. Life was good. She remembered how unhappy she'd been six months ago. Nothing to live for, almost no friends, nothing to do. Now her life was full beyond belief with so many friends; so much to do. The kids at school finally quit teasing her about Daniel. Pastor Jonas had begun preaching at the church and was quick to tell the congregation that Allie was not the only one who had talked to an angel. Still, Fanny had been right months ago—as soon as she stopped worrying about herself and started helping others, great things began to happen in her life.

Ah, Daniel. He started it all. An angel who sent her life into a tailspin and then disappeared.

"I miss you, Daniel," she whispered.

"I miss you, too."

"What? Daniel?"

"I'm here, but not in the flesh. Definitely in the spirit."

Allie jumped from the bed, arms outstretched, her plaid nightgown trailing the floor. "You're here? Really?"

He laughed. *"Do you doubt me?"*

"I do. I did," she giggled. "I did doubt you. I have been doubting you these past three months."

"Yet another doubting Thomas we have. Lady, you wound me to the core. How can you doubt the word of an angel? Did you not think I would come back?"

Allie knew he was teasing her, but she had to ask. "Are you okay?" she whispered. "You were so hurt. I was so worried. That horrible Ethan."

"Horrible, indeed. I'm all right. No need to worry. Don't I sound fine? I won't be able to appear in human form for a while, though."

"I talked to you and you didn't answer." Allie waited for a reply. "Daniel? You never answered me. What's the deal? Did I fail?"

He cleared his throat. *"No, Allie, it was I... I who failed."*

"You? An angel?"

"Michael was not happy with me."

"Who's Michael?"

"He's...my supervisor."

"Ha! Like angels have supervisors."

"*There is a hierarchy where I am.*"

"So you got into trouble, is that it?" Allie asked, sitting down on the edge of her bed.

"*In a manner of speaking, yes. So I'll be strictly ministering through my spirit form for now.*"

"Oh, I see."

"*Maybe you don't get the whole picture.*"

Allie could have sworn she felt the comforter shift with Daniel's weight.

"*There are a couple of reasons why I 'got into trouble' as you call it. I let my anger against Ethan cloud my judgment. Yet, after another battle, Ethan still lives. Truly, I knew that would be the case. Evil is impossible to conquer, no matter how hard we try. It's just that he's particularly disgusting—I want to battle him every time we meet. But that's for me to worry about—not you. At least with me no longer appearing in human form, he won't be bothering you.*"

"He won't come back...here?"

"*No, I've banned him from Friendly. While I don't trust him, I think with me not being here that he'll stay away. Besides, our project is finished.*"

"I think it turned out great! Pastor Jonas found some beautiful antique pews. Have you seen them?"

"*You all have done a fantastic job. I couldn't be happier. In fact, everyone is so pleased that a special envoy is coming to visit.*"

"An envoy of angels? Wow, wait until Pastor Jonas and the choir hears about this! There might be two anthems on Sunday mornings. Uh, Daniel, are you kidding... about the envoy?"

He chuckled again. "*No, I'm not kidding. And I must stop that. It's another reason Michael is displeased with me. He says we angels aren't supposed to tease our Earthly subjects. But with you, I have difficulty.*"

Allie laughed. "I love it when you tease me."

"*Your team of workers did an outstanding job. We admire the church bell and the way you refinished the cross. Nice touch, keeping the old one.*"

"People didn't want to take it down."

"*Mmm, yes, good point. But back to your earlier question as to why I, uh... disappeared. It also had to do with your basketball challenge. If I had stayed, and you and your teammates won District, which you did—and you and your team played fantastically, by the way—then you might have thought I somehow gave you special abilities to win. I did no such thing. Your team won the trophy strictly based on your hard work.*"

"Really?" Allie grinned. "So…like, I really learned how to play? That was me? I always thought that, you know, you helped me out. But you had nothing to do with it?"

He chuckled. *"I would high-five you right now if I could."*

"Awesome."

"You have more questions. I can feel it under my wings."

She felt his weight leave the side of the bed. "Can things go back to the way they were? Can we still talk?"

"Yes. And no."

"What? I haven't talked to you for three months. There's so much I have to tell you and, yes, questions to ask. You can't j-just leave."

"Allie," he sighed. *"It's not what I want to do. It's what I must do. I don't have a choice. I have duties…."*

"What about me? Can't I be one of those duties?" She twirled around the room, her hair dancing wildly as she reached out for him. "You can't just go away." Unexpected tears sprang to her eyes.

"I'll be back. There is the envoy to come soon and I have a personal interest in the church. I want to watch over and protect it."

Allie hesitated. "But what about me?" she asked, softly. "Don't you have an itty, bitty interest …in me?"

"Ah, but that's also gotten me into trouble with Michael."

Her mouth formed a small "o."

"Hold very still," came his whisper. *"And close your eyes."*

Allie stood still and obeyed. She felt an embrace encircle her from behind.

"There, do you feel it?"

With her eyes closed, she nodded.

"I must go now but I'll be back."

"No, Daniel, please!" she cried.

"I'll be back."

"Promise?"

He tightened his hold. *"Promise!"*

About The Author

Sommy L. Ham is a native Texan who has spent over 25 years in the writing business as a newspaper reporter, editor, publisher, communications consultant and writing tutor. She has also published numerous short stories appearing in various women's magazines. She resides in Magnolia with her husband, four dogs, four cats and her four grown children live close-by.